Readers love ASHLYN]

The Inside Edge

"Kane's pitch-perfect plotting keeps just the right amount of tension throughout, and the lively conclusion will delight readers. This is a treat."

—*Publishers Weekly*

"It is funny, poignant, at times, and very tender—a lovely story from beginning to end."

—Love Bytes

Fake Dating the Prince

"As sparkling as a diamond engagement ring, this contemporary delivers."

—*Publishers Weekly*

"Ashlyn Kane nails it in this book. The characters are utterly charming, the pacing is spot on, and this book just works."

—Joyfully Jay

Hex and Candy

"I'm just going to say it, I adored this clever little romance by Ashlyn Kane. *Hex and Candy* is clever, humorous, captivating and an absolute feel good novel."

—The Novel Approach

"Everything about this novel's presentation is unique, sharp and witty. It's also as sweet as its candy store hero, exactly the kind of novel for a light pick-me-up."

—Kimmers' Erotic Book Banter

By Ashlyn Kane

American Love Songs
With Claudia Mayrant & CJ Burke: Babe in the Woodshop
A Good Vintage
Hang a Shining Star
The Inside Edge
The Rock Star's Guide to Getting Your Man

DREAMSPUN BEYOND
Hex and Candy

DREAMSPUN DESIRES
His Leading Man
Fake Dating the Prince

With Morgan James
Hair of the Dog
Hard Feelings
Return to Sender
String Theory
Winging It

Published by Dreamspinner Press
www.dreamspinnerpress.com

THE ROCK STAR'S GUIDE TO GETTING YOUR MAN

ASHLYN KANE

Published by
DREAMSPINNER PRESS

5032 Capital Circle SW, Suite 2, PMB# 279, Tallahassee, FL 32305-7886 USA
www.dreamspinnerpress.com

Trade Paperback ISBN: 978-1-64405-993-7
Digital ISBN: 978-1-64405-992-0
Trade Paperback published October 2021
v. 1.0

Printed in the United States of America

This paper meets the requirements of
ANSI/NISO Z39.48-1992 (Permanence of Paper).

For Sibel, who kept me on course.
This book wouldn't exist without you.

Acknowledgments

I OWE debts of gratitude to several people for their efforts to help me navigate how much bending I could do to the structure of Canadian provincial and national parks while keeping the book plausible: S. Khaw, Sherry M., and Jaime Samms. Thank you so much for using your research skills, personal knowledge, and connections to help me figure this out.

This book languished for a few weeks at 99.9% finished and would have rotted there, but Morgan James provided the feedback and kick in the butt I needed to polish the rest. They're the best.

THE ROCK STAR'S GUIDE TO GETTING YOUR MAN

FIRST THINGS first. I know that "getting your man" is not very inclusive, but the other phrasings were clunky. Also, if you aren't interested in getting a partner, that's cool. This book is also for people who want to know how I ended up with a superhot trophy boyfriend and for diehard Howl fans who want to know all the dirt.

To be honest, until I sat down to write this, even *I* didn't know how I ended up here. I sure as fuck did not leave the Willow Sound of my youth anticipating that one day I would return, on the verge of a third-life crisis, only to realize I wasn't over my high school crush and decide to put a ring on it.

But now that I'm looking back, I can see the decisions I made. I know what I did right.

And the first thing I did right was go back to where it all started. So, with that in mind—here it is. Jeff Pine's personal guide to getting your man (or whatever).

Good luck.

From *The T-Bird Times*, Twin Lakes Secondary School newspaper
Issue dated May 7, thirteen years ago
T-Birds Take the Battle of the Bands
By Sarah Brown

THE BARRIE Battle of the Bands competition was held last weekend, and a group from Twin Lakes took home top honors.

Howl, a band consisting of seniors Jeff Pine (lead guitar, vocals), Tracy Neufeld (percussion), Max Langdon (guitar), and Joe Kinoshameg (bass), has been playing together for two years. This is their second time entering the Battle of the Bands contest and their first win.

Congratulations, Thunderbirds!

From *Out* magazine
Issue dated October, three years ago

IN PERSON, Jeff Pine is an attractive but unassuming boy-next-door type—five nine, with wavy brown hair, bright hazel eyes, and, unfairly, both freckles *and* a dimple. But even in an out-of-the-way coffee shop just a few blocks from his Toronto high-rise, you can catch glimpses of Howl's enigmatic, larger-than-life frontman. There's something electric in his hazel eyes, and he seems energetic but self-possessed; when the barista hands over his order, a lurid green matcha latte, they fist-bump like old friends. He never stops tapping his foot in time with the song playing quietly over the sound system, and several times I catch him tilting his head to listen, nodding a bit as though he's taking notes. It's not an affectation—he always seems embarrassed afterward. It's like he can't help himself.

Pine, now twenty-eight, has come a long way from the teenager with the chip on his shoulder who first bullied his way onto stages in Barrie, Ontario, where he and Max Langdon, Trix Neufeld, and Joe Kinoshameg attended high school.

"I had a lot to prove," he tells me, thumbing unselfconsciously at the smear of whipped cream on his upper lip. "Music felt like the only thing I'd ever been good at, but it's hard to be taken seriously when you're a short gay kid with freckles. I felt like I had to go twice as hard, swear twice as much, be twice as stereotypical rock star to make up for it."

But Pine is lucky, he says, in that his struggles have all been ones of perception, not identity. "I went through this phase in my early twenties where I was, like, almost bodybuilding. I thought if I could make my upper body look like a superhero, then bigots would have to give me my rocker cred. Which is hilarious in hindsight. I mean, just as often we're a bunch of scrawny nerds with beer guts who are obviously strung out from too much coke. But I never felt unsure of who I was. Once I stopped putting so much emphasis on things I couldn't control, like how other people see me, it got a lot easier."

What helped, he said, was following the path set forward by other out musicians—namely that there was no path. "No one's out there telling Elton John he can't rock." Among others, Pine counts Elton John, Green Day frontman Billie Joe Armstrong, and Sam Smith among those whose example he looked to. "There's no right or wrong way to be a queer musician. It's different, because sometimes we have to enforce boundaries that straight cis people don't have to. Some people think they're entitled to really personal information. But mostly I've been able to put that down as a 'them' problem."

Which isn't to say that Pine hasn't faced problems. On Howl's first North American tour, he was hospitalized with exhaustion after performing for hours in the Kentucky summer heat. Earlier this year, his boyfriend of nine months broke up with him, citing the band's grueling tour schedules and Pine's lack of availability. "And of course that ended right around the time we were in the planning stages for this album," he says, "so I was already emotionally drained, but we had to get together and we all had to pour our hearts out. I won't say it doesn't make good music, but it was hard."

The album—Howl's sixth, called *Gemini*—releases early next week and features hit singles "Blood in the Water" and "Point of View," both of which are currently charting in North America and the UK.

"And then the tour starts, and we do the whole thing over again," Pine laughs after draining the last of his latte. "Honestly, I don't know how we do it. But I love it. It's hard to believe you can be this lucky. If I could go back and tell my fifteen-year-old self, you know, not just 'it gets better' but exactly what's in store for him… I wouldn't, though. It's something he should find out for himself."

LESSON ONE
Deal With Your Shit

SORRY, THERE'S no wading gradually into shallow water here. We're jumping right in at the deep end.

Of course, this step assumes that you know what your shit is. I'm talking the real stuff—the tragic backstory, the deep-seated insecurities, the broken emotional bones that healed without being set properly.

To fix your shit, you have to know what it is.

For me there was a lot of shit, and I wanted to tackle it all at once. I wasn't connecting with Trix, Max, and Joe, my bandmates in Howl. I felt stifled by our management team. The idea of writing another album, going on another tour, or even staying in the same city with them made me want to run screaming into the wilderness.

And one day, after a brutal breakfast with Max and a rage-inducing phone call with Trix, that's what I did. I rented a cabin in the middle of a provincial park, packed up a couple guitars and some clothes and my laptop, and I left. I needed space to figure out what I wanted to do about the band, my future, my life. But really I just wanted to get away from it. Rock stars have responsibilities too, and I wanted to avoid them.

And that wasn't *all* that I needed to deal with. I showed up at this cabin in the woods expecting to leave all my shit behind for a few weeks. I should've known better. I rented a cabin twenty minutes from where I grew up.

When I showed up, all my shit was there waiting for me.

Mother *fucker*.

Chapter One

JEFF HAD misgivings right up until he turned into the driveway and the water of the Sound surrounded him on three sides—a solid, grounded, gorgeous blue, with the sky above it bright and clear. This close to the shore, the trees were sparse and the claustrophobia of the rest of the park didn't encroach. The air tasted like relief.

It was probably a good thing he was mostly there for the scenery, because the cabin wasn't much to look at—a solidly constructed square log A-frame, with a wooden porch along the front and a steel chimney out the back. Lots of windows for natural light, and a stack of firewood that'd last him 'til Doomsday. He parked the truck in a carport that also housed a bearproof garbage box and a huge plastic bin for gravel. With a little luck, he wouldn't need that in the next few months.

There was still time for everything to go spectacularly wrong, obviously. Case in point, bear box. Jeff sat in his truck with the windows down, cut the engine, and listened as the waves crashed against the rocks and Gord Downie told some unknown person to shut up about poets.

It didn't feel real yet—no hotels, no bandmates, no studio time, no practice, no interviews. This far out into the middle of nowhere, he might not even run into anyone who knew his name.

Well, not if he hadn't grown up here.

As the song faded out, a green park-ranger vehicle pulled in next to him and Jeff opened the door and got out to meet the driver. She was a young woman, midtwenties, with pin-straight dark hair, sharp cheekbones, and an easy smile. "You must be Mr. Pine?"

God, *Mr. Pine*. She didn't recognize him. He couldn't place her either. He'd probably been a few years ahead of her at school, if she'd grown up here. "Just Jeff," he corrected. "Thanks for meeting me here."

They shook hands. "Kara. And it's all part of the service."

She showed him around the cabin—a single room with a bed, table and chairs, and a kitchenette with a wood-burning stove set against the wall that led to the bathroom, presumably to keep it toasty in the winter.

God, Jeff could imagine staying there through the winter. His balls tried to crawl up into his body at the mere thought.

"GPS can get a little spotty," Kara warned as they made their way back to the cars. "What with the tree cover. Cell signal's only so-so. You probably won't get much data either. I've got a couple extra maps in the truck if you want."

Jeff smiled. "I think I remember my way around. Thanks, though." Sure, they'd probably changed things since he was fifteen, but where were they going to move the grocery? Willow Sound wasn't that big.

"Oh, are you from here?" Kara leaned back against the ranger vehicle.

He'd opened himself up for that one. "Ah, sort of." He shrugged. "We moved away when I was a teenager. I haven't been back."

Mercifully, she didn't ask him about it. Thank God, because he had no idea what he'd have said. *It's complicated*? It was actually just sad and kind of pathetic.

"All right. Well, I get the impression things don't change too fast around here." She pursed her lips around a smile in an obvious tease. "At least judging by how much people are still grumbling about the Tim Hortons that went in ten years ago."

Jeff barked a laugh. "Some things will never change. Small towns' *resistance* to change being one of them."

"So you've *definitely* been here before." Grinning, she reached into the truck and pulled out a park pamphlet. "You probably got one of these at the gate, but just in case." She turned it over and pulled a pen from her ranger cap. "Not saying the solitary life won't suit you, but if you feel like you need some company, there's a pretty good set of programs—learn to fly fish, identify plants and animal signs. There's a stargazing one, and if you're going to be around in August, you should definitely come to that because the meteor shower puts on a good show every year. And of course there's campfire night."

She handed him the pamphlet.

"Campfire night," Jeff repeated, the corners of his mouth turning up. "What, I don't look like I can build my own?" He wasn't offended; he wasn't exactly a hulking guy. He'd never quite made it to five ten, and his T-shirt was too loose to show off his arms.

"Nah, that's not it." Her brown skin flushed just perceptibly, and she shook her head. "It's more… campfire safety, an introduction to park wildlife, and then s'mores and camp songs." The flush deepened. "It's very popular with kids and people who are attracted to men."

Translation—the ranger who ran it was a hotass. Jeff smiled. "Well, who doesn't like s'mores."

She grinned back. "I'm off duty at six, so I won't be there, but tell me about it later if you decide to go. I'm sure I'll be seeing you if you're here all summer."

"I'm sure I'll get into some kind of trouble," Jeff agreed. "Nice meeting you."

She gave him a lazy salute and then climbed into the truck. Jeff watched it rumble away.

Then, absent anything else to do, he unloaded his stuff.

He didn't have much. Most of his things were in his condo in Toronto; he didn't need ten guitars out here. He'd brought two—his favorite electric Gibson Les Paul, a solid blue body he'd fallen in love with in a music store in Salzburg, and a battered old Seagull acoustic, his first love.

The cabin would be cramped enough with the three of them.

On top of that, he had a bag of clothes and toiletries, his laptop, and a heavy spiral-coiled notebook and three packs of pens. Pens were tricky; the moment you turned your back, they did some kind of battle royale until two days later you were down to one solitary ballpoint, and the cap was missing. He probably hadn't brought enough.

He *definitely* hadn't brought enough food. Or, you know, any.

And he should rectify that. One, because as confident as he was in his daytime navigation skills, all bets were off once the sun went down, and two, because if he wanted to check out Ranger Hot Stuff's sing-along, he needed to get going.

Any minute now. His stomach was grumbling. The clock was ticking. Jeff's feet were not moving him any closer to the truck. Instead they deposited him at the kitchen table, where he set his elbows against the scarred surface and dropped his head in his hands.

It had been almost fifteen years since he'd set foot in Willow Sound, but he wasn't afraid to find out it had changed. The conversation with Kara had put paid to that.

No, Jeff was more concerned that it would be exactly the same, Tim Hortons or no, that he'd walk down the street and be able to tell where he was by the cracked sidewalk under his feet or how strong the smell of hot oil from Shinny's was. He was afraid to go downtown and have people recognize him as Jeff Pine, frontman of Howl, and equally afraid they'd see Jeff Pine, the gawky fifteen-year-old who'd fled and never come back. He was afraid he'd recognize someone and equally afraid he'd meet no one but strangers.

And if he ran into Carter—

No, that's stupid. Willow Sound was small, but not so small Jeff had to have an anxiety attack about the possibility of running into his former best friend in the grocery. At least not on the first day. He didn't even know if Carter still lived here. He'd probably left for college. Lots of people never came back.

Jeff hadn't, until now.

Finally his stomach growled, deciding for him. He needed dinner and provisions for tomorrow morning at the very least. After those needs were met, he could schedule time for self-pity.

So resolved, he picked his new keys up off the counter and headed for the door.

WILLOW SOUND might've had a coat of paint or two, but the landmarks were still there. Jeff pulled into the criminally tiny parking lot shared by the grocery and LCBO and found a spot. It felt strange to drive here; he hadn't had a license before they moved. Now he knew why his dad always complained about that stoplight. In fifteen years, they hadn't fixed the timing?

He didn't realize he was sitting in his car, drumming his fingers on the steering wheel, until someone laughed outside and he jerked himself out of it. Too many memories of waiting in this parking lot for Carter to finish his shift at the grocery so they could swim or fish or hang out in Carter's basement and watch MTV. Jeff hadn't considered this complication. It wasn't like he could avoid the grocery store.

He hoped Carter didn't still work here. *That* would be awkward.

As he picked up a tiny cart near the entrance, he cataloged the differences—unlike the exterior, the inside of the store had had a facelift, and it was bright and pleasant. Jeff picked up as much fresh food as he thought he could cram into the cabin's minifridge and a great deal more shelf-stable stuff for those inevitable days when he sank headfirst into his guitar and didn't come up until midnight. He wished the cabin had a freezer, but mac and cheese in a box would have to do.

Small-town shopping had one thing going for it—expediency. The whole took Jeff twenty minutes through the aisles, without a single person asking for his autograph. He was just thinking he might escape unnoticed when he caught the cover of *Hello*, which the cashier had propped open against her till while she waited between customers. Jeff's own face happened to grace this issue, a particularly unflattering shot of him leaving the label's downtown office, freckles standing out too dark against pale cheeks and his dark curly hair mussed from the number of times he'd pulled at it in frustration. He looked like he hadn't slept in three days, for which Jeff credited caffeine, because it had been closer to a week.

He was debating whether to abandon his cart and make a run for it when a familiar voice said, "Georgia White! Is this the work ethic I inspired?" and the cashier scrambled upright, fumbling with the magazine. Her eyes caught on the speaker and she blanched.

"Ohmygosh, Mrs. Halloran. You scared me." Georgia (apparently) glanced at Jeff, then back at Mrs. Halloran, then doubled back to Jeff.

Awkwardly, Jeff turned to Mrs. Halloran as well—only to find he recognized the face as well as the voice. Mind you, last time he'd seen her he'd been looking from a different angle.

He smiled. "Hey, Mrs. H." Never would he have guessed his geriatric fourth grade teacher would be the first familiar face he saw in town.

"That's 'hello,' Jeffrey. I know I taught you proper manners." But her brown eyes danced; she had always loved gently giving her students a hard time. "Georgia, dear, those groceries aren't going to ring themselves up."

Georgia flushed. "Right. Sorry, Mrs. Halloran."

"It's good to see you back around these parts," she told Jeff sincerely. "Did you buy property out this way?"

He shook his head. He'd considered it, but what if things didn't turn out the way he thought? What would he do with it if he was on the road all the time? Cottages needed upkeep.

"Just renting for now." He didn't dare say where, with Georgia listening, and thankfully Mrs. H didn't ask. Jeff didn't know how to explain that the park, the Sound, felt like the place he needed to be, even if he'd had to bend a few rules to make it happen.

"Well, it's good to see you," she said warmly. "Though, if I can make one request? Maybe next album, at least one song I don't have to give someone detention for singing in my class?"

He felt the tips of his ears go hot. Georgia was paying very close attention to Jeff's selection of lunch meat. "Oh, well, I can't promise that." Especially since he didn't know if there'd even *be* another album. "But I'll try."

Mrs. H patted him on the shoulder. "You're a good boy, Jeffy. Your mom would be proud."

Shit, there it was. The first of many shoes he'd been waiting to drop. But he couldn't begrudge Mrs. H, who had worked alongside his mom for close to twenty years. "Thanks, Mrs. H."

She shook her head as Georgia timidly offered the total. "I think it's probably safe for you to call me Linda."

Jeff paid, signed the credit card slip with a pen like it was 2006, and gestured to the magazine.

Georgia squeaked. "Really?"

"If you promise to be this chill next time, absolutely."

Thank God for Mrs. H.

Jeff signed the cover of the magazine, right under his own face, and Georgia looked at him with stars in her eyes as he left with his bags.

JEFF TUCKED the kitchen garbage into the bear box and secured it before he considered his next move. He knew he needed to be here, in the last place he'd felt close to his mother, that he needed to spend some time excavating himself from the strata of rock star and grief. But now that he was here, he didn't feel *ready*. As much as he'd come up here for space, he didn't actually enjoy being alone. He was a social creature. He drew on a crowd's energy. Though he did sometimes get tired of putting on a show… maybe he'd be okay out here.

Maybe he could just be Jeff.

He knew it was overly optimistic when he packed the guitar into the truck, but he couldn't help it.

The sun was setting when he pulled into the lot near what the park welcome pamphlet called the "amphitheater." From the truck, Jeff could see it was just rows of backless wooden benches around an unusually large fire pit, which was already crackling. This early in the season, there weren't many campers to entertain—a handful of retirees, one younger couple, and a pair in their thirties with kids too young to be in school.

He hung back, feeling like the lone goth kid at a Hannah Montana concert. There was an odd number of retirees, though they still made an obvious group.

But he wanted a s'more, dammit, and a chance to play guitar for someone. He hadn't played solo since high school and he needed to decide if he was going to keep doing it if everything went further to shit.

Also he wanted to meet Ranger Hotass.

So resolved, Jeff hefted his guitar case out of the back seat and schlepped it to the amphitheater. He chose a seat all the way to the left, in the second row, where he could keep the guitar case out of sight. On the far side of the pit from him a table had been set up with the necessities—a cooler of water, a fire extinguisher and first aid kit, and a giant bowl of marshmallows. Jeff could almost taste the burnt-sugar goodness.

He didn't see Ranger Hotass. Was he early? That would be a first. He checked his phone. Nope. Ten minutes late. Well, Jeff had kept way more people waiting much longer, and they'd paid for the privilege. But he couldn't sit still. Maybe he'd take a short walk and come back.

The amphitheater was far enough inland to be mostly sheltered from the breeze off the water. The pine and spruce stood inky green against the twilight sky, somehow friendly figures. Jeff wondered if he'd see any moose while he was up here. Deer, definitely. Maybe a porcupine? Hopefully not a skunk.

In his meandering circuit it was just the usual—a chatter of squirrels, a chipmunk darting across the road, a hawk circling overhead before Jeff lost it to the low light. One day soon he might have to admit he needed glasses. Depressing. He should get Lasik. Jeff couldn't pull off the Rivers Cuomo look.

By the time he circled back to the fire, his guitar case was getting heavy and he'd broken out in goose bumps. He'd forgotten how chilly it could get on a May night up here.

The ranger had shown up while he was gone, and he was demonstrating proper use of a fire extinguisher as though people just had these at their campsites. Jeff couldn't make out his features from this distance, not with the firelight behind him, but he could tell the man was tall and fit, broad-shouldered and blond, with longish hair that brushed just below his cheekbones. The Dudley Do-Right type. Jeff smiled and made for his previous spot as unobtrusively as possible as the lecture moved on to keeping the ground around the fire clear of tripping hazards like roasting sticks.

"Can anyone think of anything else you shouldn't do around a campfire?"

This was obviously for the children's benefit, as he turned toward them when he asked, revealing the long line of a Roman nose.

One of the kids' hands shot up. Were all kids like that at that age, so eager for attention and approval? Jeff could hardly remember. He'd been an okay student before his mom got sick, so… maybe.

"Yes?" the ranger asked.

"Run?" the little girl said.

"Run!" the ranger echoed. "Yes, that's a very important one. Good job. What's your name?"

"Lennon."

"Very good job, Lennon," he repeated. Something about the way he said it—it was like an echo of a memory. Probably a flashback from childhood teachers—he'd been having them off and on since he ran into Mrs. H. "What do you say—is it time for s'mores?"

What self-respecting child was going to turn that down?

Jeff was debating how quickly he could get away with getting in line for a marshmallow and keep his respectability when a voice next to him said, "Are you going to play for us?"

Nope, just thought I'd lug around a heavy instrument for the exercise. Jeff bit down on the smartass remark. The last thing he needed was more bad publicity, and it wasn't a question anyway, it was a conversation starter. He was glad he'd held his tongue when he looked up and saw a woman in her early seventies, lilac windbreaker zipped all the way up, Yeti wineglass in hand.

This lady had no fucks to give about what anyone thought of her, which automatically made her way cooler than Jeff.

"The flyer said there's supposed to be singing, right?" he said. He hoped she didn't recognize him. She wasn't exactly his target demographic. "I don't want to step on anyone's toes—"

"Oh, no, you're fine. Smokey isn't fussed about the spotlight."

Jeff's lips twitched as he pulled the Seagull out of its case. "Smokey?"

She artificially deepened her voice and puffed out her chest. "Only you can prevent forest fires." She smiled as she took a seat on the bench next to him and offered her hand. "I'm Gloria."

Hell, Jeff could get away with using his own first name, right? "Nice to meet you, Gloria. I'm Jeff."

He strummed a quick chord to check the tuning. The ranger was still with the kids, helping them and their parents load up marshmallow roasting sticks. Gloria jerked her head at the group of seniors, and they ambled closer. "Don't suppose you know anything from my day?"

Jeff had cut his teeth—or his fingers, at least—on classic rock, sitting in the man cave in his best friend's basement, concentrating on the shift of strings under his skin. "I know a couple." He adjusted the high E, then checked again. Better. He plucked out an opening riff. "You know this one?"

The intro was quick—just ten seconds or so—and then it started in on the first verse. The words to "The Weight" bubbled up like something deeper than memory, like part of his DNA. It was one of the first songs he'd learned once his fingers were strong enough for a bar chord. It felt right singing it too—he'd just pulled in, and he was looking for a place to lay his head.

He looked up and caught Gloria's eye at the chorus, and she came in on cue, so he cued in each of the others in turn. But before he could finish it, someone said, "*Jeff*?"

Jeff's fingers stuttered on the strings and the melody died on his lips. He paused with his mouth halfway open, left hand still curved into a D chord, and looked up.

The man in the ranger uniform—the one whose body he had admired, whose voice had seemed familiar, stood in front of him, close enough to the firelight now that Jeff could make out his features.

Familiar features—square jaw, straight nose, smooth brow, shockingly pink mouth that had been the unwitting object of all Jeff's early fantasies.

Returning now to taunt him at his *second*-lowest moment. Fuck Jeff's life.

Oh shit, was he still staring? "*Carter*?"

Jesus, he looked—he looked like endless summer days outside, and it was like Jeff could see teenage Carter superimposed on this older, broader, even more absurdly handsome version. Which, inexplicably, had surfer-bro hair.

Gloria said, from lightyears away, "Oh, do you two know each other?"

"Yeah," Jeff said, feeling shell-shocked, at the same time Carter said, "No."

Jeff inhaled sharply, feeling the denial like a knife slipped between his ribs. But before he could make an excuse and leave, Carter backtracked apologetically, "I mean, we used to, but I haven't seen him in…." He trailed off, and everything somehow became more awkward.

It had been over a decade, but from his face, Jeff knew he was thinking about the last time they'd seen each other.

On second thought, remembering that day, maybe Jeff didn't know Carter either. "Fifteen years," he supplied. He felt like there was a band around his chest. That made Carter, what? Thirty-two? The years looked good on him.

The looking hurt, though. It brought home that they'd never talked, after. There was just that awful day, capped off with a good rub of salt in the wound, and then Jeff had run out and refused to speak to Carter, and a week later he and his dad moved. They'd never emailed, even when Jeff stopped being mad. At that point what could he have said? It wouldn't have made a difference.

Maybe Gloria sensed the tension, because she cleared her throat. "Well, it's nice that you have a chance to reconnect!"

Reconnect—God no. Jeff's life was already a turtlefuck. The last thing he needed was to mix his childhood trauma with his adult problems. Why was this happening? Was this some sign from the cosmos? *Go back to the city, kid. This place is for a you long dead.*

Except he couldn't escape the feeling that it was the cosmos that had brought him here in the first place.

"Right," Jeff said, instead of disagreeing and running away. He picked out the introduction of the song again to refocus the attention. As long as he had his little stage and his guitar, he was in control. And control was just what he needed. "So—should we try that again? Maybe we'll get through the whole chorus this time."

A few of the retirees exchanged glances, and Jeff saw the younger couple whispering to each other over a cell phone and thought maybe his cover was blown. Especially when Gloria said, afterward, "You have a wonderful voice, Jeff. Has anyone ever told you you sound like that singer from—oh, what's the band—they have that song 'Ginsberg'?"

Jeff pasted on a smile and pointedly didn't look at Carter, who was back with the kids, scooping melted marshmallow onto graham crackers. "Yeah, I've heard that a time or two." He made a mental note not to play any Howl songs. That would only invite trouble.

Not that trouble had ever needed an invitation, he thought as he glanced across the fire. Carter hadn't joined in on any of the songs, he just sat and listened. Jeff found it unnerving and spent longer than he should scrutinizing his song choices. Nothing too angry, too sad, too nostalgic.

Nothing that might give away the monstrous rending of his own heart.

Finally, after a good set, Jeff begged off. "I might be back next week," he said to Lennon, who had been delighted with his half-assed version of "Let It Go." "But I just got in this afternoon and I'm exhausted." And he was. Full-on gritty eyes, heavy chest tired. "If you're still here I'll see you then, okay?"

Jeez. He was going to bed before a three-year-old. *Guess I really do need this vacation.*

He was extra careful navigating back to the cabin in the dark. Even with the headlights, it was challenging to see the turnoff. He might really have to look into glasses. Or stop driving at night.

There was no use dwelling on any of it tonight. He put the truck in Park under the carport and was halfway into the cottage before he realized he never got his marshmallow.

Fucking Carter. That guy ruined everything.

Chapter Two

JEFF WOKE to the water-lit shine of predawn.

The cabin was cold enough that he swore his hair was trying to grow back into his scalp, but with the rest of him tucked under the covers, he was as snug as anyone could hope for. The window along the back wall had filmy curtains, but he hadn't closed them, and the washed-out sunlight reflecting off the Sound crept sluggishly through the window and suffused the interior of the cabin with an otherworldly glow.

Jeff had never been accused of being a morning person, but he sat up in bed anyway and looked out, unable to resist. A fine layer of mist hovered over the water, seeming to soak up the sun's rays and hold them there for later. A fish splashed just offshore. As Jeff watched, a kayak with a single occupant glided past the inlet, the paddle dipping silently in and out, leaving the morning undisturbed.

Jeff pulled the blankets tighter around himself and watched the sun come up, thinking back to a morning twenty years before, when it had been him and his mother in the kayak, the mist limning their skin, the future stretching out ahead of them like the water, unknown and seemingly limitless.

He was still sitting there, half dozing, what must have been at least an hour later, when his cell phone buzzed on the nightstand.

Damn. He'd sort of been hoping he wouldn't get any service. No such luck. Sighing, he reached for it and unlocked the screen.

Meeting today, 2pm, downtown offices, it said. *Last minute tour details.*

Last-minute fuck you too, Tim, Jeff thought in disgust. There was no reason he needed to be there, not to work out the set lists or wardrobe choices or whatever the fuck Tim, their manager, wanted to talk about. Tim was texting him trying to get him to come in so he could corner Jeff with Max and Joe and Trix and mention, *Oh hey by the way, remember that album that's due this summer? Well I rented you some studio space.*

Get to it. Tim and his corporate overlords didn't give a fuck about Jeff's mental health.

Not available, he texted back. *Figure it out without me.*

They could call him if they needed to.

The phone started ringing before he set it down, but Jeff sent it to voicemail and got out of bed. He was not dealing with that shitstorm until after coffee and a shower. Maybe even breakfast. He'd gotten out of the habit of eating before noon, but that was back when he slept until ten or eleven. If he was going to start clawing his ass out of bed at—he glanced at the time—barely eight in the morning, he needed sustenance.

By nine thirty he'd caffeinated, showered, and even had a full breakfast—eggs and toast and fruit. That was like, three whole food groups, four if you counted the coffee—and even though he didn't exactly feel enthusiastic about the prospect, he was at least mentally fortified enough to listen to the message.

Hey Jeff, it's Tim. Just checking in to see how you're doing, man. We'll see you in Toronto on the twentieth. Click.

Jeff deleted it. Yeah, he'd be in Toronto on the twentieth. Just like he'd be in Vancouver on the twenty-sixth and Victoria on the twenty-seventh. Just like he'd be in Calgary and Edmonton and Winnipeg in June—fuck, that was going to suck, those mosquitoes could drain a man—and Ottawa on the first of July.

And then that was it. This last leg of the tour. Jeff had said he'd do it and he would.

It was the *next* tour he was worried about.

Howl was under contract for one more album, due by the end of the summer, and a tour to follow it. If Jeff had seen their true colors as a starry-eyed twenty-year-old… well, he'd still have had to convince Max, Joe, and Trix to hold out for a better offer, to at least get their own manager. Because now he was staring down the possibility of another couple spins around the sun with Max vacillating wildly between happy and high and Trix sniping at Jeff every chance she got.

That or forking out most of his fortune to get away.

That was what he was supposed to be figuring out—whether he'd tell the three people who'd been his family the past ten years to pound salt because two of them were toxic and the label was a carcinogen. Whether he had it in him to go it alone or to start over with a new band.

Except it wasn't so much that Jeff had been burning the candle at both ends as he'd chucked the whole thing right into the fire. He was so burnt out he didn't even know if he had anything left to say.

He rubbed a hand over his forehead, willing away the tension.

His phone buzzed again, and he sighed as he picked it up.

Joe this time, the one band member Jeff could count on to put common sense ahead of personal feelings. *You coming to this thing today?*

Not if I can help it. I'm in Willow Sound.

He let that hang for a minute, watching the pulse of the three dots after Joe's name. Finally the phone rang and this time Jeff picked up.

"Hey, Joe."

"Hey, Jeff." Joe's voice was calm as always, and a little dry. "You okay?"

Jeff should've left out the part about Willow Sound, probably. "I'm fine," he said, and then he realized he was showered and dressed and breakfasted before ten a.m. and that there was an anxious knot in the pit of his stomach that hadn't been there yesterday… because now he was thinking about Howl, about their whole shitshow band and how much he loved it and didn't want to go back. "Actually, no. I'm not fine."

"You want me to come up?"

"Oh fuck no," Jeff said automatically, pure reflex. He sounded like an asshole. "Uh, sorry man, just—right now two worlds are colliding enough, you know?"

But Joe was laughing. He'd heard enough of Jeff's stories about Willow Sound in their teen years. He had context. "Relax. I get it. Just thought I'd ask. Figured if you were back in that place, you could use a friend."

Wasn't that the truth. Here Jeff was, thirty years old, rich and moderately famous in a way his teenage self had only dreamed of. His band had been nominated for three Grammys, they'd won half a dozen Junos, they'd played on every major talk show in North America. And he had no one. Not one person he could talk to.

He'd never been great at making friends—Joe and Trix and Max had basically adopted him in high school detention—and the past decade hadn't afforded a lot of opportunities to form new ones. They were always moving, touring, partying. He barely talked to his dad, who was busy with his new family.

"Jeff?"

Right. "It's cool," Jeff said. "I think I just need to be here for a bit. It's quiet. No pressure."

"Sure," Joe agreed. Jeff was pretty sure he was humoring him. "The past year's been kinda wild, eh?"

Jeff laughed sharply. "You could say that." If he never had to live through the fallout of Max trashing another hotel room—

"Maybe I'll take a page out of your book," Joe mused.

"You're still in the city?" Joe usually went back to Barrie—well, Orillia, but close enough—when they were off tour.

"Playing host to my cousin," he confirmed. "She's thinking of going into Indigenous Education at U of T. Sarah's gonna give her a tour." Sarah was Joe's longtime girlfriend. "They're calling it bonding time."

It had taken all Trix's cajoling and endless hours of tutoring to make sure Jeff finished high school on time, and he still barely graduated—not because he wasn't smart, but he knew what he wanted to do with his life, and higher education wasn't it. Still—"Good for her," he said.

"Kids these days are angrier and hungrier than we were." Jeff could practically see him shaking his head. "They don't take no for an answer."

Jeff smiled. "Good."

"Right? Anyway. I'll be at the meeting this afternoon, so I can babysit. Any particular requests?"

"No new tour dates," Jeff said immediately. "No firm commitments on anything regarding the new album. No promo commitments. I need a break."

"All right, I got you."

Some of the tension left Jeff's shoulders. "Thanks, man. I appreciate it."

There was a pause. "Look, are you sure you don't want me to come up? Sarah can manage April for a day or two without me. Just say the word."

Joe was away from Sarah enough as it was; she worked full-time and couldn't join them on the road. "I'm good," he promised. "And if I'm not, I'll call you. Take care, yeah?"

They hung up, and Jeff surveyed the kitchen. He should probably do the dishes—no dishwasher here, and he didn't want to attract mice. He *definitely* didn't want to attract anything bigger.

For the first time, he wondered who he was kidding. He hadn't done dishes by hand in fifteen years—probably not since the last time he took his turn at Mrs. Rhodes's kitchen sink before he moved. Maybe he should rent a cottage that had actual amenities. Maybe he should go back to Toronto.

While he was at it, maybe he should try making up with his bandmates before he had to play onstage with them again.

But he wasn't ready to give up. He'd been here less than a day. Was he that much of a quitter?

Actually, that was a fair question, since part of the reason he'd come here was to remember who he was before he became Jeff Pine, Howl frontman.

A question he could answer just as easily while he was doing the dishes.

He was wiping the last of the soap bubbles from his arms when he heard tires crunching on the gravel drive. Glancing out the window didn't immediately offer insight—the truck pulling in next to his had tinted windows and mud spattered halfway up the doors and could've belonged to anyone.

Could've, but Jeff would bet his Gibson he knew whose it was. Steeling himself, he topped up his coffee cup and went to the porch to meet his guest.

Jeff had thought the ranger uniform was a lot. In theory ranger uniforms should look stupid, but it was still a uniform, right? All official-looking, and Carter's fit particularly well.

The ranger uniform as viewed by firelight had not prepared him for Carter in the morning sunshine, wearing jeans and a T-shirt that looked like it had gone in the dryer one too many times. It clung to every muscle—no easy task—setting a great example for his jeans, which barely contained his thighs.

It was already cruel of the universe to throw Jeff's former BFF and unrequited crush back into his life when he was low. Did he also have to be this attractive? Honestly, was this *necessary*? Next thing you knew someone would give him a baby to hold in one extremely large hand, just to really punctuate the statement.

"Uh," Carter said when he saw Jeff standing on the porch. "Hey."

At least, Jeff thought viciously, his aviator sunglasses looked stupid. "Hey," he said back. "You know stalking's illegal, right?"

"Funny." He pulled off the sunglasses—damn it—and clipped them on the front of his shirt. Now he kind of looked like a dorky dad. Unfortunately that didn't actually make him less attractive. "Look, I come in peace, okay?" He paused, and the corner of his mouth twitched. "If I say 'I just want to talk,' does that make it better or worse?"

Jeff debated. The wound of childhood was still tender, but that was because Jeff never let it heal. He was fifteen and his mom died and if he wanted to hold a lifelong grudge against the best friend he'd caught kissing his cousin on the back steps of the funeral parlor, he would. But it wasn't as though Jeff had ever confessed his feelings. Carter couldn't know how much that hurt him.

Jeff had no reason to hold on to this pain and every reason to let it go. He'd come here to remember who he was without Howl. And a huge part of who he'd been revolved around Carter.

Besides, Jeff was not in the habit of turning away guys who looked like *that*.

"You want a coffee?" He gestured to the battered Muskoka chairs that adorned the creaky porch.

Carter nodded. "Thanks. You have creamer?"

"Now you're just getting demanding." He let himself smile a little to show he was teasing. It didn't feel natural yet, but the muscle memory was there somewhere.

Carter had his feet up on the porch railing when Jeff came back. He accepted the painted tin mug Jeff handed him. "Thanks."

"Sure." Jeff looked at the remaining Muskoka chair and debated that versus the railing. The chair felt couple-y. The railing felt awkward.

He sat in the chair and refused to fidget. "So. Long time no see, I guess."

Carter sipped at his coffee. "I don't know, seems like it was just yesterday."

Fuck, was he going to make dad jokes? Jeff refused to be attracted to that. "Really?"

"Hm. Tough crowd."

You have no idea. "I admit it crossed my mind that I might run into you while I'm in the area, but I wasn't expecting it last night. I guess you weren't either."

"You could say that." He rested the mug on the arm of the chair. "What are you even doing here? I had the impression you never intended to grace us with your presence again."

The words were confrontational, but Carter's demeanor had never lent itself to snippiness. The handful of times they'd fought as children, it'd been Jeff's temper that got the better of him or else some thoughtless oversight on Carter's part. He was too good-natured to be intentionally cruel. In any case, what he said was true and no less than Jeff deserved.

"It's kind of a long story."

Carter shrugged with his whole body, same as he always had, loose and languid. "I'm off today."

"Yeah, I guessed." Jeff gestured. "Wardrobe change."

"So what gives?" Carter pressed, as if they were still as close as they'd been as kids. "You're kind of a big deal now. Don't you have a tour to prepare for or something?"

Jeff squirmed. "Is this really what you want to talk about?"

"Hey, I'm just finding my feet here." Carter held up his hands in surrender. "We could talk about how you left and we didn't speak to each other for fifteen years instead, but that didn't seem much better."

Jeez. Jeff ran a hand through his hair. "I remember people in small towns being better at small talk."

That earned him a smile. "I remember you being a scrawny kid with a buzz cut. Things change."

"Not everything," Jeff muttered. He turned his mug in his hands, realized he was, in fact, fidgeting, and set it down next to his foot. "So, if we're not going to talk about when I left and we're not going to talk about why I'm back, do we have anything to talk about?"

Carter watched him quietly for a moment and then asked, "Do you want to find out?"

Jeff's heart battered against his ribs.

Before he could answer, Carter went on. "I mean… I understand things with Howl are kind of, uh, intense at the moment. I wasn't going to make you talk about it, and I know you're probably wary of people selling stories about you to the media, because people are gross like that. But if I wanted to do that, I still have that tape—"

Oh *God.*

"—of your eighth-grade talent show—"

The one where Jeff got a ridiculous boner onstage. Thank God for guitars—

"—and it's never seen the light of day, so."

Jeff dropped his head into his hands. "How much do I have to pay you to destroy that?"

"Are you kidding? Mom would kill me, she and Dad were so proud of you."

"I remember," Jeff said wistfully. His own father had missed it, of course—ostensibly why Mr. Rhodes had taped the performance in the first place, so his dad could watch it later, when he got home from the hospital. "What was it your dad said—something about a fishhook?"

Carter tilted his head back against the chair as though he were soaking up the midmorning sun. "He said you sang like you had a fishhook in your heart and someone was pulling it out through your lungs."

Jeff had admittedly been kind of an emo teenager. "He should've been a poet."

"He always said it cost too much to feed us, so he had to be a mechanic instead." He opened his eyes and turned to look into the trees. "He never made us feel bad about it, though. It was just a joke."

Was it? Carter had two brothers, and they were all six feet tall by the time they were halfway through high school. Maybe now that they were grown he had time to write more, since they could feed themselves. "How is he these days?" Jeff probably owed him a visit.

The expression on Carter's face made his blood run cold.

Oh God.

Carter swallowed visibly. "I'm sorry, I thought… I thought, you know, maybe you were in town for the memorial."

Jeff wanted to throw up. Carter's face was drawn and his eyes—they weren't quite glistening but there was an extra shine there.

This was what Jeff got for running away from his problems.

"Oh God, I'm so sorry." That fishhook felt like it had lodged in his throat. "When, uh, when did…?"

Carter cleared his throat. "November. Heart attack."

Right before the holidays. *Fuck.* "That's…." Heartbreaking. "I should've been here. He was important to me." You *were important to me.*

"You were important to him too."

Jeff had never doubted it. Mr. Rhodes always treated him like his own. Jeff wiped at his cheeks. None of this was going the way he'd envisioned it.

And he couldn't stand there another second while Carter pretended he was okay or he'd lose his mind.

"Do you, uh, do you want a hug?" Jeff wanted a hug. Jeff wanted, like, thirty hugs.

Carter made a noise that might've been a laugh and stood up. A second later Jeff was—subsumed, surrounded on all sides by warm cotton and smooth skin. Carter had six inches on him, which saved the hug from being more awkward, since Jeff had no choice but to turn his face against Carter's shoulder. He managed to get his own arms to cooperate enough to reciprocate, and he curled his fingers against Carter's very broad back. He tried not to inhale, knowing it would ruin him, but he did it anyway. It was like going back in time. He couldn't possibly smell the same, could he? Who still used the same deodorant at thirty-two as they did at seventeen?

It felt like they stood there for a long time. Jeff held on until he felt Carter start to relax, the tension melting away under his fingertips.

Then he pulled back. He was flirting with danger as it was. He was already fighting with his bandmates, contemplating major career changes, and running away from his problems to find himself, like some kind of rock-star cliché. He did not need to rediscover what it was like to be hopelessly in love with Carter Rhodes.

But God, he'd missed him.

He cleared his throat for what felt like the fortieth time, but before he could say anything, Carter spoke. "Look, obviously your life is complicated. We don't ever have to talk about why you left, or why you didn't…." *Why you didn't call me, why you didn't answer my email, why we didn't keep in touch.* All these years later Jeff could still read the spaces Carter left for him to fill in. Carter exhaled gustily. "But it really is good to see you, and I could use another friend."

There had to be a catch. Surely it couldn't be that easy.

But it didn't matter. Jeff needed this. He was here to find out who he was without his band, but no man was an island. Right? "Me too." He licked his lips. "When's the memorial? I'd like to come, if that's okay."

"It's the twentieth." Carter exhaled slowly. "His birthday."

Fuck, of course. "What time?" He needed to be in Toronto by four for sound check and rehearsal, and the drive was three hours, but he could probably charter a flight. That would get him there in less than an hour.

"The public thing starts at one. But Mom and Dave and Brady and I are getting together at sunrise. You could join us." He paused, and the hint of a smile returned to the corner of his mouth. "Assuming your stance on mornings has changed."

Jeff allowed himself a small laugh. "It hasn't. Didn't stop me from being up with the dawn today, though."

Carter glanced around, checking the location of the sun. The smile grew. "Forget to close the curtains?"

"I forgot how bright it can get with the water reflecting everything," Jeff admitted ruefully.

"And the curtains in there suck."

"And the curtains *suck*," he agreed. "Even if I'd closed them, I would've been flashing the fish. I was thinking I could go into town and buy something a little more substantial."

"You want company?"

Jeff opened his mouth to make a smart retort, but it died on his lips. He didn't think they were at a place where he could joke that curtain shopping was moving too fast. "You want to go curtain shopping?"

"More than I want to cut the grass," Carter said wryly. "Which is the adulting task I'll be forced to do if I go home. So you'd be doing me a favor, letting me tag along."

That was kind of transparent, as far as excuses went, but Jeff wasn't about to look a gift horse in the mouth. The foundations of his life were crumbling, but Carter was solid bedrock. He could start over from that. "All right," he agreed. "But you're driving."

Carter rolled his eyes. "I always drive."

They started toward his truck as Jeff let himself get sucked into an old argument. "In fairness, it's not like I didn't *offer*—"

"Beg, you mean."

"But *someone* was concerned about licensing and legal driving age and what his parents might say."

"*Someone* was concerned your little legs couldn't reach the pedals." Carter glanced at him sideways, an up-down glance that Jeff was not going to categorize as a once-over.

"God, you're so rude."

"Is that any way to talk to your chauffeur?"

Jeff's lips twitched as fifteen years of silence fell away. "Sorry. God, you're so rude, *Jeeves*."

Carter flipped him off and backed out of the carport.

JEFF FIGURED it wasn't just going to be curtains, and he was right; it turned out to be curtains, and a new set of linens for Carter's guest bath, and a mat for his front hallway, at which point Jeff made a comment about Carter using him for his interior decorating sense and Carter clapped back that he didn't know what he'd been thinking because Jeff didn't have sense of any kind.

He'd forgotten how easily they clicked. A few hours together and all the intervening years seemed to fall away.

Shopping turned into lunch at the fish-and-chips place that had just opened for the season, and by the time Jeff's phone chirped with a reminder that he had a phone conference in half an hour, he was basically fifteen again.

"Ah, shit," he said when the alarm went off.

Carter raised an eyebrow. "Some kind of rock-star Bat-Signal?"

Jeff flicked a rolled-up bit of napkin at him. "Conference call in half an hour, finalizing details for the show."

Carter's beer bottle clunked gently as he set it back on the table. "It's incredible how you make that sound like *root canal*."

"That's my gifted and expressive vocal range for you."

Carter rolled his eyes. "When's the concert?"

Damn. Jeff thought he'd have more time to work around this particular revelation. "The twentieth." Watching Carter's face fall made him feel like garbage, so he sucked it up and said, "I don't have to be in Toronto 'til four. Booked an air taxi for two thirty."

"What?" Carter's brow furrowed. "*When*?"

"When you were driving to the outlet." Jeff shrugged. "Why'd you think I made you drive?"

"That's—Jeff, that's so expensive."

Jeff put on his patented Media Face. He absolutely hated using it on Carter. It felt *dirty*. "Good thing I'm rich, then."

It worked. Carter made a noise of disgust. "Ugh, okay. Sorry. And thank you."

He let the false expression fall away. "It's nothing, Carter, seriously. I want to be there. Not just for you." Though Carter would've been more than reason enough.

He held up his hands. "I believe you."

"Okay." *Good. Great.* Could Jeff get a subject change?

"So should I take you back to the cabin? Do you need, like, total isolation for this root canal slash conference call?"

"It's more like a lobotomy," Jeff mused. "I should probably get back, yeah, so I can make notes and whatever." He almost said *God knows I don't trust Max and Trix unsupervised*, but he bit his tongue. Joe would be there, and Jeff trusted Joe, and Carter didn't need to be party to the band's dirty laundry. Jeff loved them. He didn't want to talk shit about them, even though they drove him up the wall. Max had been his protector all through high school, even gone so far as to be his fake boyfriend to Jeff's dad's second wedding. He never cared if anyone thought he was gay as long as Jeff didn't have to feel alone.

Jeff didn't know how it had come to this.

He shook himself and reached across the table. "Here, give me your phone."

Carter unlocked it and slid it over. It was older than Jeff's by a couple models and the Otterbox case had taken a serious beating.

"I can feel you judging me."

"What did you do to it, hit it with a hammer?" The screen worked fine, though, so obviously the Otterbox had done its job. Jeff created a contact with his information and sent himself a text.

"I… fell on it."

Jeff ran his finger down the crack in the plastic. "Are you heavier than you look?"

"While skating," Carter said.

"Well, that'll do it," Jeff said, meeting eyes with their server as she passed by. He couldn't tell if she recognized him, but she definitely knew Carter.

"Can I get you something else?"

Carter shook his head. "Just the bill, please. Thanks, Alice."

"Sure thing."

She didn't ask if he wanted to split the check, but that wasn't so strange. Lots of small places like this didn't. When she returned with it, Jeff reached for the folder but was quelled by a death stare from Carter, who apparently thought Jeff had spent enough money today. Jeff let him take it. His masculinity wasn't that fragile.

"Thanks."

Carter shrugged. "No sweat."

The drive back to the cabin was mostly quiet. Jeff added Carter to his phone contacts, then leaned his head against the window as they drove through the park, taking in the dappled sunlight and the occasional glimpse of familiar blue water through the trees.

They were just turning onto the long lane that led to the cabin when Carter said, "How'd you score this place, anyway? Usual rental contract's got a sixteen-day max."

There wasn't any accusation, just a sense that Carter knew exactly how persuasive Jeff was when he wanted something. Jeff smiled wanly. "I begged." He'd laid it on pretty thick too—*the park is a special place for me because my mom and I used to come out here before she got sick.* "When that didn't work, I made a generous donation to the artist-in-residence program."

Carter looked at him sideways. "We don't have an artist-in-residence program."

Jeff smirked. "Not *yet*."

He didn't have to look to feel Carter's wry amusement.

This time Carter didn't pull into the carport, just drove right up to the porch to let Jeff out. Jeff was left feeling wrong-footed. If they were friends again, if they were ignoring the fifteen years of silence, he probably didn't need to say thank you for today. He just didn't know what to say instead.

Carter beat him to the punch anyway. "See you around?"

Jeff offered a wry smile. "Well, you know where I live."

He nodded. "See you later, Jeff."

It sounded like a promise.

Excerpt from profile interview in *Rolling Stone*
March issue

RS: HOWL is one of the most prolific groups of the genre. It seems like every year, eighteen months, there's a new album. How do you maintain that level of productivity?

JP: When we first started, it felt like we were growing so fast, we all had so much to say. We were too excited to pace ourselves. But I think that—what did you call it, that level of productivity—that's actually damaging. Like when a kid ties a blanket around his neck and jumps off the roof of the shed. Just because he doesn't break his leg doesn't mean he's Superman. We were that kid. We didn't know any better; we just wanted to fly.

But now I think the healthy way to do it is—my mom used to garden. And she was always giving plants away, because certain kinds will self-propagate. Like every couple years the hostas got too big and she'd split them up and give them to friends, or every couple months the spider plant in her bathroom would send off this shoot that she'd start in a bud vase and it would become another little plant. It didn't hurt the plant to do it like that. They started new plants when they were ready, so it was sustainable. But when you're saying, 'okay, we need an album every year,' and you don't give that album time to develop organically—pardon the pun—what you're doing is you're just going and cutting off parts of the plants to arrange in a vase. It won't be as good and it hurts the plant.

So, I guess the short answer is, you don't. I think we're slowing down, and I'm okay with that. I'm not twenty anymore; I need to rest. I think the albums will be better for it.

RS: You've said you learned guitar as a kid growing up in Willow Sound. Can you tell us a little more about that?

JP: My mom was diagnosed with ALS when I was twelve, and my dad spent all his time with her. I would've been on my own except my neighbors—the closest thing you get to neighbors in Willow Sound—took me in as their fourth kid. Their three boys were involved in a ton of extracurriculars, so sometimes it was just me and the parents, and I'd hang out in the basement with the dad and we'd listen to music. That sounds sketchy, but it was disgustingly wholesome. And he had a guitar and he could play, and he saw that I was interested in learning, so for my thirteenth birthday he found a used Seagull at a secondhand shop and taught me to play.

RS: Howl's sophomore album, Ginsberg, raised a lot of eyebrows and drew criticism for promoting what some called a radical political agenda. How do you respond to that?

JP: [rolling his eyes] First I'd say that the people who criticized it for promoting a political agenda don't know much about history. Art has always been political, and rock has strong roots in the counterculture movement. Think back to the sixties. How many songs were about protesting the Vietnam war, racism? How many encouraged sexual liberation, civil rights, free speech? Like, have these people never actually listened to Rage Against the Machine? Or Beyoncé? I mean, come on. Is it promoting a radical political agenda to say there should be more to life than the endless grueling drudgery of trying to make enough money to survive, burning yourself out to the point where you need the panacea of drugs just to get through another day? I'm not sure that was radical even when the Beat poets said it.

RS: Howl is under contract with Big Moose to deliver one more album by the end of the summer. What's next after that?

JP: I'll let you know when I figure it out.

Chapter Three

PREDICTABLY, THE conference call was a clusterfuck. Jeff put himself on mute and tried to curb the impulse to pull at his hair as he sat at the tiny kitchen table, notebook at his elbow, phone on speaker in front of him. He owed Joe so many beers.

He didn't care how many flavors of Gatorade Max wanted. Max could request a masseuse and a personal stripper for all Jeff cared. It had nothing to do with him.

Then Trix came out with, "I want to do *416 Morning*."

Jeff frantically stabbed Unmute. "Absolutely not."

Tim said, "It sounds like a good idea—"

"It'll get people excited for the concert," Trix said. "I think you can take a day out of your vacation—"

Jeff gritted his teeth. "The concert is already sold out," he said.

"Then it'll pique interest for the next album," she said dismissively.

"I have a family commitment." If he said *I don't want to do another album* when he was here and they were all there, fuck knew what would happen. That was an in-person argument. "I won't be there. Not negotiable."

Tim said, cajoling, "Jeff—"

"I'll be at a funeral," he said sharply. "The rest of you can do whatever the fuck you want without me. I'll be there for sound check at four."

Crickets.

Joe spoke first. "Sorry to hear, man."

"If you'll text the information, Big Moose would like to send flowers—" Tim, that fucking sycophant.

"Sorry for pushing," Trix said. "That sucks, Jeff. I'm sorry. Do you need anything?"

The kicker of it was she meant it. She was so laser-focused on their music she didn't see they were making each other miserable. "I'm okay," he said. "But I need to be there. You know?"

Thankfully things wrapped up after that. Jeff hung up, debated texting Carter, then decided against it. He had leftovers for dinner, took the trash out to the bearproof box, then grabbed his acoustic and went out to the picnic table.

The sky was clear, and with the trees cut back away from the cabin, it felt huge, like it could swallow him up. Tonight he'd be able to see half the Milky Way—though maybe not as well as he would've if he broke down about the glasses. If he cupped his hands around his eyes to block out the land, he could pretend he was floating among the stars.

But that wouldn't be for hours. If he wanted to stay warm until then, he'd need a campfire. Strange how much difference a few hundred kilometers could make; it was probably nice and temperate in the city.

Jeff hadn't built a fire in probably a decade, but if you had enough paper and kindling and a big honking lighter, you couldn't go wrong. It took twenty minutes, but one of the small logs finally caught just as the wind picked up off the water.

The Muskoka chairs were too heavy to drag off the porch, but a stump close enough to the firepit served just fine. Jeff sat with his back to the fire to preserve his night vision and walked his fingers up the neck of the guitar. He played as many songs from his teenage days as he could remember. Then, on a whim, he dropped the tuning on the lower strings, because fuck it, he might as well go for the whole experience. He climbed up on the picnic table and lay on his back staring up, and plucked the constellations into existence one star at a time.

He sang until his throat hurt from the campfire smoke, and then realized he should've filled some buckets before the sun went down. He put the guitar away and used the biggest pot in the cabin to douse the flames. It took four trips.

His clothes and hair stank of woodsmoke after, but he liked it. This wasn't the sour sweat of a coke comedown or the stale vomit stench of a hangover. He crawled into bed and pulled the blankets around him in a cocoon, and when a loon called out over the Sound, he closed his eyes and slept.

THE BLACKOUT curtains were a bad idea.

That was Jeff's excuse, anyway, when he rolled out of bed at ten, still smoky, dry-eyed and dry-mouthed and feeling like he'd been on a bender even though the last alcoholic drink he'd had was at lunch with Carter.

Did yesterday really happen? Did he really make up with Carter after fifteen years via an agreement not to talk about it? A glance at his phone confirmed one new contact.

He needed coffee.

His skin didn't sit right today. He was listless—pacing as he waited for the pot to heat up, picking at the edge of a peeling callus. And the coffee didn't help. He drank it and waited for his nerves to settle, but they didn't.

He took a Clif bar out of a cupboard and tore into it outside on the porch, but the fresh air was no better. The wind had kicked up and the water was murky, choppy. It felt a little too much like Jeff did inside, and the wet slap of the waves grated something in his brain.

Crash. Your life is disintegrating.

Crack. It's your own fault.

Thwack. Your mother isn't here. You *knew* she wasn't here.

Slap. It was never about her.

Maybe he should go back to bed.

He'd had spells like this before. Usually he had at least one while on a tour, and the best thing for it was to get away from the group and do something immersive. He'd gotten a massage once, which had worked, but attempting a pedicure was an abject failure. Once, in New York, he'd wandered through Central Park until he was completely lost, and he'd felt… peaceful. Zen, even.

Thing was, he was already alone here, and he had a whole damn nature preserve to trek through, and he knew it wouldn't work. External stimuli weren't the problem. *He* was the problem.

The guitar cases sat under the kitchen table, out of the way but somehow staring at him, daring him. He'd come here to find out who he'd be as a solo artist, but he wasn't ready to meet that person yet and he couldn't put his finger on why.

Meanwhile, the countdown was ticking on the new album.

No wonder he was annoyed with himself.

He took a deep breath and exhaled slowly, then another, until he'd brought his irritation level down to a simmer and he could think around his agitation.

A shower would help. Then a drive into town and maybe even a real breakfast. Possibly brunch, by the time he got there. If he still felt like garbage, he'd think about going to see a movie or something. Crap, what day was it? Would there even be a matinee?

Whatever. He'd figure it out. But first, shower.

By the time he slid into the booth at Shinny's, he did feel slightly more human.

He still almost jumped through the roof when a familiar voice said, "Jeff!" in a tone that was the verbal equivalent of a bear hug, and he only got to his feet out of pure instinct in time to be swept into the real thing.

She hugged just like her son. Jeff let himself cling a little harder than he had with Carter, and he let her set the timetable to pull away, which she eventually did, holding him at arm's length as though to evaluate whether he'd been eating his vegetables.

"Hi, Mrs. Rhodes."

Once upon a time, he and Carter had just called each other's parents Mom and Dad, as a joke. Then Jeff's mom got sick and it stopped being funny.

"It's Ella, sweetheart," she corrected as she sat down across from him at his table without being asked. "I think you're old enough now to use my first name."

"Doesn't feel like it," Jeff said with a small smile as his server came by with another menu.

"Oh," Ella said, moving to stand, "no, sorry, we were just catching up—"

But Jeff had seen three different heads turn when she said his name, and now he was aware of more people looking his way. News traveled fast. "You can stay if you want," he said. *Please stay, I don't want to sign autographs at lunch.* God forbid someone ask for a selfie. Jeff didn't want to end up on the main character of Twitter for being rude to fans. "If you have time, I'd love the company."

It was obviously the right thing to say, because Ella smiled and accepted the menu. She ordered a drink and then set the menu on the table without looking at it. There were only so many restaurants in town; she probably had it memorized.

Jeff opened his mouth to ask her how she was, and then he remembered. There were circles under her eyes, and she looked like she'd lost weight recently, and not in the intentional way either. She must still be grieving. But should he offer condolences now? Should he wait until the right moment?

"Carter said he told you about Fred." She blinked back tears.

News traveled fast around here. "I was so sorry to hear." Understatement of the decade. "He was a great man."

"He was," she agreed as the server brought their drinks. They ordered, and the server left again with the menus. "Carter tells me you're joining us for the memorial?"

"If that's okay," Jeff said. "I'd like to pay my respects. I was… I wish I'd been around sooner."

She pulled her tea close to her. "You're here now. And of course you're welcome. Fred would have loved to have you there."

He tried to internalize that. If it was good enough for her, it could be good enough for him.

They spent a pleasant half hour chatting about nothing in particular, and Jeff felt the agitation of the morning ebbing.

"I suppose I'd best get back to the garage." Ella sighed and glanced at the time. "The invoicing isn't going to do itself."

Jeff hadn't realized she was still working. He had thought she'd retire. "Would you like a ride?"

"No, thank you, sweetheart, I drove. But it was wonderful seeing you." When the check came, Ella tried to pay.

Jeff said, "My treat. I insist. It was my pleasure. Anyway, Carter took me out yesterday."

Ella shook her head. "Yes, I know. I should be thanking you, getting that boy to take half a day from saving the world."

So Carter had grown up into a workaholic too. Somehow that didn't surprise him. He had so much of his dad in him. "It was good seeing you, Ella."

Jeff wanted to linger at the diner after she left, but the patrons in the booths kept glancing over. Any longer and he'd be inviting selfie requests. Instead, he paid the bill, left a generous tip, and slipped out the door before anyone could verify that he was *that* Jeff.

He was most of the way back to his truck when his phone buzzed. Buoyed with a weird, unfamiliar hope, he pulled it out and unlocked the screen.

And promptly considered dropping it.

Howl Guitarist Caught with Pants Down

There went Jeff's good mood. He climbed into the cab and sat to skim through the article, which included a video—with appropriate pixilation—of Max urinating on the outside of a bar in downtown Toronto. Trix was with him, just as drunk but with her pants on.

For fuck's sake. Jeff hadn't even been out of the city for three days and Max was being cited for public indecency. At least it seemed like he eluded possession charges this time. Maybe he left the drugs in Trix's purse.

Maybe they shoved it all up their noses.

Whatever. Jeff wasn't their babysitter, and he wasn't their mom. Tim could handle it, or not. And surely to God journalists knew not to ask Jeff for a comment.

He started the truck but left it in Park as he leaned back in the driver's seat and stared up through the sunroof.

"Fuck."

JEFF WOULDN'T exactly call himself a gym rat, but the fact that he ate a majority of his meals on the road several months out of the year meant he had to keep physically active if he didn't want to feel like garbage. Plus, he needed his body in good condition to keep his energy up during a concert. So after lunch, with irritation once more burning through his veins, he drove back to the cabin, changed into running shorts, and stuck in his AirPods.

An hour's worth of exercise and cottage rock put him back on an even keel. It was a warm day now, but the path he took kept him within sight of the water a good amount of the time, so he stayed cool. Just that morning he'd felt like the waves were going to drive him crazy. This afternoon they were eroding his sharp edges the same as they did to the rocks on the shore.

Well. The waters of the Sound could change pretty quick. That was what Jeff told himself.

He took another quick shower when he returned to the cabin, which was so tiny that Jeff's sweat stink would fill it otherwise. Then he took a Gatorade out of the fridge, made himself a snack plate, and went to go soak up the sunshine on the picnic table.

So things weren't going exactly as he'd hoped. That was fine, right? He hadn't written any music yet, but that didn't mean anything. He hadn't gotten up the nerve to officially quit the band yet either, but he wasn't going to do that over the phone, so that was… fine. He'd made up with Carter and now he could work through fifteen years of regret and grow as a person or whatever. Now that they were adults, Jeff could get to know him for real, and inevitably he'd find some flaw that would prove they were ill-matched, as he'd found with every person he'd dated since, and he could finally get some closure on this part of his life.

The lap of the water in his ears was a perfect lullaby. With the breeze slowly drying his hair and the sun warming his face and his muscles pleasantly buzzing with exertion, Jeff let languor overcome him.

He couldn't have said what woke him. Maybe it was the angle of the sun, or the rumble of his stomach reminding him it was time for more than just that half-eaten plate of fruit and cheese.

Maybe it was the shuffle of something in the pine needles next to the picnic table he was asleep on.

In any case, Jeff stretched languidly, relishing the twinge of muscles. He turned his head to the side, opened his eyes—

And found himself nose to nose with a bear.

Jeff immediately forgot everything he knew about bear safety. He scrambled backward so quickly he fell off the picnic table, thumped onto the bench, and rolled onto the ground.

The bear snuffled closer to the table. Oh God. Jeff was a moron. Why hadn't he finished his snack? He knew better than that. The bear box was fifteen feet away.

Which was much farther than the bear.

It was black, with a brown nose and round ears and enormous feet, and frankly Jeff was a little concerned the smell hadn't woken him, because it was a lot worse than his post-run stank. It looked at him and made a noise like an angry cow as it shuffled closer.

Jeff had only seen a bear once or twice growing up. Then again, he hadn't lived *inside* a provincial park. He was pretty sure the black ones weren't particularly dangerous unless they were mothers with cubs, and this was just one bear, so he should be fine, right? He scrambled to his feet, keeping the picnic table between them.

Something wet touched his leg. Heart in his throat, he turned around.

There was a second, smaller bear. The wet something was its nose.

The mother stood up on her back legs and roared.

Okay, yep, time to run away. Still disoriented from his sudden wakeup call, he staggered toward the cabin—only to find another tiny bear on the porch.

You gotta be kidding me.

His truck keys were inside. What was he going to do, climb a tree? No, bears could climb, couldn't they? This mama looked like she might try it. He glanced around frantically. There had to be somewhere safe—

There. The fascia under the porch had a gap in it where the wood had rotted around the nails that held it to the support post. Jeff dove in, praying the area under the porch wasn't already occupied by—God, snakes or skunks or… fuck, there were definitely spiders and other horrible crawly things. He took a deep breath and carefully pushed the fallen piece of fascia into the gap. Then he peered out through the slatted holes as the mama bear dropped back to all fours and resumed her perusal of Jeff's snack plate.

Well. This was embarrassing.

Now that Jeff was not a threat to the cubs, the bears seemed content to take their time puttering around the cabin. Jeff didn't think he'd left any other food around, but for all he knew, the bushes around the cabin were wild blueberries or something. Hell, maybe Mama Bear was tired and thought that if Jeff's picnic table was good enough for a human, it was good enough for her.

Okay, so he was stuck under the porch of his cabin until the bears moved on. So far no snakes, skunks, or other animals, and Jeff wasn't going to look around and find out about the rest. He was safe, mostly. All he had to do was… wait until the bears left.

Or—*or*! He had Carter's number in his phone. Carter was a park ranger. In fact, he could just call the park's dispatch and have them send whoever was closest to…. What did they even do with bears? Did they tranquilize them? That seemed extreme. Maybe they just scared them away? Did the park service pepper spray bears?

He felt prematurely bad about that for a split second, and then he felt a crawling sensation on the back of his leg and decided the bears could take it. He reached into his pocket for his phone….

And remembered it was still on the picnic table.

He swiped at the back of his leg without looking and prayed that whatever it was would crawl away.

So. Next time he decided to return to the town of his youth to fucking *find himself*, he was renting an apartment. He'd sign autographs at his front door if he had to. Bears he could handle. Spiders under the porch were absolutely a deal-breaker.

Canada didn't have a lot of poisonous spiders, right? So they were just gross and not, like, lethal?

Right?

Maybe he should've taken his chances with the bears.

He debated how long he should stay there, growing more convinced by the moment that a black widow was going to be the end of him and that some poor park ranger—hopefully not Carter—would find his moldering corpse a couple days later when they came to collect his garbage.

Then it registered—tires on gravel.

The sweetest music Jeff had ever heard.

Then he realized they were probably Carter's tires, and Carter was going to drive up to his cabin and find Jeff hiding under his porch because he'd been stupid enough to leave food out, and he wondered if the spiders could hurry up and kill him. Toxic venom would be a less painful way to die than embarrassment.

The engine cut out, and a moment later a door slammed. Jeff could only see legs, but they were definitely Carter's, unless the park made a point of hiring stupidly tall men with thighs that could crush skulls. "Oh, it's you," he said. Something rattled. Jeff thought Carter was leaning into the truck bed. "Come on, move along. Don't make me get the air horn. Go! Get!"

The bear rumbled loudly, but it shuffled off. The cubs ambled away with her and disappeared into the underbrush.

Meanwhile. "Jeff?" Carter called. He sounded worried.

A phantom something crawled over Jeff's calf again, and that was *it*. He pushed the lattice fascia aside and dragged himself out from under the porch as quickly as he could. Fuck dignity. Jeff wanted another shower and a Xanax IV.

"Fuck fuck fuck fuck fuck!" he chanted as he frantically tried to brush off all of his skin at once. "I hate spiders. Can you just—get them off me, please?"

To his credit, Carter didn't even smile. "All right, just… hold still?"

Hold *still*? And make himself an easier target? But Jeff managed to plant his feet for thirty seconds so Carter could check him over. Carter brushed a hand over the small of his back—which was distracting enough to jar Jeff out of panic mode; who let Carter have such big hands?—and then his ankle, and then he put both hands on Jeff's shoulders and turned him around, and Jeff closed his eyes while Carter checked his hair. If there were spiders there, Jeff didn't want to know.

"All right, all done."

Jeff opened his eyes.

"You've had a busy day," Carter observed. He wasn't outright laughing at Jeff, at least, even if amusement did color his voice. "Are you hurt?"

"Apart from my dignity, no."

Now Carter smiled. "That'll heal." Jeff doubted it. "What happened, anyway? I know you know better than to leave food outside."

Ugh. "I fell asleep," he admitted. "I went out for a run, came back, made myself a snack. I decided to eat it outside, and the sun felt nice, so I just closed my eyes for a few minutes… without finishing my food."

"Hm." The smile softened, and he shook his head minutely. "That explains it."

Jeff frowned. "Explains what?"

"The extra freckles." Carter raised his hand and lightly brushed a finger down the bridge of Jeff's nose. It lingered on the tip for a moment before he pulled it away. "And you have a sunburn."

Jeff's face did feel a little tight. Also his chest. And his pants. His whole body was wildly, absurdly primed for Carter to kiss him. Did Carter have to touch him like that?

Finally, when seconds had ticked by without Carter making a move, he found his voice. "I knew I forgot something." As the adrenaline faded from his system, he asked, "Were you talking to the bear?"

"Winnie, yeah." Carter gestured toward the cabin, and they sat on the porch. "You get to know them by sight after a while."

"And you named her Winnie. Like Winnie the Pooh."

Carter raised his eyebrows. "Who says I named her?"

"I do." The name had Carter's particular brand of wholesome stamped all over it. And he'd loved that movie as a kid.

"Fine." He shrugged in capitulation. "The first time I saw her, about five years ago I guess, she had her snout stuck in a honey jar. Someone didn't lock up their garbage properly. The name seemed fitting. This is the first time I've seen her this year. Two cubs—not bad."

Now that the terror had left his system, Jeff found himself smiling fondly. "You're such a softy."

"Hey, I'm just being a good naturalist. Nothing soft about that."

Naturalist, Jeff noted. Not park ranger. So he'd been wrong about the job title. "Uh-huh. I bet you let all the nuisance bears off with a warning about the air horn," Jeff teased. "Because you're soft."

Carter crossed his arms, playing along. "Maybe I let her off with a warning because the air horn's really annoying and I hate it and it disturbs the rest of the non-nuisance wildlife."

"Hmm." Jeff leaned back and assessed him. "Okay, I'll buy it." He shook his head. "Anyway. To what do I owe your incredibly well-timed rescue?"

"I was in the neighborhood," Carter said wryly. "And so was the bear. She has a tracking device. Dispatch radios in when she goes places she might get in trouble. I still had my radio on after my shift, so I said I'd check it out."

Of course. "So you were here to save the bear, not me."

"Oh no. I was here to save the bear from you, and you from the spiders. What were you doing under the porch?"

Jeff sighed. "Hiding. My truck keys were in the cabin, and there was a baby bear on the steps. Didn't think Winnie would appreciate me trying to sneak past the cub."

Carter glanced at the steps, which were all the way down at one end, and then at the door to the cabin, all the way at the other. "And you didn't consider jumping the railing?"

Ouch. "Just when my dignity was starting to recover." He sighed. "You working the late shift? Or can I bribe you with dinner to forget the specifics of this incident?"

"Neither, sorry." Now Carter looked embarrassed. He hunched his shoulders a little and ducked his head, as though that made him any less of a giant. The whole effect was charming in its incongruity. "Uh, I've got about a half an hour and then I've got to go...." He swallowed the last few words in the sort of mumble he used to use when his mom caught him doing something he shouldn't.

This had to be good. "Sorry, I didn't catch that."

Carter sighed and uncurled, flopping bonelessly in the chair. "I have to coach a T-ball game."

Nothing could have prepared Jeff for the mental image of six-foot-four Viking god-man Carter herding a group of ankle-biters at the least athletic team sport known to humankind. That was too wholesome. Things that wholesome did not mix with Jeff. It was like baking soda and vinegar. Jeff and wholesome together got very messy and then exploded.

"Why is your face doing that?"

"Shh," Jeff said. "I'm savoring this moment." A moment imagining a flock of five-year-olds celebrating a win by attempting to crowd-surf their coach? They probably couldn't dump a cooler of Gatorade on him like a college football team might, but they had their own individual water bottles. They could get a similar effect.

Carter rolled his eyes. "Whatever you're imagining, there's probably a lot more runny noses, kids picking dandelions, and surprise vomit."

"Yeesh. Moment ruined." He shook his head to clear away those images as well as the ones that came before them. He'd learned his lesson with Carter the first time. Carter was kind and generous and supportive, and he'd been Jeff's safe place when his life fell apart around him.

But Jeff was only safe until his stupid heart got involved, because Carter was also *straight*. The last thing Jeff needed was to rekindle his high school crush as a grown man. "Why coaching?" Then something occurred to him and he glanced surreptitiously at Carter's left hand. No wedding ring, but that didn't mean anything—

"It was my dad's team."

Wow. That was *way* worse than Carter being secretly married with a kid.

"The garage sponsors a team every year, and he always used to coach it."

"Of course he did," Jeff murmured. The man was a saint.

Carter blew out a breath. "When it came time to sign up to sponsor a team again this year, Mom got teary-eyed and started to say we'd need to ask the parents if anyone was willing to coach, and I couldn't stand the idea of her asking someone, so I said I'd do it."

Because Carter was a saint in training. Not like Jeff didn't know that; he'd put up with Jeff trailing after him long enough. "Of course you did."

That earned him a nudge from Carter's booted foot. "Shut up. I guess that means you don't want to come?"

Jeff blinked. "To watch your kids' T-ball game?" he clarified.

Carter stood and stretched, and Jeff tried not to watch too obviously to see if his shirt rode up. It didn't. "The T-ball is coincidental," he said. "There's a food truck that sells those Mennonite sausages—"

Jeff's stomach growled, reminding him he never finished his snack.

Carter smirked.

"I'll get changed."

LESSON TWO
Prepare to Reevaluate Your Assumptions

YOU KNOW what they say about assuming?

Don't get me wrong. Assumptions have their place. Without them we'd be calling the grocery ahead of time to make sure they have milk.

But every once in a while, you get this inkling that the assumptions you've made aren't serving your best interests. Sometimes something makes you look away from the tree trunk six inches from your face and realize you're in a forest.

And sometimes that invokes pants-shitting terror.

It's scary when your worldview shifts. There's comfort in the familiar. But surviving and thriving requires the ability to recognize when we're wrong and adapt to the truth. Humility is good for you.

Just don't tell Max I said that.

Chapter Four

JEFF WAS permitted to pay for dinner, mostly because Carter was busy riding herd on fifteen five-year-olds who all wanted to tell him about their week and there was no way they were going to let him walk to the food truck. Jeff wandered over himself, dropped off Carter's dinner along with a drink, and took a seat in the stands. He hoped his sunglasses would provide some level of anonymity. No one would expect to see a rock star at a T-ball game anyway.

At least, no one who hadn't grown up in Willow Sound, where the knowledge that Carter and Jeff had been thick as thieves was common and inescapable. But Jeff figured he could handle the locals.

Probably.

That was what Jeff told himself until a vaguely familiar voice said, "Oh my God—" and then quieted noticeably. "*Jeff?*"

Crap.

Jeff reluctantly tore his gaze away from the game, where Carter, in a forest-green Rhodes's Garage T-shirt, was cheering on a kindergartener to run home instead of going from third base directly into the dugout. The woman who'd spoken was Carter's age, with dark skin and short natural hair held back with a band. He was sure she'd been in some of Carter's classes—what was her name—

"It's Alyssa," she said before he could come up with it. "You probably don't remember me—"

Jeff smiled politely and shifted over on the paint-chipped bleacher so she'd have room. "You were homecoming queen my first year of high school." Carter had been runner-up for homecoming king. Jeff paid attention to things like that.

"Wow, I stand corrected." She laughed and took the seat next to him. "I guess you're here with Carter?"

It was public knowledge that Jeff didn't have kids, so either he was here with an adult who had a reason to be here or he had a problem.

"Yeah, but I've been warned to stay out of the splash zone. What about you?" He didn't want to make any assumptions.

"Oh, I'm here for the rivalry," she joked. Off Jeff's blank look, she nodded toward the opposing dugout. "My husband coaches the red team. That's our son digging for worms behind second base."

Sure enough, there was a kid kneeling in the infield, glove discarded, digging a tiny trench with a stick.

"You must be so proud," Jeff said before he could think better of it.

Alyssa wasn't offended; she snorted good-naturedly. "Honestly, I love the fact that he can just be a kid. Sure, worms are gross, but whatever. At least he's not trying to trip the runners."

Did kids do that at this age? "So, when you say rivalry…?"

"Oh, no, the kids aren't that psycho. Don't worry," she laughed. "That was a joke about my husband and my ex-fiancé coaching opposing teams."

Her ex-*what*?

"Which is also funny because they actually get along really…." Alyssa caught the expression on his face and trailed off. "Guess I stepped in it. Carter didn't tell you about the engagement?"

What was he supposed to say to that? Whatever he answered was going to make Carter look like a jerk. "In fairness we didn't really reconnect until recently." And if she had a five-year-old, chances were the broken engagement was old news.

She winced. "Sorry. I didn't mean to make it awkward. I swear there's no hard feelings."

This conversation was over Jeff's head. He decided to change the subject. "It's fine. So, was he right about surprise vomit being something to worry about, or did he make that up to impress me?"

They chatted until the end of the third inning, when the kids had a break for snacks and drinks and, Jeff thought, because they couldn't be expected to concentrate on the game any longer. Alyssa abandoned him for the red team's dugout, where her son greeted her with both hands out in front of him. Alyssa clutched her chest and telegraphed excitement. Jeff assumed the kid was holding a worm.

Meanwhile, a parent had taken over in the green dugout and Carter was making his way toward Jeff. "Clementine?" He held out a hand with four of them. Jeff refused to be distracted by how easily they fit there.

He took one anyway. "Ex-fiancé?" he said mildly, rolling the clementine to loosen the skin.

Carter sat in Alyssa's vacated spot. "I see you were talking to Alyssa."

Jeff shoved his thumb into the center of the clementine. "She recognized me. I recognized her too, I guess." He wasn't going to ask about it. It wasn't his business. And it was long over. Time to move on. "Were you going to mention you'd been engaged, or nah?"

Damn it.

Carter shrugged. "It was a long time ago. We were barely out of university."

Did Jeff get to ask why it hadn't worked out? It felt like the sort of question you didn't ask the best friend you hadn't spoken to in fifteen years. At least not until you'd been reacquainted for more than a few days.

He set the first long strip of rind next to him on the bench and peeled off the other piece. "Okay."

Carter looked over from skinning his own clementine. "Okay?" he repeated.

For a few more seconds he concentrated on scraping the pith off the first section of fruit. That gave him time to make sure his voice was steady and neutral when he said, "You don't have to tell me everything." He popped it into his mouth, then said around it, "Although if I'd found out you had a kid, I'd have been pretty miffed."

"I wouldn't keep a child a secret. Jeez, I'm not a monster."

No, he was a thirty-two-year-old man who said *jeez* out loud. Jeff swallowed. "You're big enough," he observed, which was on the mild side as far as their banter went, but he was still regaining his equilibrium.

"Ha ha." He started on the second clementine. "I guess all your relationships are kind of a matter of public record."

"Not really." Jeff spotted a seed in the next section and took a moment to squeeze it out. "I mean, I'm out, but not everyone I date is. And even when they are, not everyone wants to publicly date a rock star." He flicked the seed into the grass. "It's fun for a while, but people taking pictures of your lunch dates gets kind of old. And then there's, you know, the fact that there's a whole class of people who make their money by hinting at scandalous affairs. It's easier to keep things casual."

That sounded bitter. He shoved the rest of the clementine in his mouth to make himself shut up.

When Carter didn't say anything even when Jeff had finished chewing, he looked over. Carter was watching him with a vaguely exasperated expression, like Jeff had somehow missed the point. "What?"

He shook his head. "Never mind."

Then the official scorekeeper blew the whistle to warn everyone the game was set to resume, and Carter stood up. "That's my cue."

The game ended in a tie and with Jeff's fingers smelling like satsuma. On the way back to the park, they drove with the windows down, and Jeff leaned his head against the window frame and watched the sun melt into the horizon. Apart from the wind, the ride was quiet, but inside Jeff's head it was loud. He wanted a guitar and a microphone and an audience to sing his heart out to. He wanted a pen and a notepad and a barely lit corner of the cabin to pour himself into.

But he didn't want to look too closely at what came out.

Still, when Carter parked the truck, Jeff looked over and thought, Fuck it. It had been a nice day. He wasn't ready for it to be over. "You want a beer?"

Carter grinned wide enough to crinkle the skin at the corners of his eyes. "Thought you'd never ask."

While Jeff rooted out the drinks, Carter set to work on the campfire.

"I've got a couple chairs in the back of the truck," he said. "More comfortable than a log."

"My ass thanks you," Jeff said dryly and caught the keys Carter tossed him one-handed.

Carter clearly had more experience building campfires than Jeff, because it was burning merrily by the time Jeff had the chairs set up. They put their backs to the water to keep the smoke out of their faces, and then they clinked their bottles together. "Cheers."

Carter nodded in acknowledgment and lifted his bottle to his mouth.

A loon called out over the water, and Jeff shivered reflexively and stuck his feet closer to the fire.

"Can I ask you something?" Carter asked when the echo died down.

Suspicious, Jeff paused with the bottle touching his lower lip. "Were you waiting for an opportunity to get me liquored up to ask?"

Carter flicked his bottle cap at him. Jeff caught it. "Be serious."

Something about the way he said it made Jeff take him at face value. He let the smile fall away from his face. "You can ask me anything."

There were a lot of difficult questions on the table, but Carter asked one of the easier ones. "Why'd you come back? Why now?"

Jeff thumbed at the top of his beer label. He wouldn't have been able to answer that honestly earlier in the week—not only because he wasn't sure but because he wasn't ready to trust Carter then. Now, though…. "You've probably seen some articles about Howl?" he said. "Creative differences, uh, certain band members being intoxicated and belligerent in public…."

Carter nodded. "Sure. I tend to take it all with a grain of salt."

Saint Carter. "Well, the rumors are not exactly unfounded." He let out a long breath. "I'm sure it's come out somewhere that the four of us met in detention."

"See, that part I believed."

"Ass." Jeff rolled his eyes. One of the smaller logs cracked and spit. "I was a little…. It was hard for me when we moved. Mom had just died, I didn't have any friends, Dad was—well, you know what he was like." Inattentive at best, abusive via neglect at worst. "I barely graduated high school. Probably would've dropped out if I hadn't met Max and Trix and Joe. Not that we didn't get into trouble, obviously."

"Obviously," Carter echoed gently.

"It was kid stuff at first—underage drinking, weed. Joe never did any of it, 'cause he said if he did, Child Services might take him away from his parents. I thought he was exaggerating back then, but these days…." He shook his head. "Trix's stepmom had a prescription for… I don't even remember what. That's where it started. But I don't think any of us were addicted to anything until we finally got an album deal my second year of college." College he'd gotten into on sheer luck, with his high school grades.

He needed a break there, and Carter must've sensed it, because he redirected. "What were you even studying?"

Jeff smiled in spite of himself and tilted his head toward the sky. "Man, you're gonna laugh."

"Try me."

Well, maybe Carter wouldn't. "English language and literature. Focus in poetry, especially the poetry of the mid-twentieth century."

He didn't have to look to see the moment it connected for Carter, all the little pieces. Jeff's love of music had come from Carter's father and his love of poetry had too. Even when he couldn't bring himself to call, even when he was actively self-destructing, he couldn't turn away from the two things that brought him comfort.

And he'd pulled them together when he came up with the name for the band.

"Angelheaded hipsters," Carter said quietly, reaching out one long arm like he was going to ruffle Jeff's hair the way he had when they were kids. Instead he just touched a stray curl and tugged gently before letting go.

Jeff made his heart start beating again through sheer force of will. "Yeah, well. If I'd had any sense, I'd have named us something else. I forgot about the way the poem starts. 'I saw the best minds of my generation destroyed by madness, starving hysterical naked.' Should've been a warning."

Carter considered this in gentle silence and then offered, "I don't think that's what they mean when they say life imitates art."

Oh, what did he know; he'd studied environmental science. But Jeff allowed himself to be soothed. "Anyway. We managed moderation for a while. I got busted for cocaine possession once, though, on our second tour, and that was enough. A very expensive lawyer kept it out of the press and got the charge dismissed. But Max and Trix… I don't know. They're out of control." Or Max was out of control, and Trix was along for the ride. The difference seemed academic.

"High onstage?" Carter asked.

"Shockingly, no. At least not so far." He took a swig of his beer; even in the chill night it was getting warm. "And then there's Tim." Their asshole handler. "Back when we were young and stupid and he headhunted us, he told us the boilerplate contract terms sucked—his modified one would suit us better. We signed directly, no independent representation. Guess whose favor the contract turned out to be in." It gave Tim way too much control… and a lot of the tour proceeds and merch sales that should've gone to Howl—a big deal since recording artists made peanuts on royalties these days. "He's usually hands-off, but with the next album due and the dollar signs of the next tour in his eyes, he's decided to crawl up our asses and act as our tour manager."

Fucking Tim. Jeff finished the bottle. He hadn't even known how shitty their contract was until a movie studio had offered him a deal to score a feature animated film. Tim didn't represent Jeff, just the band. Jeff had made more on that than he did in a year of touring.

The conversation lulled, and the sounds of the night crept in—the steady crackle of the fire, the occasional off-rhythm snap of a twig or burr of rodent feet on pine needles, the drone of an early mosquito or two. Finally Carter said, "You didn't answer my question, though. Why'd you come *here*?"

The million-dollar question. "I came here to lie on my back and look up at the stars and play 'Bobcaygeon' until I turn into Gord Downie or die, whichever comes first." After a moment he raised his head. "I love my band. I love being onstage. But I don't trust Max and Trix anymore, and… I don't know. It doesn't feel right. But they're all I've had since I left here."

He wanted so badly to reach for the naked empathy on Carter's face, to allow himself to hold fast to someone who wouldn't let him sink.

He'd *wanted* to be coming back to grieve his mother, but he'd done that. She wasn't here.

She wasn't really the one he came back to find.

"So I came back," he finished, "to remember who I was before them and remind myself I can stand on my own."

Carter reached out and touched his wrist, and Jeff's heart beat allegro. "You don't have to."

"I do, though," Jeff said. "Not, like, because I think people wouldn't help me. I need to do it for me. Just like I need to decide what to do about Howl for *me*." He blew out a breath. "I meant to come out here and write an album, but once I got here, I don't know. I'm half afraid I'll write another Howl album, and half afraid I won't."

"So you haven't written anything," Carter finished.

He'd always understood Jeff better than anyone. "Getting pretty good at 'Bobcaygeon,' though."

Carter squeezed his wrist once more and let go. Jeff wondered if he'd been able to feel how fast Jeff's pulse was racing. "Well, then," he said, "let's hear it."

Chapter Five

FOR TWO days Jeff didn't see hide nor hair of Carter, even in the park. At least not in person. The night after their campfire, he got a texted picture of a garbage-strewn campsite, followed by the facepalm emoji.

Someone could've used the airhorn, Jeff wrote back.

God save us from dumb tourists, Carter replied.

Jeff spent that night violently fighting the urge to pick up his pen, playing the Seagull until his fingertips went numb, lining up his favorite songs from his adolescence one after the other.

He forgot to close the curtains again, and the sun woke him, so he sat up in bed and watched the sunrise for a few moments and heard the echo of a melody he wanted to write. Instead he picked up his phone and took a picture, let his finger hover over the Send button.

Finally he typed *Hi, Mom* and sent it to Carter.

It was too early to be awake, or so Jeff thought, but he got an answer back a moment later—a simple heart emoji.

Snippets of songs crowded Jeff's head all morning, but he put them off. Without Carter to distract him, he worried he'd give in to them eventually, so he took a drive. He could use a few more groceries and maybe something to read.

Somehow he ended up at the marina instead, contemplating a rental. He could probably only get a canoe or kayak, since he didn't have a pleasure craft license. But he shouldn't go alone. That was a big no-no for an inexperienced boater, and after fifteen years, Jeff qualified.

Maybe Carter would want to go with him one day. He pulled out his phone to text him about it and found a grease-stained selfie waiting for him.

Carter was wearing generic gray coveralls with the top half pushed down to expose the white T-shirt underneath, and he was smeared from cheekbone to neck in a way that looked deliberate. A familiar long-suffering expression sat upon his features—heavy brow, pursed lips. His eyes were laughing. *You should see the other guy.*

An entire parade of other guys could have marched naked right past Jeff playing brass instruments and he wouldn't have seen them. Jeff had received less-filthy pictures while *sexting*. The photograph drew him in. It made him want impossible things—to smooth his fingertips over Carter's forehead, trace the bow curve of his mouth with his thumb. To peel him out of that stained shirt and push him into the shower—

"Hey! Jeff, right?"

He jerked his head up. Kara the park ranger was walking toward him. He guessed it was her day off too. "Hey, Kara, right?"

She grinned. "Yeah, you remembered. What're you doing here? Thinking about renting a boat?"

Shaking his head, he admitted, "Nah, no license. I was thinking of doing a kayak… thing." *Actually I was thinking about getting my dick wet with your boss.* Jeff had thought Carter suspected Jeff had a crush on him back in the day, but if he was sending pictures like that, maybe not.

"There's rentals at the park too—a lot calmer there." She tilted her head. "Is it true that you knew the boss man back when?"

Either she'd only been hearing very selective rumors, or she was choosing to ignore Jeff's fame. Whatever the case, Jeff appreciated it. "Afraid so."

She glanced to her right, where three people around her age were launching a boat. "Hey, Rufus! We okay to take on one more?"

A man Jeff assumed to be Rufus looked over from lashing an inflatable raft to the boat's stern. "He chipping in for gas?"

Kara smiled and turned back to Jeff. "So. Let's make a deal."

Jeff had a feeling he knew where this was going. "I'm listening."

"You tell me embarrassing stories about Carter as a kid and chip in for fuel, and instead of kayaking, you get to spend the afternoon clinging to the raft while Jeri does donuts. They're *really* good at donuts."

Part of Jeff thought he should say no. He didn't know these people, and he could end up the subject of some banal tell-all. But what would they have to say about him after this? That he had unsuspected skill not falling off an inflatable toy?

Besides, it turned out he now desperately needed another distraction—this time from Carter. "Deal."

There was a short delay while Jeff went into the marina shop to buy a swimsuit and, after a moment's consideration, a giant bottle of sunscreen, and then he spent an unexpectedly pleasant afternoon with four near strangers, howling with laughter as they took turns being thrown from the raft. No one took any videos or photos of him until he asked, and that was a grinning shot with the five of them, Rufus and Justin on one side, Jeff in the middle, Jeri on the right with Kara in their lap.

Jeff looked at it fondly and then sent it to Carter, *Wish you were here.*

"What did he do?" Kara asked as Rufus piloted them back to the marina.

Jeff was relating the story of how Carter had headed off a potential bullying crisis when Jeff came out at thirteen, and he smiled at the memory. A few kids had whispered behind his back, but Jeff had had other things to worry about, and most people were nice enough to his face, largely because no one wanted to deal with Carter.

"Actually nothing. I don't think he ever had to throw a punch." He shook his head. "Gary came over all confrontational. 'Carter, I can't believe you're hanging out with this—' You can imagine how he finished that sentence. I was going into high school, and there were just enough of the right people around that you knew whatever happened was going to set the tone for what followed. And Carter just rolls his eyes and goes, 'What do you care, Gary, it's not like he'd be interested in *you*,' and that was it. Everybody took their cue from Carter."

"I thought you were supposed to be telling stories we could make fun of him for," Jeri sighed and leaned their head back against the seat. "Not, like, trying to retroactively make us fall in love with him."

Jeff froze, but no one was even looking at him. Rufus was driving, Justin was leaning against his shoulder, and Kara was sunbathing, face tipped toward the sky. It made him brave, or maybe stupid. "Carter's like that. Even the embarrassing stories just make you want to fall in love with him."

"Hmm," Jeri said, then challenged, "prove it."

This time Jeff selected the story of eight-year-old Carter attempting to save a dying plant in his mother's garden only to discover, one very painful rash later, that it was poison oak.

Jeff paid for the gas when they got back to town and bought everyone dinner to boot, and they sat on the patio at the restaurant until it got dark. By the time he returned to the cottage, he had four new numbers in his phone and reassurance in the knowledge that he did still know how to make friends, actually.

He showered off the lake water and fell into bed.

The next day he really did have to get groceries. He'd gone through the meager supplies the fridge could hold, and he needed eggs and milk and yogurt and cereal, among other things. After a breakfast of stale toast with only one egg made him feel like a sad hobbit, he went into town.

A quick peek inside the store confirmed that Georgia was working. Hopefully she'd continue to be cool. Jeff took a basket from the corral by the door and headed for the refrigerated section.

Because Willow Sound was a small town currently conspiring to make Jeff believe in a sadistic god, Carter was already there, sunglasses clipped in the V-neck of his clingy T-shirt as he double-checked to make sure his eggs weren't broken.

"How many dozen do you eat each morning, again?" Jeff asked idly, bumping against him as he reached for his own carton. "Can't remember the lyric."

Carter made a face at him and bumped him back twice as hard. Fortunately Jeff hadn't picked up a carton yet. "Shouldn't you still be in bed? I thought you rock stars were allergic to mornings."

"Don't remind me." It felt downright unnatural to be awake and doing things at this hour. "I take it this means you have two days off from naturalism? In a row? On a weekend, no less?" Jeff wasn't as diligent about checking his eggs for cracks as Carter; a cursory glance sufficed. Not obviously broken. He put them in his basket.

Carter snorted. "No. Night shift."

Jeff could feel his face contorting into an expression of extreme horror. "You have the night shift? Whose idea was that? Aren't you, like, the boss? Don't they know you fall asleep by ten?"

"Are you ever going to let that go?" He'd dropped off at nine thirty at a sleepover once when Jeff was thirteen. "I told you, I worked all day, and then I had baseball! I was a growing boy."

Oh boy, here it comes.

"You know, maybe if you'd gone to bed a little earlier—"

"I wouldn't have ended up such a shrimp," Jeff pronounced along with him, rolling his eyes as he added a tub of butter to his basket. "My height—which is completely normal for a man, by the way, you're the freak here—couldn't possibly have anything to do with the fact that neither of my parents was tall."

"Definitely the sleep," Carter said sagely.

Uh-huh. They moved together to the next section and fell naturally into step. "So do you just not ever take days off?" Jeff paused in front of the healthy cereal. The store didn't carry his favorite brand, and he wasn't familiar with one of the two options they did have. "Hey, do you eat this?"

"Take the Morning Crisp," Carter advised, grabbing a box for himself… and then he moved on to the next shelf without answering the first question.

Jeff smelled an evasive maneuver. "So that's a 'no comment' on the days off?" he called as Carter rounded the endcap to go to the next aisle.

Two steps later he almost ran right into him as Carter did an abrupt about-face and beelined back down the cereal aisle.

Jeff blinked. "Where's the fire? Is someone asking about your self-care routine in aisle three?"

Carter gently but firmly took his elbow and marched him down toward the other end. Jeff let it happen, utterly bemused and bursting with curiosity. "Just come with me. Please."

It wasn't like Jeff was putting up resistance. "Where are we going?"

"Small change of plan," Carter said. "Do you mind coming back later?"

"Like how much later?" They were in sight of the exit now. "I need food for lunch. My bread is stale."

"I will hand-deliver you groceries for two weeks if you leave with me right now."

But now Jeff's curiosity was piqued. "When are you going to have time to buy groceries for me? You barely even have time to sleep."

He'd stopped, and now Carter was facing him, shoulders hunched a little like he was hiding. "Jeff—"

And then someone else said, "Carter?"

Jeff turned to take in the newcomer, and Carter… sort of slipped behind him.

The new guy was a little taller than Jeff and more solidly built, with dark blond curls and a pink slash of a mouth parted in recognition—first of Carter, but then his gaze lit on Jeff and his eyes went wide.

Maybe Jeff should've let Carter hustle him out of here.

Behind him, he could feel Carter's resignation. "Hey, Pacey."

Wait, *Pacey*? Like that guy on *Dawson's Creek*? Jeff had never actually met anyone whose parents named them that, which meant this man wasn't local, or at least he hadn't grown up here.

Pacey cleared his throat and looked pointedly from Carter to Jeff. "Sorry, am I interrupting?"

"What?" Carter said, faux casual—way too faux for Jeff to fall for it, though he didn't know about Pacey. "Uh, we were just grocery shopping."

Pacey looked for all the world like the next words out of his mouth were going to be *aren't you going to introduce me to your friend*, at which point Carter was going to lie to at least one of them. It didn't take a genius to figure that out. "And I realized I lost my phone somewhere on the walk in," Jeff filled in before Carter had to profane himself. "Carter's going to help me look for it. Right, Carter?"

He chanced a look back just in time to see Carter's expression go from resigned-deer-in-headlights to unlooked-for-relief. "Uh, yeah. Maybe you dropped it on the way over from the bakery?"

Whatever. Jeff could play along. "Yeah, I did stop to take that selfie with the bear claw." He set the basket, eggs and butter and all, down on the reshelving table.

Carter mustered an anemic smile for whatever hell demon from his past Pacey was. "Nice seeing you," he said, putting his basket next to Jeff's, and they walked out of the store together.

Jeff was kind of worried Carter was going to have an anxiety attack, so he didn't ask the question right away, instead steering him down the street in the direction of the bakery.

When they were half a block past the grocery, Carter started to unclench. He dropped onto the bench in front of the pharmacy and put his head in his hands.

Jeff strongly wished he had a Frappuccino or something to sip on while he waited for Carter to collect his wits, because he was lining up any number of caustic one-liners on the same theme and having a difficult time choosing between them, and a Frappuccino would pass the time. But finally Carter raised his head—not enough to look at Jeff, but at least so he was gazing across the street and not at his shoes—and said, "Thanks," his voice laden with all kinds of trouble.

Jeff decided on the straightforward route.

"So," he said conversationally, "who was that?"

Carter sighed heavily. "Pacey McNaughton. His family owns a summer cottage about fifteen kilometers down the road."

Obviously not the information Jeff was looking for, but sometimes you had to be patient with Carter or your suspicions would grow into conclusions and then you'd have way too many emotions to deal with on a public sidewalk at not even ten in the morning. "And how do you know Mr. McNaughton?"

Finally Carter looked up and met his eyes. "How do you think?"

Patience had never been Jeff's strong suit. "Well, Carter, my *first* thought was 'Wow, that is definitely Carter's ex-boyfriend,' but then I thought, 'Nah, that can't be it, Carter definitely would've told me if he was into dudes.' You know, like fifteen years ago, or at least last week."

Carter's mouth flattened into a thick line. "That's not fair."

I'll fucking say, Jeff thought, narrowly tamping down on a surge of panic. Because it was one thing to have been in love with Carter fifteen years ago, knowing he was unavailable. It was another thing to crush on him now when they'd be going their separate ways by the end of the summer. And it was something entirely different to realize the bedrock he'd based his assumptions on was actually quicksand.

Then Carter went on, "I'm not famous, okay? Maybe you don't remember what it's like, but for the rest of us, it's not like there's one *Vanity Fair* article and then you never have to come out again. You have to keep doing it again and again and again. Forever." His nostrils flared a little, and the corners of his mouth turned down. "And sometimes the longer you know someone, the harder it is."

Bullshit. He couldn't have told Jeff back when the two of them were thick as thieves? Carter had been Jeff's confessor. It stung that he hadn't trusted Jeff enough to reciprocate—not back then, and not in the past few days either.

But that was Jeff's problem, not Carter's. No one owed it to anyone to come out before they were ready.

He sank down next to Carter on the bench, all his fight replaced with guilt and hurt. "You're right. You're absolutely right, I'm being a shithead, proving your point for you. Sorry. I didn't mean to make it more difficult."

But in typical fashion, Carter was already finished being angry, because he waved off the apology. "It's fine. I know if I'd mentioned it that day we went for lunch it would've been fine. I just get…. Well, this isn't the only time it's happened, obviously."

"Obviously," Jeff said. "And I mean, you're mostly right that I don't have to come out to people, but it's not like everyone in the world knows my face. Sometimes I do have to. And it does get tiring correcting people's assumptions."

Carter smiled wanly. "Thanks."

Great. Now that they had *that* out of the way—"So, you and Pacey." He propped his chin on his hand and batted his eyelashes. "He seems dreamy. Tell me everything."

"Ugh." Carter shoved him playfully. "You're the worst. It was a summer thing. I would've been… twenty-five, I think?"

Jeff and Howl had just been hitting their stride, booking international tours, starting to get recognized. He reached past the feeling of shaken foundations for the surer ground. "Carter Rhodes," he said, mock scandalized. "You had a relationship with a *summer resident*?"

"*You're* a summer resident," Carter pointed out.

That set fire to something in Jeff's guts, but he ruthlessly stomped it out. "How dare you. I am a *hometown boy returned to his roots*."

"For the summer," Carter said, heavy on the implied eye roll. "In a rental cabin."

Does that mean you're going to date me next? Jeff bit down on *that* before it could escape his dumb mouth. "So what happened? That didn't feel like 'oh well, summer ended, it's been nice knowing you but see ya later.' That felt more like 'I left your things on the lawn and somehow they mysteriously caught fire.'"

Carter laughed and spread his ridiculously long arms over the back of the bench. If Jeff wanted to, he could lean back too, and it would be like Carter had his arm around him. "God, what kinds of breakups have you had? I promise you no one has ever set anything of mine on fire."

No, of course not. Jeff couldn't see how Carter could ever make anyone that angry. "You're just not trying hard enough."

"I didn't realize inspiring arson was the goal." He shook his head, sobering. "It was, uh. It was my birthday and he wanted to surprise me, so he got me tickets to a concert."

Jeff's stomach did something very uncomfortable.

"It was a whole thing, you know, we even drove into the city for it, got a hotel room. Looking back I think he was maybe a little more serious about the relationship than I was and I didn't pick up on it."

Jeff didn't have to ask what concert. He keenly remembered being aware of the fact that he was doing a show in Toronto on Carter's birthday. "That's always awkward," he said, hoping his voice didn't sound as strangled as it felt. His palms started to sweat. Since when was it this warm this early in Willow Sound?

Carter glanced at him sideways and Jeff could hear his unvoiced commentary on how often Jeff was perfectly aware that he was the less serious person in a relationship. "He already knew I liked the band because I had their CD in the car—"

"I am three thousand years old," Jeff said. "Remember CDs?"

Carter ignored the interruption as though determined to get this story out. "So we had really good seats. Not first row or anything, but close. And at first it was really great. We both liked the music, and it was a great show, but um…."

Jeff was going to melt right through the bench. Possibly with embarrassment. Probably with something else.

"There was some weird technical difficulty, maybe an amp blew a fuse or something. You'd know better than I would."

Ha ha, Jeff thought hysterically, completely unable to laugh at Carter's stupid in-joke.

"Anyway, most of the sound went out—everything but one mic and the lead guitar. So while the tech guys worked on that, the lead guitarist had one of the crew bring out a stool and he plugged in this beat-up sunburst guitar I'd seen about a million times—"

"Fuck," Jeff said quietly, but at least they were now both acknowledging, if not the elephant in the room, at least the fact that elephants existed.

"—and played my favorite song on my birthday."

"You always were kind of a sap," Jeff said automatically. Teenage Carter had loved to play the Wallflowers' "The Difference" at top volume in his beat-up truck, windows rolled down as he sang along. In retrospect maybe a song about people remaining the same despite the passage of time was a little on the nose for that concert.

"I like what I like," Carter returned. Jeff was going to die. "I, well, I sort of had an unpredictable reaction to that, and then I had to explain to Pacey that actually I know that guy in the band, we grew up together. He… jumped to some conclusions."

It was too much information to process. Jeff couldn't even guess what that meant. "So instead of your romantic birthday surprise, you broke up?"

Carter winced. "It was a really long drive back to Willow Sound."

"Fuck," he said again. Then he recontextualized running into Pacey in the grocery store and repeated, "Oh *fuck*—"

"Hey." Carter derailed his panic with a hand on his wrist. "I don't care what he thinks, okay? And just because it didn't work out between us doesn't mean he's going to go, I don't know, attempting to sell a nonstory to a tabloid."

Jeff took a deep breath and attempted to internalize it all. "Okay, but he definitely does think we're boning. I could tell just from the way he was looking at me earlier. This"—he gestured between them, intending to indicate the lasting trauma Carter had just inflicted on Jeff's psyche—"only reinforces that I am definitely right about that."

"Maybe," Carter allowed. "Do you care? We can go tell him the truth."

Oh *hell* no. Now that Jeff knew there was a chance, however slim—and he was desperately trying to bury the quiet but insistent notion that Carter 100 percent knew Jeff had sung that song for him, that if he did he'd almost certainly guessed that Jeff had sung hundreds of songs for him, many of which he'd penned himself—he wasn't letting Pacey McNaughton think he had a second shot. "Nah. He broke up with you. He doesn't deserve the truth." He paused. "He *absolutely* would've set your shit on fire, though."

"Oh, no doubt," Carter agreed, nodding. "Dodged a bullet on that one."

They grinned at each other, and just like that, everything was fine.

Well. Except Jeff still didn't have any groceries. He sighed and got to his feet, then pulled Carter up after him. "Come on. I think you owe me ice cream."

IF JEFF expected things to be weird after that—awkward or different in any way—he would've been disappointed. But things didn't change much, at least not outwardly. Carter still worked way too much—apparently "night shift" meant, like, birdwatching for owls or something, which was kind of cool, but when he wasn't at the park, he was filling in when his mom needed him at the garage. And Jeff was still avoiding anything that even remotely resembled writing, because if he picked up a pen, he would be forced to confront his feelings about Carter being bi. He'd have to think about what it could mean that Carter touched him *all the time*, that he texted Jeff just because. That he'd sent him a selfie that belonged in the centerfold of a certain kind of magazine.

Jeff didn't have the emotional bandwidth for that and he couldn't afford to have his heart crushed again. He was perfectly happy sublimating, thank you very much.

In Carter's somehow still-existent off hours, they managed to make time for the odd lunch or dinner or campfire.

This morning brought something slightly more athletic.

"Tell me the truth," Jeff demanded as they made their way down one of the more treacherous hiking trails, which wended along the rockier part of the shore. "How do you have time to stay in shape? We've established that you don't even have time to sleep."

"You think being a park naturalist is all driving around and eating donuts?" Carter teased as he easily scaled a boulder.

"I mean, that's how *I'd* do it." He was debating where to grip for the best leverage when Carter's hand came into his field of view. He took it without thinking and let Carter help him up. At the top, Carter steadied him with a hand on his hip. "I know it's not *all* driving around, but it's not all wilderness hikes and kayaking either."

He was proud of himself for getting out a full sentence with the distraction of Carter touching him.

"No," Carter agreed a heartbeat later, drawing his hand away as he turned back to the path. "But I mean, when I'm not here, I'm at the garage, and that still gets pretty physical. And you know me. I'm not good at sitting still."

"Have you ever *tried* it?" Jeff countered as Carter hopped down to the next rock. "You never know. You might find out you like it."

"A rolling stone gathers no moss."

"What's wrong with moss? Isn't moss, like, key to the ecosystem?" Jeff slipped a little but caught himself. "Hey, hold up, would you? If I break something, Tim's going to have kittens." Mean, ugly kittens.

Carter looked back, expression mock contrite. "Sorry," he said. "I always forget about your short little legs—"

But his words cut off abruptly and the contrition on his face morphed to surprise and then dismay as he went sideways. There was a clatter of rocks and then a splash.

Fuck! "Carter!"

"Ow," came the sound from the other side of the large outcropping.

Well, at least he was conscious. Jeff carefully picked his way around until Carter came into view. He was breathing, no obvious trauma, lying on his back in a shallow pool of water. "Are you okay?" It didn't look like he'd hit his head, but God knew his skull was thick enough. It might not bleed on the outside.

"Yeah." Carter groaned as he propped himself up on his elbows. "Foot got stuck and I lost my balance. Not the greatest look for a naturalist."

"Lucky you're out of uniform today," Jeff quipped. He backed up toward Carter's feet, partly to get a better look and see if he'd twisted anything but partly so he wouldn't stare at Carter's non-uniform—a white T-shirt that was now completely translucent. "You can fly under the radar." He knelt next to Carter's feet, wincing at the cold water on his knees. "Which one got stuck?"

"The right one." Jeff looked up in time to catch Carter's grimace as he rotated his foot, and then had to look back down quickly, because staring up the length of Carter's body while he lay prone like that would lead to madness.

Jeff wasn't a medic by any stretch, but the foot didn't look like it was moving with the range of motion it should. "That doesn't look good." Definitely bad enough to warrant a trip to a doctor, maybe even X-rays. "Think you can stand?"

"Yeah, if you help me up." Carter groaned and bent his left leg up toward his ass. "Come give me a hand."

Jeff rose and stepped closer, mindful of the loose stones under his feet. He made sure he had solid footing before he leaned down and grasped Carter's hand. He could see Carter's nipples through his shirt—tiny little brown-pink buds that were hard with the cold. "Ready?"

Carter nodded, and Jeff pulled. Unsurprisingly, Carter was heavy. Equally unsurprising, he was strong as fuck. He got upright with his weight balanced on his left foot, his wet right side plastered against Jeff.

"How are you so heavy?" Jeff asked in an attempt to distract himself. Despite the damp, Carter's body was hot and firm and clean-smelling. Jeff had to resist the urge to turn his face into his chest and just… inhale. "Seriously, do you eat bricks?"

Carter panted with exertion, his chest pressing against Jeff's shoulder as he braced him. "What do you think I wash down those dozen eggs with?"

Great. He was a giant with a possibly broken foot and he was making jokes. Unbelievable. "What's the plan here? Do you think you can put weight on it, or are we going to need to call an ambulance?"

They hobbled together for a few steps to more even ground, Jeff chanting to himself the whole time that he could freak out later. But when they got to the soft, loamy forest floor, Carter took one step and went ashen. Jeff caught him under the shoulder and helped ease him down to sit on a fallen log. "So that's a no on walking."

Carter's chest heaved as he breathed through the pain. "I can try it again. Just give me a minute."

Jeff looked skeptically at his foot, which he was not even putting any weight on while sitting down. "Unless you plan on crawling instead—*that was not a serious suggestion*—I think we'd better make the call."

Carter groaned. "No, it'll take forever to get the ambulance down here, and the roads aren't exactly designed for it. And the sirens are disruptive to wildlife." He shifted on the stump until he could worm his hand into the pocket of his athletic shorts, which Jeff was now unavoidably aware were also wet and clinging obscenely. It wasn't like Jeff hadn't seen Carter's dick before, but that was close to twenty years ago, and he hadn't had a sex drive at the time, so it didn't count. Finally Carter produced a soggy set of keys. "Here. Go back to the truck and drive it up the road. If we head inland from here, I think I can make it with your help."

Carter's truck was parked maybe a kilometer and a half from there. Jeff could get to it quickly on the forest trail—much more easily than he would over the rocky shore. He was lucky they hadn't been farther along in their trek. "All right," Jeff said dubiously, glancing once more at Carter's ankle. "Sit tight."

Jeff didn't exactly run to the truck. He was distracted enough to know that wasn't a good idea; they'd really be up shit's creek if they *both* hurt themselves. But within ten minutes, he'd moved the truck to the closest spot to the trail. A quick check of the glove compartment revealed some ibuprofen and a basic first aid kit, and he grabbed those along with a half-empty bottle of water from the cupholder, which he shoved in his pocket.

Carter was approximately twenty yards closer to the road than Jeff had left him, perched on a lichen-encrusted boulder.

"What part of 'stay put' did you not understand?" He looked even worse than he had before, sweat beading on his forehead, face twisted with obvious discomfort. *Idiot.* Jeff thrust the bottle of ibuprofen at him. "Take these. Now."

He expected Carter to argue, but he really must feel like crap, because he took two and washed them down with the remaining water without comment. Jeff sat on the ground in front of him and positioned the first aid kit next to him. "There's a tensor bandage in here, but I wasn't exactly a Boy Scout. You know how to use one?"

Carter nodded. "You're gonna have to take my shoe off. Sorry. If I'd known, I'd have gotten a pedicure."

Jeff untied his laces and loosened them, then braced his left hand on the back of Carter's calf and worked the shoe off as gently as he could. Carter's sock was soaked, so that came off too.

The red, nasty swelling started midway up his foot and ran all the way to the ankle. "All right, next step?"

"Start wrapping at the toe. Try to keep the bandage from folding and make it tight. The idea is to compress it to stop it from swelling."

Jeff propped Carter's foot on the first aid kit and got to work. He wound the bandage over and under, keeping his touch light and the bandage taut. Finally he pulled the flimsy aluminum butterfly clip out of the first aid kit and hooked the end in the stretchy material. "I always thought these things seemed poorly designed." But it held.

Standing, he picked up the shoe with the sock stuffed inside and the first aid kit in one hand and offered Carter the other. "You need a minute, or are you ready?"

Carter grabbed on and pulled himself up. "Let's get it over with."

Limping down the trail was significantly easier than Jeff anticipated—maybe not so much for Carter, who was probably working harder than he needed to to avoid putting too much weight on Jeff. "Does this remind you of that one three-legged race?"

Carter huffed with exertion or laughter as they inched closer to their destination. "Don't make me laugh. Next time I'm choosing a taller partner."

Better than allowing Jeff to suffer the indignity of Carter practically dragging him over the finish line. "Next time maybe just watch your step."

They reached the truck, and Jeff moved the passenger seat all the way back so Carter could get in.

Jeff got in the driver's seat and took out his phone.

"What are you doing?"

"Getting directions to the nearest clinic."

"I'll be fine," Carter insisted. "Just take me home and I'll ice it."

Yeah, right. Jeff remembered watching one of Carter's high school hockey games where he took a hit to the head that should've kept him out of the rest of the game. He decided to continue to play, only to fall flat on his back five minutes later. Carter wouldn't go to the doctor if he was bleeding out from an arterial wound.

"Sorry, can't hear you," Jeff said as he started the engine. "Too much horsepower. Hey, isn't this thing super environmentally unfriendly?"

"Jeff—"

Finally Jeff's phone managed to get a good enough signal to direct him to the nearest urgent care center.

"Follow the road for two kilometers," Google instructed.

Carter groaned. "Fine. But don't take me there. The one up the highway has an X-ray clinic attached, if you're so determined to play nurse."

Now there was a mental image. A little role-play could be sexy, definitely, but he had a sudden mental image of snapping on a latex glove and intoning, *Just a little prick*.

Fuck, he was going to laugh. That wasn't the impression he wanted to give, but it was bubbling up inside him anyway, edged with hysteria. He clamped his lips together and fought down the impulse.

"Shut up," Carter said grumpily, finally causing Jeff to lose the battle against the snicker. "What are you, twelve?"

"You're lucky I didn't tell you to bend over and cough."

"Guess I left myself wide open for that, huh?"

Jeff could not have this conversation while driving on a twisty road where he might hit a deer. Or a tourist. "I hate you."

"No, you don't. Turn left here."

It was forty minutes to the clinic, so Jeff called ahead to make sure they could accommodate Carter. A cheerful reception clerk informed him that yes, the X-ray machine was working and the tech was in, and scheduled an appointment.

"This is really unnecessary," Carter tried again.

"Shut up."

First they had to see a GP, which was mostly a formality. Dr. Rutledge asked Carter to rotate his ankle and flex his foot. She grimaced and wrote the order for the X-ray. "Just take this next door," she advised. "Shouldn't be too long."

Carter managed to make his own way into the X-ray room, and for a few minutes, Jeff sat in the waiting room with his phone out, debating whether to call someone. Carter's mother? It wasn't really his place. Joe? He could, but what would he say?

Then the X-ray tech popped her head out into the waiting room. "Mr. Pine? He's waiting for the video call from the radiologist at the hospital in exam room two. You can wait with him if you want."

All right, then. He pocketed his phone and followed her inside.

"Sure I'm not violating your medical privacy?"

Carter gave him a flat look. He had his foot elevated on the chair across from him. "I figured you wouldn't believe me if the doctor says I'm fine unless you heard it from their mouth," he said tiredly.

Sometimes it was uncanny how well they knew each other. Jeff sat. "I should've brought a snack."

As if on cue, Carter's stomach rumbled.

Jeff looked at it accusingly. Carter's shirt was only barely damp now, but it didn't matter. Jeff would never forget the view, whether that was a blessing or a curse.

"Bricks," Carter said. He had circles under his eyes, and the strain on his face was clear.

"We should've had Dr. Rutledge prescribe you something for the pain." Why hadn't he thought of that sooner?

"Better this way," Carter said. "If I need surgery or something."

Jeff startled. That was the first time he'd acknowledged this might be an issue worthy of medical attention. Carter really must be in pain. "Are you—"

The video monitor pinged with an incoming call, and the feed flipped immediately to a thirtyish man in a white coat, who was looking at another monitor off to his left. "Hello, I'm Dr. Lall," he said without looking at the camera. Then he turned his head, sat down on a rolling stool, and moved closer to the camera. "So, which one of you has the broken foot?"

Jeff pulled up the notes app on his phone and dutifully recorded the doctor's instructions—rest, ice, compression, and elevation for the first forty-eight hours; a cast with crutches or a plastic walking boot whenever Carter was mobile; and absolutely no driving for at least two weeks, until Carter's simple fracture had healed enough that he could wear a stiff shoe if he absolutely had to drive.

Carter looked ready to argue until the doctor explained, "You could be charged with careless driving. That's up to a two-year license suspension. Not worth it."

Jeff could already tell it was going to be a fun two weeks.

"The more you keep off it, the faster you'll recover," Dr. Lall went on. "Do you have someone who can help you out at home?"

He was looking at Jeff when he said it.

"I don't need—"

"He does," Jeff said, long past caring if anyone recognized him and thought he and Carter were an item. "What do I need to do?"

Chapter Six

THEY WERE both exhausted and starving by the time Carter directed Jeff to pull into his driveway. Willow Sound didn't have delivery, but they'd ordered takeout and picked it up on the way, along with the painkillers Dr. Lall prescribed, which Jeff had already bullied Carter into taking.

Carter's house was a neat bungalow just outside town, with a cheerfully overgrown lawn and a detached two-car garage that, knowing Carter, was full of sports gear, an ATV, a snowmobile, and maybe a boat, with nowhere to park the truck.

Jeff backed in so Carter could get out on the side closest to the house, and he pretended not to notice Carter glaring at him for it. To be honest, he was a little surprised it had taken this long for his mood to sour completely. Carter was nothing if not independent to a fault.

Apparently the other thing Carter was… was a complete slob.

"Dude." Jeff crowded into the entryway behind him. He could certainly see why Carter had stopped there. Any attempt to make his way farther into the house would invite aggravation to his injury via the multiple tripping hazards. Laundry baskets, dirty clothes, a recycle bin—why did he have that in the house?—boots, running shoes, flip-flops, and the empty box for a toaster provided a natural obstacle course to get from the front door to the kitchen table. Or the couch, for that matter. "Have you been playing The Floor is Lava?"

He expected Carter to get snippy, but his shoulders just slumped and he rubbed his forehead with his right hand. "You might have a point about me overextending myself."

Gee, you think? Jeff took a deep breath and let it out slowly. "Just… stay here and try not to fall over while I make a path."

By the time Carter was settled on the couch with his foot up and a plate of food, Jeff was several items deep in making his to-do list—clear out the junk, hire a service to take care of the yard, look into housekeepers, consider and possibly throw away everything in the fridge.

He was halfway through dinner when Carter finally said, "You don't have to stay, you know." He was only poking at his food. "I can get Mom and Brady to help for a couple days, and then I should be fine on my own. You didn't sign up for this."

I would if you asked me. There wasn't much point denying it to himself. "You did, though," Jeff said. "You decided to be friends with me. You're stuck with me now."

The painkillers kicked in after dinner, leaving Carter dozing on the couch, which gave Jeff time to look around. The rest of the house wasn't as bad as the hallways and living room—the kitchen was cluttered but not dirty, and the bathroom was clean. Aside from a stray pile of laundry, the bedroom was acceptable. Jeff stripped the sheets and tossed them in the washing machine just because, and told himself he was not allowed to have a crisis about it. He triaged the worst hazards and left a few voicemails with various service providers, then loaded their plates into the dishwasher and pushed Start.

Finally he sank into a chair at the kitchen table and rubbed his hands over his face.

What the fuck was he doing?

He'd come here to make peace with his past, to integrate it into who he was, to learn from it—not to return to the same lovesick teenager he'd been. Not to repeat his mistakes—not to tear open the wounds on his dumb scabbed-over heart and rub salt in them. But trying not to fall in love with Carter was like trying not to get wet in a hurricane. If that was his goal, then he needed to cut Carter out of his life for good.

But that hadn't done any good the first time, and Carter needed him now. Jeff wouldn't abandon him. It didn't matter in the end if Carter loved him back. Having him in his life was worth the occasional lapse into heartache and yearning.

But he really should not get anywhere near a pen, because he'd spilled enough of his secrets already. He was sure Carter had guessed most of them, and it wouldn't be fair to be *more* obvious and still expect Carter to maintain the fiction that Jeff only wanted his friendship.

The friendship was enough, of course. It had to be.

The dryer buzzed, and Jeff made himself repeat the words to "O Canada" over and over in his head while he remade the bed, to prevent any other thoughts from intruding.

Then he went to wake Carter.

"Hey." He touched Carter's shoulder, sleep-warm and firm. He didn't expect Carter to turn his head toward the touch, and he was completely unprepared for the soft, sleepy-eyed look Carter favored him with afterward. "You want to try sleeping in an actual bed? Your couch is seriously not up to the task." Carter had his broken foot propped on the armrest and he still had to contort himself in order to squeeze onto the couch.

"Ugh." He scrunched up his face as he returned to consciousness. "Dry mouth."

That'd be the meds. "I'll get you a glass of water." Then he wouldn't have the impulse to tuck Carter in.

But it was almost worse to walk into the intimacy of Carter's bedroom while he was already in bed, long body stretched out over his California king, right foot propped on a pillow, uncovered.

His T-shirt and shorts were on the chair next to the bed, and now Jeff's eyes couldn't stop following the line of Carter's calf to his knee to his thigh where it disappeared under the sheet. The view a few degrees north wasn't any better. Carter had only pulled the sheet up to his waist, so his bare chest was exposed—well-defined pecs and visible if not perfect abs. Jeff's mouth was a little dry too.

He cleared his throat. "Water," he said unnecessarily as he set the glass on the nightstand.

"Thanks," Carter mumbled, his voice already rough with sleep.

"I'm, um. Do you mind if I borrow something to sleep in?" Jeff still smelled like hike.

Carter lifted his hand and pointed. "Second drawer on the left."

The second drawer on the left turned out to be plain white T-shirts and boxer briefs. Jeff stared at them for far too long and then took the pair on top and closed the drawer a little too quickly. "Thanks." He had to get out of there. "I'll be on the couch. Yell if you need me."

THE MORNING brought unanticipated new levels of compartmentalizing. The couch was a nightmare, half because it was too small even for Jeff to sleep on and half because it smelled like Carter. That hadn't stopped Jeff from sinking into an aching, immersive impressionist painting of a dream, full of sound and smell and color and touch, the shape of Carter's palm against his cheek and his back under his fingertips. He'd woken to the phantom touch of Carter's mouth on the side of his neck and decided that, as Carter's guest, he had the right to the first shower of the day.

He didn't even consider cold water. He bent his left arm against the shower wall and leaned his head against it. As the heat sluiced over him, he took himself in hand and pretended Carter was touching him, his body pressed to Jeff's back, his lips murmuring sweet encouragement into Jeff's ear, his thick cock sliding between Jeff's cheeks, not pushing in, not yet, just a presence and a promise.

He squeezed his eyes shut when he came and then he washed up quickly, trusting the water and the scent of bodywash to destroy the evidence.

By the time he was out of the bathroom, Carter was awake and mobile, though he didn't look happy about it.

"You look like crap," Jeff said, frozen in place because Carter was wearing boxers and a T-shirt and Jeff was wearing a towel, and he had to say *something*.

"Didn't sleep well," Carter rasped. Jeff believed him—his eyes were heavy-lidded and he was standing in the hallway, kind of staring.

"You need coffee," Jeff decided. If Carter kept looking at him like that, Jeff's towel was going to fall off. "I'm just—I'll let you have the shower." And he squeaked past him down the hallway and thanked any god who'd listen for the built-in shower seat in Carter's bathroom so he had no excuse to volunteer for a sponge bath.

He didn't want to put yesterday's clothes back on, so he was swimming in a T-shirt of Carter's and shorts that hung past his knees when Carter's mom showed up five minutes later.

"Carter?" Had they not locked the door, or did she have a key? "I brought you some groceries—oh, Jeff."

Jeff could see her taking in the details—the fact that he'd just showered, that he was wearing Carter's clothes, that he'd just emerged from Carter's bedroom—and putting two and two together to get sixteen. "Good morning, Ella," he said. How did you convey *by the way, I'm not sleeping with your son* with any degree of tact?

She beamed at him. "I'm so sorry to intrude."

"Oh, you're not," Jeff said quickly. "I just didn't want to leave Carter alone overnight with a broken foot, so I slept on the couch."

He tried not to notice her smile dimming. "Of course. You were always such a good friend to Carter."

Jeff almost laughed out loud. Carter had always been the one taking care of him—scaring off his bullies, distracting him from his mother's illness, offering his own family when Jeff's couldn't take care of him. "He was always a good friend to me. He's in the shower. I was going to make some coffee, if you want some."

OBVIOUSLY CARTER wouldn't be doing much driving or physical labor for a while, but apparently there was still deskwork to take care of. Jeff wasn't sure how he was going to get anything done, since he'd peeked into the home "office" in Carter's second bedroom to find mostly workout equipment and a folding table that had seen better days… like the nineties. Carter had asked his mom to swing by the park office to pick up his laptop, so Ella drove Jeff back to his cabin.

When the silence in the car had stretched on for going on ten minutes, Ella said, "You know, when I asked you to try to get him to slow down, this isn't what I meant."

Jeff snorted in spite of himself. "Beggars can't be choosers." He glanced at her. "You're not going to have trouble without him at the garage, are you?"

"No, actually, this is a blessing in disguise." She signaled to turn into the park entrance. "Katie's looking to go back to working part-time now that the baby's old enough to be in day care. She actually has accounting experience, so I can hand over most of the office stuff to her, and that frees up Brady for physical labor." She smiled. "He's been whining about desk duty for three months. This'll make everyone happy."

That sounded like a pretty good solution… except for one thing. "What about Carter?"

Ella shook her head and slowed the car so the gate attendant could see her park pass. They waved her through. "Carter has always felt like he has to take care of everyone else. He likes to be needed. Fred was like that too; he lived to help others. But Carter never wanted to work at the garage."

Jeff nodded in response and went back to gazing out the window until they pulled up outside his cabin. "Thank you for the ride. I'll see you at the memorial?"

"It'll be good to have you there." She took his left hand in both of hers. "Carter might not say it, but it means a lot to him that you're coming. And Fred and I always thought of you as a son."

Jeff knew she needed to say that as much as he needed to hear it, but that didn't stop it from hurting—reminding him of the sting of his own dysfunctional family and the torch he'd been carrying for Carter at the same time. "I've never thanked you properly," he said through a suddenly thick throat. "For everything." His chest constricted. "If it hadn't been for Fred buying me that guitar.... It sounds stupid, but I swear it saved my life."

"It isn't stupid, dear." She squeezed his hand. "He was so proud of you and what you accomplished. I know it would mean a lot to him if...."

Jeff turned in his seat and took her other hand as well. "Tell me," he urged. "Anything. After everything the two of you did for me...."

"You always were a good boy." She gave him a brave smile. "Would you bring your guitar to the memorial? Not the public one, just the boat service. And would you play something for Fred?"

His eyes burned. "Yes," he said immediately, voice rough. "Yes, of course I will."

They went their separate ways. Jeff thought they both needed to catch their composure.

He had plans to check in with Carter later, but in the meantime, he did have a concert in a few days and he should at least make sure he remembered how the songs went. On top of that, he had to choose something to play at the memorial. He needed this vacation, but he wasn't going to shirk his obligations.

He'd just finished going through the acoustic half of the set list when Joe's name cropped up on his caller ID.

Jeff's stomach sank as he answered.

"What's up, Joe?"

"Hey, buddy. Just wanted to give you a heads-up."

Great. Jeff raised a hand to his temple to forestall the incipient headache. "How bad is it?"

"Max and Trix convinced Tim to book *416 Morning* on the twenty-first. Or, I don't know, vice versa."

"Jesus Christ, why?" Jeff burst out, anger flaring. "That's the day *after* the concert. After that we're going out West. What's the point?"

"I've got my suspicions." He sighed. "Rumor has it they want to add a show in Toronto."

What a surprise. "Timeline?"

"Possibly the day of the show, maybe between the Winnipeg and Ottawa dates."

"They know we have to approve this shit, right?" The number of concert dates was specified in the contract.

"Yeah, they do. Except remember that concert that got canceled because of that electrical fire?"

Fuck. Jeff had forgotten. "All right. I'll keep an ear out for Tim. How are Max and Trix? Any fallout from the whole public urination thing?"

"You know Tim. He's convinced all publicity is good publicity."

Unless it was Joe making a statement about Indigenous sovereignty, treaty rights, and systemic discrimination, or Jeff making one about queer representation, or Trix talking about misogyny in the music industry…. "Tim's a windbag."

"Yeah," Joe said. "Listen… when you're in town, you think we can get away a couple hours, just the two of us? There's something I want to talk to you about."

That sounded ominous. "Something bugging you?" Jeff's stomach did an unpleasant twist. "You and Sarah are okay, right?"

"We're fine. And it's nothing you need to worry about." A voice spoke in the background, too far from the mic for Jeff to catch it. "Look, I've gotta go, but call me if you need to, all right? If they go for the twenty-first, we can probably make a case that it's too last-minute if we present a united front."

The problem with the twenty-first was that it cut down the time between the Toronto show and the one in Vancouver. At that point it almost didn't make sense for Jeff to come back to Willow Sound between concerts.

Jeff really liked being in Willow Sound. He *needed* to be in Willow Sound. So that was a problem.

"Thanks, bro. Talk to you later."

So that put a damper on the afternoon practice.

Sure enough, true to Joe's prediction, Tim called half an hour later. Jeff let it go to voicemail, then texted Joe.

Do it the 21st like they want, or hold out for something in late June?

Joe texted back a few minutes later. *Might as well get it over with.*

Jeff set his phone back on the table, trying to tamp down his disappointment. It was probably for the best. A week away from Carter would help restore some of his equilibrium. He could get a little distance from the situation and figure out….

Figure out what? Jeff didn't need a week in Toronto to decide if he wanted Carter. He'd known he wanted that since he was thirteen.

Figure out if he was going to do something about it, now that he knew a relationship with another guy was explicitly a thing Carter was interested in?

How could he, though? They lived different lives. Jeff was on the road all the time—*needed* to be on the road all the time even if he decided to leave his band and do his own thing. Carter loved his home, loved his family. Jeff couldn't pull him away from that. And that was assuming Carter would ever consider him anything more than a friend, an additional brother. There was a lot stacked against them.

The phone rang again, and Jeff picked it up without looking. "Did you tell them the twenty-first?"

Silence. Then, "Did you hire someone to cut my lawn?" Another pause. "And weed my garden?" A final accusatory silence. "And power-wash the garage?"

"They had a promotion," Jeff said. "Hi, Carter."

His mind supplied the visual of Carter's eye roll. "Hi, Jeff. What's the twenty-first?"

"Another test of my patience." When Carter didn't immediately respond, he clarified, "Second concert date in Toronto. Unfortunate contract loophole. Are you pissed about the landscapers?"

"*Landscapers*? I thought they were just cleaning up."

"Don't get your panties in a bunch." And that was a horrible thing to say out loud when he was wearing Carter's underwear himself. He should probably change. "What did you want me to call them? *Lawn maintenance professionals*? Kind of a mouthful."

"I'll give you a mouthful," Carter muttered. Jeff's dick twitched in his borrowed shorts. "I want to be pissed."

"But you're not."

He exhaled. "No."

Jeff sensed there was more there, but he didn't know how well his probing would be received. Carter had always been at his most prickly when he was annoyed about being vulnerable—sick or injured or, for one miserable, memorable month the summer he was fifteen, heartbroken from his breakup with Marina Thompson. "Do you… want to talk about it?"

Another one of those annoyed pauses. Then, begrudging but not particularly snippy, "About what?"

"Just… don't bite my head off, okay?"

"When have I ever?"

Jeff didn't bother responding to that. "I just noticed that, uh, you've kind of been letting the house get a bit… I just want to make sure you're okay." *I know your dad died, and you idolized him, but are you depressed?* seemed like a stupid question.

This time Carter's silence was softer. "I'm okay," he said after a moment. "It's… okay, do you want to hear something dumb?"

Everything that comes out of your mouth is dumb. But this wasn't the time. "You can tell me anything."

Carter breathed in sharply enough Jeff could hear it. "When Dad died, there was a lot to do—not just funeral arrangements but practical things like covering his shifts at the garage and making sure the shop's bills got paid on time, ordering supplies. And I couldn't help with the grief, you know? I couldn't make that better for Mom any more than anyone could make it better for me, but doing the practical stuff made me feel like I was helping. And then I kind of forgot to stop doing it."

"Classic Carter," Jeff murmured. "You're almost lucky you broke your foot, you know. Now you *have* to slow down."

"I think I've slept more in the past day and a half than I have in the past month," Carter joked.

"That's horrifying," Jeff said. "You need to sleep more. And that's coming from a professional musician who's been on cocaine benders." He paused and, in the interest of honesty, amended, "Okay, one cocaine bender."

"Yeah, yeah." He cleared his throat. "You're not still…?"

"No. I told you I quit and I meant it. Kind of loses its appeal when someone derails right in front of you. Plus it fucks up my sleep."

"All right," Carter said quickly. "Just checking."

He couldn't help being a mother hen. Jeff wondered if it was a middle-child thing or a Carter thing or both. "So how's the foot today?"

"It hurts and I'm bored." His voice held a heavy note of self-deprecation. "I've never been good at doing nothing, and after the past six months, I'm *really* not good at doing nothing." He paused. "Also, I just remembered something else."

"Hm?" Jeff asked.

"I'm supposed to coach T-ball tonight."

And that was how Jeff found himself swinging into Carter's driveway at six with a stack of foil-wrapped sandwiches in a bag on the seat and a couple bottles of Gatorade in the cupholders. Carter limped out of the house toward his own truck.

Jeff rolled down the window. "Get in, loser. I'll get the camp chairs and equipment."

Carter looked between Jeff and his truck, then sighed and followed instruction. Any moment now Jeff would be canonized for performing a miracle.

When he got in the truck, Carter shoved a bag at him. "You're going to need this," he said sweetly.

Jeff opened it to reveal a forest-green T-shirt with Rhodes's Garage printed on it, in size Carter. He swallowed. "Gosh. You shouldn't have."

"There's a whistle too. Really pulls the outfit together."

"I regret our friendship," Jeff told him as he put the truck in Drive.

Carter leaned smugly back in his seat, eyes closed and face turned toward the evening sunshine. "No, you don't."

He really didn't.

They got to the ball park before any of the kids and their parents. Jeff set up one of the camp chairs in the dugout across from the end of the bench so Carter could put his foot up, then passed him a sandwich. "All right. What exactly does T-ball practice consist of, anyway? Not sure if you remember, but team sports were not exactly my forte."

Carter looked up from unwrapping his dinner and smiled fondly. "If I recall, you were definitely one of the dandelion-pickers." He raised the sandwich to his mouth and took a bite. Jeff didn't know what to focus on—how wide Carter could open his mouth or the little smear of mayonnaise at the corner of his lips—so he turned his attention to his own dinner. "Practice is practice. Warm-ups, stretching, catch, what passes as batting practice."

"I literally do not know the proper way to hold a T-ball bat," Jeff pointed out.

"That's all right." Carter grinned. "Neither do they."

Setting up the tee did turn out to be within his wheelhouse. After all, Jeff had many years' experience setting up the band's equipment, which was a lot more complicated than a few pieces of crappy plastic. He set a whiffle ball thing on the tee and propped a few bats against the backstop, and then he heard a car pull into the parking lot.

Time to get changed.

Jeff walked back into the dugout and reached behind him to pull his shirt over his head. He'd changed out of Carter's T-shirt and shorts before he left the cabin, and now here he was about to put Carter's clothes back on. Probably better if he didn't examine *that* too closely before hanging out with a bunch of children. "So you're gonna help me remember everybody's name, right?"

He popped his head out from under the hem, the shirt still half on his arms, and stopped dead.

Because Carter was watching him with hot eyes, the irises almost consumed by blown pupils. There was plenty of sunshine left, so it wasn't the low light making him look at Jeff like Jeff was about to star in his favorite adult video.

Jeff's mouth went dry. He could feel the heat of that gaze on his skin as he dropped his shirt on the bench.

"Don't worry." Carter dragged his gaze up from the line of hair that led down from Jeff's navel. "I'll help you with whatever you need."

Jeff wet his lips, caught in Carter's gaze. Something pulled him inexorably closer. The heat in Carter's eyes hooked into his belly and curled in the tension inside him.

It would be so easy. They were so close now. Another step and Jeff could touch him—could brace a hand on his shoulder, lean down—

A car door slammed and the spell broke. Jeff realized he was a recognizable famous person standing shirtless in a public dugout looking for all the world like he was about to do something that could get him arrested, and he quickly reached for the team T-shirt.

Carter was still watching him when he finished putting it on, though the fire in his eyes had been banked. Everything about his expression said, *Later*.

So that wasn't going to be a huge distraction while Jeff had a dozen kids to look after, or anything.

Everyone seemed to arrive more or less at once, and they piled into the dugout in their team shirts.

"All right, kids," Carter said, in a slightly louder version of his campfire-safety-talk voice, "I want you to listen up, okay? I had a little accident this week, and I'm not supposed to do too much standing yet. This is Coach Jeff. He's going to help me out today. So listen to him and don't give him a hard time if he forgets your name, all right?"

Jeff was having a hard enough time remembering his own name. "Thanks, Carter." He turned to the kids. "All right. Let's start with some warm-up laps. Who likes to run?"

Every kid raised their hand. Bless them.

"Me!"

"I do!"

Well, running, at least, Jeff could do. "All right. Let's all run some laps together to get our muscles ready for practice. Ready, set, go!"

Running a kids' T-ball practice was a surprisingly good workout, between the running and the jogging between kids and chasing after stray whiffle balls. Only one kid cried, because another kid put gum in his hair when Jeff wasn't looking.

"Amanda!" Crap, was that her name? Whatever. "What are you doing?"

"Uh." Amanda put both hands behind her back, but the gum gave her away, stretching between—oh, who was the other kid? Miller? Molson? Some kind of beer name—between the other kid's head and her hand. "Nothing."

"Christ," Jeff muttered. Were parents watching this? No, they were mostly gossiping. A few of them glanced at him from time to time, or at Carter, but he was pretty sure that had nothing to do with Amanda and Beer Kid. "Okay—Miller?"

The kid sniffed. "Morgan."

Okay, so it was Rum Kid, not Beer Kid. Fine. "Morgan. If you hold really still, I think I can get the gum out. Amanda?"

She looked up at him with wide brown eyes.

"Drop the gum, please, and go see if Coach Carter needs help doing the batting order for practice." He didn't know if that counted as a punishment, but at least it got her away from this poor kid.

The gum hadn't gotten in too far, so it was mostly just gross and not a disaster. Jeff pulled a dinner napkin from his pocket and picked up the bulk of it. "Okay, Morgan, I can get most of it out, but I might make what's left in there worse, or I can get out my pocket knife and cut a little bit of your hair and get all of it right away. What do you think?"

One little snip later, Morgan's tears dried up and Jeff made a trip to the garbage to dispose of the gum.

"New rule," he told Carter, who was holding back an obvious laugh.

"Oh?"

Jeff flicked his gaze to Amanda. "No gum during T-ball practice."

Carter grinned.

Practice ended at seven thirty, and the parents came by to thank Jeff for stepping in or to commiserate with Carter about his injury. Jeff was 99 percent sure most of them had known Carter in high school, and even Jeff had had classes with one or two. He got the vibe they'd been sitting around deciding who was going to ask if Jeff and Carter were *together* together, and he had no interest in them getting an answer before he did.

"Nice seeing you guys," he said as he threw the last of the equipment in the bag, "but it's been a long day and it's about time for Carter's knockout painkillers. Maybe I'll see you in a couple weeks."

Carter raised an eyebrow at him as they walked toward Jeff's truck together. "Subtle," he said.

"Hey, it worked."

That buzzing energy he'd felt between them in the dugout returned on the drive, but Jeff kept his hands on the wheel and his eyes on the road, even if he couldn't help his wandering mind.

What would happen if he got out of the truck at Carter's? Would Carter invite him in? He couldn't be imagining the way Carter had looked at him, and he knew himself well enough. His own desire would've been plain. Hell, he was getting hard now just thinking about it.

Were they really going to do this? How much could Carter physically manage with a broken foot?

Fuck it. Jeff was thirty seconds from pulling the truck over and blowing him on the side of the road.

But then, suddenly, they were in Carter's driveway, the truck's engine ticking as it cooled. Neither of them had spoken since they left the diamond.

Finally Carter said, "D'you wanna—"

Jeff's damp fingers slipped a little against the plastic as he unbuckled his seat belt. "Jesus yes."

LESSON THREE
Make Room for New Things

GET YOUR minds out of the gutter. Not like *that*. Or at least, not only like that.

In theory, dealing with your shit should leave space in your life for happy, nonshit things. In practice, those spaces fill up with grocery shopping and cleaning behind the couch. Yes, even rock stars get dust bunnies.

New relationships need space to grow—shared hobbies and shared time. A drawer in the dresser, not just room in your… heart (stop snickering). But it's easy to let those spaces get cluttered with less important stuff. The weeds of life. Jobs, family, friends, chores, and so on are all *necessary* parts of life, but they're also *established* parts of your life. They have roots already. They're strong enough to survive a little neglect. New relationships, not so much.

Chapter Seven

SOMEHOW THEY managed to get inside the house. Jeff had half a second to be fiercely glad he'd cleared away the clutter, and then Carter caged him in against the wall with his huge body, tilted Jeff's face up with one enormous hand, and crushed their lips together.

Jeff opened under the onslaught and clawed at Carter's back and chest as Carter plundered his mouth with a rough, frenzied kiss Jeff had waited more than a decade for. He bit back on a whimper, trying to be conscious of Carter's bad foot, but his knees threatened to buckle with every rasp of Carter's five o'clock shadow or sting of his teeth over Jeff's lips.

Carter wanted him. Carter wanted him bad enough he was trying to devour Jeff against the wall of his house when he'd broken his foot the day before, when there was a perfectly good couch twelve feet behind him. The knowledge was great for Jeff's ego—and his dick—but his conscience made him turn his head until Carter was mouthing at his jawline, biting down his neck.

Jeff shuddered, curling his hands at the small of Carter's back, pulling at the fabric of his shirt. "Carter—*fuck*—we should, the couch."

Carter ignored him and slid a hand down Jeff's chest until he was cupping Jeff's balls, his wrist and forearm pressed tight to Jeff's dick. Jeff's cock twitched and he tilted his head back farther against the wall, giving room for Carter to bite lower. He closed his mouth over Jeff's Adam's apple, just the brief score of teeth and tongue, enough to boil Jeff's blood in his veins. He bucked against Carter's hand, helplessly turned-on.

Carter shifted his weight and then hissed against Jeff's neck, and that cut through the lust. Jeff jerked away just a little, forced his fingers to release Carter's shirt, and pointed. "Couch. Now."

He was definitely getting that sainthood, because Carter went.

As soon as Carter sat, Jeff was in his lap, knees braced on either side, careful not to rest his weight on Carter's right leg. Jeff could feel the press of Carter's hard cock through his shorts, but it was hard to focus with Carter's hands bracing his ass, long fingers a centimeter from Jeff's asshole, with Carter's tongue in his mouth again. Jeff wanted to grind into his lap and get them off that way like teenagers on a second date, but he didn't dare. Too much pressure on Carter's foot could break the spell. Jeff couldn't risk it.

Instead he braced his left arm against Carter's shoulder and reached between them with his right hand, finally getting to touch Carter in the way he'd fantasized about for so long. His cock felt hard and huge under the slippery fabric of his shorts, and Jeff stroked him through them and bit at Carter's lips and tongue.

"*Jeff*," Carter broke the kiss to say, and Jeff was hit with a bolt of lust so strong he thought he might come just like that.

"What do you—" he asked, desperate to make Carter make that sound again, but that was as far as he got before Carter put one huge hand on his head and pushed him down.

Oh fuck yes, Jeff thought as he went to his knees between Carter's thighs, and only realized he'd said it out loud when Carter said, "You're gonna kill me."

"You're gonna like it," Jeff promised, and if he wasn't gentle when he pulled Carter's shorts down his thighs, Carter didn't complain any more than Jeff did when Carter pushed him down on his cock.

It was even bigger up close, long and fat and flushed and dripping. Jeff wasted no time taking the head into his mouth, sucking, making it as wet as he could, letting his spit drip down the length of it. Carter kept his hand in Jeff's curls, setting the pace, like he *knew* Jeff went crazy for that.

Jeff's erection was leaking all over his own shorts, but it could wait.

"Jeff," Carter said again, like it was the filthiest word in his vocabulary. His cock leaked a glob of precome on Jeff's tongue and Jeff lapped it up and then slid his mouth down as far as it could go. The angle wasn't right to get him all the way down his throat, but he would have to work up to it anyway.

Until then, Jeff sucked, hollowing his cheeks. He wrapped his right hand around the part of Carter's cock he couldn't take down. Then he closed his eyes and took in every obscene *uh* that fell like filthy pearls from Carter's lips. Jeff's face was wet with precome and drool and his eyes stung with tears from the perfect bite of Carter pulling his hair, and he'd never been so turned-on in his life.

Finally, too soon, Carter's thighs tensed and he arched against the couch. His hand tightened in Jeff's hair. "Gonna come," he said, and then the pressure left Jeff's head, but fuck that. Jeff grabbed Carter's wrist, encouraging him to hold Jeff down.

Carter's dick jerked in Jeff's mouth and he groaned, "God," in a voice that went right to the pleasure center of Jeff's brain.

Yeah, Jeff thought as he worked Carter's shaft as much as he could while Carter guided his head, hips thrusting up minutely until he came, gasping, flooding Jeff's mouth with come faster than he could swallow it. It seeped out over his chin and hand, hot and slick. Finally Carter pulled Jeff's head back until he could only reach the tip, and he licked up that last drop of come before Carter dragged him onto the couch to straddle his left leg.

Then he tugged him into a kiss, smearing come between their mouths as he pushed his left hand into Jeff's shorts. Jeff bit at Carter's mouth as Carter closed a hand around his cock, worked the elastic down with his wrist, and pulled him out.

He didn't even register that Carter had stopped kissing him until he said, "Spit," and brought his hand to Jeff's mouth.

Jeff spat. Carter thumbed the rest of his release off Jeff's chin and added that too, and then he closed his hand around Jeff's cock, sliding over him tight and slick and perfect.

It looked obscene, the way Carter's hand engulfed him. Jeff's dick was average size, but Carter's hands were so big, he could touch Jeff almost everywhere at once. And he was watching Jeff intently with smears of his own come on his face and his softening cock glistening with Jeff's spit between his legs.

Jeff was about to congratulate himself for lasting more than five strokes when Carter moved his other hand back between Jeff's legs and fingered his hole through his shorts at the same time he thumbed across the head of Jeff's cock. He catapulted into orgasm and a litany of stupid noises fell from his mouth as Carter wrung him dry, stroking and stroking until Jeff was so sensitive he pushed his hand away, heaving for breath.

Carter didn't break his gaze even as he raised his hand to his mouth and sucked the come off his thumb, because apparently it wasn't enough to wreck Jeff physically. *Jesus fuck.*

Under the serene silence of life-altering filthy sex, Jeff became aware of a backing soundtrack of blind panic. What had he just done?

He'd only just gotten Carter back in his life and now he'd put that in jeopardy, hadn't he? Jeff wasn't exactly Mr. Successful Interpersonal Relationships. He couldn't even figure shit out with the band who'd been his family for half his life. What made him think he could pull it off with Carter?

Carter was too important to risk for sex, even brain-leaking-out-your-ears, throw-away-everything-you-were-wearing sex.

Which, speaking of, Carter was still watching him with hooded eyes. He raised his hands to the hem of Jeff's—technically Carter's—shirt and tugged gently, smearing it with come. "You look good with my name on you."

Jeff was going to self-immolate. This was not at all how he'd ever expected this to go. He felt not just wrong-footed but impossibly young and unprepared. He'd spent fifteen years establishing himself, building a band, building a brand, forging this new identity out of the crumbling garbage of his past, and now all he wanted was the right to wear Carter's name.

If he was honest, it was the same thing he'd been yearning for when he started the band in the first place—for someone to claim him as their own. For Carter, specifically.

If Carter didn't mean that seriously, the way Jeff wanted him to—or if he did and it didn't work out—this thing between them would destroy him.

Jeff was still trying to come up with words—not even necessarily words to address everything he was feeling; he'd settle for words that made a reasonable response to what Carter said—when he heard the scrape of gravel and then a clatter of aluminum. He and Carter exchanged panicked glances, and the words Jeff finally managed were "Did you lock the door?"

Carter shoved at him, and Jeff scrambled up, belatedly remembering he needed to help Carter up after him. Carter's shorts were still around his thighs, which made his lopsided wobble toward the bedroom a bizarre combination of hilarious and erotic, with the firm bubble of his ass sticking out underneath his T-shirt. Jeff would've laughed at the absurdity, but he was too busy shoving down panic.

"Uncle Carter?" came a prepubescent voice.

Jeff stripped off the ruined shirt, then used it to mop up whatever he could. God, he was a mess. They both were. "Uncle?" he hissed. "I thought Brady's kid was, like, six months old!"

"That's Charlie. She's Dave's oldest." He tossed Jeff a clean T-shirt.

Dave played professional hockey and was only in town through the off-season. "It's May!" Jeff whisper-yelled as the front screen door banged open. "The playoffs are still on."

"Not for the Devils," Carter said wryly. "They must've gotten in today. They were going to come for the memorial if…." He waved a hand. "Otherwise we'd have postponed."

Jeff pulled the clean shirt on. "I forgot nobody locks their door here. Or calls first." He looked at his shorts, which seemed to have escaped contamination by way of a miracle.

Meanwhile Carter was attempting to pull a new pair of shorts over his walking boot. "Yeah, well, welcome to the family."

Jeff didn't have time to panic about that either, because the voice called again, "Uncle Carter?"

"Hey, Charlie," Carter yelled back. "One second." He glanced over at Jeff. "What's our play here?"

Jeff looked up and met his gaze. "How old's Charlie?"

"Twelve, I think?"

Old enough to be suspicious about her uncle coming out of the bedroom with someone else. "You want me to go out the window?"

Carter rolled his eyes. "Come on." Before Jeff could protest, he opened the door and wobbled out. "H—oof!"

There was a spindly prepubescent clinging to Carter's chest not ten feet from where Jeff just came his brains out.

"Ow," Carter said after a moment. "Careful, please, my foot's still sore."

The kid pulled back and Jeff caught a glimpse of hair that was a few shades closer to peroxide than the usual Rhodes blond, shaved on one side and cut in a long bob on the other. She was wearing athletic shorts and a sleeveless shirt. It didn't take a genius to guess why she might be anxious to see Uncle Carter. "Oh my God! What did you do?"

"Hiking accident." Carter edged past her toward the couch.

Jeff was still considering making a break for the bedroom window when Charlie's gaze moved up from her uncle and landed on him. "Oh." She looked from Carter to Jeff. "I didn't know you had company. Sorry."

The window would have been a better choice.

"It's okay," Carter said quickly. His ears were red, because of course they were. He could casually introduce Jeff to the filthiest sex of his life without the faintest shred of shame, but as soon as it came to acknowledging it to someone else, bam! Instant flush. Jeff wished that weren't so fucking adorable. "Charlie, this is my friend Jeff. Jeff, my niece Charlie."

Charlie raised her hand in an awkward wave. "Hey." Then her eyes widened and she said, "Wait, Jeff as in *Jeff Pine*?"

Ohhhh fuck. "Uh," said Jeff.

"Like this dumb hick town's most famous queer person Jeff Pine?"

Please don't hug me when I smell like come. "Guilty?"

"Oh my God," she said. Then, obviously putting the pieces together, "*Oh my God*, Uncle Carter, are you—is this—?"

Jeff was not going to have a panic attack in front of a tiny fangirl, even if she was Carter's queer niece.

Finally Charlie finished in a hissed, obvious stage whisper, "*Are you having a secret relationship with a rock star?*"

Carter threw a helpless look at Jeff, but what was Jeff going to do? He didn't know anything about kids. He literally cut gum out of a kindergartener's hair an hour ago. "It's complicated," Carter said, which deserved an award for Understatement of the Year. "Look, Charlie, it's great to see you, but can you give us a minute?"

She looked back at him, then at Jeff again. Jeff hoped she hadn't realized that if you peeled back the layers of his rock star persona, all you'd have was a guy who'd been in love with his best friend since eighth grade. "Sure, Uncle Carter. Um, I'll just wait outside."

The screen door banged shut behind her, and somehow Jeff made himself walk the rest of the way to the couch, because Carter really shouldn't be getting up again so soon. He dropped down onto it and put his face in his hands… which still smelled like spit and come. Jesus.

"Hey," Carter said gently, touching his shoulder. "Relax, okay? Charlie's dad's a professional hockey player. She knows better than to post things on social media."

Jeff had not even gotten that far into his list of things to freak out about. "Right now I'm a little more concerned about your mom." He took a deep breath.

"What?" Carter tilted his head. "Come on, Mom loves you."

Yeah. That was the whole problem. Jeff needed her to keep loving him, no matter what happened. "Look, this is… a lot."

Carter froze and his face closed off. He withdrew his hand. "Sorry, I…."

It hadn't even been five minutes and Jeff was fucking up. Bad enough he'd put that guarded expression on Carter's face. He needed to fix this before it got worse. "I just, I came out here for… space, and perspective on my life, and to figure out who I am when I'm not, you know…." He waved a hand vaguely toward the door. "Jeff Pine, Willow Sound's most famous queer person."

Carter raised an eyebrow.

"Yeah, I know." He rolled his eyes. "But the thing is, I don't know who I am without *this* either, and when you're already having an identity crisis…."

Carter's face shuttered further. "You don't have to explain."

"Yes I do." Jeff huffed out a breath. "I wasn't expecting this, all right? Don't get me wrong. It's a good surprise. I just need space."

Some of the guardedness fell away, and he nodded. "Okay. I can respect that." He clenched and unclenched his right hand. "Uh, are you still… I mean the memorial's the day after tomorrow. I'd understand—"

"I'll be there," Jeff said quickly. "I wouldn't miss that. I already hate that I wasn't here before."

"Okay." Carter sagged a little. "Okay. I'll see you then."

"Yeah." Jeff stood up. "I'll see you."

Charlie was sitting on the lawn next to a powder-blue bike. She looked up from her phone when Jeff walked out.

Jeff had never had a more awkward walk of shame. He raised his hand in a wave.

Charlie returned the gesture. She didn't look any more comfortable than he felt.

So the memorial would be interesting.

Jeff got back in the truck and started the engine. He needed a shower and a beer, or maybe one of those weed gummies he picked up before he left Toronto. He needed a good night's sleep and a little distance from Carter, from the way he looked at Jeff, the way he touched him.

He needed clarity.

He went back to the cabin intending to accomplish all of those goals, but when he unlocked the door, all he could see was his notebook sitting untouched on the kitchen table next to the unopened package of pens.

Jeff should shower. He *needed* to shower. But.

But he needed to process too, and he'd always processed best on paper. There was no point waiting. It was going to come out of him one way or another, and at least if he wrote it out, he'd have control over how.

He sat down at the table and pulled the notebook toward himself.

When the pen touched the paper, it seemed to operate of its own accord.

Firelight, wrote the pen.

Jeff had written his share of torch songs. The band's early days were full of them. He'd been trying his best not to think about it, because then he'd have to wonder if Carter knew those songs were about him. It seemed impossible now that he didn't.

Those songs had been full of Jeff's adolescent lust and yearning, and he'd meant them. People felt that when he sang them.

"Firelight" was in a different category. If Jeff's other songs were torch songs, this was an inferno, and he wove that allegory into the fabric of the lyrics. He struck a match to light a candle to see by, but the sudden brightness blinded him; he started a fire and burned up because the flames that kept him warm drew him in and they were only safe at a distance.

But every time I hear your voice
Every time I see your face
I know I never had a choice
I go right back to that place 'cause
You draw me in like firelight.

He dropped the pen after four verses when a loon called out over the Sound and broke his concentration. Shivering, he stood and went to the window, surprised to find the sun had set. The sky was red-orange, fading quickly to indigo, and the stars were winking to life one after the other, as though the loon had called to them.

Except it hadn't been calling to them, obviously—because the high, haunting cry came once more, and this time another call answered.

"Shower," Jeff muttered to himself. He couldn't get maudlin about a couple of birds, even if they did have a beautiful love song.

THE NINETEENTH was drizzly. Jeff woke up to the patter of rain on the cabin roof, sat up long enough to confirm the Sound was foggy and gray, and collapsed back into bed for another two hours.

When he could no longer ignore nature's call, he got up, put on a pot of coffee, and flicked on the space heater. Without the sun to heat the room, the air held a definite nip.

Jeff took the Seagull out of its case, changed the strings, and banged through an old standard with heavy strumming to stretch them out. Then he retuned at the kitchen table and watched through the screen door as the outside world got a little soggier.

He spent half an hour working through the song he'd play tomorrow, making sure his changes felt smooth, and then another twenty minutes singing softly and an hour toying with the solo.

Then he washed his face and made himself eat breakfast.

The rain didn't let up all morning. Jeff's phone stayed quiet, which surprised him. Despite last night's promise, he'd expected a check-in from Carter. When it didn't come by noon, he found himself thumbing open a text message. Did Carter need anything? Groceries? Company? Someone to grab the remote off the far table?

But he knew it wouldn't be fair to send a text when he'd asked for space just yesterday, so he closed the message without sending anything.

By two he needed to get out of the cabin, rain or not. He grabbed his truck keys and a sweatshirt and then, after some consideration, added his pen, notebook, and guitar case and trudged out into the damp.

With the passenger-side window open just a crack, the day seemed less claustrophobic. Jeff grabbed a late lunch at the diner where he'd eaten with Carter's mom. It was nearly deserted due to the weather, but when he'd been sitting in the back booth with his notebook and a plate of crumbs for half an hour, the bell above the door jangled.

Jeff looked up out of habit to see Charlie Rhodes slip inside, hair plastered to her head. She met Jeff's eyes and did a deer-in-the-headlights impression.

Jeff knew the feeling.

"Hey, hon." Tasha, the server, topped up Jeff's coffee. "Shouldn't you be in school?"

Charlie opened her mouth, her face set in an expression Jeff recognized as *about to get in trouble*, mainly because he'd worn it for most of his adolescence. "It's all right, Tasha, she doesn't go to school here." If he got on her good side, maybe she wouldn't grill him about her uncle.

Tasha glanced at him askance and then back at Carter's niece. "Oh, Charlie," she said. "I didn't recognize you with the haircut. I like it."

Charlie's face lowered its weapons. "Thanks."

"What can I get ya?"

She perked up. "Coffee?"

Oh boy. Jeff tapped his pen on his notebook and ducked his head to hide a rueful smile. It was like looking in a mirror that went back in time.

To her credit, Tasha didn't laugh. "Sure. Coming right up." But she grabbed the pot with the orange around the top—decaf.

They sat there quietly for a while—Charlie at the counter, spinning the mug she'd had all of two sips from, Jeff in the back booth, tap-tap-tapping the end of his pen on his comp book. Finally Tasha said, "I could turn the radio off, you know."

Jeff blinked and raised his head to meet her eyes. "Sorry?"

Sheepishly, she gestured above to the decrepit sound system piping out tinny twenty-year-old Top 40 hits, then to the guitar case under the table. "I could turn it off if it's bothering you. I figured you didn't want to leave your guitar in the car or whatever, but look. There's nobody in here but me and Charlie, and there won't be until the seniors start coming in for their early bird specials."

At the mention of her name, Charlie glanced over. She looked away again just as quickly—still a little starstruck.

Tasha must have seen the internal struggle on his face, because she sweetened the deal. "Tell you what. I'm going to turn the music off. I've heard this song twenty times today already anyway and I'll lose my mind if I have to listen to it one more time. Then I'm going to go in the back and hide until someone rings a bell." There was one on the counter, the kind Jeff associated with library desks. "Be cool and don't tell Grandma."

Her grandparents still owned the diner. Jeff remembered her at about ten, coloring in the same booth he sat in now.

"All right," Jeff agreed at last, smiling wanly. "Promise I won't let Charlie dine and dash."

Tasha winked at him, slung her dishtowel over her shoulder, and disappeared into the back. A moment later, the music cut out.

Sweet silence… for now. He pulled out the guitar case and unlatched it, careful not to glance over at his audience. "You don't mind, do you?"

Charlie whirled on the stool, obviously a little surprised Jeff was addressing her directly. "Uh, no, it's cool. I guess."

Oh, she *guessed*. Jeff kept a lid on his amusement—he wasn't laughing at her and didn't want her to think he was. He slung the strap over his head and nudged the case back under the table. For a few seconds, Jeff absently tuned the guitar, keeping his eyes on the tabletop. He strummed a G chord, then a C minor. The high E was a little flat, so he tightened the peg.

Eventually Charlie said, "What're you doing? That doesn't sound like a song."

He looked up, half startled, to find Charlie watching him, coffee forgotten. "Tuning. Each of the strings has to be set to the right note. Otherwise this"—he strummed an A—"sounds like this." He detuned the G and B strings and strummed again. They both winced at the discordant sound.

"Oh." She paused as Jeff brought the guitar back into tune. "How do you know what note it should be?"

"Practice," Jeff said dryly. But then he realized that wasn't a helpful answer. "When I was your age, I used a tuner. It's a little microphone that registers the frequency…." Too technical. "It tells you what note you're playing." Better.

The conversation lapsed while Jeff worked through the intro he'd been putting together. But his throat stuck on the lyrics. Sure, Charlie knew that he and Carter had a thing…. That was kind of the problem.

Damn it. He needed feedback and the only person available was a preteen. Hopefully Charlie had inherited the Rhodes family trait of being nonjudgmental. "Hey, can I ask you something weird?"

Charlie eyed him warily. "How weird?"

"Not, like, gross weird, it's—" He let out a long breath and decided to start at the beginning. "I'm writing this song about… coming back home, I guess. Coming back *here*." A thinly veiled metaphor for coming back to Carter, but she was twelve; she didn't have to know that. "Do you leave and come back every summer?"

She nodded, her drying hair sticking to her cheek. "Yeah. We moved a lot more when I was younger, but we've been in New Jersey for a while. But we always come to visit Grandma and—"

Shit. They both realized they'd wandered into an emotional minefield at the same moment. Charlie turned and fidgeted a napkin out of the countertop dispenser. Jeff pretended not to notice.

When he felt like he could speak again without betraying himself, he said, "Your grandfather was really special." He cleared his throat. "He's the one who taught me to play, actually."

Charlie turned around again. Her eyes were just a bit red. She bit her lower lip. "He promised to teach me this summer."

Boom. Maybe it was time for a strategic retreat. But it didn't seem fair—Jeff was the one who'd brought it up. He thumbed absently at the low E and searched for the words.

"Why d'you wanna know?"

Blinking, Jeff looked up again. He'd lost the thread of conversation.

Charlie must've interpreted his confusion, because she clarified, "About leaving and coming back. Why d'you wanna know?"

"Because that's what I did, I guess. Except it was just one time coming back, a long time later. It isn't going the way I thought it would."

She narrowed her eyes, but there was a smile hiding at the corner of her mouth. "Because of my uncle?"

Jeff knew that was going to bite him in the ass. "*Maybe*. Partly." He shrugged. "It's not weird for you? Coming and going all the time, I mean, not the part about your uncle." Best not give her any openings.

"It isn't weird," she said, but then she amended, "It *wasn't* weird until this time." Because Fred was gone.

Yeah.

Plucking out a simple riff, Jeff searched for words. "I wasn't sure what to expect when I came back here. I think I sort of thought everything would be the same, which is ridiculous. People change, people move. I'm not staying in my parents' old house or anything." He thumbed the low E a few times.

Charlie pulled her knees up onto the stool and slung her arms around them. "The weird thing is that it's, like, *mostly* the same, but not everything. It's not fair. If everything was different or everything was the same, it would be less weird."

"Yes!" That was the exact feeling Jeff had been trying to put into words. He'd traveled back in space, but he'd also expected to go back in time. Part of him felt as though he *had* gone back in time, which made the whole thing that much more confusing. "That's it exactly. Except, I don't know. I'm different too, I guess."

"Wouldn't know what *that's* like," Charlie muttered, tossing back her short hair.

Jeff barked a laugh and only grinned wider when he caught the pleased smile spreading across her face.

Then he looked down at the instrument in his lap—the battered secondhand well-loved thing, Jeff's prized possession. The one Fred had bought for him.

He'd come out here to find himself, but maybe he wasn't supposed to rediscover who he used to be. Maybe he should focus on the kind of person he *wanted* to be.

Jeff cleared his throat. "So, hey. Do you still want to learn to play guitar?"

BECAUSE THE universe could occasionally be merciful, it didn't rain the next morning.

Jeff rose before the sun, showered and dressed, then hit the Tim Hortons drive-through on the way to the marina. He kept the radio off for the drive and pulled into the parking lot at five to six, bearing a box of coffee with a sleeve of cups and a dozen breakfast muffins.

Carter's mother was in his dad's old truck, backing the boat into the water, but Carter and his brothers were standing awkwardly at the nearby picnic table, hands in pockets, shoulders hunched against the morning chill.

They all looked up when Jeff pulled in, but Carter looked away again quickly and returned his attention to what had to be Dave—he was too tall to be Brady, even if he wasn't as tall as Carter.

Jeff took a deep breath and let it out slowly. No pressure. Just a bunch of guys he knew half a lifetime ago and their mom.

He opened the door and swung himself out of the cab.

Brady greeted him first, with a handclasp-turned-backslap-hug—very straight bro. "Good to see you again. Shit circumstances, though."

Jeff was already having flashbacks to his mom's funeral. The awkward platitudes sounded just as terrible coming out of his own mouth as they had to his ears back then, but what else was there to say?

The world didn't have words big enough for this kind of truth. "I'm so fucking sorry, man. Your dad was one of the best."

Dave was next. Jeff hadn't known him that well, since he was four years Carter's senior and had already been drafted into the NHL by the time Jeff graduated elementary school, but he shook Jeff's hand. "Thanks for coming," he said gruffly. "It means a lot to Carter."

He could've just gutted Jeff with a fish knife. It would've been kinder.

That left Carter, who didn't say anything. Jeff didn't either. They met eyes, and then Jeff nodded and they hugged, and if they both held on a little too long, Carter's brothers probably weren't going to be shitheads about it today.

Eventually Jeff pulled back just as Ella got the boat trailer lined up perfectly. Dave and Brady went to help launch it, and Jeff said, "I could use a hand with a few things."

He and Carter got the stuff loaded while Ella was parking, and then they were all aboard, making for open water.

"Where's everyone else?" Jeff asked.

"Katie's with the baby," Brady said. "She's not too sure yet about bringing a six-month-old on a pontoon." He gave a tired half-smile. "Plus, when you have a six-month-old, you don't wake them up if you don't have to."

Dave nodded his agreement over an enormous bite of muffin. "I remember those days. Couldn't get Charlie out of bed either. And Brit gets motion sick. But they'll be there this afternoon."

Privately Jeff thought a smaller audience would make his task easier anyway. He held the guitar case between his knees. Pressed against his left side, Carter was a steady, solid line of warmth.

Finally they must have reached Fred's favorite fishing spot, because Ella cut the motor.

It was a calm day, and the waves of the Sound lapped gently against the hull. Ella sat down between Dave and Brady, and they all avoided looking at the urn of ashes sitting on the console next to the boxes of coffee and muffins.

After a moment she asked, "Is there a pumpkin cream cheese one in there? He loved those."

"I set it aside already," Brady said.

"Don't bother saving him a coffee," Carter said with the ghost of a smile.

Dave raised a hand and covered a laugh. "God, he used to bitch about their coffee."

"In his defense," said Jeff, "it is… not… good."

"You're just not putting enough cream in it."

They sat quietly for a few moments. No birds called, and no other boats were around.

Finally Ella stood up and picked up the urn. "All right." The muscles at the corners of her jaw bunched and released, but she kept her composure. She turned to face the water. "Well, you finally did it, Fred. You got all your sons to get together on your birthday to go out on the boat. You can thank the Boston Bruins for that, though I know you'd hate doing it."

"Harsh, Mom," Dave muttered, but he smiled wanly.

"Even Jeff is here."

Jeff figured that was his cue. He turned to the side and set the guitar case on Carter's lap to open it. Carter held it for him while he withdrew the instrument.

"Things haven't been the same without you, and I don't expect they ever will be. You left a hole." She cleared her throat. Brady wiped discreetly at his eyes. Next to Jeff on the bench, Carter inhaled shakily.

"We miss you," Ella said. "We miss you every day. But we're going to be okay." She bit her lip and met Jeff's eye, and he took that as his cue.

He slipped the strap over his head and stood.

Jeff had played for crowds of thousands. He'd played on no sleep, after being on the road for months on end, he'd played with a fever. In the early days, he'd played four- and five-hour sets.

Playing "Landslide" for an audience of four living people and an urn of ashes proved the most difficult performance he'd ever given.

There wasn't any fanfare afterward. Jeff put away the guitar, Ella opened the urn, and everyone took a handful of ashes to scatter. Brady offered Carter the muffin, and he hefted it in his hand.

"Happy birthday, Dad," he said. Then he drew his arm back and launched the muffin into the lake.

Chapter Eight

BACK AT Ella's, the healthy adults adjourned to Fred's man cave to begin the process of curating items of interest for the memorial. Due to the walking boot, Carter was remanded to the kitchen table. Every so often a family member delivered a box to sort through.

Jeff didn't exactly feel as though he belonged, but he was invited to the study, and he thought Brady even expected him to come in—but Ella took one look at his face when she suggested it and sent him upstairs with Carter.

Mixed blessings—when it was Charlie's turn to bring up a box, she tromped extra loudly up the stairs, like she wanted to make sure they heard her coming. Every time she slid something onto the table, she smirked at Jeff, but he refused to break first.

Besides, their détente was hilarious.

"Sorry," Carter murmured as he lifted a forty-year-old LP out of the box to inspect the label. "I'm sure this isn't exactly what you meant by space."

Only Carter could sound sincere in that apology at his own father's memorial. "For once in your life, stop being a martyr," Jeff grumbled. "Not everything is about you. And despite what you may have been led to believe, not every rock star thinks everything's about them either."

Carter's lips twitched. "All right."

Jeff had always known Carter's dad was sentimental. He'd never made a secret of it. But it still surprised him how many keepsakes the man had—programs from Dave's first hockey tournament, bits of science projects (mostly Carter's), a shell from a trip he and Ella had taken to Florida when Carter was twelve. A room service menu from their honeymoon. Even, preserved in the pages of a volume of poetry—Ginsberg, of course—two tickets to Howl.

Jeff spent long enough staring at them that Carter noticed, and he wordlessly held out his hand.

Jeff gave them over and watched Carter smooth his thumb over the date and time. Third row. Those seats would've cost a fortune.

"I would have gotten him tickets," Jeff said hoarsely. He would have given the performance of his life if he'd known his hero was in the audience. "VIP passes. Booked his hotel room."

Carter shook his head. "He wanted to pay."

They lapsed into silence, sorting—Goodwill, scrapbook, or sale—with the records to be maybe divided among family and interesting tchotchkes set aside to display for this afternoon. Carter put the tickets in that pile. Jeff didn't argue.

Under the Ginsberg was a Moleskine notebook with yellowed pages. Jeff lifted it out and opened the cover, half expecting another ledger of home improvement expenses—being sentimental did not preclude Fred from being a packrat—only to find, cryptically, a date range from Jeff's teenage years. When he set the book on the table, it fell open further, and the pages flipped as something in the book pushed them back. Jeff put his thumb in to keep the page as the item fell out.

It was an envelope with a few pictures in it, apparently depicting the day he and Ella moved eighteen-year-old Carter into his dorm in Toronto. Jeff smiled at it. Ella and Fred looked just as he remembered them, while Carter was skinnier, a little gawky. Of course Jeff remembered him being handsomer than he was. The three of them had their arms around each other and were grinning widely at the camera.

Jeff set the envelope aside and pulled the book closer. The page was dated a few years later than the photographs, so they likely weren't related. Under the date, he read—

Little fish has a big mouth
and bigger plans.
Hook line and sinker:
foolish fishers fling him back.
A gamble, a sting, a breath held,
a barb removed, another scar.
Little fish's belly fats with wasted bait—
he won't be little forever.

"Jeff?" Carter asked. "Are you okay?"

Jeff slammed the book closed, his heart in his throat. "I'm—I need some air."

Running away twice in three days. He was going to beat his old record at this rate.

Carter eventually caught up to him on the back deck, clomping outside with a grimace. "Kind of rude to make me chase after you with a broken foot," he teased gently.

Pacing frantically, Jeff ran both hands through his hair. "Kind of rude of me to be more needy than a dead father's sons at his memorial service, so I'm just hitting it out of the park all over."

Carter frowned and stepped closer, and Jeff instinctively stopped walking. He didn't want to step on Carter's foot. "Hey." He put a hand on Jeff's elbow and coaxed his arm down. Jeff didn't relax. "We've had six months to process. And Dad… he was your family too. You're allowed to grieve him."

"Am I?" It didn't feel like it. "I left, Carter. I didn't—for fifteen years I didn't call him, I didn't email. I acted like he was dead to me. Do I really have a right to be here? After everything?"

"Did you stop loving him?" Carter asked. He wasn't holding Jeff's elbow anymore, he was holding his wrist. When had that happened? "Because he didn't stop loving you."

Fuck. "Maybe he should've." Jeff bit the inside of his cheek hard as he scrambled for composure. When he could speak without his voice breaking, he said, "I know he didn't."

"He was proud of you."

"I didn't do anything to be proud of."

"No?" Carter brushed his thumb over the thin skin on the inside of Jeff's wrist. "You made a career doing what you love. You've been successful. Your music is good. A couple Grammy nominations. That's nothing to be proud of?"

Jeff shivered. He wanted to tug his hand away but couldn't muster the strength. He felt frozen. "I'm a coward."

"Are you?" Had Carter moved closer? He was all Jeff could look at now, and he could scarcely breathe. "Your music is brutally honest. You sing something and people feel like they know all your secrets. That takes bravery."

Did Carter feel like he knew all Jeff's secrets? "Maybe," Jeff said. "But when it's time to act, I run away." He'd run away fifteen years ago, afraid of what loving Carter might do to him, and he'd run away earlier this month, afraid of what would happen if he let himself continue loving his band.

Finally Carter let go of him, and the rest of the world rushed back in.

"Actually, can we talk about that?" Carter's eyes went shadowed, and his voice seemed heavy. "About the day you left, I mean."

Suddenly weak-kneed, Jeff lowered himself to sit on the deck stairs before he could fall. His throat constricted with panic. "I thought you said we didn't have to talk about that."

"Yeah, well." Carter dragged over a chair one-handed and planted himself in it. Even as panic-stricken as Jeff was, he had to admire the sheer strength that took—the chair was solid pine. "That was when I was afraid you'd run away."

Jeff squeezed his eyes shut, dug his nails into his palms, and leaned back against the deck rail. "And now?"

"Now I know you're going to run away. The only thing that matters is if you come back."

Jeff really wanted to come back. He took a deep breath, held it, let it go. He opened his eyes. "All right," he said. "You want to talk about what happened, so we'll talk about it." If he dug deep, maybe he could be as honest as Carter seemed to think he was. After all, everyone knew anyway, didn't they? Jeff only liked to pretend they didn't. "I'll start. I walked outside to get some air after my mom's funeral, after my life fell apart, and you were sitting on the back stairs of the funeral parlor kissing my cousin."

If he was being brave, though, truly brave, he couldn't leave it there. "In case the subtext wasn't clear—" He swallowed and looked right at Carter. "—that broke my heart a little."

Carter was the one person Jeff had always trusted not to hurt him. Jeff had no claim to him, but the betrayal of that trust had devastated him all the same.

He thought he'd feel different after admitting it, but he didn't. Maybe he felt like he'd admitted it so many times by now, onstage in front of thousands, that it was old news.

Carter gave him a pained look, the corners of his mouth tightening and turning down. "I kind of figured." But he didn't look away. "I'm sorry. It was a stupid thing to do. Can I… elaborate a little?"

Elaborate? "Is there more to say?"

Carter lifted a shoulder, repositioned his leg, grimaced, repositioned it again. "I don't want to say something like *excuse*, because I don't have an excuse. I have… motivations, I guess? Extenuating circumstances? I want to give you the whole picture."

For God's sake. "I think I got the picture pretty clearly," Jeff said, dry and a bit stung.

Carter opened his mouth.

Jeff cut him off. "Yes, okay? Fine. *Elaborate*."

It could hardly make things worse.

"Your life was falling apart," Carter said. "That's how you put it. Your mom died, your dad was making you move.

"But—God, this sounds awful with this much hindsight, don't think I don't know that. But I was seventeen, and my life was falling apart too. My best friend's mom died and there wasn't anything I could do to help him. And he was going to move, and all the plans I'd had for that last summer before university were gone too. On top of everything, I knew I wasn't the person everyone thought I was, but I wasn't ready to tell them so."

Well, that cut some of his resentment off at the knees. Jeff licked his lips. "You're right, that's a lot to deal with." Was he saying…?

"I know it doesn't excuse the way I hurt you." He leaned forward and clasped his hands between his knees. "But when I kissed—oh God." He stopped and dropped his head into his hands. "Crap."

His ears were bright red, and Jeff wondered what had him so flustered. And then he realized—"Oh my God, you forgot her name!"

"This is so embarrassing." He lifted his head just enough for Jeff to see his eyes. "But I guess it proves my point. I didn't want to be different. I did a shitty thing trying to convince myself I didn't have feelings for you, and then you caught me and any chance I had went up in smoke." He dropped his hands again and let Jeff see his sad, resigned smile. "At either thing, or so I thought."

Okay. He was definitely saying that. Jeff pressed his lips together and waited for him to come right out and admit it.

"Nothing to say?" Carter said.

He cleared his throat. "Uh, doesn't seem like you're done." His mouth tried to make a shape, but it couldn't pick one. The lower half of his face just sort of twitched aimlessly. "I mean. I've pretty much said it all. Publicly."

But Carter wasn't going to let Jeff off easy. He reached forward, and Jeff automatically reached back until Carter was holding his hand. "The thing is, I should be over it, but I'm not. When you showed up again, I thought, well, it's been years and people change, and I wasn't going to risk losing your friendship again if it turned out we'd changed too much or I'd just been romanticizing the past." He glanced away and then back again. "I figured this was my chance to figure out what might've happened if I didn't mess it up the first time."

Jeff swallowed. "What makes you think it would've worked out?" he asked, because somehow talking about the past felt a lot safer than talking about *now*. "You weren't ready to come out. I was a grief-and-hormone-fueled ball of resentment. And you were leaving for university anyway. I would've hated being the boyfriend back home." He'd have felt like a kid. "It was doomed. Like, don't get me wrong, I'd have been into it. But it would've been a train wreck."

"Then maybe we're lucky we waited."

Jeff's fingers clenched reflexively and his heart thudded in his throat. How could Carter be so sure about this, so calm? "What makes you think now will be any different? I came here because I'm a mess, Carter. Again or still."

"Well, we've basically been dating since you got back," Carter said gently, and he smiled when Jeff started in surprise. "I'm confident that my feelings haven't changed. I can be patient while you draw your own conclusions."

Jeff stared at him, sure that he couldn't possibly be real. Saint Cinnamon Roll Carter Rhodes, the world's sweetest and most patient man—unless he was getting a blow job.

But now that he thought about the past few weeks, he felt stupid. The lunches, the T-ball games, the hikes in the woods. The way he'd *touched Jeff's face*. Romantic campfires just for the two of them and the park's sixteen billion mosquitoes. "You were *stealth dating me*?"

Carter laughed, which was unfairly devastating at this distance. "I really didn't think I was being that sneaky. But yes. I've had feelings for you since before I could acknowledge I'm bi even to myself. So I thought, you know—you're here for the summer. Why not give it a try? I'm not willing to spend the rest of my life wondering if we could've had more. I want to know for sure."

"Fuck." Jeff weaseled out of Carter's grip and steepled his hands in front of his mouth. "You really… for that long?"

"Maybe not as long as you," Carter admitted, which was more of a blow to Jeff's dignity than his ego. It had been nice believing Carter had been oblivious to his feelings, at least before Jeff started singing about them on the radio. "But yeah."

"Jesus." He shook his head, and a smile started to creep over his lips despite his misgivings. Maybe things had gone to shit fifteen years ago, but Jeff had forgiven that, consciously or not. And maybe his life was still a mess, but his life would always be a mess. That shouldn't stop him from living it. "You know, if you'd told me this in high school, I wouldn't have lost my V card to that guy from robotics club."

Carter's eyes went molten in an immediate and obvious tell.

"Oh no," Jeff said, wagging his finger. "No, okay. Ground rule, no jealousy shit. Except for hot sex purposes. I live a public life. No nonsense or we might as well give up now."

He expected Carter to react with chagrin or defensiveness, but instead he got a brilliant, wide smile. It took Jeff a second to recover from it and ask, "*What*?"

"Just—yes?" Carter said. "You set a ground rule, so that means yes, right? You're going to date me for real?"

"Apparently we were already dating anyway," Jeff said. He was going for mock sour, but he just sounded… smitten. He was so screwed. He'd never been able to say no in the first place, and now—

"Do you still—um, I mean, we can take it slow if you still want space."

For God's sake. "I mean, yes, I'm probably going to need a little space. But how much slower can we possibly go? It took fifteen years to get to second base. At this rate if we ever move in together it'll be at a nursing home."

"We can get matching slippers," Carter promised, eyes dancing.

Jeff gave up. The man was actually perfect. "You're not going to be wearing slippers for a while," he pointed out as he stood up. That put him between Carter's knees.

Carter moved his hands to bracket Jeff's hips and looked up, his expression inescapably fond. Jeff kissed him, curling one hand around the back of his neck. He tasted the curve of his smile and drank in the sun-warm scent of him as Carter tucked his fingers into the back pockets of Jeff's jeans.

It was probably for the best, Jeff thought distantly as Carter nudged his mouth open to deepen the kiss, kneading and pulling at Jeff's ass until he stumbled closer, that he hadn't known Carter would be like this. He would never have learned to play guitar if he'd known. He'd have been too busy jerking off all the time.

He was debating whether the deck chair could hold both their weight when he heard the soft rumble of the patio door opening. "Carter, sweetheart—"

Jeff jerked reflexively out of the kiss, mortified, and he might have stumbled down the stairs, except Carter had a solid grip on his ass. Carter just chuckled and dropped his head against Jeff's chest.

"I'll come back later," Ella said, all amusement. "Just wanted to let you know that guests are starting to arrive." And she closed the door again to leave Jeff to die of embarrassment in peace.

"Tell me now," Jeff said, "before I get in this any further—does being a cockblock run in your family?"

Carter wrinkled his nose. "That seems unlikely, biologically speaking. Kind of against natural selection."

"So we're just unlucky."

"Well." He smiled and pulled his hands out of Jeff's pockets, but only far enough that he could rub his thumbs into the divots of Jeff's pelvis. "I don't know if I'd go that far."

Jeff shivered involuntarily and offered his hand instead. "Unfortunately, I think I have to take a rain check on proving it." He "helped" Carter to his feet, which mostly meant they held hands while Carter stood under his own power and then loomed sexily. "Come on. You need to go greet people, and I…." He took his phone out and looked at the time. "I only have another twenty minutes before I need to leave for the airport, and I should actually offer my condolences to your sisters-in-law." Preferably without an awkward boner.

He ended up standing in the living room with the family to greet the guests. If any of them found it strange to see Carter's former best friend or the frontman of a famous band in the Rhodes family home, Jeff couldn't tell.

People were still arriving for the open house when Jeff finally couldn't delay leaving anymore and got up. "I'd better go or I'll miss my flight," he said wryly.

"You literally chartered it," Carter pointed out, but he didn't otherwise object. He didn't get up either, which would've been fine even if he didn't have a broken foot, because Katie had handed him the baby—thus fulfilling Jeff's prophecy—so she could prepare something in the kitchen. Carter took the baby's arm and gently waved it.

Jeff was absolutely fucked. "I'll see you in a couple days."

"Bye!" Katie poked her head out from the kitchen. "Safe flight."

He caught Carter's eyes for one last lingering smile. Then, more reluctantly than he wanted to admit, he got in the truck and drove away.

Chapter Nine

HIS USUAL car service picked him up at Billy Bishop airport and took him right to the venue, so he didn't have time to panic. Of course, that didn't mean he didn't do it anyway—not about the concert, not about being onstage, but about being around Max and Trix again.

But when he opened the door to the green room before rehearsal, it was to good-natured laughter, the kind he hadn't heard in months.

"I don't think you can rhyme *purple* with itself any more times," Joe said wryly, which led Jeff to understand he'd arrived just in time for one of their pre-show "songwriting" exercises. "Disqualified."

"Boooooo." Max wadded up a piece of paper and tossed it at him. "Like you can do better."

"Whirlpool?" Jeff suggested, setting the Gibson case against the wall. He frowned, considering. "Urinal?"

"Now there's a combination," Trix laughed. She twirled a drumstick. "Good flight, Jeff?"

"Beats flying commercial." He dropped onto the couch next to Joe and pulled a guitar from a nearby armchair. "What did I miss?"

"Aside from Little Max's TikTok debut?" Trix rolled her eyes. "Not much. We're very boring without you, you know."

"Very boring," Max said, like butter wouldn't melt. "How was Willow Sound?"

"Oooh, yes." Trix gave up her seat at the makeup table at the far end of the room to sit cross-legged on the rug in front of the couch and stare up at him like a kid at story time. "How *was* Willow Sound? Did you see *Carter*?"

Jeff felt his cheeks going red. "Uh—"

"Oh my God," Joe said. He set his guitar aside and immediately turned to Jeff with his full attention. "You didn't tell me you ran into him!"

"I cannot believe you guys remember his name." Jeff threw his head back against the couch so he didn't have to look into anyone's eyes.

"Dude, of course we remember the boy who *broke your heart.*" That was Max. "Like, remember that night after we broke into the Top 100 the first time with that song that was definitely about you perving on him in the lake—"

Jeff covered his face.

"—and Trix got drunk and said 'we should send that guy a thank-you card, what was his name again?' and you said—"

"All right, yes, okay!" He dropped his hands so he could glower at them more effectively. Of course Max remembered. He'd offered to drive to Willow Sound and punch Carter in the face enough times, as a teenager.

"Anyway, you ran into that guy?" Trix said. "I was just teasing, but seriously. You saw him? Did you, like, slap him for kissing that girl at your mom's funeral, or was it more awkward, like, 'hey, just so you know, none of those love songs were about you'?"

"Is he still hot?" Joe asked.

"Fuck you, whose side are you on?" Jeff grumbled.

"Nah," said Max suddenly. "Don't tell me you finally hit that."

"Or let that hit you," Trix said. "We don't judge."

"We absolutely do not judge," Max agreed. "And also, we want details."

Joe raised his hand. "I don't."

"Overruled." Trix propped her head in her hands. "Come on, seriously. I know he broke your heart. What happened? Did you get an apology? I mean, he was your best friend."

All right. "I got an apology," Jeff acknowledged.

Shockingly, giving an inch did not satisfy the inquisition.

"Good," said Joe. "About time."

Trix nodded. "I'm glad. You deserve some closure. Although, like, don't let it stop you from writing another angsty song about it if the mood strikes."

Jeff was just basking in that nice warm feeling of validation that you get when your friends prove you'd done a good job choosing them—a feeling he admittedly hadn't had in a while—when Max said, delighted, "You got *laid.*"

"No!" Trix said. Then she looked at Jeff's face. "Wait, yes? *Yes*?"

"If I tell you, can we get started rehearsing already?" Jeff needed to warm up.

Joe put his hands over his ears.

Max and Trix leaned forward like puppies hoping for table scraps.

"Yes, I got laid," Jeff said. They didn't need more details. He stood up, guitar in one hand, and offered the other to Trix. "Now can we practice, please?"

Trix let him drag her up. "Aww. Jeffy. We missed you too."

IT WAS possible, Jeff knew, to be a technically proficient performer and make a good career as a musician. But if you wanted to be a superstar, you had to love it. You had to feed on the roar of a crowd, you had to crave it, you had to feel lost without it.

There were days Jeff forgot that he was that guy—the one who fed, who craved, who got lost. But one hit of the stage at a full house and it all came rushing back and flooded his brain with dopamine.

"Good energy tonight," Joe said, standing in the wings beside him.

"*Great* energy tonight." Max corrected bounced on the balls of his feet.

Jeff would've worried about him if he weren't like this before every performance, which felt unfair—he was literally just thinking about his own adrenaline rush, about how much he loved the anticipation of stepping onto the stage and holding your breath as the fans cheered you on. Everyone else was excited too.

But everyone else wasn't a drug addict, so.

Their opening act, an alt-rock group from Winnipeg with a style a little softer than Howl and a lot less polished, closed out their set to decent applause, and the stage lights went dark.

There was a little resetting required—different equipment, different settings for the sound mixing—but it was a well-oiled machine by now.

The cheering started when Trix walked out, visible to the audience only as a slender wild-haired silhouette backlit against the curtain as she made her way to the drum kit. Max followed as he always did, all the way across to the far side of the stage, guitar slung across his back.

Joe and Jeff did their preshow fist bump, and then Joe joined them.

Jeff gave it a few seconds, soaking it in. Then he slung his guitar around until he had it by the neck in his left hand and walked out to center stage to a deafening roar.

The tech crew had left everything where it should be. Jeff plugged in and gave the nod to the sound engineer backstage, who turned on the juice.

It felt a little like *he'd* been plugged in, like he had twenty thousand volts running through his blood, lighting him up from the inside. But the stage was still dark.

They'd been opening this tour with "Blood in the Water," one of the singles from the latest album, and it always got a great reception. But this afternoon at practice, after the first number, Trix had flipped a drumstick on the snare and then said, cheekily, "We should do 'Seventeen' instead."

Because Jeff was a sentimental asshole, he'd agreed.

The thing about concerts was that they were for fans, and fans talked. They knew to expect "Blood in the Water." Giving them "Seventeen" made them feel like this concert was special, like *they* were special. And they let Jeff know how much they appreciated it when, instead of the distorted, trembling opening chord of "Blood," he plucked out the retro-sounding twangy intro of the band's first number-one single.

The roar reached deafening levels… and then went silent.

Trix came in with the thud of the drum just after the third measure. Joe and Max joined in two bars later. But the lights stayed down until Jeff made friends with the microphone and sang, like someone was pulling his heart out through his mouth with a fishhook, "I met a man with kindness in his eyes, I met the truth in the ache of a long goodbye."

The lyric was supposed to be about a *boy*. Jeff didn't doubt people would notice. But it felt right. Maybe he wasn't about to go on television and tell the world or anything, but a little update wouldn't hurt.

He caught Max's eye and then Joe's after the second verse. They nodded, and as the chorus started, Jeff backed away from the mic and let the audience carry it, filling the venue with the words Jeff had written.

So yeah, he loved his job.

By the time the song ended on a ringing chord that reverberated throughout the space, the mood was electric and Jeff was pulsing with the heartbeat of twenty thousand fans.

He grinned into the microphone, full of joy, and glanced sidelong at Max. "Hey, Toronto, long time no see."

Sure, it was dumb, but Jeff loved pleasing people, and sometimes pleasing people meant being kind of dumb. The crowd roared back.

"Did you miss us?" Joe asked.

Another roar.

Jeff didn't have to glance over his shoulder to know Trix was looking at Max. "D'you think that was a yes?"

And more, louder cheers.

"We missed you too," he said. "We're gonna let Trix sing you this one."

Fuck, he loved this—the lights, the noise, the way things fell into place. He and Max and Trix and Joe just *clicking*, feeding on each other. Walking their guitars across the stage to share a mic for some slick harmonies, ad-libbing the extra-profane verse in "Heavenly Bodies" the way they always did because it had been deemed too hot for radio but they were too pleased with themselves to leave it out.

If this version left Jeff's bandmates wondering what exactly he and Carter had been up to in Willow Sound, they didn't call him on it while he was onstage.

They wrapped the night with "Ginsberg," because if you couldn't scream about fucking the establishment with twenty thousand strangers who'd paid hundreds of dollars to see the same concert as you, then when could you? Jeff felt the irony of it in his bones, but the truth was, he might be rich, but he'd never be the man.

When they filed into the green room, Jeff felt as good and as loose as he had after any concert in their early years, before everything started going to shit. He high-fived Max and hugged Joe, even though both of them were soaked with sweat, and he planted a wet kiss on Trix's cheek.

"So that didn't suck," he said cheerfully.

Joe stripped off his shirt and flung it at him. Then he dug on the wardrobe rack for a clean one. "Who was it who told you you had a way with words, again?"

"My third-grade teacher." Jeff threw the shirt back and followed it with his own. "Ugh, I think I'm getting sweatier with age."

Trix kicked her minidress into the laundry pile. "Don't even start. If I'm still doing this in fifteen years, I'm gonna need a freakin' snorkel."

Joe laughed. "Charming."

There were two showers just off the green room, and by the time Jeff had had his turn, Trix was toweling her hair dry at the table and Tim was going over the details for the morning show.

"I'll have a service swing by to pick you up at five. *Don't* be late."

Jeff shuddered.

Max made a face. "Guess we're not going out tonight."

"You guys were the ones who wanted to do *416 Morning*," Jeff pointed out. "And now we're all going to suffer."

"Sleep when you're dead," Trix advised.

That had been Jeff's motto at twenty, but ten years later, his body did not function the same way. "I'll die if I don't sleep, is more like it." He stifled a yawn. Usually he was jittery for an hour or so after a show, but tonight he just wanted to climb into bed. Apparently the rural life had made him soft.

It couldn't have anything to do with the fact that he hadn't stayed up past eleven in two weeks.

"Well, don't forget your stuff." Trix pushed his comp book at him across the table and motioned to the guitar by the door. They were playing a different venue tomorrow.

He was half-asleep when the car pulled up in front of his building, and he made it inside on autopilot alone—impressive since he barely spent any time there. He was most of the way into bed before he remembered to check his phone, but he took it out, thinking the least he could do was text Carter before bed.

Instead he saw a message. *Call me when you get this after the show? I'll be up.*

How could he resist that?

The phone rang only once before Carter picked up, sounding warm and sleep-worn. "Hey."

"Hey, yourself. 'I'll be up,' he says."

"I was awake," Carter protested. There was a sound like a few small *foom fooms*, like the air huffing out of pillows. Sleeping on the couch, probably. Or "resting." "Mostly. Healing a broken bone is surprisingly exhausting."

"We don't have to talk. To be honest, I'm not exactly bursting with energy myself." He closed his eyes and put his feet up on the mattress. It felt good to be off them. "Nice to hear your voice, though."

"You should probably rest yours," Carter said wryly. "Was it a good concert? You sound like you deep-throated an elephant."

Jeff blinked at the ceiling. "That's… evocative." He was pretty sure he couldn't handle an elephant. He could barely handle Carter. "And generous." But he definitely was a little hoarse.

Heh heh. Elephant. Hoarse.

Possibly he was a little punch-drunk.

"You know what I meant." He could almost see Carter's ears turning red.

"It was a good concert." He smiled. "I have to go do this talk show thing tomorrow. It's possible someone will ask a question about my personal life. Would it bother you if I'm vague?"

"Do what you gotta do," Carter yawned. "I'm probably not prepared for the level of chaos that would descend upon my life anyway. And people at work will be nosy."

Kara was definitely going to be nosy. Jeff could guarantee it. "Are you going back tomorrow?"

"Desk duty," Carter confirmed. "But at an actual desk. And I get to do campfire night, albeit with an assistant to do the literal heavy lifting."

"Good," Jeff said. "I worry about you sitting at home. I have this image of you deciding to remodel your house while your foot's broken."

"You're not far off. I was so bored tonight I almost started peeling the paint off the back door. It's chipping."

"You could get a new back door," Jeff pointed out, his eyes drifting closed.

"There's nothing wrong with it. It just needs a coat of paint."

And someone with the time and energy to sand and paint it, Jeff thought but didn't say. And new weather stripping. And to be completely reframed because it leaked air around the edges. If Jeff had noticed that much in two days…. "Uh-huh."

"Anyway, it'll be nice to get back to doing something that at least feels like it's making a difference."

Jeff opened his eyes and made himself sit up against the headboard. This seemed, from the actual uncharacteristic undertone of bitterness in Carter's voice, like it might be important. "What do you mean?"

"I don't know…. It's dumb."

Far be it from Carter to imply he was anything other than entirely satisfied with the hand he'd been dealt. "It's not dumb," Jeff said, fully awake now. "I want to understand, okay?"

"It can wait until the morning—"

"Carter."

Carter laughed through his nose. "Fine, you win." There was a soft thud. "I probably told you back in the day I wanted to get into conservation, right?"

"I seem to recall you mentioning it a time or two." Or seven, or a hundred. Teenage Carter was evangelical about habitat preservation.

"Well, that didn't exactly change. I did a master's in eco-conservation. But academia is…."

Of course Carter had a graduate degree, the nerd. "Competitive and underpaid?" Jeff suggested. He didn't have firsthand experience, but he did actually read.

"Yeah. And if you don't do something right after you graduate, or if you don't do a PhD, it's difficult to get back into the field. I started working with the parks service and thought, you know, at least it's related. I track wildlife populations, invasive species, climate change markers, that sort of thing. I make recommendations to keep tourists away from nesting threatened species, that kind of thing."

"Except now you're stuck inside," Jeff finished.

"I don't have enough spreadsheets to pretend I'm doing science. There's only so much I can do from a chair, so I'm assisting with the regular park maintenance admin. Scheduling and dispatch and phone nonsense."

"I'm sorry. That sounds… honestly, I can't relate at all, but it sounds boring. And I'm sure the actual pain of having a broken foot doesn't help."

"Plus my boyfriend left me all alone to field invasive questions from my family."

Jeff snuggled down onto his side and curled his knees up. The bed felt too empty, which he didn't have an excuse for. It wasn't like they'd even gotten as far as being in one together. "That's rough." He paused. "I miss you too."

"I'll see you soon," Carter promised. "I mean—I will, right? I know you have to go out West after this."

Jeff should stay in Toronto, but after fifteen years of waiting, he wasn't willing to sacrifice another minute. "I'll be back before I head out there. At least for a day or two."

"Good." He sighed. Or maybe it was a yawn. "I should let you get to bed. I know you have to be up early."

"And you need to go back to sleep."

"I told you, I was awake."

You shouldn't have been. "Good night, Carter."

DESPITE THE late night, Jeff woke up refreshed and ready to face the world—or at least, he would be after a shower and some coffee. Even Toronto was quiet in the hazy liminal light of predawn. Jeff got in the car to find Tim's PA waiting for him, which was a mixed blessing—she'd brought a lemon-honey tea and a breakfast sandwich, but she also had an agenda. Tim sometimes sent her in his place because Jeff wouldn't hesitate to push back against Tim, but he felt bad doing it with Dina. It wasn't her fault Tim asked her to do his dirty work.

"Morning," Jeff said, resignation creeping into his voice despite his best efforts.

"Morning," Dina chirped back as she handed over his breakfast, blithely unaware of—or at least not reacting to—his mood. "So I'm supposed to prep you for the show. The hosts sent a list of topics they want to cover, questions they want to ask, that sort of thing. I'm here to make sure we're all on the same page."

She was here, Jeff thought sourly, to convince him to make verbal commitments about the album progress he had so far been unwilling to make to Tim or anyone at the label. He sipped his tea. "Let's hear it."

"Right. Well, first, obviously, details of the concert tonight. Limited tickets are still available, it starts at eight. Echo Beach."

Tonight would be a smaller, more intimate affair, and outdoors too. Hopefully the weather held; outdoor concerts were Jeff's favorite to play.

But he knew all the information about the concert already, because he was a damn professional. "Right," he said, motioning her to go on.

Dina's smile didn't dim. "They're also going to want to promote the Canada Day concert, especially since that'll be televised on CBC. They have all the details for that, so you just need to make some nice comments about how you're looking forward to celebrating the birth of our country."

Ugh, that sounded pretentious. Jeff knew his job, and alienating white Canada by pointing out that the country had a long way to go before it was anywhere near as great as it liked to think it was was something he could do artistically in a song but not in plain language during an interview. Unfortunately.

But he did like a party, and *everybody* liked a day off work, and giving a free concert to hardworking people who liked music was something he could get behind. He'd become a master of strategic phrasing. "Got it."

Dina scrolled down on her phone. "Next order of business. Max's, um, incident."

"I'm not handling that," Jeff said flatly. "If Tim expects me to smooth that over, he can kick rocks. That's what PR firms are for."

Flattening her lips, Dina tried again. "We've asked the hosts to avoid the subject, but should it arise, we'd like you to play it off as a harmless mistake. Max paid his fine. No one was injured—"

"Except the half a dozen people who had to see his dick when he whipped it out in public," Jeff said. "Getting high out of his mind in a public club was a 'mistake' when he did it seven years ago. Now it's a habit. If they bring it up, I'm leaving it for Max to handle." No matter how well Max had behaved himself last night.

He could see Dina clenching her jaw, but she could obviously sense he wasn't going to budge, because she just said, "Let's move on. With the tour set to wind down in the middle of summer—which is already unusual—people are going to be wondering when you might be in the studio next."

Jake bit into his breakfast sandwich and made himself chew it twenty times before swallowing so he wouldn't grit his teeth.

He still kind of wanted to bite her head off instead. Well, Tim's by proxy. "If they ask about it, I will tell them the truth, which is that we haven't started writing it yet."

Dina cleared her throat. "It's been eighteen months since the last album—"

Yeah, Jeff was aware they'd been touring on this album for a year now, hence the lighter schedule, thanks.

"—and you're under contract. Your fans want some good news they can sink their teeth into. Something they can look forward to."

"You mean the label wants to squeeze another record out of us and they don't care about the personal cost."

"Jeff—"

"Dina." Jeff hated to be the guy who interrupted, but this line of conversation wasn't going to get them anywhere. "You can tell Tim that he does not want to know what will happen if the label pushes this issue right now. Yes, we're under contract for another album. I'm aware of that. I'm not going to make up details about progress on it because there hasn't been any, and I'm not going to lie." There were probably too many *I* statements in there to get away with without raising suspicion, but if people weren't suspicious about Jeff's commitment phobia by now, then they weren't paying attention.

Dina didn't say anything. She looked down at her phone, her mouth pursed.

Jeff exhaled. "I'm not trying to be difficult. I know you're just doing your job, and Tim gave you this job because he's too much of a chickenshit to do it himself. But I'm not a gullible kid anymore. I know my way around the business, and I'm not going to let anyone push me around. Life's too short."

Finally she nodded slowly and dropped her phone facedown on her lap. "Sorry," she said after a moment. "I hate when Tim does this to me, but I need this job."

"I get it," Jeff assured her. "No hard feelings, like I said. But you should probably advise Tim that if he tries any nonsense, it's not going to go over well."

"Noted." She picked up her phone again.

They pulled up at the studio a few minutes later, and Jeff submitted to being made up for television and then prodded into the appropriate outfit by the stylist Tim had sent over. Joe, Max, and Trix were there too, most of them preverbal at this hour.

"Did you three get any sleep at all?"

"I crashed five minutes after I got home," Trix said through a yawn. "I just hate mornings."

"Well, have some more coffee. This was your idea."

Joe didn't look much better. "I *tried*." He tilted his head back so his makeup artist could get to work on the oversize baggage beneath his eyes. "Sarah couldn't sleep, so she and my cousin stayed up all night watching dance movies in the living room."

"Aren't you, like, the designated adult?" Max was already through with the whole hair-and-makeup routine and had been vacuum sealed into his skinny jeans. "Can't you just tell them to… not?"

"I'm gonna give you a minute to think about what you said." Joe rolled his eyes. "I'm really in the habit of telling my partner she can't watch TV in the middle of the night if she can't sleep. Give me a break." He swallowed the last word with another yawn. "Anyway, I'm supposed to be the fun one. I'm walking a line here. Gotta make sure I'm cool enough that April comes to me if there's trouble."

"You don't think she's taking advantage a little?"

Joe's reply was lost in another yawn.

Despite the early hour, the show got off to a smooth start. Trix took some ribbing for not being a morning person, which everyone laughed at, especially when she pointed out, "Jeff's normally the worst of us. I don't know what happened."

"I went to bed early for two weeks is what happened. It was awful." He'd loved it.

"Jeff's been on an artists' retreat," Max said sagely. "Except it's just him and the loons. Actual birds, I mean."

"It's peaceful," Jeff defended, laughing.

The hosts looked at each other with knowing smiles, and then Shae—that was her name, right? Shit, Jeff couldn't remember suddenly; he was never awake in time to watch this show—said, "We've got some pictures, actually, of how peaceful it can be."

They showed a shot taken from somewhere in the park—a loon on the water at dusk, with the Sound glowing orange-red in the dying light. Then there was a lovely foggy morning in the forest, with a silence so thick you could hear it.

The third picture was a shot of a downtown street around midmorning, on a bright clear day that highlighted the care the shopkeepers took with their storefronts.

Or it would've, if anyone bothered to focus on anything other than the two figures sitting on the bench on the sidewalk.

The photograph was taken from an angle, so you could see Carter on the right, his arm stretched out over the back of the bench, his head thrown back in laughter, and Jeff sitting next to him wearing a smaller, teasing smile, just enough to dimple a bit, his eyes glittering with fondness.

"Wow," said the other host, Gisella. "I'd get up early too."

Fuck. There was no way Tim didn't know about this. He probably set the whole thing up and deliberately excluded Jeff from knowing about it to get a "genuine reaction" since he knew he wouldn't get what he wanted on the album front. Jeff didn't have a single doubt he did it as a way to prove he could make Jeff's life difficult if Jeff didn't fall in line. The subtext was clear—*Bring me that album or I'll make your life hell.*

Tim had never understood that Jeff was a professional shit disturber.

"So, Jeff, who's the guy?"

Jeff sighed internally but pasted on his Professional Media Smile. "That's my friend Carter. We went to high school together." He gestured at the photograph and said, "Obviously we still enjoy giving each other a hard time."

He said it definitively enough to imply that follow-up questions would be shot down in a truly awkward fashion, so the hosts let it pass and moved on to Joe, who was working with an Indigenous nonprofit group that promoted the preservation of traditional art forms.

Eventually the topic moved on to that night's concert.

"I'm going home after this to have a nap," Max admitted. "Gotta be ready. Eight o'clock. Opening band starts at seven. Some guy called Aiden Lindell?" He was faking not knowing the guy; they'd played the same stage before. Jeff was pretty sure they'd only been able to book Aiden because he lived nearby.

"I love Aiden's music," Gisella sighed. "And he's easy on the eyes too."

Jeff couldn't argue with that.

"What about after the concert?" Shae prompted. "Any plans to be in the studio any time soon?"

Gritting his teeth, Jeff opened his mouth to give the line he'd promised Dina he would, but before he could say anything, Trix spoke.

"No concrete plans yet, but I'm sure it'll be soon. I've seen Jeff scribbling in his comp book, which usually means he's actually got three or four songs ready to go. I guess all that time up north was good for something. Now the rest of us just have to do our parts."

He was going to kill her.

"Trix is exaggerating how far along those songs are," Jeff said. "They're really mostly lyrics right now." A lie. "Besides, I wouldn't want to write a Howl album without, you know, Howl."

In other words, *back off, that's not for you.*

"What people don't know is that for a professional musician, Jeff is like, super modest," Max piped in. "He'll tell you something's not ready, but Jeff's version of 'not ready' is another musician's demo." He grinned, not the least repentant, and for a moment, Jeff wondered if he was doing it on purpose. "Writing an album with him is a huge rush because you go in with a handful of proto-songs, and it's like he hears how it could be. Don't get me wrong, everybody's got their bit to do and we're all good at it, but Jeff has the magic touch."

Jeff took it back. That sounded like Max trying to butter him up. It wasn't going to work—he was pissed and he was going to stay that way.

He kept his mouth shut for the rest of the segment unless someone addressed him directly, knowing it was making the interview awkward and stilted and not giving a ripe shit.

As soon as filming wrapped, he ditched his collar mic and stormed back to the green room, actively fuming. Trix was hot on his heels—when he attempted to slam the door behind him, she caught it and held it open.

"What the fuck, Jeff?"

He whirled around. "I could ask you the same thing!"

"What crawled up your ass?" She planted her hands on her hips. "You've been acting fucking weird since you got back from Willow Sound."

I've been acting "fucking weird" since I had to give Max Narcan in January, he snarled internally. "I don't know, Trix, maybe I don't appreciate being committed to things I haven't agreed to—"

She rolled her eyes. "In case you forgot, we have an album due in less than two months, asshole. So sorry for trying to light a fire under your ass—"

"—or maybe I don't like it when people I'm supposed to trust go through my shit."

"Since when do you care if I go through your comp book?"

Since he'd started wondering whether he had a future with his band. "Since when do you unilaterally answer questions for the whole band?" he shot back.

That landed—she flinched and crossed her arms defensively. "Just because you're the lead singer—"

Jeff had never been the type to trash a hotel room, but he was starting to see the appeal of breaking things on purpose.

"Trix," Max murmured from behind her, touching her shoulder. "What's going on?"

"Nothing," she spat. Then, half as harshly, "Nothing. Jeff's just being a dick about nailing down a timeline for the album, and he's pissed I forced his hand." Her mouth went sharp. "Hope Carter's prepared for those commitment issues."

Fuck, Carter. On top of all the other shit, he had to warn Carter that people outside his family were going to be asking questions now too. "I'm out of here," Jeff snapped. "Don't fucking call me. I'll see you at sound check."

LESSON FOUR
The Truth Will Set You Free, But in, Like, Absolutely the Most Terrifying and Inconvenient Way Possible

HERE'S A shocker for you—famous people are liars.

We lie about how much we do yoga and how much we do coke and tell people we were on a retreat when we mean we were in rehab.

But the music is honest.

When we're onstage, we're wearing makeup and outfits specially selected by someone whose job it is to convey things about us through clothing. It's the work of several people just to light the band properly. Everything is deliberate.

Everything *has* to be deliberate, because the performers are raw and exposed. Performing live, doing it well, requires vulnerability and trust.

Someone once told me all good stories are true. It's the same with music. If your song doesn't come from a place of honesty, it's probably not very good. It might be fun, it might be catchy, it might even win you a Grammy. But it won't resonate with an audience the way a true story will.

The problem is that sometimes the truth will break your heart.

Chapter Ten

JEFF WALKED three blocks before he calmed down enough to call Carter. He ducked into Starbucks for a latte, carefully avoiding the gaze of the other morning patrons, then stepped back outside and hailed a taxi.

Hey, he sent. *Don't suppose you get the local Toronto morning show up there?*

He practiced his meditative breathing while he waited for a response. In, two, three, four; hold, two, three, four; out, two, three, four. Again. Again.

Finally Carter's reply brightened the screen. *Watched the YouTube upload. Should I call?*

Some of Jeff's tension uncoiled. *Not yet. In a cab. Call when I get home?*

Ok.

He gave the driver a huge tip for making it back to his condo so quickly, then stalked into the elevator, his thumb already hovering over the Call button on his phone. He would've pushed it, but he didn't get service in the elevator.

Finally—

"Hey," Carter said immediately, before the phone even had a chance to ring. "Are you okay?"

Jeff's knees gave out and he found himself sitting against the door to his condo, legs straight out in front of him. "No."

"Which part?"

Jeff thunked his head against the door, swamped with guilt. "Is it terrible if I say I don't really care about the picture of us right now? I mean. I'm not happy about it, I didn't know it was going to happen, and I'm going to have someone's head on a plate for blindsiding me with it. And I'm sorry you got dragged into this." He paused and swallowed past the thickness in his throat. "Fuck, apparently I do care about that too."

"Hey, hey," Carter said gently. "It's okay. I don't care, all right? It's not like people around here haven't wondered for the past fifteen years."

Jeff groaned and ran a hand down his face. "Sorry. Again. I didn't exactly consider the potential consequences for you when I was writing all those songs about how"—*in love with you I was*—"bad I wanted to bone you."

Carter snorted. "Apology not accepted. I don't think that's what tipped people off."

Probably not. "*Anyway*. That's tangential."

"You're angry with Trix."

"I'm furious with Trix. With Tim too. I specifically told his assistant I wouldn't be fielding any questions about a new album, and the hosts went ahead and asked anyway, which means either they went against his wishes—possible but unlikely, because they like booking celebrity musical talent—or he conveniently forgot to pass that message on."

"Or he did it deliberately and Trix was complicit."

Jeff's stomach twisted. "Yeah. I mean, of the likely scenarios, that's the one that's getting to me."

"I'm sorry. You must feel really betrayed."

He felt… yeah. Exactly like that. "I know we're under contract for another album. I know the deadline is looming. Max and Trix have been bugging me about it. But it feels like it never ends. Album, tour, repeat. They want, like, a two-year cycle. That's just not enough time anymore. I want to enjoy *life*." He wanted to spend time with someone who wasn't in his band. He wanted to be able to date. He wanted Carter, specifically, and he couldn't see how he'd ever be happy if he only got to see him a few months of the year.

"Yeah," Carter said meaningfully. "I know."

Okay, Jeff thought, going warm. Well. Good.

Then Carter cleared his throat. "But uh, okay, don't take this the wrong way. But you are under contract for that album, right? Or… how does that work?"

Jeff closed his eyes. "Yeah," he said on a long exhale. "I mean, there's ways out of it, but they're expensive. And it feels disloyal—not to the label, fuck those guys, but to Joe and Trix and Max. I love them. I love making music with them. But rock stars aren't the easiest people to live with. It was dumb to think I could just avoid the problem by not starting another album. Which probably doesn't help my case with anyone."

There was a pause and then Carter said, "How do you mean?"

He rubbed his hand over his head. "I could've told the truth. 'Hey guys, I know we've been family for fifteen years, but I'm not sure I want to do this with you anymore. Have a nice life.'"

"You could just… bring up the idea that you want to slow down?" Carter suggested carefully. "Uh, sorry if you've already tried it. I'm not clear if you want help solving the problem or just someone to vent to."

"Could you stop being disgustingly perfect for two seconds?" Jeff muttered under his breath. "I have asked, though, as it turns out. It didn't amount to anything the last couple times because we were contracted to deliver albums by certain dates. Which is still happening now. We agreed to a maximum number of tour dates per album, like, eight years ago when we were young." And full of energy. And stupidity. "With stipulations that dates could be added in certain increments over such-and-such a timeline if sales warranted. Same thing with the new album schedule." Which was where they were now.

"That sounds… not good."

"Yeah, it *is* not good." Twenty-two-year-old Jeff hadn't thought about getting a lawyer. "Anyway. There are multiple issues here. The first is Trix and Max and Joe not knowing I'm thinking about leaving. The second is Tim will do anything to get another album because we're a golden goose, and he's shown he's willing to exploit my personal life to get me to play ball."

Carter sucked in a breath. "You think that's what the photo was about?"

"I'm not *sure*." Jeff stared at the ceiling. "But it makes the most sense. I didn't know that was coming. Why not prime me for it? By blindsiding me, the hosts risked alienating me and potentially other celebrities who might be interviewed on the show. That's not worth it for a two-second reaction. Maybe if they had a picture of me sucking your dick."

"Jesus." Carter made a strangled noise.

"Which means they thought I'd been prepped for it. Because Tim *should've* prepped me for it. He didn't. Trix and Max didn't seem surprised, though."

"Hmm."

Jeff's butt hurt. He should probably get up off the floor. "What?"

"I was just thinking," Carter said, "that you should fire this Tim guy."

"Right?" Maybe that was something he could bring up, at least—that he did not want to re-sign with Big Moose, period, after this album if it meant working with Tim. "Anyway. Tell me about your day so far. Hopefully it's been better than mine."

"Hmm. Well, it's pretty early, but guess what? Dave's already been over." If a tone of voice could roll its eyes, that was what Carter's was doing. "He's appointed himself my personal trainer while I'm nursing the broken foot."

"Oh Lord." Jeff had a nightmare flash of Dave tying a dumbbell to Carter's walking boot. "Do I need to stage an intervention? I think I have Kara's cell phone number."

Carter laughed. "No, it's fine. It's actually helpful—he's had foot injuries before, so he knows all the exercises to keep as much mobility as possible. Plus, if I had to stop working out for six weeks, I would lose my mind."

"True, but—" Jeff glanced at the clock. "It's still only eight in the morning."

"Yep," Carter agreed cheerfully.

"*Ugh.*" Jeff might be becoming a morning person, but he didn't have to *like* it. "And now what? Are you getting a ride in today?"

"Dave dropped me at the office after our workout. I'm just sitting down to open my work email. Well. Technically I was already doing the sitting-down part."

"Uh-huh." Jeff was skeptical of exactly how much of the recommended sitting down Carter was doing, but he didn't have much leverage from Toronto. "Anything good?"

The sound of office chair wheels, then the clack of a keyboard. "Let's see." Click, click. "A couple repair orders—we've got some rotting boards. Safety hazard. Aren't you surprised by how glamorous my job is?"

Jeff snorted. This wasn't even Carter's regular job. "Shadow me for a week and you'll see true un-glamor, trust me." Tour buses plus Taco Bell. *That* would take the shine off rock stardom.

"Automatically generated email from our weather stations with climate data," Carter continued. "Oh, look—spam." *Click.* "And—jeez, what was *she* doing up at four in the morning?"

"You got an interesting one?"

"Maybe. It's from my friend Emily. We went to school together. She was one of the good ones—managed to at least give the impression she wouldn't shank you for grant money."

Jeff couldn't tell if he was joking. "She sounds nice."

"Mm-hmm. I guess she's also one of the lucky ones, because her email's asking for data."

Translation—any other person would have been jealous his friend still got to participate in active climate science and he didn't, but Carter was too sweet.

In any case, Jeff had lost him—whatever this request was, his curiosity was piqued and he was now in full science mode. "All right, I'm going to let you go and try to shower off this morning so that I don't break any guitars onstage tonight."

"Hmm? Oh. Sure. Thanks for calling."

Jeff shook his head. "Talk to you later."

Then he dropped the arm with his phone into his lap.

There was only so much wallowing he could do, and he'd already done most of it. Trix and Tim did a shitty thing, but Jeff wasn't doing himself any favors either. He needed to come up with an album timeline and touring schedule he didn't hate, evaluate whether he could do it with Howl, or find a way to get out of doing it.

Knowing that it would likely spell the end of his time with the band.

He couldn't do all of that in an afternoon, but he couldn't do *anything* if he didn't start somewhere. With a new objective in mind, Jeff pulled himself up off the apartment floor. He had work to do.

BY THE time Jeff's car service dropped him at the venue, he had fifteen minutes until sound check and Tim was obviously about ready to light into him.

Before he had the chance, Jeff handed him a business card. "You're right, I'm borderline late. If you've got anything to say about it, please contact my lawyer."

Tim's face went from apoplectic to pants-shitting dread and back again. "Your *lawyer*?"

"Monique Huberdeau. She's reviewing Howl's contract as we speak to determine whether there's been a breach on your part. Because if I find out that you knew that photograph would be used on the show this morning and you didn't tell me, and the contract says you should've, we are done."

"Who the fuck do you think you are?" Tim sputtered, turning red.

Jeff took his sunglasses off and, channeling Carter, hung them on the front of his T-shirt. Time to out-douchebag the douche king. "I'm a motherfucking rock star, Tim. I don't know where you got the idea you could walk all over me, but it ends now." Then he clapped him on the shoulder. "Now where's my band?"

Joe, Trix, and Max were already on the stage, waiting for him.

Jeff's stomach twisted into knots. Trix was sitting at the drumkit, elbows on her knees, leaning over with her sticks held loosely in her hands. Max and Joe stood stage right and stage left respectively. The atmosphere was one of persevering awkwardness.

And most of it was Jeff's fault.

"Hey," he said, taking the stool that had been left at center stage. "Can we talk for a minute?"

Joe met his eyes and nodded incrementally. Max pulled his own stool closer and sat. "Sure."

Trix let out a long breath. "Whatever," she said, shoving her drumsticks into her right boot. "Can't imagine what we have to talk about."

But before Jeff could say anything, one of the techs popped up from the side stage. "Sorry, I don't mean to interrupt, but we've got a limited window here and we still have to do sound check for the opening act. Any chance we can get started?"

Fuck. Jeff pinched the bridge of his nose. He needed to eat something and get some Advil or tonight would destroy him. "Yeah, okay. First things first." He blew out a breath and met Trix's eyes. "After the show?"

For the first time he noticed she looked tired. Obviously she hadn't been to Makeup yet. "Yeah." She nodded and pulled the drumsticks out of her boot. "The show must go on, right?"

"Ready to rock," Joe confirmed, plugging in. "From the top?"

Something always went wrong during sound check. Broken guitar strings, accidental feedback loop, mic stand tipping over. Jeff took it as a good omen—things going wrong in sound check meant they *wouldn't* go wrong during the show.

This time, when Trix was retuning the tom to avoid sympathetic vibration of the snare, one side of the lug broke off. She pulled her hand away and stared at the offending plastic—only the rods were metal—and swore. "What the fuck. Mass-produced piece of shit."

"That's a new one," Max said. "Hey, Wilma!" He leaned over the side of the stage, where the tech crew was working on… something. If it didn't happen onstage, Jeff didn't know about it. "You got a pair of Vise-Grips?"

A moment later someone handed up the appropriate tool, and Max walked it over to Trix.

With a minimum of fuss, Trix resolved the problem. "Can I keep this 'til after the show?" she yelled.

Someone raised a hand in a thumbs-up.

They finished just in time to yield the stage to the opening act, and Jeff let himself be hustled to Wardrobe and Makeup. Joe sat in the chair next to him and submitted to being airbrushed, while Nancy tousled Jeff's curls.

"I could give you a little trim," she offered, "if you think it's getting a bit long."

Jeff had a sudden flashback to Carter's hands in his hair. "Ah, no. I think I'm keeping it for now. Thanks, though."

When their techs had left, Joe swiveled toward Jeff. "Look, are we going to talk about this? Because I can't help but feel like I'm missing something."

"Yeah. That's my fault." Jeff fought the urge to fidget with his hair by sitting on his hands and glanced both ways before lowering his voice. "I'm pretty sure Tim is up to some manipulative shit. There's no way the hosts of that show used that picture without him knowing, so why didn't Dina tell me about it? Why didn't he tell them no?"

Joe's eyes widened. "You didn't know that was coming?"

"I didn't even know that picture *existed*."

"I'm sorry, man. That's messed up." Now Joe was looking around too. "Not that I've ever exactly been his biggest fan either. Can't say I'm surprised."

"Yeah, well. We got saddled with him when we didn't know better. But if we'd been smart a little sooner, maybe we could've been free a while ago." Maybe a different manager would have gotten Max into rehab—*real* rehab, the intensive kind, not a wishy-washy two-week program where he'd just use the whole time anyway. Maybe a different manager would have supported Joe's activism.

Maybe a different manager wouldn't have worked Jeff until he was burned up as much as he was burned out.

"You don't want to do the album," Joe said, understanding dawning.

He might as well admit it. "Not if it means working with Tim." Jeff debated for a moment, but in the end, if he couldn't trust Joe, the whole thing was shot anyway. "But I know it's too much to ask everyone to consider breaking our contract. Meanwhile, I told Tim if he needed to talk to me he could go through my lawyer."

Joe whistled. "That's going to cost you."

Not as much as it'd cost to get out of their contract. "It will be worth it." Besides, hopefully it was a short-term solution.

"Yeah, I guess it will." Joe worried at his lower lip for a moment. "So. Are you as worried about Max as I am?"

Max *and* Trix, yeah. Maybe more so. Jeff grimaced instead of giving in to the urge to rub his eyes. "Yeah." He'd been hoping, stupidly, that being away from the crush of the tour would mellow him out. But for Max, the problem was never the tour. "After the show?"

"Yeah." Joe nodded once, face tight, and then clapped Jeff on the shoulder. "Come on. Let's go out with a bang."

Jeff could have let the past day spoil the show. He was furious with Tim and half sick over Trix and Max. But fans had paid stupid amounts of money to be here tonight, and they deserved him at his best.

Besides, outdoor concerts were always special. Jeff liked the way the night breeze could carry his voice, the way it rippled through the crowd. Until recently, he'd loved the sense of security he received from the people around him. He could make a misstep and Max would catch him, add a verse and Joe would be there, lose the beat and Trix would find him back.

He always wanted to feel that way onstage with them. He hadn't even considered leaving until he realized he didn't feel it anymore. Somewhere along the way, they'd lost themselves and each other. All he could do now was try to bring them back.

The outdoor stage wasn't quite dark yet. This time of year, it wouldn't be for another hour. So Jeff walked onstage in a beautiful twilit May evening, guitar in hand, and joined his band.

Max met his eyes first, blessedly clear and sober. Trix gave a nod, terse but not solemn. Then Joe, who raised his eyebrows and thumped out a quick riff—*Are you ready?*

Jeff looked out into the audience—a sea of cell phone lights and swaying bodies. At least one person had a really fragrant blunt, but it wasn't likely to bother even Max.

Jeff's fingers shaped the chords, major one, major four, minor five, diminished seventh, but he didn't strum. The guitar made just enough sound without it for the audience to recognize the song.

"I hear you like Shark Week," he said, because he was a hopeless nerd.

The crowd cheered anyway. A microphone bestowed a lot of power.

Jeff stepped back and turned to nod at Trix, and she raised her sticks for the count. One, two, three, four—

Jeff had always loved this song. He and Trix had written it about their parents, obliquely. Trix's mom had narcissistic personality disorder. Jeff's dad was frankly just a shit parent. Jeff had never tried to put a label on it. The chorus pretty much said it all anyway:

I should've known you'd smell the blood in the water
I should've known you'd find the moment to strike
You were the priest, I was the lamb on the altar
I'm not naïve, I just forgot what you're like

The chorus grew progressively angrier as the song went on, with Trix joining him in a two-part harmony that culminated in shout-singing, a technique that had taken them years to do well. Tonight Jeff felt the strain on his vocal cords and knew the fans could hear it and feel the raw emotion the words evoked for him.

And for Trix.

This was what had bonded them, once upon a time. It hurt to sing it now and think of her instead, knowing she was probably doing the same. But audiences responded to honesty, and when the last notes of the song faded away, they were on their feet, hollering, the sound echoing in Jeff's ears even past his noise-reducing earpieces.

He took a moment to catch his breath and happened to look back and found Trix's gaze by accident. She inclined her head.

Good enough, Jeff thought, and subtly cued Joe for the bass intro of "Ginsberg."

The tension on the stage might feel uncomfortable to Jeff, but it hadn't impacted the audience. If anything, they had more energy than Jeff could remember from any other show in the past two years.

The first set ended on "I Like the Thrill," Max's homage to e.e. cummings. Jeff yielded center stage and let him get into it in sensuous, crooning detail while Jeff, Joe, and Trix took turns with breathy backup vocals. As the last orgiastic harmony faded into the finally fallen night, the crowd ignited in cheers. Jeff was glad for them that it was dark now. The song tended to put people in a certain mood.

They didn't have a lot of downtime while the tech crew prepped the stage for the second set of the show, which had different lighting needs due to a stronger focus on acoustic numbers. They also had to roll out the piano for Joe as well as Trix's second drum kit, which had a slightly different tuning.

They reopened with Joe at the piano under a bright spotlight, tickling through the delicate intro of "That Summer."

As the melody transferred to Jeff, Joe's light went out and another came on, illuminating Jeff standing on the piano, feet shoulder-width apart, guitar cradled against his hips, head bowed.

The sound of five thousand people losing their shit would never get old, even if Jeff couldn't see them: if he opened his eyes under the spotlight, he wouldn't be able to see to get down from the piano when the spotlight moved.

Trix came in, the heat of the spotlight left his skin, and Jeff carefully jumped down as Joe sang about his childhood adventures climbing trees and terrorizing his grandmother's chickens.

Unlike the show the night before, they stayed mainly with recent releases, bantering back and forth with snippets of history—how the songs came to be, who suggested what lyric, who was responsible for what songs.

With one or two songs to go, Joe was back on bass, picking out a muted background leitmotif as he quipped, "If the song's about breaking the law, Trix probably wrote it."

Trix groaned theatrically but tapped out a rimshot anyway. "Just because I wrote out my fantasy of keying a cop's car—"

"Also that one about breaking into a museum," Max put in.

"That was for a movie."

"What about 'Catch Me'?" Jeff asked innocently. "How many speeding tickets do you have again?"

She snorted and made a face at him. "Since when are you such a narc?"

Jeff played a minor ninth to indicate his disagreement with the statement.

Max picked up the thread. "Joe's songs are all pretty personal. Life experiences."

It wasn't a secret or anything, so Joe just nodded. "Max, you know, he's a little of everything. A poem he read, a place he's been, a woman he—"

"Treated very respectfully," Jeff broke in because he knew his cue.

"Respected all night long," Joe continued.

Trix tapped out a quick beat—tom-tom-tom. "And then there's Jeff."

Oh boy.

Jeff felt his face going redder under the bright lights of the stage, even though he'd seen this coming. It had been one thing before, when he could pretend that the songs were just songs, not written about anyone in particular. Now—well, Carter must at least suspect they were mostly about him. Which was fine. Except Carter's entire family also knew. Most of Willow Sound would follow.

Jeff had made some choices.

"Hey," said Max, "do you guys know what a torch song is?"

Giving up the pretense of not being embarrassed, Jeff let his guitar strap hold the instrument's weight and covered his face. "Guys—"

"You know that phrase 'carrying a torch for somebody'?"

Jeff dropped his hands. "You're the worst."

He wasn't really mad—this kind of banter, especially at smaller shows, helped give them a little break to change gears between songs, and showing off the chemistry between them was important. For some fans it was that, as much as the music, that drew them in, that made it worth the price of admission.

And to be honest, Jeff had missed it too.

"Jeff has two gears," said Joe. "Scathing social commentary, and love songs that make you want to peel your face off."

"Wow," Jeff deadpanned. "You really know how to sell it."

"Just telling it like it is."

"Jeff loves love." Trix picked up her mic as she came out from behind the drum kit and gestured to someone just offstage. One of the tech crew walked out with a stool. Another followed with Jeff's acoustic, which he'd already finished with for the set.

Or so he'd thought.

"And I happen to know," Trix went on, taking the guitar from the stagehand, "that he's been working on something new to share with us."

She had to know what she was doing. She had to be aware of the position she was putting him in. But none of it showed on her face or in her demeanor as she smiled winsomely—for the audience, but *at Jeff*—and held out the instrument. "You guys wanna hear it?"

You bitch. Jeff fought the urge to clench his teeth in fury.

The crowd, obviously, went apeshit.

Trix had backed him into a corner. If he didn't deliver a new song, *he'd* be the asshole—and he risked rumors of a Fleetwood Mac style rift following them for the rest of the tour. Every music blog would speculate about their feud. They'd bring up Max's public intoxication arrests, poke around with the (true) theories about his drug addiction, probe any comment Jeff had made in the past year for meaning. Someone would be the bad guy. Fifty-fifty it was him.

Or he could play a song.

The part that pissed him off was he couldn't remember—if he played it onstage, did Big Moose automatically own the rights? They'd been so young when they signed the extension to their contract, he couldn't remember.

But fuck it. Either way this would be the last song they ever got from him.

He took the guitar, but he didn't smile. "All right," he said as the tech moved his mic stand closer. He sat; it was easier for a song he hadn't played a hundred thousand times. "This might be a little rough because no one's heard it yet."

Not even the man he'd written it for. Jeff cared about the copyright more than the money, but what he cared about most was that this was the first song he'd be performing that he could've openly played for Carter and said, *This is for you.* And he hadn't gotten the chance.

He vowed he'd never let her steal another opportunity. Carter would just have to put up with Jeff's half-finished musical love confessions.

He cleared his throat and checked the tuning—it was perfect, but he fidgeted a little anyway, to buy time. "I guess you could call this a torch song." Normally he'd have ducked his head in a combination of genuine and affected embarrassment. But this song didn't embarrass him. His feelings for Carter were nothing to hide or be ashamed of anymore. So he just gave a half smile and said, "This is called 'Honey, Time.'"

It didn't take him long to settle on the introduction. He wanted something mellow and ringing, with gravitas—a different feel from most of Howl's work. It didn't surprise him that the not-quite-end product was reminiscent of early 2000s Coldplay, since that had been Jeff's go-to when he was a teenager wallowing in feelings he didn't know how to express.

He let the introductory riff ring, that delay pedal doing its job to reel people in; he could feel the eyes on him. Apart from the sound of the guitar, the stadium was utterly silent.

"It rained the day that I met you—that's what my mom said, and I guess it must be true." The memory made him smile. "Left our coats on the hallway floor. Should have known then. You were six and I was four."

As the verse shifted into the chorus, he stuttered on the frets, cursing himself in his head, but the audience didn't make a sound. Unnerving. He hadn't played new music live like this since before they had a label. But the gentle sway of cell phone lights in his periphery kept him going. "Honey, time was never on my side until now. Honey, I could never meet your eyes until now."

Another verse, another chorus, his heart pounding in a way it hadn't since his first live performance at fourteen. Then the bridge: "You were raised by a man who knew it takes strength to be tender. Yeah, he raised me too, but I was never as strong as you were."

Then the home stretch—final verse, final chorus. "Honey, time is on our side now. Honey, look me in the eyes… now."

The last word ended on three plucked strings that sang gently in the otherwise still night. Then, somehow, at the same time, a breeze kicked up and ruffled the hair at the back of Jeff's neck, and he shivered and raised his head as the spell broke.

Jeff had never seen so many cell phones used as lighters. The noise built the same way as the breeze, with a whistle or two first, and then applause, and finally hoarse, jubilant howls that went on for minutes, until Jeff started to feel embarrassed for real. He stood and handed the guitar off to the first tech who appeared as another gave him back his electric and took the stool away.

"I guess that's gonna be a single," he offered. Not Howl's, though, if he had anything to say about it.

The noise made him grin, though inside it felt grim. He slipped the strap of the electric over his head and rolled his shoulders. "Now—should we turn the volume back up?"

He let the way he felt shine through when he turned to meet Trix's eyes behind the drum kit. She registered his expression and then looked down, ostensibly to fuss with the snare.

Well. There wouldn't be an encore tonight.

When Jeff left the stage after the final number, he handed his guitar to a stagehand and beelined for the green room. He didn't make eye contact with anyone. He didn't check to see if Trix was following, or how far back Max and Joe were until he was in the room and he heard the door click closed.

He whirled.

Trix stood with her arms crossed, looking every bit as angry as Jeff was.

"How fucking dare you," he said.

She opened her mouth.

"No, really," Jeff said. "I want to know. Where the fuck do you get off? Who the fuck are you to decide when my songs are ready to be performed?"

"You have *half an album in there*, easy," she shot back. "Were you planning on writing the whole thing yourself?"

That couldn't be her problem. "Are you worried I won't leave enough room for your tracks?" he asked incredulously. "I don't get it. This morning I was pissed you pushed about the album so your response was to push again with higher stakes and make me perform a new song that you had no idea would be ready in front of five thousand people? Walk me through that decision process."

Trix slammed her palm against the door. "What the fuck else was I supposed to do, Jeff? You fucking *abandoned* us like we had some kind of disease. You've refused to talk about album development for *six months*. I'm sorry, but I have a career to think about, you know? You obviously need a kick in the ass to stop trying to make things perfect and sit down with us and start collaborating."

"You obviously have forgotten the entire concept of *boundaries*!" Jeff thundered. "We had this argument this morning! Plenty of bands take more than eighteen months between albums! I am *tired*, Trix! I am tired of being on the road all the time. I love playing with this band. I love our music. But when I ask for some space to get my head straight, suddenly I'm the bad guy? I am tired of not having the time or energy for anything else. If this is enough for you, that's great. But it's not, for me."

"So, what, you just get to make that decision for all of us?" she snapped. "Unilaterally? Because there's three other people in this band. In case you forgot."

That was low. "How could I," Jeff hissed, "when one of them keeps *stabbing me in the back*?"

"Maybe if you'd paid some goddamn attention, you would've seen it coming!"

Fuck! Jeff fought the urge to break something. He threw his hands in the air instead, palms forward. "That's it. I'm done."

Trix went ghost white, taking two steps away from the door, toward him. "We have four more shows—"

"And I'll be there," Jeff said coldly. "I will be there for every dress rehearsal, every sound check, every concert. But that?" He gestured toward the stage. "That was the last new song I'll ever play onstage with Howl, I promise you that." He didn't care what it cost him. "I hope it was worth it."

He yanked open the door, still incandescent, to find Tim standing next to the door, looking distinctly unwell. Jeff smiled nastily at him. "Consider this my notice."

He didn't want to mean it. He'd never wanted to mean it. But how could he stay after this? He loved being onstage, but it took a certain amount of fearlessness and a huge amount of trust, not only in himself and his abilities and the fact that he had something to say, but in the people up there with him. If he couldn't trust Trix not to push him over the edge, he couldn't play with Howl anymore.

And there went the past fourteen years of his life and most of his savings, just like that.

God, what was he doing, walking away from this? He felt sick. Had he eaten before the show? Not that it mattered—he could hardly keep anything down now. Better to just go home and….

He'd burn that bridge when he got there. For now, going home would be enough.

Chapter Eleven

IN THE car, he let his brain turn off and leaned against the window, his hair, still damp from a fast and furious post-show shower, tickling his cheek and forehead. He didn't need to play the whole night on an endless loop. If he let himself think about it, he'd only feel worse.

He should've stayed in Willow Sound. Instead of an audience of five thousand, he could've had a couple dozen around a campfire, with Carter next to him for some unprofessional but pleasantly rumbly harmony. Besides, he didn't trust Carter not to overdo it if he didn't have supervision. Sure he *said* someone else would be handling the physical aspect of campfire night, but Carter had never been that great about delegating. He was probably walking kids over to the s'mores table, showing parents and teens the different ways to lay kindling.

Or maybe not. It was late now. Carter had probably gotten a ride home, and now he was sprawled in bed, wondering if Jeff would call. Maybe he'd even decided to give his ride a break and just asked to be dropped at Jeff's cabin, and it was *Jeff's* bed he was lying in—

The car pulled to a stop and Jeff shook himself. No point in idle daydreams. "Thanks," he told the driver as he climbed out. "Have a good night."

She waved at him as she pulled away into the darkness.

Jeff shouldered his gig bag and managed his acoustic in his left hand so he could dig for his keys with his right. Nigella, the doorperson, offered a friendly smile as he approached. "Good evening, Jeff." He hated being called Mr. Pine. "Good show?"

"Uh," Jeff said. He didn't want to be rude, but he didn't have the energy to lie to her either. "I think that depends on the metric."

"My B." She winced as she reached out to take a guitar so Jeff didn't have to wrangle two at once. "You want me to send somebody for ice cream, or?"

He opened his mouth to answer, but before he could, a hulking shadow in the darkness next to the condo entrance stepped forward.

Nigella already had her hand on her radio by the time he was within five feet. "Jeff, do you know—"

The man shuffled closer, gait uneven, until finally the light spilling from the entrance to Jeff's building illuminated his face.

He has got to stop doing this to me.

Carter apparently had not shaved that morning, and since he was genetically related to Bigfoot, that meant he had what would've been three days' beard growth on any other man. Jeff was extremely into the whole look—the flannel shirt with the sleeves rolled up, the nice jeans that fit really well except where the walking boot ruined the line, and particularly the way Carter looked at him like the rest of the world didn't exist.

Jeff half felt like he'd summoned Carter with the power of his own yearning. He couldn't keep himself from moving closer until he could see Carter's face clearly in the low light.

"You're missing campfire night," was all he could think to say. "You love campfire night."

Carter gave him a soft look. "Jeff."

Jeff's heart fluttered against his rib cage. Oh no, Carter couldn't do this to him tonight, when Jeff's evening had been such a disaster. He deserved his own day, untainted by this clusterfuck.

But the implication made him feel better anyway. He cleared his throat and turned to Nigella. "Sorry, Nigella, that was rude of me. This is Carter. He's my…." Best friend, boyfriend, soul mate. "He's with me."

"Oh," she said, visibly relaxing. She looked Carter up and down and then said to Jeff, "Nice."

Carter made a vaguely embarrassed noise.

Oops. He hoped she didn't think Carter was a sex worker. Oh well, she'd work it out eventually. "Um, could you do me a favor and have the guitars brought up? No hurry. Tomorrow morning's fine."

The knowing look she gave him made him squirm. "Of course. Whatever you need."

Jeff needed to escape scrutiny, ASAP. "*Thank you,*" he said gratefully. Then he gestured Carter to precede him inside.

He looked just as good in the bright light of the lobby. He still walked a bit off-kilter, but the boot had a thicker sole than most shoes. For a few seconds, Jeff *watched* him, and then Carter turned around and looked knowingly over his shoulder, and yep, Jeff had completely forgotten how to act like a human being.

Jeff cleared his throat. "So, are you stalking me now?"

"I tried doing it the easy way," Carter said, full lips pursed against an obvious smile as they got into the elevator, "but someone wasn't checking his text messages."

Oh. Right. Jeff hadn't looked at his phone since he left the venue. He figured the dozens of text messages were from people he didn't want to talk to.

The mood from the concert tried to creep back in as Jeff hit the button for his floor. "It's been a long, shit day, to be honest." The doors slowly closed. "I—"

He stopped talking when Carter's big hand slid along his jaw. "I know," Carter murmured.

Did he know he was turning Jeff's knees to jelly?

He shouldn't have been able to loom like that with a broken foot, Jeff thought. It wasn't fair. But he couldn't bring himself to be upset about it, because when Carter kissed him, his day improved immeasurably. He melted into it as much as he could without clinging, wary of putting undue weight or stress on Carter's foot.

That was difficult to remember when Carter smelled so good. His beard prickled against Jeff's lips, a raw, sensual almost-pain that brought blood to the surface of Jeff's skin, further sensitizing it. The contrast of soft lips and rough hair set his nerves alight.

The elevator stopped. Carter didn't, right away, which Jeff would have been fine with, except he didn't want to wait any longer to get into his apartment. The doors were closing again when Jeff flung out an arm to stop them.

"Mmf," he said against Carter's mouth.

Carter gently bit his lower lip.

Never mind Carter, *Jeff* needed to sit down. Summoning his willpower, he pushed Carter's chest. Then, when Carter had backed away enough that he could form actual words, he pointed. "This is my floor."

Carter tilted his head toward the hallway. "Lead the way."

Which apartment was his again?

Muscle memory came through. Jeff unlocked his door and they went in. "Just leave your shoes on," he said, which in retrospect was kind of stupid, because they were pretty obviously going to take their clothes off.

Carter gave him a pointed look, one eyebrow raised.

"Shoe, then," Jeff corrected. His tongue felt too big for his mouth. "You're not taking the boot off until you're horizontal, and the height difference has to be awkward without a shoe on the other foot."

Carter smirked at him and beckoned him closer. "You're not going to give me the tour?"

"What," Jeff said, snarking on instinct, "you don't think you can find it?"

Laughing, Carter let Jeff hustle him farther into the apartment. Why had he ever thought he needed so much space? Sure, the view of the skyline was incredible, but in retrospect, there were way too many steps between his door and his bedroom.

That was probably why they ended up on his couch, with Jeff half pinned against one arm and Carter supporting himself above him on his good knee, the casted foot balanced on the floor. Carter took his mouth again, a merciless onslaught that left Jeff gasping when the kiss broke and Carter moved down his neck.

"Carter—"

Carter mouthed his collarbone, then paused and inhaled. "Why do you smell like Irish Spring? Never mind, I don't care." And then he sat back enough to pull Jeff's shirt off.

Jeff had already opened his mouth to demand reciprocity when Carter slid his hand down his chest and stomach until it rested on the fly of his jeans. He flicked his eyes up to Jeff's. "May I?"

Was he serious? Jeff half wanted to say *no, because I can do it faster*, but all that came out was an affirmative-sounding moan. He made himself nod for clarity.

Carter didn't waste time. As soon as he had Jeff naked, his hands were everywhere—his sides, his chest, his nipples, his thighs. Jeff could feel the heat in his gaze like a brand raking over his skin, and he rolled his hips into it instinctually. But when Carter reached for his cock, Jeff grabbed his wrist.

Shit. Now he had to explain.

"Uh," Jeff said, face hot. How to word this. The fire in Carter's gaze had only intensified. "Not to make assumptions." He licked his lips. "But if you want to fuck me, you shouldn't touch my dick yet."

Carter's gaze went to Jeff's hand around his right wrist, then to Jeff's cock, lying plump against his stomach but not all the way hard.

With his other hand, he rubbed a small circle high on the inside of Jeff's thigh. "Oh?"

Jeff fought the urge to writhe, but between Carter's scrutiny and the teasing touches, he was too turned-on to be embarrassed. "It's better if I come that way," he panted, fighting the urge to buck into Carter's hand. "Like, a lot better?" Should he just come out and say *I'm pretty sure I can have multiple prostate orgasms on your dick*? "Ah!" Carter had weaseled out of Jeff's hold and was tweaking his nipple. "I stay hard after or, uh, during"—depending on his partner's stamina—"and then I jerk off and come again and it's really—"

Jeff stopped talking. He'd met Carter's eyes again, and Carter looked—ravenous, and also like Jeff had just told him he'd solved global warming.

Jeff shivered. They definitely should've fucked years ago.

"Really what?" Carter prompted after a moment. His voice had gone smooth and dark.

Jeff wet his lips. "Why don't you find out?"

Carter never could back down from a dare. He moved both hands to Jeff's hips and caressed the divots of his pelvis. "Turn over."

Every thought Jeff had ever had evaporated in his haste to obey. Shit, why didn't he keep lube in the living room? Surely every civilized person—

Carter put both hands on Jeff's ass, and Jeff dug both hands into the arm of the sofa like he might fall off.

"Okay?" Carter asked, close enough that the puff of the words whispered over Jeff's skin.

Jeff was already trembling. "God yes."

Then Carter pulled him open, thumbs on the sensitive skin that covered the seat of his ass. Jeff dropped his head to the arm of the couch when a single dry digit teased briefly over his hole. His breath came in uneven pants and he was already spasming reflexively when Carter let out a low sound and leaned forward.

The rasp of sharp stubble on Jeff's sensitive skin came just before another soft puff of air, this one directly over his hole. Finally he felt the damp, soft press of Carter's lips, and then the slick heat of his tongue.

"Oh God," Jeff whispered into the couch.

Carter didn't react except to lick again, soft and wet, moving his mouth gently over Jeff's opening. His beard burned the insides of Jeff's asscheeks, a counterpoint to the sweetness of his tongue.

Jeff's bones melted like butter in a hot pan. His mouth dropped open and inhuman sounds came out of it—formless vowels and breathless stutters and whimpered pleas that never made it all the way into words. Carter didn't push in yet, even though Jeff was sure he could've. He was just getting Jeff *wet*, making him soft so he could—so he could—

"Uhh," Jeff said quietly when Carter moved his mouth up just a bit to kiss the top of Jeff's cleft and the very edge of his rim while he smeared his thumb through the slick spit over Jeff's opening. He moved it in a tight circle, barely pressing. "*Uh*," Jeff repeated as he tried to spread his legs further.

Carter chuckled against his hole, causing another involuntary spasm, and then took mercy and hooked both thumbs just inside the ring of muscle. His hands were huge, but Jeff could not have been more ready for the stretch. He gave over to it and let Carter hold him open for his mouth.

But Carter didn't seem to be in any hurry. He moaned against Jeff's asshole like this was the hottest thing he could imagine, then stabbed his tongue in short, shallow fucks into him, wet and filthy. The prickly hair around his mouth was setting Jeff's hole on fire.

"*Carter*," he gasped, already trembling.

"Mm," was Carter's reply, low and satisfied and utterly devastating. He pushed his tongue deeper, leaving Jeff clawing at the couch, eyes open but unseeing. In and out he worked it, until Jeff was so sensitive he thought he'd scream.

Then he pulled back, shifted again, and hooked a thumb in deep. He tugged gently at first and then, when Jeff said, "Fuck yes, *more*," he pushed deep and pulled Jeff open wide.

"Jesus," Carter muttered roughly. He spat on Jeff's hole, which was devastating, and then rubbed it around with the other thumb to make sure everything stayed slick. "Are you always like this?"

"Uh," Jeff said, half stalling for time, half because Carter had just pulled his thumb out and replaced it with a long finger. He swallowed and searched for words. "Kinda, yeah."

"That's so hot."

Jeff was going to say something about that—*Carter* was the one who was systematically destroying Jeff's brain cells—but then Carter curled his finger unerringly across Jeff's prostate. Jeff cried out and bucked against him, demanding more.

"Found it," Carter said with a smirk Jeff could hear.

Jeff wanted to reply, but Carter put his mouth back on Jeff's hole and swallowed any comment he could have made.

It didn't take long for his orgasm to build. Carter had a talented mouth, and he kept teasing Jeff with his tongue, lapping around the edges of his hole as he fucked him with two thick fingers, with spine-tingling accuracy. And in truth, Jeff had always been easy for it. He was blessed that way.

Carter rubbed his scruff over Jeff's left cheek, then ran his tongue up the same spot. "Close?" he asked.

Jeff would have nodded, but it was taking all his voluntary muscle control not to collapse against the arm of the couch. "Uhhh-huh," he managed as he squeezed his eyes shut.

"Good," Carter murmured. He scissored his fingers, stretching Jeff open, and then licked between them, flicking his tongue over Jeff's hole.

"Oh fuck," Jeff panted. His knees and shoulders shook. "That's—*fuck*, uh, uh, uh—"

Finally Carter thrust in a third finger, rubbing all three hard over Jeff's prostate gland, still mouthing around the abused muscle, and Jeff lost it. He shook through his orgasm, gasping, clenching down on Carter's fingers. Then he collapsed against the arm of the couch, wrecked and ready for more.

Just as soon as he could get his knees under him.

Carter kept licking and thrusting until Jeff was sensitive enough to try shivering away, and then he pulled back. Jeff heard him wipe a hand down his stubble.

"Jeff, oh my God. Turn around?"

With a little help from Carter manhandling him, he did, letting his legs fall open to Carter's gaze. Carter licked his red, swollen lips and raked his gaze down Jeff's blotchy red chest to his cock, which was glistening with precome and still obviously hard.

"May I…?"

Jeff nodded, dazed, and they both watched as Carter ran his fingers through the fluid coating Jeff's dick. Jeff fought not to squirm or buck, but God. He still wanted so much.

After two long, torturous strokes, Carter rasped, "How long until you can come again?"

Had he not been listening? "Ten seconds to get to the bedroom, another thirty to get lube?"

Carter let go and awkwardly leveraged himself to his feet, leaving Jeff starving for touch. "Which way?"

Fucking *finally*. Jeff pointed and then got up too.

He left Carter to strip while he grabbed the supplies. When he turned around, Carter was shirtless—as mouthwatering a sight as it had been last time, and maybe better because Jeff could appreciate him from a bit farther away, the definition in his pecs and abs and the red-gold curls that highlighted them.

The pants, however, seemed to be a problem.

"I hate this stupid boot," Carter muttered, cheeks red.

Jeff realized the problem—he couldn't get his pants off without removing the boot first. And there was no way he was fucking Jeff with the boot off; Jeff had known him too long. That would 100 percent result in further damage.

"Fuck it," Jeff said. "Half-clothed sex is hot anyway." As long as he could get his jeans down enough to get his dick out, Jeff didn't care. "Get on the bed."

"Bossy," Carter said, but he knelt on the bed anyway, with his foot hanging off the side to keep pressure off, and gestured for Jeff to come closer. "Come here and kiss me."

Jeff wouldn't be refusing that invitation anytime soon. Slightly unbalanced on the soft mattress, he leaned in until he could meet Carter's mouth. Another shiver went through him at the taste.

But he didn't have a chance to fall into it—Carter gently pushed him backward and Jeff gladly went.

Was he really about to do this? After fifteen years?

It only took Carter a handful of seconds to shove his jeans down to his hips. In that time, Jeff opened the condom and pushed himself up on one elbow so he could stroke Carter to full hardness. Carter must have enjoyed himself on the couch almost as much as Jeff had, because he was dripping precome.

Carter put his hand on his wrist. "Condom?"

Jeff handed it over and grabbed a pillow from the head of the bed. He barely had the pillow situated under his hips before Carter nudged the slick head of his cock against his hole.

Oh God.

"Fuck," Jeff said. His eyes closed as he arched on the bed. Of course Carter was like this. "Come on, please—"

He pushed the head in and Jeff hissed in pleasure, body opening easily, only for Carter to pull back and tease him again.

Jeff opened his eyes. "Carter. It's literally been fifteen years. Are you seriously going to play just the tip?"

Carter blinked down guilelessly.

"I will put you on your back and ride you," Jeff warned.

Carter smirked. "Don't threaten *me* with a good time."

But then he finally, *finally* pushed inside, and Jeff's body lit up like a firework even as Carter's mouth dropped open and his face went slack.

"Fuck," Jeff said, shifting his hips up into it. He wanted it all. "Anyone ever tell you you have a big dick?"

When Carter laughed breathlessly, said dick shifted just right. "I've had a few complaints."

"Not from me. As long as you move it—"

Carter moved it.

"No complaints," Jeff gasped, planting his feet so he could move in counterpoint.

"Jeff." Carter groaned and set his hands on Jeff's hips to control the pace. "Thirty seconds, you said?" He sounded strangled.

Jeff would've laughed, but Carter started fucking him like he meant it—deep, firm thrusts that stretched Jeff perfectly. The skin around his hole was still prickling from Carter's facial hair, and the sensation of Carter's cock gliding past the ring of muscle was almost too much.

He gasped and writhed on the bed, clamping down, trying to gauge how close Carter was. He looked lost in pleasure, mouth slack, pupils blown, and he was fucking into Jeff like his life depended on it, his heavy balls slapping between Jeff's cheeks.

"Do you—" Jeff's words cut off when Carter nailed his prostate just right, hard enough to make Jeff fist his hands in the sheets and arch his back. "Do you want to race?"

"I want to watch you come for me."

He was never going to get over Carter being so unabashedly straightforward in bed. Jeff nodded frantically and scrabbled at the covers to find the lube. Every time Carter fucked into him, his hard cock bounced on his belly, a delicious sensation that had him riding the edge of orgasm.

"Next time," Carter said, his steady thrusts making it very difficult for Jeff to get the cap open, "I'm going to do that."

Jeff would be riding him, then, because he was afraid if Carter shifted his grip, he'd fall off the end of the bed. "Whatever you want," he said, *finally* getting a slick hand on his cock. "Just please—please—"

Carter bit his lip, visibly straining. He tilted his head back toward the ceiling as though even the sight of Jeff would push him over the edge. "Please what?" he gasped. "What are you waiting for?"

"*You*!"

Carter's hips snapped forward brutally. He relinquished his hold on Jeff's hips to plant his hands farther up the bed and brace himself on either side of Jeff's shoulders. His firm stomach brushed against Jeff's fist and cock as he stroked himself, the coarse hairs teasing against Jeff's head. Jeff met each thrust as best he could, but Carter was wild now, out of control.

Jeff tangled his free hand in Carter's hair and yanked him into a desperate, clashing kiss.

Carter made a pained sound against his mouth and bit his lip just this side of too hard. Then he broke the kiss and pressed his forehead to Jeff's as he came, huge cock spasming, balls twitching against Jeff's hole.

"Oh God." Jeff had never felt this desperate—this *full* with pleasure. He squeezed his eyes closed to relish every inch of Carter inside him, every hypersensitive stretch of skin where they were touching, Carter's slightly sour breath, the unmistakable scent of come. "Carter!" he cried out as his orgasm crested.

Carter pushed up in time to watch him, big palms on the insides of Jeff's thighs as Jeff erupted. He clenched hard around Carter, milking him further.

Eventually it was too sensitive and Jeff had to pull his hand away, coated in his own release. He wiped the remainder on his thigh—he was due for some cleanup anyway—and looked up at Carter, their chests heaving in time.

Carter's face reflected Jeff's thoughts perfectly—head empty.

"God," Jeff said aloud to the ceiling, possibly repeating himself. He was still gasping for breath. "If this is what you're like with a broken foot, I need to start working out more."

Carter collapsed next to him on one shoulder, laugh-groaning. "What can I say? You bring out the best in me."

Jeff made a show of looking down at the condom that hung drooping off his cock.

"Classy," Carter said.

Unfortunately, however little energy Jeff had remaining, cleanup was necessary. He was impressed he hadn't simply passed out after his second orgasm, but he could not sleep like this. And since sleep now seemed particularly imminent, he hauled himself to his feet. "I'm gonna clean up. You want a cloth, or are you coming too?"

Carter nodded as he sat up, but then gestured to the situation with his jeans and walking boot. "I'll be a minute."

Jeff's muscles protested every step to the en suite. He closed the door to wipe himself down, use the toilet, and wash his hands, and opened it before he brushed his teeth. Carter came in, now wearing only boxers and the boot. He dropped the condom in the trash and reached for the soap.

"You don't happen to have a spare toothbrush?"

It took some rummaging, but he found one. Then he got to truly appreciate how tired he was, because he didn't have the mental bandwidth to freak out about the domesticity of a scene he'd been longing for half his life.

He wandered back into the bedroom while Carter finished up. "Is one side of the bed better for you?" A broken foot could definitely fuck with one's preferred sleeping arrangements.

"I'll take the left, if you don't mind."

Jeff was a middle-of-the-bed sleeper, a habit born of many years of sleeping alone, so he shrugged. "Sure."

They climbed in. Carter arranged a couple of Jeff's decorative pillows under his right foot, then turned on his side to face Jeff.

Jeff lay on his side too, soaking in the reality of the moment. "So." He tucked his hands under his cheek. "What brings you to Toronto?"

Carter pretended to give this serious thought. "Well, I heard on TV this morning that this band I like was having a concert and there were still tickets available. They're pretty okay, I guess. And the lead singer is hot."

Jeff made a face at him. "Wait, you bought tickets? I would've gotten you a comp. VIP access." He didn't have the energy to waggle his eyebrows, so he just implied it with his voice.

Carter shook his head against the pillow. "I wasn't sure I'd be able to make it." Right—campfire night. "I didn't want to disappoint you. I knew you were already having a bad day. I wanted it to be a surprise."

"It's a good surprise," Jeff assured him. He frowned, his foggy, orgasm-addled mind struggling to put together… something. "Wait," he said again, "you went to a concert with a *broken foot*?"

"The venue is accessible. I called and made sure. I had a seat and everything."

"Which you sat in the whole time, I'm sure," Jeff grumbled. Yeah, right.

Carter didn't bother to confirm or deny, but he did reach out to the bed between them. Instinctively, Jeff reached back and joined their hands. "Mostly." That soft expression, the one that made Jeff feel like he was swaddled in warm cotton candy, had returned to his face. "I did have to stand up close to the end, though. I wanted the full experience for the new song."

The new song Jeff had written for him—the one he'd poured his heart into, the one he'd been so upset he wouldn't get to play for Carter first.

It was kind of a blessing, really. This way he'd never have to wonder how Carter would feel about it. After all, he'd skipped campfire night.

Still, his throat was a bit thick when he asked, "Did you like it?"

Carter laced their fingers together. "I loved it."

Chapter Twelve

JEFF WOKE up feeling… normal.

Given the events of the night before, he half expected to feel like crusted-over crap and half like he was walking on a cloud, so the equilibrium was weird.

But Carter wasn't in bed, which was unacceptable. Jeff felt robbed of a snuggly morning after. Though cuddling with a walking boot on did present a challenge.

In any case, now that he was awake, he wasn't going to stay in a bed that didn't have his boyfriend in it. He made a quick detour to the bathroom and then went in search.

Carter was on the floor in the living room, doing crunches in his boot and boxers, because he was a deeply flawed man who did not know how to relax. But Jeff wasn't going to interrupt him to complain. He watched for a few seconds—he had his own flaws—and then made a strategic retreat to the kitchen for coffee.

When he returned with two mugs a few minutes later, Carter was sitting on the couch like a normal person, looking at his phone. "Oh. Hey," he said. "I didn't hear you get up. I didn't wake you, did I?"

"I sleep fine on a moving tour bus," Jeff said wryly. He handed over one of the mugs. An idea was taking root in his head, and he wondered if he could pull it off. "You, however, don't seem to sleep enough no matter where you are."

Carter shrugged at the accusation but didn't deny it. "It's hard to get comfortable with this thing on. I thought about taking it off at night, but uh…." He took a suspiciously quick sip of his coffee.

"But you did it once and it was a bad idea?"

Apparently realizing Jeff wasn't going to let him off the hook, he admitted, "I rolled over in the middle of the night and woke up in agony."

Yikes. Jeff hoped he hadn't injured himself worse. "Well, anyway, I—" He frowned. "Did you bring a bag?" Come to think of it—"How did you even get here? You can't drive."

"You're not the only one who can book a flight. It's May Two-Four." Right—the long weekend on which rich Torontonians typically traveled to their cottages to open for the season. Plenty of air traffic out of Toronto, plenty of empty seats to fill on the return.

"But no luggage?" Jeff was confused.

"I didn't want to presume."

Ridiculous. "What was I going to do, put you in an Uber?" He shook his head. "Never mind. You're here now. Can you stay a few days? I don't know what your work-from-couch schedule looks like."

"Ha ha." He considered. "If I had my laptop, yeah, I could stay a few days. I sort of thought you'd want to go back to the Sound, though."

He did. But if he kept Carter away, he might have to actually slow down and relax. Besides, it could be fun hanging out with him in the city… and Jeff knew just where to take him first. "What are the chances of someone being able to bring said laptop?"

"Uh, I actually think Mom was planning to come into the city for dinner and a movie with a friend."

"Perfect." Jeff set down his coffee mug and picked up his phone. He winced at the number of unread text messages and set it to Do Not Disturb. "See if she's willing to bring it for you and then I'll take you to breakfast."

Carter blinked at him, making his eyes wide. "What, you're not going to make me breakfast?"

Jeff gave him a flat look. "I've barely been home in weeks. Unless you'd like a side of penicillin with your dry toast, I think treating you to breakfast is the better option here." Though he could always get something delivered….

Before he could suggest it, Carter stood and held up his phone. "I guess I'll get dressed."

Oh well. If Jeff had his way, they'd have plenty more chances to enjoy extended mornings in. He looked back down at his phone screen, intent on discovering a restaurant option near his real destination. But before he could get past the first word, Carter spoke again.

"Although…."

Jeff jerked his head up.

"I *could* use a shower," Carter said. "And it's so hard to reach my back with a broken foot."

Jeff dropped the phone.

LATER, CARTER glared at him in the medical supply store and said, "You lied to me."

"I never said we weren't going to buy you a knee scooter." Jeff ignored him to speak to the shop associate. "Is it big enough? I'm not sure how to tell."

"That's our largest model," she told him. "Adjustable handlebars and knee rest. Oh, but if you want my advice, you'll upgrade the wheels. The little ones are prone to tipping if you hit even a piece of gravel wrong."

Carter gave Jeff a *look*, but Jeff could not resist. "I absolutely want to pimp his ride."

"Jeff, I'm not going to use—"

Jeff put on his talking-to-the-press smile and turned to the associate. She was wearing a name tag, he noticed. "Jen, would you give us a minute, please?"

"Sure. I'll be behind the cash desk if you need me."

"Thank you so much."

He waited until she'd taken a few steps, then turned back to Carter. "Look, aren't you going nuts not being able to walk significant distances?"

Carter's brow furrowed in a pout. "Sure, but…."

"But what? You'd rather use crutches because they're more manly?" Jeff let his tone of voice convey how absurd that was. "Sounds kinda… sexist? Ableist?"

The pout developed a guilty tinge. At least he knew he was being an idiot. "I'll look stupid."

"You'll look like a man who's letting himself heal properly," Jeff countered. He wheeled out a smaller display model and tested it out. Not bad for comfort or size. "*I'll* look stupid." He'd have to make sure Jen had enough product in stock in case someone else who really needed a scooter came by, but—

"You're *not* going to ride around on a scooter." Carter shook his head. "Point made, I'm being ridiculous. I'll use it, okay?"

"Good," Jeff said. "I'm getting one of the cool ones you can stand on. Come on, let's go find Jen and get you some off-road tires."

Whatever his initial protests, Carter enjoyed himself throughout the rest of the morning. Jeff was pretty sure he needed the illusion of independence as much as anything. After an hour of wheeling around the Eaton Centre while Jeff bullied him into more expensive versions of his usual wardrobe—he wanted to get Carter into some designer threads, but Eaton Centre's offerings were easier to access—Carter was cheerful and relaxed.

He was also enjoying Jeff being his bag boy.

"I don't know," he said seriously as he wheeled past Indigo. "I could use something to read. Maybe a couple hardcovers."

Jeff had given up on his own scooter after Carter allowed him to buy a year's worth of underwear. "I'll buy you an e-reader. More tree-friendly."

Carter looked over at him and grinned—and nearly ran someone over.

Whoops.

"Oh my God, I'm so sorry." Carter fortunately had managed to keep his feet, and so had his victim, who hadn't been looking where she was going any more than Carter had.

"No, are you kidding, I just about knocked you over." The woman was maybe five five, with a round face and round-framed glasses. "Are you okay?"

"Fine," Carter promised. "No harm done. You're sure you're all right? I didn't run over your toes or anything?"

"Nah, I'm good, see?" She stuck out her foot to show off a pair of Doc Martens.

"Hey, maybe you should've tried a pair of those," Jeff said, teasing.

It turned out to be a mistake, though, because when she focused her attention on him instead, she rotated in his direction enough for him to identify her Howl T-shirt.

"Oh my God," she said. "You're Jeff Pine!"

Jeff glanced around. The mall wasn't too crowded, but he didn't want to clog up the walkway, so he nudged Carter's shoulder until he scooted closer to the wall.

"He is." Carter grinned like this was the most entertainment he'd had all week, which was rude. Jeff had done an excellent job entertaining him in the past twelve hours particularly.

"Oh my God. Would you, I mean—shoot." Her face fell. "I wish I had a Sharpie or something, you could totally sign my T-shirt."

Jeff normally carried one, but he had a lot on his mind this morning. "Selfie?" he offered instead.

"Yes! A selfie! God, you must think I'm so old-school. Oh man. I'm sorry I'm being such a nerd. I just… I've loved your music since I was a kid."

Jeff loved his fans, but that comment made him feel about a hundred years old, and he could tell Carter noticed, because he laughed. He tried to cover it by offering, "I could take it if you want."

"Thank you, that would be so amazing! My friends are gonna flip their shit!" Beaming, she turned her gaze back to Carter to hand him her phone, and—

Crap.

"Hey," she said as Carter turned the phone around, "you wouldn't happen to be that guy from the picture on *416 Morning…?*"

Busted.

Carter glanced at Jeff, who shrugged. This was Carter's call to make. "That's me," he said, holding the phone easily in one enormous hand. Jeff needed to not focus on that while they were in public.

Jeff maneuvered to stand beside his fan, then belatedly realized he didn't know her name. "The man with the scooter who tried to run you down is Carter," he said. "And I'm Jeff, obviously, and you are…?"

"Oh! Chrissy. My pronouns are they/them."

"Nice to meet you, Chrissy. You want any particular pose for this photo?"

They bit their lip. "Um, is it okay if you put your arm around my waist, and I'll do the same?"

Jeff had had many more invasive requests, and some who hadn't asked. "Sure. We'll make Carter jealous."

Carter rolled his eyes, but Chrissy seemed not to be paying attention. "I can't believe this is happening."

Carter took the picture and handed them back their phone. They looked at the picture and flushed prettily. "This is so great. Thank you, really."

"It's no problem," Jeff assured them. "Anything for a fan." Not *really* anything, but they didn't need to know that.

Chrissy took a step back and pushed their hair behind their ears. "So, like, I'm sorry because this totally isn't my business, but you joked about making him jealous, and I was at the concert last night, and it seems like maaaaybe you're seeing someone new?"

Now Jeff saw some panic creep into Carter's features. But the cat was pretty much out of the bag now.

Easy for Jeff to say. His cat had never even been in the same room as the bag.

"It does seem like that," Jeff agreed, which was polite, not an outright lie, and vague enough for plausible deniability.

"Wow," Chrissy said. "Well, that song last night was awesome, so if, you know. I'm really happy for you." They paused. "And now I totally have to go because I'm being obnoxious and also I'm going to be late for work. But thank you again. Just…. Howl means a lot to me."

Jeff pasted on a smile. "It means a lot to me too." He hoped he sounded more casual than he felt. "Have a good day, Chrissy."

Because all of a sudden Jeff wasn't.

Beside him, Carter was sagging too. It was time for phase two of Carter's rehab plan.

"I want shawarma," Jeff said. "To go."

Carter's stomach growled on cue. Jeff still knew him. "That sounds awesome."

AS JEFF had planned, Carter's eyelids started to droop when they were halfway through lunch at his kitchen table.

"Why don't you have a nap?" he suggested. "You look like you could use it."

It was a mark of how exhausted Carter must really be that he didn't snark or argue. He lay down on Jeff's couch with his right foot elevated over the arm and fell asleep within minutes.

Jeff quietly cleaned up their lunch dishes, then sat down at the table and took out his phone again. He had messages from Joe, Tim, Max, and Trix. He wasn't ready to deal with Trix, he sincerely meant it when he told Tim to talk to his lawyer, he couldn't talk to Max without having a breakdown himself… but he couldn't abandon Joe.

What's going on with you and Trix? Are you okay?

Then, half an hour later—*I know I said we needed to talk but it seems like maybe now's not a good time?*

Jeff couldn't leave him hanging indefinitely. *I am so sorry. Being a shitty friend.* He sent that, then bit his lip as he debated what more to say. *Trix forced me to play a new song live onstage that she'd never even heard as some kind of power move. Idk whats going on. U got any idea?* Maybe Tim was paying her to pressure him into getting the album done?

Jeff thought about Max's habit and wondered. It was possible. Addicts did shitty things. But there was only so much coke you could put up your nose before you dropped dead. They made good money. Surely it couldn't be that dire, that he needed to hit Trix up for cash?

Before he could spiral too far down that rabbit hole, he needed to grow up and deal with the last text. *Sorry I flaked on u. Talk in VAN?*

For a moment he only got blinky dots. Then—*Wtf. No clue. Van works. Take er easy, ok?*

That was the plan. Sort of. Jeff sat down in the armchair across from the couch and spent half an hour losing himself in his notebook.

At two, Carter's phone buzzed on the coffee table. He didn't even stir. Jeff picked it up and took it into the kitchen to answer. "Hi, Ella."

"Jeff. Is Carter indisposed?" she teased.

"He's napping," Jeff said. "I didn't want to wake him. Are you here?"

"About five minutes out, according to the GPS."

Jeff made arrangements to meet her and offered her his parking pass since his truck was still at the airport. He was on his way back inside with Carter's laptop bag over his arm when he spotted a familiar figure in the lobby.

Trix.

Objectively, she looked terrible. Her hair was greasy, rolled into a sloppy twist on top of her head, her Chucks were dirty, and she had dark circles under her eyes. Without her usual makeup, he could see a zit forming along her jawline, and from the redness around her eyes, she'd either been crying or she was high as a kite.

Maybe both.

"Jeff." She stood when she saw him and took a step forward, her phone clutched in both hands. "I've been trying to get ahold of you, I just…."

Jeff waited.

She dropped her hands to her side in defeat. "Can we go somewhere to talk?" She swallowed visibly. "I… I owe you an apology and an explanation, but I don't want to do it here."

Jeff didn't want to do it in his apartment either. "Carter's napping on my couch. His foot's broken because he's an idiot."

Trix winced. "Practice room?"

Jeff didn't like it, but at least it was soundproof. "Fine," he agreed. "Come on."

Carter was still out cold when he opened the door, so he tore a page out of his comp book and left it on the coffee table. *Working some stuff out with Trix in the practice room. Help yourself to whatever if you wake up.—Jeff*

Then he joined Trix and closed the door.

Jeff's music room was the second-largest room in the apartment. It had its own lounge furniture as well as a drum kit, piano, and a selection of guitars. But Trix was sitting on the plush rug near the low table, her arms wrapped around her knees and her chin resting on top of them. He hadn't seen her look like that since her platonic date ditched her on prom night to hook up with the captain of the football team.

He was still pissed, but he needed to know what was going on. He grabbed a couple bottles of water from the mini fridge and sat on the rug across from her.

"So." He cracked open the bottle, then closed and reopened the cap a few times to have something to do with his hands. "Where do we start?"

Trix picked up her own water and slid her thumb under the paper label. "I know where it really starts, but first…." She took a deep breath and finally looked up, her eyes haunted. "What I did to you—the way I've been treating you—is shitty. I knew it was wrong, and I did it anyway, and you're right if you hate me. I'm sorry." Another deep breath, and she opened the water bottle. The cap clattered to the floor.

Instead of drinking from it, she set it closer to the center of the table, crossed her legs, and waited.

Jeff still didn't understand, and he was still angry. "Okay. I'm willing to listen." To be honest, she was freaking him out.

"Right." Trix rubbed her palms on her thighs. "Remember when you called me in April? You'd had that breakfast with Max, and money went missing from your wallet while you were in the bathroom."

Jeff had thought nothing of leaving it on the table since Max was right there and they were waiting for the check. He'd had a thousand or so in cash on him because he'd made an appointment to look into a used guitar he'd had his eye on. Only when he'd emerged from the washroom, Max had taken care of the check and was talking with some shady-looking guy Jeff didn't know. He handed Jeff his wallet and Jeff pocketed it and hadn't noticed until he went to buy the guitar that the cash was missing.

"I called you and asked you if Max was using again." He'd just been through rehab in January.

She nodded miserably. "I said I didn't know, but I knew he was. Is."

Jeff exhaled, uncapped his water again, and took a small sip. "How bad?" Max and Trix had always been closer than the rest of them. Jeff had thought that would change, once. He'd figured a few years on the road together and they'd gel more. And they had, but not as much as he'd thought.

"That's complicated." She peeled the rest of the label off the bottle. "It's…. He does okay when we're on tour, you know? He doesn't use while we're working."

Jesus. Jeff thought back over the past ten years and realized that was true. Max had never missed a performance, never shown up high when they were working on an album. "Was that what this was about this whole time?"

She bowed her head.

"Trix, that's—that is so fucked. Max doesn't use while we're working, so we have to work 24-7-365?" He could feel the rage simmering below the surface, born of years of helplessness and feeling in the dark and months of Trix manipulating him.

"I know—" she said, but he cut her off.

"Do you?" She'd been counting on him trading his well-being for Max's, indefinitely, and in the end it wouldn't even *work*. "This is like putting a Band-Aid on a bullet wound."

"I *know*," she said again, and this time her voice broke and Jeff shut up. Maybe he should let her get through whatever she had to say, and then he could tell her that he was still leaving. "Jeff. I've been awful to you and to Joe. I've been trying to fix my mistakes, but I just keep making more of them."

With effort, he kept his cool. He took another deep breath, then a long sip of water, and made himself count to four. "I'm not sure what you thought you could fix by trying to force an album out."

"The thing is, it's my fault." Finally she pushed the water bottle to the far right side of the table, out of reach. "I'm the reason Max is an addict."

For once in his life, Jeff heard the warning bells and slowed his roll. He put down his bottle too. This seemed like something to visibly devote his full attention to. "What do you mean? You got him hooked on drugs?"

She laughed sharply at that, then wiped at her face. She wasn't crying, but she looked hunted. "No. Well, yes, I guess, if you count sharing my stepmom's Xanax. I meant it's my fault because I… because something happened to me, and Max…. Max was the only one who knew about it. And I made him swear never to tell." When she inhaled, her chest shook. "And I think he really needed to tell someone."

Something about the way she said it made the hair on Jeff's arms stand up. He wasn't sure he wanted to know what she was going to tell him, but if she'd been sitting on it this long—it had to be close to twenty years—then maybe her need to tell him outweighed that. "Tell someone what?"

Sallow-faced, she kept her gaze on the table. "When I was nine, my parents split up. I mean, you knew that. Um, and I went to live with my mom, and when I was eleven, she married my stepdad."

A nauseating ball of ice formed in Jeff's stomach, though he couldn't have said why.

Trix blew out a quick breath. "My mom's a narcissist. Which you know. My stepdad made her really happy, though. And he was great to me too. I thought, okay, my mom's kind of a bitch but this isn't so bad."

Jeff's heart pounded. He felt sick.

"Anyway." She shook her head. "They let me do whatever, you know? I didn't really have chores, they didn't care about my grades. I started hanging out with some older boys because at least they paid me attention. I was twelve, I guess, or thirteen."

"Trix…."

She inhaled sharply through her nose. "No, I've gotten this far. I have to—just, I have to.

"You can probably guess what happens when a dumb girl starts hanging around with older boys. I probably should've… I should've just stuck to Max, but I only hung out with him when the guys were busy because he wasn't *cool*. I was so dumb."

Finally Jeff mustered the courage to reach across the table. He caught her hand in his. "Trix. You were young, not stupid." But his mouth caught on what more to say. *If someone took advantage of you. If they did anything you didn't want.* Even if she *did* want. Jesus. She was a kid.

He couldn't get anything else out. He didn't want to put words in her mouth, and his own was too full with horror.

She gave him a broken smile. "I kinda was, but thanks." She squeezed his hand once and let go. "Anyway, I…. One day I was at Max's place. His parents weren't home. His mom was working and I think his dad had a fishing trip or something. Suddenly I got this stomach cramp, really bad, like I was going to shit myself. Except I knew I wasn't. I just wasn't letting myself really know."

Jeff's hand trembled as he took a sip from his own water bottle. He didn't interrupt. He couldn't.

"I must've freaked Max out with the screaming and crying. He broke the lock on the bathroom door and found me in the bathtub. He must've thought I was dying."

"Jesus," Jeff said finally as unexpected tears sprung to his eyes. His hand sneaked out again without his input and wrapped around hers. "That's…. I'm so sorry you went through that alone."

This time she didn't pull her hand away. "I wasn't," she said, meeting his gaze for a moment. "I had Max. He helped clean—"

Their gaze, and her voice, broke. "It was the size of my fist. I couldn't look at it, so Max got rid of it for me. I think that's the worst part, that I couldn't look and that Max had to."

She cleared her voice, wiped at her face again. Come to think of it, Jeff didn't think he'd ever seen her cry.

He guessed not much would register, after what she'd been through.

"I never told my mom, but she must've figured it out somehow because she—" Her throat worked soundlessly for a moment. "She said she couldn't have a slut like me around the house. Didn't want the competition."

"*Christ*." Jeff wanted to hit something.

"I moved in with my dad and stepmom," Trix finished, "and that… that was it. Max never told. Neither did any of the boys. I guess they would've been in big trouble if they had. So I never got a reputation."

As if that mattered, Jeff thought, but then, it did, didn't it? When you were a preteen girl. Of all the things to have to worry about. Fuck. "Why tell me now?"

She lifted one shoulder in a minute shrug. "I've been treating you like shit. Even if I've been dealing with things—or not dealing with them—that doesn't excuse the stuff I did. You'd be right to leave the band. I fucking deserve for you to leave, or to kick me out of it, or whatever. But I don't want you to, so I have to do what I can to fix it."

Jeff rubbed his face with both hands. He didn't know if there was anything they *could* do, at this point. "This is a fucking mess."

Her face fell. "Yeah. Welcome to my life."

At least this explained why she and Max were always so close, why it felt like Joe and Jeff were always on the outside. "All right. We need a plan."

At that she jerked her head up. "A plan." Hope lit her voice.

"Max is getting worse." He'd stolen from Jeff, almost certainly to buy drugs. He'd definitely used while Jeff was in Willow Sound. He could be using right now. Jeff didn't spend enough time with him outside of their gigs to know anymore. "He has to be, or you wouldn't have pushed for the album so hard. Right?"

"It's pretty bad. I made him move back in with me."

"Narcan bad?" He needed to know what they were dealing with.

"Not since February."

That was bad enough. Jeff downed half his water bottle. "He needs to go to rehab. Not outpatient rehab. Something with actual counselors and security."

Trix bristled. "He needs to be a part of any discussion involving his future."

Jeff didn't have a comeback for that, because she was right, he couldn't just go around deciding Max's life for him. It wouldn't work if Max didn't want to quit. He held up his hands. "You're totally right. I just… I'm not an expert, obviously, but he's been to rehab before and it didn't take. It seems like he needs more drastic measures."

She massaged her temples. Somehow in the past hour, she seemed to have gained a number of fine lines around her eyes to go with the dark circles beneath them. "The trouble is, sometimes asking him about it can push him to use. I can work on it incrementally, but if we confront him… it could go really bad."

"Play it by ear?" he suggested. "Maybe at the end of the tour…?"

"Yeah." She leaned back against the seat of the couch. "This might suck."

Jeff snorted involuntarily. "Probably not any more than the past few months. Years. Tours."

Trix lifted her head and looked at him. "You're that tired?"

Instead of answering right away, Jeff let himself think about it. "I'm burned out," he said slowly. "Part of it is this thing with Max. Part of it's just… I think you and Max aren't the only ones who've had stuff you didn't deal with, you know? It's catching up to us, or at least it's catching up to me. I feel like if I don't take the time to get myself right, it's just a long slow slide downward."

They sat in silence for a moment before Trix said, "I'm sorry I didn't know."

"Trix, are you kidding me right now? Don't apologize. Christ."

For a second, her face froze halfway between apologetic and surprised. Then, absurdly, she started to giggle. She put her hand over her mouth and looked shocked at herself, but the laughter started to slip past her fingers until Jeff caught it too.

"Fuck," she said, gasping against the side of the couch, "Jeff, we are *so fucked-up*, oh my God. We have so many issues we could start an archive."

Jeff was lying flat on his back, laughing silently and clutching at his stomach because he couldn't get a deep enough breath to make noise. Tears rolled down his face. He honestly couldn't tell if they came from mirth or catharsis.

Finally he gathered himself enough to flop over on his side so he could look at her around the end of the table. "What are we gonna do in the meantime?"

Trix lay on the floor too, her hands tucked beneath her cheek. "I don't know. I mean, write an album, usually. That'd keep us all busy. Keep Max's nose clean, so to speak. Except I don't deserve to collaborate with you right now, so there's that. And also, I get the feeling Tim's been playing you?"

"Not particularly *well*," Jeff said, "but yeah. He's a dick. I would rather gnaw my own foot off than let him make another dime from our work. But getting out of our contract is going to be expensive."

"Didn't you just hire a fancy lawyer?" she asked. "I mean… that's something lawyers look into, right? She could theoretically help us find a way out of it. Find another label even."

Well… maybe? "That could solve some of our problems."

"Like the fact that all the songs in your comp book are love songs?" Trix suggested, smiling gently.

"Not all of them," Jeff protested. "None of them are particularly… rock-y." Which, yes, their label would likely have issue with. They'd want at least a couple bangers.

The gentle smile turned up sharply and she laughed. "Oh my God. Jeff. You're writing a *cottagecore album.* You pulled a Taylor Swift!"

Oh God. He had even written those songs in a cabin in the woods. He raised his hands to his face as he laughed. "In my defense, people love those albums."

Trix turned over onto her back and sighed at the ceiling. "I can just imagine you singing about Carter's cardigan."

"Don't jinx it," Jeff warned.

She tilted her neck and met his eyes. "You're really for-real gone on him, aren't you? Like, not just a high school crush."

"Literally every love song I have ever written is for him. That one I said was about that guy Brian I dated for a couple months? I lied." He smiled wanly. "I am really for-real gone."

"I'm happy for you," she said after a moment. "You deserve it."

It was coming up on dinnertime when they pulled themselves off the floor. "Do you want me to check if Carter's still sleeping?" Jeff offered. "I could ask him to relocate to the bedroom if you don't want to meet him right now." He wouldn't blame her.

But Trix shook her head. "No, it's okay. I made my bed, I can lie in it." Then she smiled. "Besides, I'd like to meet him."

Jeff knew that look. "And by 'meet' you mean 'ogle'?"

"I have no idea what you're talking about." She stood up and reached a hand down to Jeff. "Come on, you can introduce us, and then I'll get out of your hair and you can take advantage of his after-nap energy."

Sure enough, Carter was awake, fussing with something that smelled amazing in the kitchen. "Jeff?"

"Hey." Jeff poked his head through the open pocket doors and into the galley-style kitchen. "You up for meeting another quarter of Howl, or is that too much rock-star exposure for you for one day?"

"Hmm." Carter put down the spoon he'd been using and tottered over for a kiss. "Say 'exposure' again."

"Oh God," Jeff heard from behind them, and he sighed and turned around.

"Trix, this is my boyfriend, Carter." Jeff glanced up at him as he stepped forward to shake Trix's hand. "Carter, this is Trix, aka Tracy Neufeld."

Trix smiled genuinely as they shook hands. "Hey. Jeff's told us… pretty much everything until a couple weeks ago, but give us time."

Carter snorted a laugh. "Thanks for looking after him for me."

"Excuse you," Jeff said, "which of us needed the other to clear a path to the couch for him when he broke his foot?"

Carter allowed that to pass without comment.

Trix, though, gave them both a knowing look. "Jumping right to the old-married-couple impression, I see."

"Something like that," Carter agreed, but the sideways glance he cast at Jeff—all heat and promise—gave lie to his words.

Jeff wanted to do about three things at once—shuffle Trix out of the apartment, make sure dinner wasn't going to explode, and tackle Carter into the bedroom—but he didn't get a chance to do any of them, because Trix's phone made an obnoxious chirp. Frowning, she pulled it out. "Sorry, just let me…," she mumbled.

Carter's phone vibrated in his pocket only a few seconds later. Jeff felt left out until he realized he'd left his on silent.

Then, with some trepidation, he took his phone out of his pocket too.

The screen showed a slightly alarming number of notifications. If there was anything really important, it would come through his texts.

In this case it turned out to be from Carter's mom, which wasn't worrisome at all.

It was a link to a Buzzfeed article with the unpromising headline "Howl Frontman's Summer Fling?"

Jeff scrolled without reading and eventually came to the Twitter screencap he'd been expecting. The tweet had over two thousand likes and had been retweeted nearly as many times. It showed two pictures side by side, one of Jeff with Chrissy from that morning, and the other the one of Carter and Jeff that had come up on *416 Morning* the day before.

Chrissy's text more or less confirmed the source of the article. *Look who I ran into at Eaton Centre! This tall handsome guy who looked kinda familiar offered to take the picture for us. It was THIS GUY from that pic on @416Morning!*

"Looks like you've been found out," Trix said as she shoved her phone back in her pocket. She looked between them and shook her head. "Uh, so I'm going to leave you to… talk about that. It was nice meeting you, Carter."

"Yeah," Carter said, obviously still distracted by his phone. "You too."

Jeff saw her to the door, aware that Carter was still facedown in surprise fame.

"I hope he gets over it fast," Trix offered.

"Are you… do you want me to call you an Uber? Should I call Max for you?"

She shook her head. "I'm actually in better shape than when I came over. Promise."

Jeff nodded and decided to take her word for it. "Okay. Well… call me if that changes."

"I will." Then she threw her arms around his waist. "I'm still sorry for what I did to you. It's okay if you're still mad. But thanks for listening anyway."

Startled, Jeff stood frozen for a moment but then hugged her back. "Any time."

When he returned, Carter was back in the kitchen, staring into a bubbling pot of pasta. Jeff touched his waist, pressed a kiss to the back of his shoulder. "Hey. You okay?"

Carter put the spoon down and pulled Jeff to him. "Yeah. I mean, I'm kind of used to it?" he said ruefully. "Famous brother. It's not totally unfamiliar territory."

Right, and Carter and Dave looked enough alike that he'd probably been mistaken for Dave a few times.

Being the brother of a famous person was a little different from dating one, though. "This is probably going to be slightly more invasive."

"I'm a big boy," Carter said, bumping his pelvis pointedly against Jeff's. "I can handle it."

Jeff fought the urge to look down. He was afraid if he moved everything on the stove would boil over.

But Carter interrupted his train of thought with a tilt of his head. "Everything okay with Trix? Things seemed kind of tense onstage last night."

Of course Carter picked up on that. Jeff sat on one of the kitchen stools and hooked his feet on the bar underneath it. "She didn't exactly ask me if it was okay to make me play a song I'd written that she found in my notebook when I foolishly left it in her grasp."

"What? *Crap*." The pasta pot boiled over. Carter took the lid off and turned the heat down, then stirred frantically until the danger passed. "What the hell, Jeff?"

"Yeah, that's what I said too." He shook his head. "She came to apologize and… explain, I guess. There were mitigating circumstances. It still wasn't okay, but *we're* okay."

Carter still looked a bit like he wanted to chase Trix down and defend Jeff's honor, or the honor of his song, but he let it slide. "If you say so."

"I do."

Which brought Jeff to his next topic of conversation. "So listen… you can say no."

With a soft-focused look nonetheless sharp enough to cut right through Jeff's bullshit, Carter said, "Can I, though?" Then he switched the burner off on the pasta sauce and the pasta. "What am I allowed to say no to?"

Jeff cleared his throat. "Well, you have your laptop now. And you have the go-ahead to work from home for a little while…."

Carter drained the pasta. When he'd finished and Jeff still hadn't gone on, he prompted, "You know you have to actually ask me something in order to give me the opportunity to say yes or no, right?"

"Come on tour with me," Jeff blurted.

Carter sloshed a few penne noodles over the side of the strainer onto the floor. "Seriously?"

"Maybe not the whole tour," Jeff backpedaled. "I mean, you'd be welcome. But at least to Vancouver and Victoria. It's beautiful, and you—" *You need a vacation.* Nope, if he framed it like that, Carter would find a way to back out. "Maybe it's selfish of me," he said instead. "But

I'm not ready to let you out of my sight yet if I don't have to. I can have my travel agent book you on our flights."

Carter left the pasta in the strainer and turned around to face Jeff. "You don't think I'll be a distraction?"

"You'll definitely be a distraction," Jeff said wryly. "But maybe not a bad one." He fought the urge to look down at his hands and mostly managed to meet Carter's gaze. "We're gonna write another album. I don't know what we're going to do about recording or producing yet. I hate our label. But writing would be a lot more fun with a muse around, so…."

He didn't know why he felt so vulnerable—it wasn't like Carter didn't know that song was for him. But he still didn't relax until Carter dumped the penne into the sauce, stepped across the kitchen, and cupped his face to kiss him. "I have to double-check with work," he said when he pulled back, "make sure there's no weird tax thing. But if they say it's okay… then yeah. Why not?"

Jeff grinned. "Really?"

Carter kissed him again. "Really."

Okay. That gave Jeff *options*. That gave him time. That gave him….

An erection. Okay, it was Carter kissing him again—his cheekbone and then his dimple and then his ear and then his neck—that was doing that.

"Hey," Jeff said, suddenly finding himself sitting on his own kitchen table, "pasta reheats well, right?"

Carter laughed against his mouth and let himself be led to the bedroom.

LESSON FIVE
Decide Who You Want to Be

TYPICAL SELF-ABSORBED advice from a rock star—50 percent of a relationship's success is up to you. Which begs the question: Who are you?

That summer, I hardly knew. Was I the kid who'd left town at fifteen and never looked back? Or the exhausted thirty-year-old who crawled home to lick his wounds?

Was I the frontman of Howl, the rock star, the guy in the band? Or was I a budding solo artist?

Most of the time I didn't even know which of those guys I *wanted* to be, so I focused on being Jeff the boyfriend. (Don't do that. It's stupid.)

You can't define yourself by who you're dating. But you can decide what's important to you—the job, the mission, the message, the ethics, the people. And you can make your choices accordingly.

Does this really help you get your man—your *person*? I think it does. I think it's important that the people in a relationship come to some kind of consensus on what the best version of themselves looks like.

Besides, this way, if the relationship ends prematurely, at least one of you will still like you when it's over.

Chapter Thirteen

CARTER WAS visibly uncomfortable on the plane, even in business class, even with the heavy anti-inflammatories the doctor had prescribed. Jeff felt bad about it—Carter was only on the stupid plane because of him—but whenever he opened his mouth to apologize, Carter gave him a look and said, "Don't."

And then, instead of apologizing, Jeff had to say, "So if I chartered us a private jet, do you think we could—" and then Carter shoved his dinner roll into Jeff's mouth.

"No private jets," he said firmly. "Sure, it's mostly huge companies that are responsible for climate change, but that's a bigger carbon footprint than I'm comfortable being a part of."

Jeff took a bite of the dinner roll and set the rest down on his tray. "I could just jerk you off under the blanket instead," he offered, voice pitched low. "You know. As a distraction."

This turned out to be a mistake.

Most of the discomfort melted right off Carter's face and was replaced by what Jeff could only describe as evil lust. "I have a better idea."

Carter apparently took Jeff's words as a challenge to get him as worked up as possible without touching his dick. Between the tray table and the blanket Jeff had thrown over his lap out of habit when he sat down, no one could see anything, but he was intensely aware of even the slightest twitch of Carter's fingers as he gently, teasingly massaged his way from Jeff's knee to the top of his thigh. By the time he reached Jeff's groin, Jeff was frozen in his seat, afraid to move lest he shove Carter's hand down over his crotch and buck against it until he came.

When he was sure he couldn't take another second, Carter drew his hand back, and a flight attendant came around and took away their dinner trays.

"I hate you," Jeff hissed, flushed all over and aching in his jeans.

"No, you don't," Carter said blithely as he stowed his tray table. He glanced over and smiled evilly. "Thanks for the distraction. It really helped."

Jeff gritted his teeth until the flight attendant's cart had gone by and he could escape to the bathroom.

Apart from that, the flight was uneventful. They landed in Vancouver and deplaned to find a postcard-perfect day waiting for them, the late afternoon sun washing everything with warmth. The water in the Strait of Georgia was a deep, glassy blue, and the Coast Mountains rose in the distance, capped with snow.

The view from their hotel room was just as nice.

"Wow." Carter wheeled his scooter over to the window and set his laptop bag down on the desk. "Swanky."

"Only the best for you."

Carter half turned to give him a look at that, because yeah, Jeff had booked the room before he knew Carter was going to be sharing with him, but whatever. He'd also upgraded after Carter said yes.

Carter sat at the desk while Jeff tipped the bellhop. Then Jeff flopped onto the couch in the sitting room and stretched. He was still worked up from the flight. "Sooo… plans?"

Carter swiveled toward him, hands between his splayed knees. Jeff was tired, part jet lag, part travel, and he still kind of wanted to crawl across the room and put his face in Carter's crotch. "I was actually about to ask you that. I've got a couple things I need to check on for work, but I didn't know if we had dinner reservations or…."

Jeff had been thinking maybe romantic room service, but a night out could be good. In fact, a night out would preclude Carter from spending the whole evening on his laptop the way he had yesterday in Toronto, as though he were trying to make up for not being present for work in person by working twice as many hours.

"We should go out," Jeff decided. They didn't have a lot of time in BC—the first concert was tomorrow, then the follow-up the next day, and the day after that they'd fly out again, Carter back to Willow Sound and Jeff and the rest of Howl to their gig in Calgary. "I'll look for something close by."

"Sounds good." Carter was already unpacking his laptop. "Do you mind if I work for a few? I'm pretty sure I'll have another email from Emily. She's been trying to track the impact of climate change on wildlife populations across Canada's parks, but the data's kind of a raw mess. I'm trying to help her track down better sources."

Jeff had no idea if that was part of Carter's actual job or if he was just such a keener that he couldn't help himself, but he waved his hand. "Have at it. It's early for dinner anyway. The longer we wait, the less jet lag will suck."

"Thanks."

Unfortunately, Jeff had underestimated his own exhaustion and Carter's commitment to work. He fell asleep on the couch googling restaurants and woke up an hour and a half later to Carter touching his shoulder.

"You were saying about the jet lag?" Carter said, amused.

"Mmph." Jeff rolled his neck to try to work out a kink. Outside, the setting sun burnished the mountains in red-gold. "You woke me up in time for the show."

Carter lowered himself onto the cushion next to Jeff. "I guess they do sunsets okay out here too."

"You still want to go out for dinner?"

Jeff's stomach rumbled. Apparently their light lunch on the flight wasn't enough to satisfy. "Yeah, but it might be a little tougher to get a reservation now. Let me just…." He shook out the pins and needles from his arm and picked up his phone.

Then—"On second thought," he said, and he got up and used the hotel phone to have the concierge make a reservation instead.

"Wow," Carter said again when he wheeled into the lobby at the upscale restaurant the concierge recommended. "Probably a good thing you took me shopping."

Jeff had been mentally high-fiving himself since Carter stepped out of the hotel bathroom in fitted blue slacks that strained across his thighs, a plain white henley, and a gray sweater with a snap collar and detail at the shoulders that drew attention to just how broad they were. It was almost like Jeff had been paying attention all along to the things his stylist told him.

"You definitely look like a snack," Jeff agreed, borderline lascivious.

Before he could say anything more scandalous, the maître d' arrived to take them to their seats. Carter folded the handle on the scooter so it fit under the table and looked around. "You trying to impress me or something?" But he smiled like it didn't bother him in the least that Jeff was about to drop several hundred dollars on a dinner Carter would've struggled to afford.

In response, Jeff batted his eyelashes. "Is it working?"

Carter laughed softly. "I don't know. I've seen you pick gum out of a five-year-old's hair. What's *this* going to prove?"

He probably had a point, but whatever. They still had to eat. "That I care about sustainably sourced local salmon?"

Another huffed laugh, accompanied by a look so tender that Jeff, who made his living baring his soul in public, felt uncomfortably naked.

Dinner was nice. Carter was enraptured by the food and Jeff and seemed oblivious to the world beyond their table. Jeff made him try the fancy wine just because, then grinned when he wrinkled his nose and ordered him a beer instead.

As far as dates went, Jeff thought it was going well—until he'd paid the bill and they stepped outside to find a handful of paparazzi waiting for them.

Carter, who had been wheeling over the threshold when the first flashbulb went off, faltered and lost his balance, cursing when his booted foot hit the pavement. Jeff reflexively grabbed the handle of the scooter before it could roll off.

Shit.

"Carter?"

Carter had taken a step backward into the vestibule of the restaurant. Cursing mentally, Jeff backed up too, until the doors closed and they had a semblance of privacy.

For someone who was one of the calmest, most impossible to ruffle people Jeff had ever met, Carter looked positively *bothered.* His skin paled under his early summer tan, his mouth went tight, and his eyes took on a hunted expression.

"Are you okay?" Jeff reoriented the scooter so Carter could use it. "You didn't hurt yourself, did you?"

Carter shook his head, some of his color returning. "No, uh, it turns out the shop assistant was right about how jarring it is when you hit something unexpectedly and fall off, but no damage, I don't think. Just an adrenaline spike."

Thank God. "Sorry about this." Jeff nodded at the sharks outside. "It happens sometimes." More so on tours than at home, where people were more or less used to seeing him, and usually only if someone tipped them off; Jeff wasn't *that* recognizable. "I should've warned you."

"It's not like you knew they were there," Carter pointed out.

"No, but…." He might as well rip off the Band-Aid. "Between the Twitter thing and this—it's going to be obvious now that we're together, so you're going to get to deal with all the fun of being a rock star's boyfriend. Sorry about that."

As suddenly as his composure had left him, though, it returned. Carter propped his knee back on the scooter and shrugged. "It was bound to happen eventually." Then he added wryly, "On the plus side, no one will be assuming I'm straight for a while."

The glass is always half full, Jeff thought. "Okay. So do you want to go out together, or do you want me to get in the car and come back for you? Or we can ask if there's a back exit." It wouldn't be the first time he'd sneaked out of a restaurant. At least this time it didn't involve Max being high out of his mind.

Carter deliberated. "You don't have a preference?"

Maybe with someone else. Maybe once upon a time. But—"Unfortunately, when it comes to your mom knowing I wrote seriously dirty lyrics about you when I was practically a teenager, the cat's already out of the bag. After that, the rest of the world isn't so scary."

Carter's easy laugh was born of surprise. It was no less addictive now than it had been when Jeff was a high school freshman. "It's my brothers you should've worried about."

Oh Lord. Jeff was an only child technically, but he remembered what Brady and Dave were like growing up. Best to focus on something else for now. "How do you want to do this? If you didn't have the scooter, I'd just hold your hand."

Carter had the nerve to look disappointed they couldn't do that, and Jeff's heart made a noise like a rubber chicken. "Should've gotten one big enough for two."

Now there was a mental image. Jeff grinned. "All right. Let's try this again, eh? Don't try to answer any questions, it just encourages them."

"This feels so rude," Carter grumbled.

"Taking flash photographs of someone without their permission is rude," Jeff pointed out. "Don't flip them the bird, though, you're not Chris Pine."

"Mom would disown me." He huffed as he wheeled back up to the door. "All right, let's do this."

Jeff stayed just in front. The tabloids already knew his face; a shot would be useless to the photographers unless they could see both of them.

"Jeff, is it true—"

"Over here, Jeff—"

"Can you confirm—"

"—rumors of an underground sex club—"

Oh, dammit. Jeff didn't need eyes in the back of his head to know that would get Carter to turn around. Sure enough, by the time Jeff caught his wrist, the photographer already had a shot of his face and a quote of Carter saying, in a deeply disparaging tone, "*Really*?"

Frankly after the past week, Jeff wouldn't be all that surprised to find out Carter belonged to an underground sex club—though he *would* be impressed if you could find one in Willow Sound. "Come on, in the car." He urged Carter in front of him.

Carter must have realized his mistake, because he got in the car first without argument. Jeff left the scooter for the driver to deal with and climbed in after Carter. When he closed the door on the paparazzi, the *chunk* of it seemed very loud, punctuated by a sudden cessation of noise from outside.

"Sorry," Carter said after a tense half second. "That was pretty obvious bait, right?"

Jeff shrugged. "Yeah, but I could've warned you. Should've, even. You didn't give them anything they could use, except maybe a shot of your pretty face."

"Ugh." Carter slumped in his seat as the car started to move. He was sullen for a moment and then cracked, "I knew I should've gotten my brows waxed."

Thank God for Carter's even keel. Still. "I should probably call my publicist," Jeff said apologetically. "Release a statement." He'd been hoping for a little more time to settle things with Carter before he had to do something so practical and unromantic, but he didn't see a good way out of it.

He didn't even want to think about what would happen if they broke up. Everyone would know how serious he'd been, wouldn't they? People would find out Jeff and Carter had known each other forever and put two and two together. If they broke up after that….

But he was being stupid. Cart before horse. If they broke up, people talking about it would be the least of Jeff's problems.

"Sorry," Carter said again. "It's weird. It's not like I didn't know you were famous, right? Except that it's not how I think of you. I keep forgetting." He smiled. "I'll get used to it."

Jeff wasn't convinced, but that was his own problem. "I hate that they ruined our date night—the first night we got to spend together where we *both* knew it was a date."

Carter slid across the seat until their shoulders touched. "Hey." He jostled into Jeff's side and gave a lopsided grin when Jeff looked up. "Night's not over yet."

Jeff was going to have to start eating his Wheaties to keep up once Carter's foot healed.

Whatever. It'd be worth it. "You say the sweetest things."

"Of course," Carter said, mock serious. His eyes turned dark and heated. "I have to do *something* to make up for all the nasty things I'm going to do to you."

"Hmm." Jeff grabbed Carter's hand before it could elaborate on what Carter meant by *nasty things*. "What if I want to do the nasty things to *you* this time?"

Carter squeezed his fingers. "I think we can work out a schedule."

THE NEXT day marked the official start of the album-writing-and-planning session. Somehow everyone had figured out Jeff and Carter had the biggest room, which led to Joe, Max, and Trix showing up at the door around ten thirty.

They were lucky Carter had already started his workday, citing a request from Emily to track down some data from one of the other parks.

"You couldn't call first?" Jeff asked as he stepped aside to let them in.

Max propped the case for his acoustic against the couch. He raised an eyebrow at Jeff, then noticed Carter sitting at the desk, broken foot propped up on the overturned garbage can, gently swiveling back and forth as he waited for someone to take him off Hold.

Joe rolled his eyes at Trix. "I told you."

Carter took his foot down and turned his full attention to his phone. "Hey, is this Seanna Clarke?.... Hi, this is Carter Rhodes from Great Bear Lake. I'm wondering if you've got data on...."

Jeff made a "keep it down" gesture and lowered his voice. "I know I said we'd write today, but are we going to do it here? We don't have a drum kit in the hotel, for starters. And Carter's here."

"Thank you," Carter said. "I appreciate it." He ended the call. "Uh. Hi again."

"Right," said Max. "Real jobs."

With an eloquent eye roll, Carter closed his laptop. "At least nobody makes up lies about me joining an underground sex club in order to get a reaction photo." He paused and reconsidered. "Or they didn't until last night."

Jeff had just gotten off the phone with his publicist a few minutes before Trix knocked on the door.

"Well, you're officially famous now," Joe said. "Congratulations, I guess."

Carter made a face.

"It could be worse," Joe went on. "When Sarah and I started dating—"

Oh God, no. "Carter doesn't need to hear that story," Jeff interrupted.

"Sarah would probably be embarrassed anyway," Trix agreed, backing him up. "So, you know… maybe don't."

"*Anyway*," Jeff cut in, "this is kind of Carter's place? For doing work?" As in the whole reason Jeff upgraded the suite—okay, apart from the romantic gesture—was to accommodate him. They weren't just going to kick him out.

But Carter smiled and tucked his laptop into his bag. "It's okay. There's a business center downstairs with complementary coffee and everything. You can't exactly bring a guitar down there."

"We could work in another room," Joe pointed out. "We have three of them."

"Nah," Carter said easily as he gestured at the window and, therefore, the mountains and the water visible through the late morning fog. "Kinda sick of the view anyway." He'd confessed the previous night over dinner that he found it hard to concentrate on anything except how gorgeous it was. Jeff couldn't wait to bring him back sometime when he could actually enjoy it properly—hiking, kayaking. God, maybe they'd even camp. Jeff could survive for two days without hot water.

Probably.

"Are you sure—"

Carter cut Jeff off with a kiss on the cheek. He was getting pretty good at moving around with the cast on. "I'm not the only one who has to work," he said. "I'll be fine. Text me if you're getting lunch?"

Jeff nodded wordlessly, his ears hot for no reason he could name.

Then Carter collected his scooter and wheeled himself out.

As soon as the door shut, Trix dropped into an armchair, giggling. "Oh my God, Jeff."

"*Wow*," said Max. "I thought she was exaggerating. But no. You really do have it that bad."

"Don't be jealous," Jeff grumbled. He collected his guitar and comp book from the bedroom and made his way back to the sitting area.

"I think it's nice," Joe offered. "However, I am never sitting anywhere near the two of you on a plane again—"

"Jeff!" That was Trix, actually scandalized, but smiling.

"It wasn't my idea!" Jeff blurted.

Max threw his head back and howled, slapping his knee. "Oh my God. I never thought I'd see the day you met your match, but Carter has *all* of your numbers."

"You're the worst." He tossed the comp book on the table. "Does anyone else have a comment to make about my boyfriend, or can we get to work now?"

Joe raised his hands. "Not me. I came to work." He produced his phone and set it on the table. "I brought track recordings and everything."

"Oh, a professional," Trix teased. She pulled her drum sticks out of her boot and set them on the table, then pulled a few throw cushions off the couch and sat on the floor. "Some of us have to improvise. But I've got some ideas."

Jeff opened his notebook to a fresh page. "All right, then. Conceptually, what do we have?"

Starting with Joe, each of them listed the song ideas they had been working on. An album needed a mix, but it also needed cohesion, something that would tie it together musically, thematically, or at least tonally. They couldn't just split an album fifty-fifty with Jeff's love ballads opposite Trix's bangers. They could do one that was a mix of ballads and Joe's anecdotes, maybe, but that really would be almost cottagecore, for them.

And then there was Max, who'd apparently been sitting on seven nearly complete songs written in actual musical notation. He took the pages, dogeared at the edges, out of the bottom of his guitar case and put them on the table.

Jeff felt like an asshole. "Okay, I'm getting the idea that I was late to the party on this one."

But Max shrugged. "We're here now," he said, as though it were really that easy.

Maybe it was. Maybe it could be.

Trix blew out a huge breath. "So—thoughts for themes? Do we want to make lists?"

The business of whittling the album down from forty or so potential tracks to the ten to fifteen that would make the final cut took the remainder of the morning. By twelve thirty they were so into it they didn't want to stop, so Jeff texted Carter that they were getting room service, and he should come up and join.

Carter texted back a picture of a plate with a half-eaten sandwich. *I got hungry. Sorry! I don't want to break your stride anyway.*

He was probably right, since Jeff didn't actually see the text until almost two, when he texted back a heart emoji.

Finally, around three, they wrapped up. There was still sound check and warm-ups and whatnot to go over. Trix shoved her drumsticks back into her boot and grabbed her hoodie from where she'd flung it over the back of the couch. "Meet you in the lobby at five?"

"Sounds good," Jeff agreed absently. He stared at the chaos that had become the coffee table—a haphazard mess of yeses, nos, maybes, and revisions. His eyes felt gritty.

The door closed, and Jeff realized Joe was still there. "Hey, so I was hoping…?"

"Shit!" Jeff tore his attention away from the paperwork. "Yes. Sorry. We were going to talk, and I've been flaking." Partly because of Carter, but partly because he thought he might know what Joe would say, and he didn't know if he'd like it—wasn't *ready* to know if he'd like it.

But it wasn't fair to make him wait.

"You've been a little preoccupied," Joe agreed. Of course he got it; he got *Jeff* better than anyone except maybe Carter. "This won't actually take long. I just… I wanted to talk to you first."

"Yeah, of course." Apart from Carter, Joe was Jeff's oldest friend. "I get it. Things are, um, not always good right now." Hence his apprehension.

Joe looked pointedly at Carter's empty desk space and smiled slightly. "I don't know… some things are pretty good, right?"

In more than a decade performing with them, Jeff had never been roasted by his bandmates so consistently. "I thought you didn't want details? You don't want me to contest 'pretty good,' do you? With something like… incredible, mind-blowing, energetic—"

"Please stop," Joe laughed and brought his hands up to cover his ears.

"—voluminous—"

"Gross."

Okay, that was probably TMI. "Anyway." Jeff leaned back on the couch, feigning nonchalance. "What's—"

"Sarah's pregnant," Joe blurted.

Jeff's mouth fell open. Words tumbled out without forethought. "Oh shit, no kidding?"

Apparently this was a happy occurrence, because Joe was smiling proudly, his cheeks a little flushed. "Yeah. We found out a few weeks ago. That's why she's been having a hard time sleeping lately. Being pregnant is uncomfortable even in the first trimester."

So it was early still. "Wow. Hey, that's great. Congratulations." Jeff snapped out of it and stood to pull him into a hug. "You're gonna be great parents."

"Thanks. My mom's really excited. I keep telling her it's early…."

Parts of Trix's confession came back to him. Jeff did his best to keep them compartmentalized in the back of his mind, not to let them intrude on this joyous moment. "How early?"

"Nine weeks." Joe blew out a breath. "But Sarah's thirty-two, and it's her first pregnancy, and she's high-risk because of her diabetes, so she's kind of freaking out."

Translation—Sarah was fine; Joe was freaking out. "Oh man. That's got to be hard, with you touring. I guess she probably didn't want to come with, though, huh?"

"She can barely sleep in our own bed," he said ruefully. "I got a text at three her time because I wasn't there to use as a body pillow."

"Rough." But this didn't seem to be the whole story. "So—is that it? Not that a baby isn't a lot, it's amazing, it's huge, but I sort of got the feeling you weren't done."

"That's the other reason I wanted to talk to you first. I know you're on the same page. I need to stick around Toronto for a while when this is done. At least 'til the baby is born, maybe longer."

Ah. "No tour," Jeff said.

"I'm gonna be a father," Joe said, and there was something fierce and happy in his voice. "I don't want to miss it. Sarah will have some mat leave, but she wants to go back to work after. Her job is important to her."

Jeff heard what he didn't say loud and clear. Sarah's job was important to her… and that was important to Joe, maybe more so than his own job. "The band will still be here after the baby's born. When they're in school and stuff." They were already talking about finding a way to ditch Big Moose. That meant they could ax the grueling tour schedule too.

Theoretically.

Or they could be stuck doing the tour without Joe.

He wanted to be reassuring, but he wasn't sure that was what Joe was after.

"Will it?" He gave Jeff a searching look. "We both know things have been rough for a while. You need a break. Max—"

A toilet flushed, and he broke off. "Carter didn't come back yet, did he?"

Swallowing his dread, Jeff gave a slow shake of his head. "No." Come to think of it, he hadn't seen Max leave. He'd just assumed he'd sneaked out when Trix had.

But that was stupid. His guitar case was still over by the door. Which meant—

Water ran in the sink. Then the bathroom door opened and Max came out. "Hey. Did Trix leave?"

Shit. Jeff hoped he hadn't overheard anything. "Yeah man, she said she wanted a shower before sound check."

"Cool. I'm going to head out too. If I'm lucky I can catch a nap." He paused to collect his guitar and looked at Joe. "You coming too? If we don't clear out, I don't know how Jeff'll get laid again before the show."

"Hey," Jeff protested weakly.

Joe grinned and bumped his fist. "Get it, brother. I'll see you downstairs, yeah?"

Carter came in a few minutes after they'd left, just as Jeff was climbing out of the shower and into bed for a quick nap of his own.

"Jeff?"

"In the bedroom," Jeff called as he burrowed into the sheets.

Carter wheeled into the bedroom. "Productive day?"

"Mm-hmm," Jeff said. He wanted to tell Carter Joe's news, but if he went into it, he'd never get any sleep. "Talk later? You want to lie down with me?" After a beat he added, "No funny stuff, mister. I need my beauty sleep. Come cuddle me."

With a snort, Carter sat down on the bed. A moment later, after removing his shoe, he curled awkwardly around Jeff. "Better?"

"Mm-hmm." The weight of Carter's arm across his waist settled something inside him. Suddenly his eyelids were heavy. "Wake me up at four thirty?"

Carter pressed a kiss to the edge of his jaw. "Okay."

Chapter Fourteen

Giving a concert when your boyfriend was backstage with an all-access pass was a new experience for Jeff. Off the stage everything felt precarious; he was walking on eggshells making sure he didn't let on about Joe maybe leaving or about the impending intervention with Max. But on the stage, he felt like they owned it again. He felt like he had in the beginning, when they were young and full of energy and hope and joy.

Tonight, with Howl beside him and Carter waiting in the wings, Jeff could take on anything.

The full roar of the crowd at PNE—just over five thousand—only proved him right.

Some nights you just knew. The transitions clicked, the banter came smoothly, the energy just kept building. Tonight was one of those nights when nothing could touch them. From the moment Trix's vocals joined his on "Blood in the Water," Jeff had goose bumps. They blistered through a few earlier anthems, and when Joe took over lead vocals for a protest song, the whole venue rang as the audience shouted the lyrics at the tops of their lungs.

When the song wrapped, Joe glanced over at Jeff and shrugged helplessly, grinning. Jeff knew that look; he'd given it to Joe and Max enough times. Joe had put so much into the song that he needed a break or he wouldn't be able to sing tomorrow.

"Thanks for that, Joe," he said into the mic once the cheering had calmed enough for anyone to hear him.

The cheers picked up again.

Joe bowed.

"Always love following an act like that."

That earned him some whistles and laughter, and he glanced over his shoulder at Max and raised his eyebrows. "I think we might have to deviate a minute here. Joe needs a breather."

Trix picked up the thread. "What do you suggest?"

Jeff thought of rearranging the set list a little—they could just move up the songs that featured more of Max's vocals, or they could omit Joe's from the songs they'd settled on—but he'd turned around completely to see Trix, which meant he could see Carter in his director's chair backstage, wearing the headset that would keep the speakers from deafening him… and Jeff didn't become a rock star by not seizing every opportunity that came his way.

The last time he'd played a song he'd written just for Carter, he hadn't even known Carter was watching. This time he could really pull out all the stops.

"Maybe we should slow it down a bit," Jeff suggested. He let his fingers pick out a few of the opening notes from "Heavenly Bodies"—but he did it at three-quarter speed. "Hey, Trix, you think you can…?"

He couldn't see her eyes because of the lighting and the angle, but he could hear her eye roll in her voice. "Sweetie, please. I think I can follow that. Although if we're editorializing…." She beat out the usual rhythm for the song, and then she swapped the tom for the snare and put a heavier emphasis on the bass, which she hit *just* a bit late.

"Oh my God," Max said, half laughing into the microphone. The new beat evoked nothing so much as straining bedsprings and a headboard hitting the wall.

"I love you guys," Jeff said sincerely. "Trix, count us in?"

She gave a throaty chuckle into the mic and followed in a breathy, low voice, "Two, three, four—"

Suffice it to say they didn't even consider doing the radio edit. By the time Jeff wrapped up the guitar outro—which sounded more like a person wailing in ecstasy than ever before—the noise from the fans was mostly wolf whistles.

He wiped his wrist across his forehead, using the sweat-wicking band he had there to avoid getting drips in his eyes. But before he could even look back and check to see his effect on Carter, Trix laughed. "Hey, Jeffy, I think you're needed backstage."

What?

When he turned around, two of their tech crew were red-faced with mirth and Carter—Carter was standing, flushed, beckoning with one finger.

Well, that cat wasn't going back in the bag. He might as well take advantage. "'Scuse me just—one second," Jeff said, and a huge cheer went up as he unplugged and strode back just outside the range of the stage cameras.

Probably some of the fans could still see from this angle, if they were sitting to the right of the stage, but fuck it. Jeff had just enough time to sling the guitar onto his back before Carter slid both hands into his hair and yanked him into a kiss.

Between the energy from the stage and the energy pouring in through Carter's lips, the buzz of his stubble and the heat of his body, Jeff expected to burn up like a book of matches. He opened his mouth and Carter swept his tongue in for a brief, hard, dizzying moment.

Just as suddenly, he pulled back, his expression sheepish. "Hope you don't mind the interruption?"

Jeff swayed on his feet, held upright mostly by Carter's hands in his hair. "Umm." Interruption?

Finally the howling of the crowd filtered through his brain.

Oh. Right. "Nooo," he said slowly as his brain kicked back into gear. "I mean, I probably shouldn't make it a habit, but this is your first all-access concert. I understand being simply overcome with lust—"

Carter stopped him with a finger against his lips. "Don't ruin it."

"—but you'll have to wait 'til after the show." Jeff grinned and took a step back. He held eye contact until he almost tripped over a cable, then jogged back upstage. He picked up the patch cord and plugged back in, still beaming, and only realized when he accidentally caught his own face on one of the huge screens that Carter had made a fairly obvious mess of his hair.

He cleared his throat into the microphone. "Ah, sorry about that, something needed my attention—"

Max hooted. "Yeah, Carter's—"

"*Anyway*," Joe said. "You were saying, Jeff?"

"I was saying…." Jeff didn't remember what he was saying. "Trix, what was I saying?"

"I think you were just going to play the intro of the next song, actually."

That sounded like a good plan. Jeff snapped his fingers and pointed. "I knew we kept you around for a reason."

The show wrapped with the same wild energy it started with, following a huge encore of "Ginsberg" that shook the building. As they left the stage, Jeff bumped both fists with Joe, high-fived Max, and spun Trix in a very sweaty hug.

"Seriously," he was telling Joe as they reached the green room, "you fucking *killed it* tonight. You set the tone for the whole show. I think I still have goose bumps—"

"Oops," said Trix. "I think I left my phone in the wardrobe room."

"I need a drink," Joe said, about-facing. "There was a water cooler this way. C'mon, Max, I'll show you where it is."

The abrupt exodus left Jeff a little bemused—until he opened the door to the green room and Carter yanked him inside.

"Hi," Jeff said breathlessly.

Carter hooked his fingers in Jeff's belt loops and pulled him carefully backward. "Hi."

He backed up until he hit the ottoman in the center of the room, where he sat.

Jeff swallowed.

Slowly, Carter thumbed the skin above Jeff's waistband. He looked up with dark eyes and pulled Jeff closer still. "Yeah?"

"Uhhh," Jeff said. Between the show, the kiss—which had suddenly flooded back to him—and the way Carter was looking at him now, all heat and hunger as he licked his lips, he could hardly think. "Did—the door?"

"I locked it," Carter assured him. His fingers were on Jeff's fly now.

"Thank God."

Jeff had been on a loud stage in front of thousands of screaming fans for hours. Even with the hearing protection he used, he could barely hear the tick-tick-tick of Carter pulling down his zipper tooth by tooth. But he could feel the vibration each sound made.

He'd been half-hard since the kiss. Now, with Carter watching him intently and reaching into his jeans, *half* was a distant memory.

"Oh my God," Jeff whispered.

Carter ran the backs of his knuckles over Jeff's cloth-covered erection. His mouth twitched into a slight smirk when Jeff shuddered at the touch and his cock jerked. "I kinda wanted to do this against the wall." He slid his hand into Jeff's boxers and withdrew his dick. "But kneeling is a no-go right now. So try not to fall over."

Jeff opened his mouth to answer, but Carter opened his mouth and put it on his dick, and words weren't going to happen any more than

Carter kneeling. A moan punched out of him when Carter licked the tip of his cock.

In his years as a rock star, Jeff hadn't exactly been celibate. He'd had his share of hookups backstage, especially in the early days. But he'd never felt a rush like this, standing in the middle of the green room with Carter watching him intently, his gaze every bit as hot as his mouth.

Jeff's knees trembled, but Carter braced him with strong hands on his hips and took him down deep, and really, the knees weren't going to hold out for long… but they didn't have to.

"Carter." The word came out helpless and turned-on. Without thinking, he reached out to brace himself. His hands landed on Carter's shoulders, which only made Carter eye him hungrily, as if in challenge.

It was over embarrassingly quickly. Carter knew just how to touch him, and the way he flicked his tongue against the underside of Jeff's cock proved his undoing. Jeff came with a groan, emptying into Carter's mouth, his knees shaking.

Carter worked him through it until Jeff had to push him back, oversensitive. "God, I guess you liked the show?" he said, half falling onto the ottoman.

Carter wiped the corner of his mouth—distracting. "It had an effect."

Jeff snorted and tried to muster the energy to put his dick away. "Evidently."

But Carter shook his head. "Not just sexually. It's wild to see you out there doing your thing, you know? In your element." He ran a hand through his hair. "I don't know if I can explain it right. It was one thing to watch you do it from the stands as a fan, even as someone who'd known you before. It's something else to be there for sound check, to watch you put songs together from scratch, to know what happens on the fly. What's the phrase—'born to the stage'?"

He seemed so earnest about it that Jeff would've blushed if his system could've coaxed any blood to his cheeks. "You think so?"

"Jeff." Carter tilted his head. "You are a literal rock star with multiple platinum albums. But even if you didn't have those, something special happens when you go onstage. It's just different, seeing it from this side."

Jeff didn't know how he was supposed to keep his heart in his chest. It was a lost cause anyway; it had belonged to Carter since the day they met. "You're too good for my ego." He leaned his head on Carter's shoulder.

"Pretty sure there are multiple Top 100 songs about how much you want my dick," Carter said, warm rather than wry, "so, same, I guess."

Jeff muffled his laugh in Carter's sleeve.

LIKE ALL good things, their time in BC had to come to an end. Two days later they packed up their things and did one last check of the hotel suite.

"All good?"

Carter was frowning slightly when he came out from checking the bathroom, but he said, "Yeah."

They both got distracted by the view again, and Jeff found himself gravitating to Carter's side to take it in one last time. "We'll come back," he promised. "I've got most of the summer off. Pick a couple days you don't have to work once you're free of the plastic menace and I'll let you take me hiking."

Carter looked down. "You will, huh?"

Jeff squeezed his hand. "I'm generous like that."

They had an hour or so together at the airport, which they spent in the first-class lounge because people kept trying to take pictures; they had in fact made the front page of the internet, and that always meant more attention. Carter pretended not to notice as they each grabbed a paperback to read on the plane, but Jeff didn't miss the way he kept ducking his head, then looking over his shoulder every other minute.

So the first-class lounge refuge it was.

Twenty minutes before Carter had to leave for his flight, he started digging through the pockets of his carry-on. Jeff stopped scrolling through Twitter. "What's up?"

Carter frowned. "I can't find my painkillers."

Jeff blinked. Carter hadn't mentioned being in any pain over the past few days. But when he opened his mouth to ask, Carter cut him off with a shake of the head. "I'm fine now," he clarified. "But when I called him before I flew to meet you in Toronto, my doctor said the flight might cause some discomfort. He wasn't wrong. He wrote me a prescription for something to take before takeoff, but now I can't find them."

"I have some Advil," Jeff offered. "Better than nothing."

"Thanks."

They had another few minutes before Carter had to leave for his flight, but Jeff couldn't think of what to say. The irony was not lost on him.

"So, I guess you should—" Jeff started, at the same time Carter said,

"Have you booked your flight—"

They both stopped. Carter quirked up one corner of his mouth. "How are we so good at being together, and so bad at hello and goodbye?"

Jeff rubbed his palm on his thigh. "I don't know, lack of practice?" he suggested. "We were joined at the hip for almost ten years, and then nothing. It kinda makes sense."

Shaking his head, Carter pushed himself to his feet. "We should practice sometime we're not in an airport, maybe."

Jeff stood too and glanced around the first-class lounge. Its only other occupants had plenty to distract them—phones and laptops and headphones. No one was paying them any attention. "No time like the present," he said, and he stood on tiptoe to press a quick kiss to Carter's mouth.

Or he meant it to be quick, at least, but Carter didn't let him go right away. He caught Jeff by the waist and kept him pulled close in a deep, thorough kiss that had him swooning. When he pulled away, he rubbed his nose along the length of Jeff's in a gentle caress.

Jeff was so in love with him it was stupid.

He cleared his throat. "Ah. I'm back in Willow Sound the day after we play Winnipeg. June 9."

"I'd meet you at the airport, but I still won't be able to drive," Carter joked.

"You're a mess," Jeff agreed—and the irony of *that* wasn't lost on him either. "I parked at the airport anyway."

"Right." Finally Carter released him, took a step back, and mounted the scooter. "Call me?"

"Uh, obviously." Jeff had proven pretty conclusively that he couldn't live without him. "Time zones permitting." It'd be pretty late in Ontario by the time Jeff wrapped a show in Calgary.

A garbled announcement came over the speaker, and Carter made a face. "I really do have to go. Text me when you land?"

What a sap. "Of course. You too."

Statement released to Twitter and Instagram
May 29

HI EVERYONE,

Since by now our pictures from last night's dinner are probably making the rounds on social media, I might as well come clean. Yes, I'm seeing someone new. Yes, my best friend from high school. (I know, but clichés exist for a reason.) Yes, that's him with me in that picture from 416 Morning. Yes, that was us together at the restaurant, which was a very nice first date aside from the invasion of privacy.

Anyway, feel free to speculate about which songs I wrote about him. It's not like he doesn't already know.

Lots of love,

Jeff & Carter

Attached is a photograph taken in selfie mode—Jeff and Carter pressed cheek-to-cheek, grinning, with a filter of bubble hearts.

CR: LANDED in Willow Sound. Getting a ride home from Mom. Feel like I'm 15

JP: Before or after you dated whatshername?

CR: During, obviously

JP: WHEELS down in Calgary. Gonna buy a cowboy hat for reasons

CR: Just the hat?

JP: Didn't think you'd approve of the leathers

CR: You've seen me eat steak

JP: So should I get the boots too or just the chaps?

CALGARY WAS a shit show.

Joe's voice was absolutely shredded. Unless he was on the phone with Sarah, he barely spoke outside of sound check and shows, to preserve what remained. Their flight was delayed two hours due to a mechanical problem, and everyone was cranky. Trix got food poisoning from something in the airport.

That left Jeff and Max together, and they hadn't hung out just the two of them since Max stole a grand out of Jeff's wallet.

They ended up in the hotel bar watching NHL playoffs over plates of good steak with sad, limp salad. Jeff did his best not to flinch when Max ordered his third beer. Three beers wasn't even out of the ordinary for *Jeff*, so he didn't feel like he should judge.

"So, what do you think?" Max said.

Jeff did his best to divert his attention from the tie game between Winnipeg and Colorado and focus back on the conversation, which was about… shit. Best touring locations? "Uh," he started, hoping to buy some time.

Fortunately Max apparently hadn't been finished. "I just think it would be really cool to start the next tour in the UK, in a bus, you know? Things are pretty close together there, it'd just be neat. Like a working vacation."

The next tour. Jeff's heart sank. He felt like such an asshole. It wasn't fair to string Max along like this. He needed help, not *handling*.

The thing was, Jeff knew exactly what would happen if they broke the news that they wouldn't be doing another album after this until Max got clean again. And that was a few hours of Max faking it very convincingly until he OD'd. So he said, "You got any destinations in mind?" and let Max spin his wheels. He wanted to see Bath and Stonehenge and Dublin and Edinburgh and Manchester—Max had specific taste in English football clubs—and half a dozen rock landmarks along the lines of Abbey Road.

"Were you a travel agent in another life?" Jeff asked somewhere around the bottom of his own third beer, and Max blew a raspberry.

So *that* part of Calgary went okay. By the time Jeff got back up to his room, he knew Carter would be in bed, but he had an actual email waiting for him, so things weren't all bad.

Hey,

Feels super weird to write you an email after fifteen years, but I know how you feel about voicemail and I'm not secure enough in my masculinity to send forty unanswered texts. So: email.

Everything's fine here. Nothing burned down. Someone did replace my back door, which is a little bizarre. You wouldn't know anything about that?

Charlie wants your autograph. Dave's pretending he's not butt-hurt that you're her favorite Willow Sound famous person. Mom and I have a bet on whether he's going to try to buy her a pony. Personally I think Charlie's going to convince him to get her a dirt bike.

Katie started working at the garage, and she already has things sorted to where my services are no longer necessary. It's weird having free time. The house is too quiet. I hate it.

In other news—well, "news"—the Gazette's decided to try its hand at clickbait-style articles. Check out this one. I feel like Mrs. Bially would've had a thing or two to say if one of us ever turned in a newspaper article like that.

I'm back in the office starting tomorrow, still not allowed to drive, though. Bet I get a lot of requests for Howl songs at campfire night.

If someone asks for "Heavenly Bodies," I'm out.

Carter

That made Jeff laugh. The idea of Carter having to sing that, knowing Jeff had written it about him—yeah, he could see how that would be a bit much. He hit Reply.

Thank you for not forcing me to check my voicemail. You're the best.

I definitely do not know anything about your back door or its Energy Star efficiency rating or the fact that it is made of mostly recycled materials, and I certainly don't know whether your previous back door ended up at Habitat for Humanity. Very mysterious. Maybe you have a secret admirer.

I'll pick Charlie something up from the merch table and sign it for her. Gotta keep my #1 fan happy. Maybe I can find a Howl dirt bike. That'd really cheese Dave's cheddar. Make up for that time he put my underwear in the freezer.

He paused there and clicked the link for the *Gazette* article.

Hometown Heartthrob

By Zachary Schmidt

Anyone who's lived in Willow Sound for any length of time has heard the name Jeff Pine. At thirty years old, Pine is one of the most recognizable musicians in North America, and he got his start right here. It's no surprise the town has long held Pine as one of its favorite sons.

To the disappointment of many, though, the affection has been one-sided. Pine hasn't returned to his hometown since he left at fifteen... until now.

Music media across the country have speculated on what kept him away, but here at the Gazette, *we're more interested in what brought him back. And the answer to that question seems to be our very own hometown heartthrob, Carter Rhodes.*

Whether the relationship lasts remains to be seen, but this reporter hopes we'll see more of Pine in Willow Sound either way.

Suddenly he wasn't smiling anymore. Why would someone write this? It didn't seem right in a close-knit town like that. Jeff had felt more or less safe from tabloid-style exploitation there, and now.... His stomach turned. Reading such callous disregard for Carter made him sick and furious.

Idly, he wondered what it cost to buy a small-town newspaper these days. It couldn't be much, surely. The *Gazette* was a once-weekly paper, otherwise online only. It couldn't have much circulation.

Buying a newspaper so you could fire someone because they were mean to your boyfriend was probably only likely to make people talk about Jeff in bigger papers, though. Maybe he could have a word with the editor instead. Or with Mrs. Bially. She'd tear a strip off someone for sure.

Remind me to cancel my subscription to the Gazette, *and tell your campers I'll do "Heavenly Bodies" for them next time I'm in town.*

J

Jeff went to bed in a decent mood, thinking of his inevitable reunion with Carter and fantasizing about a private getaway when neither of them had to work.

He woke up to a text that pushed the good mood right into the gutter. *Winnie was spotted this morning with only one cub. Tracker's not working.*

No doubt Carter was taking that personally, and he couldn't even go out and look for the missing one. *Oh no. :(Are they old enough to leave their mother?*

He was pretty sure he already knew the answer.

Not til next spring.

Shit. *I'm sorry. I hope it turns up.*

Alive, Jeff didn't add.

Later, after the band had eaten and gone over the day's itinerary, Jeff had a few free minutes when he figured Carter might be on lunch break. But when he called, it went to voicemail. He hung up without leaving a message.

Jeff hadn't heard back from him by the time they left for soundcheck. Joe had seemingly recovered from straining his voice, and he sounded almost back to normal. Trix didn't rush to the bathroom even one time. Max and Jeff got halfway through a song, met eyes, and finished it out before they both rushed for the comp book because they'd had the same idea for one of their new songs.

By the time they surfaced from their tweaking and he remembered to check his phone, he only had half an hour before Makeup.

1 missed call

2 unread texts

They were all from Carter.

Nothing yet today, the first one said. *Could be that she was just out of sight.*

The second one said *Charlie wants to know if you're gonna sign my door.*

Jeff smiled. *Sign no. Christen maybe.* He sent that, then glanced at the time and grimaced. *Gotta get ready now, Makeup in 30.* He wanted to add something else—*miss you* or *wish you were here* or something more sentimental—but they didn't seem to be doing that. He didn't want to make Carter feel pressured to come with him on tours. Carter had his own life and his own work he was passionate about.

Anyway, it wasn't like Carter could possibly not know how Jeff felt about him. Literally anyone who listened to the radio knew.

So he turned off his phone and went to grab a quick shower.

"Blood in the Water" went fine—not Jeff's personal best performance, but the thing about performing live was every show was different. That was kind of the point.

Jeff's earpiece crapped out in the middle of the second song after an eardrum-piercing feedback shriek, and he floundered for two measures because it took him that long to find the beat of the music under the ambient noise from the venue.

The techs got him a backup piece before the next song, but Jeff was rattled. It shouldn't have fazed him; that sort of thing had happened all the time when they were starting out and had shittier equipment. Back then he never would've missed a note.

He'd gotten soft.

The crowd laughed when Jeff explained, apologetically, "Amazing how easy it is to take for granted that the tiny speaker in your ear won't start screaming at any moment." He glanced over his shoulder at Joe. "Do we dare try something else?"

The next song went smoothly, and Jeff had just about put the earpiece incident behind him. Then Joe tripped over a cord that should've been taped down. He didn't fall, thank God.

Near the end of the first set, as Jeff was starting to relax again, Max started acting strangely.

First he was just slow on the changes. Then he nearly wandered off the side of the stage. By the time Jeff realized he was drunk or high, they were halfway through a song.

Max had a problem. Jeff knew that. But in ten years, it had never interfered with their jobs. As far as Jeff knew, he'd never used before or during a show. Why would he start now?

Jeff caught eyes with Joe, who looked just as worried as Jeff felt. He couldn't spend too much time looking at Trix, because that would put his back to the audience. Instead he headed toward Max, still playing, to share his microphone for some of the harmony, and managed to surreptitiously—he hoped—turn the volume down on the guitar.

Jeff took over the rhythm guitar part until the outro, when he switched back to lead.

Then Trix cued the tech crew to bring the lights down one song early. Jeff yanked out their patch cords and looped Max's arm around his neck. "Come on, buddy, let's get you backstage for a minute."

Trix met them just behind the stage, worry writ large over her features. "What the hell is going on tonight?"

Jeff deposited Max in a chair and handed his guitar off to a tech. Max slouched to one side but didn't fall off, conscious but woozy. "I don't know," Jeff said grimly. "But this is ridiculous. Have we just lived such a charmed life that the law of averages is catching up with us, or what?"

Had Max been using during shows this whole time and he'd just gotten very good at hiding it? That would fucking figure, if the wheels were about to fall off now, with four shows to go in the tour.

Jeff, Joe, and Trix looked at each other. Then they turned to Max.

Finally Trix stepped forward and knelt next to the chair. "Hey, Max. You seem kind of out of it. Are you okay?"

"I didn't, I didn't." He blinked slowly, then finally managed to finish. "I didn't take anything. I swear."

Trix looked up at Jeff and shook her head. "I think he's telling the truth. This isn't… he doesn't get like this. He gets loud, manic. You've seen him."

Unfortunately. Max was more likely to attempt a double back handspring than sway onstage and nearly fall off it. And now he was listing so far it didn't seem like he'd be able to stay on his chair.

Joe took a step forward, gently touched Max's wrist, and then yanked his hand back. "Jesus. He's burning up."

"I don't feel so good," Max groaned and clutched at his stomach.

Jeff had just enough presence of mind to reach down and yank Trix to her feet before Max leaned over the side of the chair and barfed all over the floor, spattering their shoes.

"Fuck!" Joe jumped back in surprise. "Okay, get the on-site EMTs down here," he said to a nearby tech, who nodded and touched her headset. "You think it's, like… the flu?"

"It's June," Trix protested. She took a step back as the EMTs arrived. "So probably not the flu, but what if… I mean, I thought I had food poisoning, but…."

Before Jeff could answer, one of the EMTs stepped in. "We've seen a few cases like this. There's a nasty norovirus going around." She grimaced as Max groaned again, and she and her partner got him on the backboard. "This is the worst case I've seen, though, if that's what it is. He needs the hospital for sure."

That just figured. And of course now Jeff and Joe had been exposed too, not to mention the tech and whatever poor custodian got stuck cleaning up.

"All right. Shit." Jeff took a step back and looked around. "Where the fuck's Tim? We need a game plan."

He showed up just as the EMTs were ready to take Max to the waiting ambulance. "What happened?" He looked at the stretcher, then at the vomit, and came to the predictable conclusion. "Don't fucking tell me—"

"They think it's a virus," Jeff said impatiently. "Apparently there's a stomach bug going around. That must've been what Trix had yesterday."

Before he could find a way to make it about him, Trix jumped in. "Someone needs to go with Max to the hospital." She looked at Tim and crossed her arms. "And someone needs to figure out if we're finishing this concert and how."

Jeff mimicked her posture. On his other side, so did Joe.

Finally Tim raised his hands. "All right, all right. I'll go with him."

Good, Jeff thought. *That's your fucking job.*

"I'll see if Erica can step in for him," Trix said, gesturing toward one of the techs. "Text me updates."

Tim stalked off after the EMTs, already on his phone.

As soon as he was out of earshot, Joe said, "Why have we put up with him for this long?"

"'Cause we signed a stupid fucking contract that tied us to him when we were barely more than children." At the time, they'd jumped at the chance to skip a step—they should've gotten a manager first and then that person should've been their advocate at a label. Instead Tim was a corporate shill who took advantage of them for his own gain. Jeff blew out a breath. "Okay, uh, first things first—I think we should all go wash our hands and possibly take some vitamin C?"

Joe looked up as a custodian came trundling down the hallway with a cart. "Hey, man, thanks for coming. What's your name?"

The custodian blinked in surprise at being addressed directly by the talent. "Uh, it's Kyle."

"Kyle, I'm Joe, this is Jeff and Trix. We just want to tell you I think the guy who threw that up is probably contagious with a stomach bug, so if you've got a face mask and extrathick gloves or something, uh, you probably want to use them."

"Thanks, yeah." Kyle withdrew a paper mask from one of the compartments on the cleaning cart. "Always be prepared."

Jeff made a mental note to find a way to tip him before he left. "Awesome. Okay, we're gonna go… decontaminate."

A quick wardrobe change later, Jeff led a very subdued group back onto the stage. Between their concern for Max and their substitute guitarist, they never did recover the energy. Jeff would've rated their performance a C+ at best.

Naturally the tabloids would be all over Max leaving the concert too. It wouldn't matter that he was feverish and dehydrated. He had a history of drug abuse. That was all trashy websites needed to generate clicks.

He was already pissed when he returned to the green room, so when he opened the door to find Tim—who should've been at the hospital—holding Jeff's phone, Jeff went nuclear.

"What the fuck do you think you're doing?"

Tim swore and fumbled the phone. It fell to the floor.

"First of all, that's mine," Jeff said. "And I'll be asking for your pathetic excuse of a lie in a minute. But more importantly, why aren't you at the hospital?"

Half a second later, he felt Trix and Joe behind him. "What's going on?"

"Tim was just about to explain why he's not with Max," Jeff said, deadly calm now. "Considering he left here with a high fever and barely conscious."

Tim huffed. "Max is fine. When I left he was sitting in the ER with an IV drip, waiting for admitting."

Alone, in a hospital, where the doctors might not know about his history of drug use. Where no one would know the contact information for his family if he lost consciousness. Fantastic. Jeff strode across the room and picked his phone up from the floor.

The screen glowed with a request for his password.

He gritted his teeth. "This was off when I left it."

What if Tim had cracked his password? Jeff didn't doubt for a second that he'd go through all Jeff's messages looking for leverage. Anything he could find in order to force Howl to sign another shitty contract once this one was up. Anything to keep them under his thumb.

Jeff didn't have anything about Trix's past in there, but he couldn't remember everything on his phone. Eventually Tim would have found something he could use—something someone had said out of context, a sext from an old boyfriend.

His stomach turned. What if Carter had sent something? Jeff would do anything to protect him from the fallout a dick pic would bring. And doubtless there were a few on Jeff's phone if you looked hard enough—not Carter's, but he didn't exactly expect Tim to be truthful about it.

"The fuck," Trix said. "Should I call Security?"

Tim bristled and reached for his ID badge. "You can't—"

"No," Joe interrupted. "I think Jeff should call his lawyer."

That sounded like a better idea. "On the way to the hospital," Jeff decided. "Max shouldn't be alone. He should know we have his back."

Chapter Fifteen

JEFF UNLOCKED his phone as Trix called a cab. No new text messages, but he did have an email from Carter:

I'll give you $20 if you cover "Rock Star" instead.

Despite the gravity of the situation, Jeff smiled. But that faded after a moment too, when he thought about what it might be like for Carter to exist in a world where all the songs Jeff wrote about wanting him played on the radio and everyone knew they were about him.

Jeff admitted to himself with a mounting sense of guilt that it might be awkward. At least the newer songs were full of love and longing. He didn't need to write any more teenage sex fantasies, subtle or overt, when the actual real-life experiences went so far beyond anything he could've imagined.

He could probably even convince Trix and Max to pare them out of the setlist too. And Joe would understand.

It was late in Toronto, but maybe having an expensive lawyer on retainer meant they'd take your calls at all hours, or maybe she was just still awake.

"My favorite rock star," she said. He could just picture her in her uptown high-rise office, drinking a glass of wine with her feet up and watching the lights through the floor-to-ceiling window. "What can I do for you, Jeff?"

He exhaled slowly as he marshaled his thoughts. He didn't want to come across as reactionary or overly emotional. He was fed up with Tim's machinations and he wanted them to stop. But if they could use that behavior to get out of their contract, so much the better. "Max caught some kind of virus and had to go to the hospital. Tim was supposed to be with him, but when we got offstage, I caught him in the green room with my phone. It was off when I left to play the concert and he'd turned it on. I'm pretty sure he was trying to get into it."

"That's a serious accusation," she said, but her voice was level. "I don't suppose you have proof."

"Not unless the green room's under surveillance, which I doubt." He glanced beside himself at Trix. "Joe and Trix were there, but they didn't see anything until he dropped the phone. And there'd be no way to prove what he was trying to do with it anyway."

A keyboard clacked in the background. "Now you're thinking like a lawyer. We have a couple options here. Do you have a minute to talk?"

"Uh, one sec." Jeff muted the mic and asked the driver, "How long to the hospital?"

He glanced at the GPS. "Thirteen minutes."

Jeff went back to the call. "Yeah, I've got some time."

"Great. I'll get down to it." More clicking. "No proof means we don't have a lot of wiggle room to file a criminal complaint. You could try something in civil court. I'd have to look closer at your contract; there might be a loophole he could use. But that would take years, and in the meantime, you're suffering. Or we just document all the shit he's put you through and take it to the label and say, 'Fix this.'"

Frowning, Jeff tapped the fingers of his free hand against his knee. "That doesn't sound all that useful."

"That's because you're not looking at it from a PR perspective." There was a creak and then a thud, as though she'd just rotated her chair and taken her feet down off her desk. "The last thing a label like that needs is a scandal from a huge star alleging poor treatment. But I might actually have a better idea."

Hope? Was that the strange, tiny, slightly buoyant feeling rising in his chest? He cleared his throat. "Oh?"

"I mean, a properly worded document from me outlining your issues with Tim lets them know we're holding a trump card—that you're willing to talk about the reason you're dragging your feet on the album, which will hurt their chances of signing other talent. That's a solid backup plan if you don't like this one."

"Okay." He nodded automatically. "That seems… I mean, that gets me out of dealing with Tim the fastest. I'm pretty sure he was looking for something he could use for blackmail in my phone, so the sooner he's out of my life, the happier I'll be. So what's the other idea?"

"I need time to put that together, and we can only talk about it if you get the whole group to agree that leaving Big Moose is what you want to do. *Don't* talk to anyone else about it, okay? It's the kind of thing where, if the label gets word of it, they're likely to ruin things. In the meantime, as a backup plan, can you email me a detailed list of your grievances? Ask the other band members if they have anything to add. I can get on it first thing tomorrow if you send it tonight. Okay?"

It sounded like it actually might be, one day in the future. "Yeah. Thanks, Monique." He didn't want to get too into the details in a car where the driver could overhear.

By the time they arrived at the hospital, Max had been moved to a room and was sitting up in bed, pale but lucid and conscious. "Hey," he said when they came in. "Wow, are visiting hours not a thing anymore?"

"Jeff charmed the charge nurse," Trix said. "He had to sign her boobs and promise we'd be out of here in ten minutes, though."

That was a slight exaggeration—no autographs had been exchanged—but whatever. It made Max laugh weakly. "She knew she was barking up a sunflower, right?"

Jeff rolled his eyes. "Funny." But he was glad Max felt well enough to joke. "What've they got you on, anyway?"

He wanted to take the words back as soon as they came out, but before he could extract his foot from his throat, Max answered. "Something for the fever, plus IV fluids and some kind of painkiller? I think. I had a wicked headache. I'm probably gonna pass out soon."

"We won't keep you up," Joe said. "You scared the shit out of us, though. I thought you were gonna fall off the stage."

Trix sat next to the bed. "Why didn't you say you weren't feeling well?"

For just a second, something dark passed across Max's face. "I don't know, I just… I thought I could play through it. Guess not." He grimaced. "I hope I didn't get any of you sick."

Joe and Trix exchanged glances. Then Trix said, "We actually think I might've given it to you. I guess Joe and Jeff are going to be watching themselves the next couple days."

Hooray.

"Echinacea and vitamin C cocktails," Joe said dryly. His voice sounded hoarse again. Jeff hoped it was the same vocal strain he'd been dealing with all week. "Washed down with lemon-honey tea. The glamorous life of a rock star."

"Better than an IV," Max pointed out.

The charge nurse came by then to kick them out, because Jeff really *had* only negotiated for ten minutes. Trix handed Max his phone and he thanked them, and then they walked down to the lobby.

"Well. What next?" They were supposed to be driving to Edmonton overnight on the bus, but they couldn't leave without Max. And Jeff didn't want to be on a bus with Tim. They had a day off between concerts. They didn't have to leave tonight.

"I'll book us hotel rooms," Joe offered.

"I'll figure out where our stuff is."

Trix blew out a sigh, then gestured at the pharmacy down the street. "I'll go find you guys some immune boosters."

IN THE morning he remembered he needed to talk to Carter. First, though, he lay in bed and took stock of his body—no strange feeling in his stomach, no fever, no strange aches or pains.

Maybe he'd escaped norovirus.

A quick trip to the bathroom, and then he grabbed his phone and sat against the headboard, listening to the rings.

Carter picked up on the third. "I read the news. Are you okay? What happened?"

Right—it was later in Ontario. Carter had probably seen something about Max's sudden disappearance from the show this morning. "Max caught norovirus. Stomach flu, basically, except he was stupidly feverish and didn't tell anyone and almost fell off the stage." Even now Jeff felt drained from the ordeal, and he wasn't even the one who was sick. "The hospital kept him overnight, but he texted this morning to say they're discharging him around noon."

"I'm glad he's all right. But are *you* okay?"

Jeff opened his mouth to say yes, but the lie wouldn't come. "Honestly?" He plucked at the bed covers. "I don't think I caught norovirus, at least. But I'm…." *Fuck.* He wasn't supposed to tell Carter anything was amiss. But a few of the details wouldn't hurt, right? "I caught Tim trying to break into my phone, basically, and I'm worried about Max, and…." And he was making everything about him. "It's kind of a lot to handle. Distract me, would you? Did you find your bear?"

Carter sighed. "Not yet. That's not so unusual, though. We don't get sightings every day. I just worry."

No surprise there. Carter was always soft like that. "What about everything else?" Jeff frowned. Their time in Vancouver seemed so long ago already. "You were doing something for your friend—Emily?"

"Oh—yeah, that's a… I mean, we make jokes about government inefficiency, but if you knew the truth, you'd probably become a libertarian."

Jeff barked out a startled laugh. "I doubt it, but I can imagine. I take it it's, uh, not going well?"

Carter hummed. "It's going okay, really, just getting multiple people at multiple different parks—national and provincial—to collect the same data and then put that data in the same place and make it accessible to people who want to use it for science is apparently more of an undertaking than I realized."

What a surprise that he'd bitten off more than any reasonable person would chew. Jeff leaned back and tilted his head toward the ceiling. "You know you're supposed to be recovering from breaking a bone, right? Not finding more work for yourself?"

"I like working." Stubborn. "Besides, this is… I don't know. It's not what I thought I'd do with my life, but it feels a little more important than lecturing tourists about littering."

Jeff knew Carter's job was more than that, but that wasn't the point. The point was that Jeff worried too, largely about Carter's pathological inability to actually relax. But saying *please slow down before you work yourself into an early grave the same as your father* would be unforgivably cruel. Jeff disliked himself for so much as thinking it.

He'd have to come up with a way to approach the problem from another angle. In the meantime he just said, "It's good that you're doing it. It *is* important."

"Thanks."

Before Jeff could say anything else, his phone beeped, and he checked the call ID. "That's my lawyer calling, sorry. Following up on the whole Tim thing. Call you later?"

"Obviously. Tell Max get well soon from me."

Jeff smiled. "Thanks, I will."

As usual, Monique got right to the point. "Jeff. Did you get a consensus from the group?"

He exhaled, nodding. "Yeah. I think they were already unhappy with the pace and the pressure and the whole contract… situation." They'd signed young, and their cut of royalties wasn't what it should have been, and they didn't have an advocate for their own interests. "But seeing how Tim treated Max and his invasion of my privacy—they're on board."

"Good. Like I said, this can't leave the group or the deal will be dead in the water. I'm talking injunctions, lawsuits, blackballing—they will make your lives hell. But I've found a way to get you out of your contract."

Jeff's breath caught. "Seriously?"

"Here's the thing. When you signed your extension, they forgot to update your exit clause. You were already big. You know what the penalty is now?"

"Enough." They could afford it if the other band members had saved the same way he had, but he knew Max hadn't and he wasn't sure about Trix. Jeff could pay it only because he'd written and recorded songs outside of their contract with Big Moose, but doing so would wipe out his savings. "It's not a practical option."

Monique hummed. "Not for you, maybe. But for a competitor label?"

Oh. Jeff licked his lips, intrigued now. "How would that work?"

"That's the tricky part. I'd rather explain it to all of you at once. In the meantime, do you want to talk about the red herring? I think you'll like it."

Whatever Jeff was paying her, she had earned every cent. "God, yes."

"So the label's calling Tim back to Toronto. They're going to send someone else out with an NDA. Don't sign it until I've looked at it and okayed it."

A weight Jeff had been carrying for years seemed to vanish from his shoulders. "*Seriously*?"

"Seriously," she said. "After what he pulled, he'll be expecting something. If we do nothing, it's actually more suspicious. And if you're taking action against Tim specifically, and you act satisfied with that, they won't expect the follow-up. You've got some leverage at the moment, so any requests for who they do or don't send in his place? I don't know who you've worked with."

He only needed to think about it for a second. "Dina—I think her last name is Youssef? She's sort of Tim's underling, but she's good otherwise. She knows us." And if he could force the label to promote her, so much the better.

"Got it." In the background, her keyboard click-clacked. "I have a few details I want to finalize before I talk to the group, but just hold tight. This is going to work."

"*Thank* you," Jeff said. He wasn't going to put himself through another Tim. He hung up feeling lighter than he had in weeks.

Word came through Monique that Dina would meet them in Edmonton, and then Trix got a call from Max that he'd been sprung. By early afternoon they were on the highway heading north, Max dozing in his bunk, Trix deeply engrossed in Animal Crossing. Jeff played a couple hands of Speed with Joe, but about an hour into the drive his phone started buzzing constantly in his pocket, and finally it was too much of a distraction and Joe beat him.

"Best five out of seven?" Joe smirked.

Jeff pulled his phone out and checked it—four texts from Carter.

Maybe Joe saw it in his face, because when he said, "Rain check?" his voice was very dry.

Flashing a grateful smile, Jeff climbed into his own bunk—literally climbed; his was above Max's—and drew the thick curtain. It wouldn't give him total privacy, but it did a fair job muffling sound if he wanted to have a phone call.

The first message from Carter read *Second bear sighting. Only one cub.*

Shit. That wasn't good, but it was followed by *False alarm, apparently that was Tutu with her cub.*

Who was naming these bears? Jeff made a note to ask if Carter had named that one too.

The third message read *Why do I suddenly have 1000 new Twitter followers?*

And—that, okay, that was concerning. Jeff didn't even know Carter *had* Twitter. Honestly it seemed like something he'd hate.

You don't even follow me! was the last message. *How did they find it?*

Well… that was easily answered. Jeff tabbed over to Chrome, typed *Carter Rhodes Twitter* into the search bar, and screencapped the result. Then he pasted it into a text message.

We released your name as part of the announcement. Remember? You were going to lock down your Facebook page?

For almost thirty seconds he got nothing more than three blinking dots. Then: *Ah.* Followed by *What do I do now?*

Jeff opened Twitter just for the hell of it. He winced—there was more than one tweet about last night's performance and how bad it was, not to mention speculation on what drugs Max had taken and whether the norovirus line was a coverup.

And then there was a tweet he was tagged in that answered all his questions.

Okay, was anyone going to tell me @jeffpineHOWL's new side of beef is an actual honest to god forest ranger, or was I supposed to find that out by myself?

The tweet quoted Carter's personal account, which had retweeted the official park account's picture of him in uniform handling… was that a baby opossum?

He took another screenshot and sent that too.

SIDE OF BEEF????? Carter replied.

That shirt is kinda tight, Jeff pointed out. *Not a criticism btw.*

I'm a naturalist! he complained. Then, *Now what?*

Jeff rolled his eyes. *Locking your Twitter is a thing.* He should probably do it soon, though, because that tweet already had over five hundred retweets and it had only been posted half an hour ago. *Or you could lean into it.* Carter's Twitter handle was @crhodesbearlake. Like, if he wanted people to be able to internet stalk him—or, frankly, real-life stalk him—he couldn't have made it easier. *Change your name to @smokeybearlake and start posting educational videos.*

Funny.

Jeff thought so.

LESSON SIX
Let Go

THERE'S A reason they call it falling in love. Not *climbing* in love, not *careful and gradual descent* into love. Falling. A terrifying, uncontrolled, unintentional downward movement.

But there's that moment before you hit the air, when you're teetering on the edge, arms windmilling. There's that stretched-out second when you know you could go back. You could dig your fingers into the cliff face and walk away intact.

And sure, you don't want to let go without having some reasonable hope that things will work out the way you want them to.

On the other hand, you can't expect someone else to jump if you're not willing to fall yourself.

Easier said than done, though, right?

Chapter Sixteen

EDMONTON WENT better than Calgary. Neither Max nor Joe was 100 percent, but they were both improving. They fussed with the set list to give Joe's voice more of a break and made sure Max stayed hydrated, and if it wasn't a great show, at least Jeff didn't feel like he had to avoid Twitter.

Which turned out to be a good thing, because the overnight drive from Edmonton to Winnipeg was long and Jeff was too anxious over the potential of getting out of their record contract to sleep for more than a few hours on the bus, and catching up on Twitter early the next morning led to an incredible discovery.

@smokeybearlake started following you.

Jeff almost hit his head on the top of the bunk. "Oh my God."

Max must not have been asleep either, because he poked his head out the side of the bunk. "What?"

Half hanging over the side of his bunk, Jeff hit the Play button on his phone and handed it down so Max could watch the video—posted to Great Bear Lake's official Twitter account—of Carter in full Public Service Announcement mode, describing the importance of not transporting firewood from areas with emerald ash borer, how to build a campfire, and how to put it out again safely.

The video had a thousand likes. Carter's quoted tweet of it from his personal account had fifteen hundred.

Max laughed quietly so as not to wake the others. "That is the most wholesome shit I've ever seen. Tell me he's not Dudley Do-Right all the time."

With a cough, Jeff pulled his phone back up. "No comment?"

This time Max had to muffle his laughter in a pillow.

Jeff went back to Twitter and followed @smokeybearlake. Then he texted Carter. *Trying to get more famous than me???*

This was your idea, Carter pointed out.

You should do the next one shirtless.

They made it into Winnipeg around lunchtime and checked into their hotel. Max and Jeff had adjoining rooms, which Jeff discovered when he dropped his bag on the chair next to the bed only to hear a knock from his left.

Jeff opened the door and Max poked his head in. "Huh. My room's way nicer than yours."

"What?" Jeff pushed past him into Max's room… which was a mirror image of his own.

"Made ya look."

Ugh. "I can't believe I fell for that. You're the worst."

Max was still laughing when Jeff closed the door in his face. He fell into bed and woke up three hours later to a text from Dina. *Managed to rent practice space for tonight*, followed by the address and details.

THANK YOU, Jeff replied, all caps, because they really did need to get to work on writing that album.

He really needed to find them a manager like her. Maybe then he wouldn't feel so paranoid all the time.

A quick rinse later, Joe and Trix had given a thumbs-up to meeting in the lobby, but Max hadn't responded.

Probably still sleeping, he sent the group chat. *He's got the room next to me, I'll get him.*

He toweled off his face and hair, threw on a pair of jeans, and then rummaged through his bag for a T-shirt. He frowned when he spotted one he didn't remember… and pulled it out only to discover it was Carter's T-ball shirt.

He ran his thumb over the letters of *Rhodes's Garage* and smiled. Had Carter left this in Jeff's bag on purpose?

Feeling sappy, Jeff pulled it on, shoved his feet into his shoes, and knocked on their adjoining doors.

No answer.

"Max?"

Jeff opened his side. Max's wasn't latched, just most of the way closed. "Max?" he called again as he pushed the door open. "Are you in—"

His heart stopped.

On the floor in front of the coffee table sat Max, hunched over with his arms around his knees. He was staring fixedly in front of him at three long white lines. A small bag of powder and a razorblade lay next to them.

For several long heartbeats, Jeff couldn't speak. His tongue felt thick in his mouth. Finally he whispered, "Max?"

Max blinked slowly. He didn't move except to raise his head the tiniest increment. His eyes looked hollowed-out and desperate.

Carefully, Jeff lowered himself to the floor on the opposite side of the table. His heart thudded painfully against his ribs. "Max, buddy, what's going on?"

Max took a deep, shuddering breath, then let it all out, heavily enough that some of the coke blew across the table. In the back of his mind, Jeff knew he was fucked if anyone found them like this, but he couldn't leave Max. Not now. "I…." Max swallowed and put his hands over his face, digging the heels of his palms into his eye sockets. His shoulders shook, but he didn't make a sound.

Finally he pulled his hands away. His voice cracked when he said, "I think I need to go to rehab."

Relief washed through Jeff like a tsunami, leaving his eyes wet, but grief rendered him speechless. A lump formed in his throat, and he swallowed around it. "Max—"

"I saw it," Max said. "When I was sick onstage, I know you guys thought—I've never used before a show. I've wanted to, God, but I never. I wouldn't do that to you. Because you're my friends." He clenched his hands into fists. "And then I thought, 'Max, you fucking asshole, of course they think you'd do that.' I stole from you. I stole from your *boyfriend*. I made you and Trix and Joe clean up my messes. And ever since then, all I can think about is…."

Three lines of coke.

Jeff wiped a hand over his mouth. "What…." He stopped to clear his throat. "What do you want to do?"

He couldn't go on like this.

"I don't know. Not…." He waved a hand to indicate the table. "I don't want to leave the band. But I think maybe the band is leaving without me. I think maybe it should."

Fuck. Jeff's eyes burned again, but he blinked it back. "It's not because of you."

"It's not *not* because of me," Max countered. "Look. I heard you and Joe talking, so I know…. He's got other things to worry about."

Jeff opened his mouth to correct him, but Max went on as though he didn't care.

"And Trix? You think drummers like her come around every day? She thinks I don't know, but she's been talking to some other women in music. They're stupid if they don't ask her to sign on, and she'd do it in a fucking heartbeat if it weren't for me." His face twisted in a rictus of misery. "Because she thinks it's her fault I'm like this."

Swallowing, Jeff reached into his pocket for his phone. This seemed like the time to have some backup. It buzzed in his hand, now, but he didn't want to draw attention to it. He left it where it was. "Trix knows…." What? That Max didn't blame her? That it wasn't really her fault?

"Does she?" Max asked. He didn't give Jeff time to respond. "And you. You keep asking for more time off. I get it. I do. God knows the only reason I've been able to keep up this long has been going up my nose."

This wasn't how Jeff wanted things to go. He'd really thought…. He didn't know what he'd been thinking. Joe needed a year or more off, realistically, or else a complete rethinking of their usual touring style, and Max needed to flush his system.

Trix—maybe some time away from them would be good for her.

And Jeff?

Jeff loved the stage. He loved the music. He loved his band.

But that wasn't all he loved.

He never thought he'd be sitting on the floor in Max's hotel room, watching him *not* do drugs, when he finally realized his band was going to fall apart.

That maybe Monique couldn't save them.

His heart sank as he realized the depth of his own failure. Max had always been there to support him when Jeff needed it most, and Jeff had flaked when Max needed him to return the favor.

That ended now.

Jeff cleared his throat and gestured at the table. "Do you, um—if I get rid of this, are you going to go through withdrawal?" But maybe that was the wrong question, or the right question but the wrong priority. "I mean, we can get you into a place before the show. What do you want to do?"

In his pocket, his phone buzzed again. The window for the two of them to act without Trix and Joe finding out was closing. And God knew Dina didn't need to deal with this on her second official day as their tour manager.

"Flush it," Max said all at once. "I want it out of here. But I can't—you'll have to do it. Sorry."

As if Jeff cared about that. He jumped up and glanced toward the bathroom. He didn't want to let Max out of his sight in case he changed his mind, but… at some point he had to trust him.

Max hadn't locked his door. Hadn't even closed it. Jeff had knocked.

Max had wanted Jeff to find him. He wanted Jeff to stop him. Jeff figured that was more reassurance than most people got.

In the end he grabbed a washcloth, wet it, then pulled the bag out of the garbage can and brought that with him. He swept the neat lines into the can, then emptied the little plastic bag in as well. In the bathroom again, he pulled Carter's shirt over his nose and closed his eyes as he gently ran a slow stream of water into the can.

Then he tipped the whole thing into the toilet and flushed.

The liner went back in the bin. The washcloth went in the garbage.

After a moment's thought, he put the garbage can in his room and brought his own to Max's.

Then he washed his hands with soap and water all the way up to his elbows.

He must have taken too long, because before he'd dried them, Joe and Trix showed up at the door.

Knock knock knock. "Max? Jeff? Are you guys in here?"

Wetting his lips, Jeff poked his head back into the main room. Max hadn't moved. "Hey," he said quietly. "What do you want me to do?"

For a moment Max didn't move, but then he exhaled shakily and rubbed his hands over his face. "Let them in," he said quietly. "I want to tell them the truth."

NEEDLESS TO say, practice did not happen.

Instead, Trix and Joe and Jeff and Max piled into the same bed, the way they had when they were too broke to afford two hotel rooms, and called Jeff's lawyer.

"You're sure you're all on board with leaving," she verified. "And you're willing to keep the rest of this conversation to yourselves only."

They all met eyes, each sitting cross-legged on their own corner of the bed. One by one, they nodded.

"We're sure," Trix said. "What do we have to do?"

Monique outlined the plan. "If you're all in agreement, then for the sake of this arrangement, I'll act in the capacity of your manager. We'll need to sign paperwork to that effect before anything goes forward, but I've found a competitor label willing to pay the exit penalty on your contract."

Max looked at Trix, and before Jeff could explain, she said, "That means they'd pay the fee for not delivering the final album."

"Why would they do that?" Joe smoothed back his hair. "I mean, it's a lot of money."

"It is," Monique agreed. "It is, essentially, an enormous advance on your next album and tour. Which means they'll only do it if you can deliver an album to them—the album that should be going to Big Moose—before that due date. And they'll want at least one guaranteed album after that."

"And we'll have to tour again," Trix said, looking at Jeff.

He winced. He'd been hoping for something that would let them put that off longer, something that would give them time to recover. Time for Joe to be a dad. Maybe Trix could get some therapy.

Perhaps Monique understood that disappointment, because she said, "Yes. However, they're willing to sit on the start of the next tour. It would begin next summer, with some promotion gearing up in the spring, most of which could be coordinated from Toronto."

Jeff looked at Joe, who looked at Max, who looked at Trix. Trix and Jeff met eyes.

"That sounds… doable," Jeff said.

Trix nodded in agreement. "Yeah. Except, uh, the album's due at the end of August."

"Not anymore," Monique told her. "We need it by the end of July. Just for insurance."

Oh great, no pressure, then. Seven weeks. Plenty of time… if Max wouldn't be missing several of them for rehab. Jeff glanced at Max, then Joe, then Trix. Joe blew out a breath and said, "Okay. I think we can make that work."

At least they had a bit of a head start.

Then Monique dropped the next bomb. "Good. Here's the next thing. Don't do any work where the label is paying for the space."

Shit. Jeff was really glad now he'd upgraded the hotel room in Vancouver at his own expense. "Okay?"

"It's a long shot, but they could claim that renting practice space counts as investing in the final product. We don't want them to have a leg to stand on. So wherever this gets written, wherever you record the demo, you do it on your own dime. Preferably somewhere the label won't find out about it, to forestall legal shenanigans."

Now that would be tricky. There was no way to know which employees at the recording spaces they usually rented were in contact with people at the label. Something could come up at any time. So nothing in the city, then.

"I think I have an idea," Jeff said after a moment. "Let me call you about it later, though, okay?"

Max cleared his throat. "In the meantime, can you look into something else?"

When they hung up, they cued up *101 Dalmatians* on hotel pay-per-view. Jeff had Dina cancel their practice rental.

Then they ordered an obscene amount of room service and settled in.

"You're sure you're okay playing tomorrow," Trix asked for maybe the third time.

"I'll be fine," Max promised, closing his eyes. His beef lo mein noodles slid off his chopsticks, and he cursed. "Just don't leave me alone."

They were actually pretty lucky, Jeff thought, that they'd accidentally gotten adjoining rooms.

He didn't pick up his phone again until Max and Trix were in bed for real, curled up facing each other, talking quietly. Then he retreated to his own room, but he didn't close the adjoining doors all the way.

He missed Carter. He wanted nothing more than to call and tell him everything—Joe's impending fatherhood, Max's journey to sobriety, the potential dissolution of the past ten years of Jeff's life.

But that wasn't a conversation to have on the phone. Carter had enough on his plate with healing, helping his mom, coaching T-ball, saving the environment. Jeff wasn't going to be one more problem for him to solve, one more drain on his mental and emotional resources.

With the door open, he couldn't even sext, so he couldn't be a physical drain either. Talk about a bad time.

I miss you, Jeff wrote. He stared at the words for a moment but didn't hit Send. Finally he added *See you in two days* and sent it.

He was almost asleep when the reply came, and he squinted at the bright light from his phone now that his eyes were accustomed to darkness.

I'll be here.

Article from *Winnipeg Lifestyle* website
June 9
Howling Good Time

EVERY ONCE in a while—not often, maybe once a decade or so—you experience an event and you know there's something special about it. Last night's concert at Bell MTS Place was one of those times.

From the moment the curtain went up, Howl held the audience rapt. While frontman Jeff Pine, 30, has long received most of the credit for the band's popularity, penning and voicing the majority of their hits, last night his bandmates displayed every bit as much passion, charisma, and talent. Bassist Joe Kinoshameg had the stadium on its feet during "Water for Oil." Drummer Trix Neufeld led a hair-raising a cappella version of "Gemini."

But it was rhythm guitarist Max Langdon who stole the stage. As a general rule, concerts should not involve silence. When he took center stage to debut "Last Call," you could have heard a pin drop.

"Last Call" was the last number of the evening, an emotional, heartrending ballad utterly unlike Langdon's other work. Taken on its own, it's a beautiful song with a strong depth of feeling and an unforgettable hook.

Taken in context, though—Howl has yet to announce another album, despite the fact that this is the second song to debut onstage this concert cycle and their contract with current label Big Moose Records includes one likely due this summer—it sounds like goodbye.

Chapter Seventeen

BY THE time the prop plane touched down in Willow Sound, Jeff was ready to get on his knees and kiss the dirt.

Not because the flight was long or bumpy or anything like that—but because for the first time in a long time, he felt like—how did the Eagles put it? Like he was already standing on the ground.

This was where he wanted to be.

Well, almost.

He had the vague idea that he didn't have any food left at the cabin, so he swung by the grocery store on the way and picked up a few essentials. On a whim, he also picked up two six-packs of craft beer and a nice bottle of wine. Jeff liked it, even if Carter didn't.

It was tempting to drive to the rangers' station, but he knew Carter had been busy with work, so he went to the cabin instead. He put away the groceries, replaced the sheets on the bed with the ones he'd brought from his condo, and wiped down the thin layer of dust that had accumulated on the counters and kitchen table.

Carter was the first one he texted—*all settled back in at the cabin.* He attached a picture of the beers he'd put on ice in a half-size Igloo cooler.

But after that he went through the whole group. He checked in with Joe about Sarah, who'd had an ultrasound that morning, and got back a surprisingly detailed image of a fetus that was—awesome but also kind of creepy. *Doctor says the baby's healthy.*

That's great!! he texted back.

He texted Trix next. She was meeting up with a couple girlfriends for a spa weekend. She sent him a selfie that involved cucumbers, a face mask, and a glass of champagne.

Nice, Jeff sent back. *Have fun. Remember to hydrate.*

Max was supposed to have no contact with the outside world for the first week of rehab, so Jeff couldn't text him anything. Instead he took a picture of the sun reflecting off the Sound and sent it to Max's email address. Then he leaned back on the picnic table and closed his eyes.

The gentle lapping of the water. The sigh of the breeze through the trees.

The crunch of gravel under tires.

Jeff smiled, eyes still closed, and soaked up the sun for one more minute.

Then the truck door slammed and he turned around.

Carter stood next to the truck, holding the dreaded walking cast in his left hand. Apparently he'd traded it out for the stiff-bottomed Birkenstock the doctor had suggested if driving became unavoidable. Jeff was going to give him shit for that, absolutely, on both fashion and health and safety principles, but, like, not right now. He had other priorities.

"Nice boot," he said pointedly, because Carter was still wearing half his usual ranger footgear. "Wanna—"

"Oh my God," Carter laughed. "Come here and kiss me. I'm not limping all the way over there."

Jeff didn't have to be told twice. With long, hurried strides he crossed the space between them. Then Carter dropped the boot to the ground, wrapped both arms around him, and dragged him into a kiss.

Maybe he shouldn't have—probably Jeff should encourage him to show a little restraint when he wasn't even wearing his walking boot—but Jeff couldn't do anything except enjoy it. Carter was warm and solid against him. He tasted a little like a three-thirty coffee break, and he kissed Jeff like he knew all his secrets and would take them to his grave.

The scent of him filled Jeff's nose—vaguely piney bodywash and the lingering aroma of shaving cream, because apparently he'd cleaned up the edges of his beard just for Jeff. And it all *fit*—Carter's hands at the small of his back, his lips on Jeff's, his tongue in Jeff's mouth, his chest under Jeff's fingers. The warm sun on the side of his face, the breeze off the water, the ground under his feet.

It fit.

But he only allowed himself to indulge for a minute before he broke away, because Carter was not wearing the appropriate footwear for Jeff to swoon in his arms. "Come inside?" he offered. "I got stuff for dinner."

The look Carter gave him, fond and a little wry, said he wasn't fooled. "Dinner, eh?"

"Mm-hmm." Jeff picked up the boot and gestured toward the cabin, trying not to hover as Carter carefully limped along next to him. "What's weird about that?"

Their hands brushed as they walked, and Jeff deliberately slowed his steps to keep time with Carter's. Carter tangled their fingers together. "Kinda thought you were thirsty."

What a loser. Jeff liked him *so much*. "Terrible." He shook his head and opened the door for Carter to precede him into the cabin. "Is that the best you can do?"

Carter didn't bother with subtlety. He went straight to the bed and bent to unlace his boot. Then he kicked it off, leaned back against the pillows, and patted the mattress beside him. "Why don't you come find out?"

So that was how it was going to be. Jeff kicked off his sandals and set the boot down. "Tell me, do you practice those cheesy dad jokes when I'm not around?"

"I know how into that you are," Carter said, casually unbuttoning his shirt without breaking eye contact, "so I figured I'd really spend some time perfecting it and making those videos—"

"Oh my God, you asshole." Jeff had had to muffle some embarrassing noises into his pillow when he'd watched the last one, in which Carter demonstrated the importance of sorting recyclables by making perfect three-point throws into the appropriate bins. He had a feeling Carter was joking, but Jeff *was* into it. He had a *problem*.

"—so you wouldn't forget what you were missing out on." Carter smirked and dropped his shirt on the floor.

If Jeff broke his foot, his muscle tone would disappear in a week, because he would spend his entire life sitting on a couch. Carter looked like he hadn't missed a workout. And he was laid out like a buffet in Jeff's bed, legs a mile long, looking good even with a farmer's tan, eyes daring Jeff to come closer. Tease him back.

Jeff hadn't seen him for a week. He was half-hard from a kiss and watching Carter's lazy strip show, and Carter's dick was tenting his pants. They could tease each other later. *Now*—"Can I fuck you?" he blurted before the words had a chance to pass through any kind of filter.

Carter smirked and put his hands behind his head. "I don't know, can you?"

Well, he'd walked right into that. He pulled off his own shirt. "Take your pants off, oh my God."

They were both naked by the time Jeff joined him on the bed and crawled carefully next to him on his left side to avoid his injured foot. "You have lube around here somewhere, right?" Carter asked, all mock concern.

Did Carter think he jerked off dry? "What's wrong with you?" Jeff asked nonsensically, and then he put his hand on Carter's jaw and caught his lips for a kiss.

It felt sweeter and less desperate than the other times they'd been in bed together, but Jeff didn't have enough data to guess why. He knew he got worked up easily when it came to getting fucked, and Carter obviously enjoyed getting him that way. He couldn't tell if this hazy, lazy, saccharine moment owed its existence to a comparative lack of urgency or if they were both just feeling kind of sappy.

Didn't entirely last, though—by the time Jeff got around to maneuvering between Carter's thighs, he felt plenty urgent. He lifted Carter's right leg with a kiss to the ankle and set it on his shoulder—catching a budding grin from Carter in the process, because Carter was a giant and it really did look ridiculous, but Jeff said, "Don't start" and slid a slick finger into him.

Carter did not start, unless you counted a bitten-off hiss and a sudden arch of his back.

Jeff was still learning to read his body, so he slowed down to pay attention. Carter was hot and tight around him, but there wasn't any tension in his face, and he hadn't gone soft. Good signs, but Jeff didn't get where he was by being satisfied with *good*. He thrust gently, turned his face to kiss Carter's calf again, and hid his smile against his skin when Carter's cock jerked.

Flushed now, Carter looked up at him through hooded eyes, and—

Everything ran together after that—Carter's soft groans of encouragement, the musky scent of sex in the air, the velvet heat of his body around three of Jeff's fingers before Carter handed him a condom. Somehow Jeff put it on. He must have, because moments later he was sinking into Carter, pleasure lighting up his nervous system. His stomach clenched and his mouth dropped open and he wanted to close his eyes, but he needed them open; he was still watching Carter, still reading his cues.

Carter looked completely *gone*. His head had fallen back against the pillows, and the muscles of his stomach were visibly tight, like he was already riding the edge of orgasm. When Jeff could convince his ears to register anything over the rushing of his own blood, he could hear the rough hitches of Carter's breath and the slide of their skin and the gentle thud of the ancient headboard against the log wall.

Jeff couldn't last, not with the way Carter felt around him, beneath him, the hot slide of his body. But he was determined to see Carter lose it first. Somewhere in the rumpled covers, he found the lube. It wasn't easy to get it open one-handed and pour some in his palm when he couldn't take his left hand from Carter's leg, but he managed. His thighs burned from the slow, careful pace he'd set, but he needed to be precise. He'd asked for this and he intended to make it perfect.

Carter's breathing was louder now, and he'd braced his arms on the headboard for leverage to move into Jeff's thrusts. His hair fanned out in a halo on the pillow, and a beautiful flush painted his chest. When Jeff wrapped slick fingers around his dick, his body tensed. It only took a handful of strokes to make him come, openmouthed and breathless, all over his chest and belly and Jeff's hand.

It was too much for Jeff. He tumbled into orgasm, muffling his cry in the crook of Carter's knee.

For several heartbeats Jeff didn't move, just caught his breath and *looked.* Carter's chest was still heaving with exertion, and while Jeff had to appreciate the effort he put into keeping up that muscle definition, now that he was *really* looking, without Carter distracting him with cheesy lines, he could see the dark circles under Carter's eyes. Still biting off more than he should chew, Jeff guessed.

He kissed the inside of Carter's knee again and slowly pulled out, careful to keep the condom in place. If Carter wouldn't take care of himself, Jeff would have to do it until he could. He gingerly eased Carter's leg back to the mattress, then settled next to him on the bed and nosed in for a kiss.

Carter hummed against his mouth with an utter satisfaction that would have made Jeff zillions of dollars if he could figure out how to use it in a song. He smoothed his left hand up Carter's flank, over his chest, to the corner of his jaw, and then let his fingers tangle gently in Carter's hair. He'd never had it this long as a teenager, thank God. Jeff would have chafed his dick right off.

"Turns out, yes," Carter said eventually, when the kiss had broken and Jeff had sunk into the pillow to finish rebooting his brain.

Jeff blinked three times, and then he got it and groaned. He lifted his head. Carter's cheeks were rosy, his lips bitten red, and his eyes were a little glassy. "You're the worst," he said fondly and leaned in for one more kiss. Then he rolled to his feet to get a cloth. "Why do I like you?"

"You have a fetish for dad jokes and park uniforms?" Carter guessed a moment later.

"I do like the way the pants have to beg your thighs for mercy." Jeff disposed of the condom, cleaned himself up, and returned to the bed to wipe Carter down.

"Your face is doing a thing," Carter accused.

Jeff glanced up and took in the pursed twist of his lips. "I don't know what you're talking about." Carter had come spattered all the way up to his shoulder.

Now Carter laughed outright. "You're so *smug*."

"Oh, look who's talking," Jeff scoffed as he tossed the washcloth in the direction of the bathroom. "Mr. Looks Like a Lumberjack, Fucks Like a Porn Star."

Carter cackled. "I should put that in my Twitter bio."

"Can you even say 'fuck'?"

"Not where my mom will see it."

Jeff remembered being a teen, trying to remember to keep it clean around Carter's parents even though Jeff's dad didn't care. He hated being on the receiving end of those disappointed looks. "Do you think I can convince her the radio edited out a bunch of times I said 'fudge,' or has that ship sailed?"

"She's seen you in concert, so I'm afraid you're out of luck. Unless you were on your best behavior that night."

Jeff didn't have a best behavior. "What's plan B?"

Carter snorted and nudged him with his good leg. "Go bring me my boot. I heard you were making dinner."

THE THING was, Jeff knew he and Carter had a lot to talk about. He and the rest of Howl were still working out what they wanted to do—a discussion that essentially had to wait until Max's therapists decided they weren't a threat to his sobriety. He didn't think Carter would particularly care if Jeff went from his rock-star boyfriend to his kind-of-sort-of-unemployed rock-star boyfriend, but he should still tell him.

And then there was—well, he'd told him what went down with Tim, but he hadn't filled him in about Max, or Joe's news. Or that he'd had his lawyer call a Toronto real estate agent. The market for selling a condo could be volatile, but whatever. Jeff had paid cash; he wasn't going to be upside-down on his mortgage or anything.

And he wanted to get up to speed on Carter's life too—he wanted to know if they'd found the bear cub that had chased Jeff under the porch and how the T-ball team was doing with their coach still laid up with a broken foot and if Carter had sorted out the research data problem and how many hours of sleep he was getting a night.

Except of course Carter was still doing too much, especially now that he'd decided it was okay to drive if he wore an ugly sandal, and while Jeff thought he was actually a pretty good communicator most of the time, he felt like he was falling down on the job because neither one of them could keep their hands to themselves.

And then there was the whole thing where selling your condo and moving back to your hometown at thirty because you'd finally admitted to yourself (and anyone who had a working internet connection) that you were in love with your best friend was kind of a huge, terrifying deal. Jeff was pretty confident Carter felt the same—like, sometimes the way he looked at Jeff made Jeff want to pinch himself, because Carter went all-in on the heart eyes—but he didn't *know*.

How did you even say to someone, *By the way, no pressure or anything, but I'm upending my entire life so I can be close to you. Please don't think I'm clingy*?

It wasn't *just* so he could be close to Carter—there were other factors—but still. Communication was important and Jeff was going to make an effort, damn it. So, the day after he got back from Winnipeg, after his welcome-home-from-work kiss had turned into welcome-home-from-work riding Carter on the couch until his legs were jelly, he gingerly repositioned himself—he was going to have to start stretching his hip flexors before sex now—and then rested his head on Carter's shoulder. "Hey. How was your day, honey?"

Okay, maybe his delivery needed some work. Carter laughed silently, and his body shook with it as he tilted his head back on the couch. "Really?"

Jeff was offended. "What?"

Carter slouched down until their heads were touching. He basically had to sprawl halfway across the couch to manage it, because he was offensively tall. "It's getting better all the time."

Jeff took it back; he wasn't offended anymore. "Sweet talker." But he actually wanted a serious answer. "For real, though. I know you're worried about Winnie's cub. I didn't want to ask over the phone…."

Sagging a little more, Carter said, "No news. Winnie's tracker's not working, so we can't just stalk her across the park. It's all wait and see."

Damn. "Sorry." Jeff squeezed his hand. "Sucks."

"Yeah." Carter sighed. "I'd like to go look for her, but I can't exactly scooter around in the wilderness, off-road tires or no. Plus there's"—he waved his hand—"the general clusterfuck that is the national and provincial parks' data collection."

Jeff had heard a few variations on this theme by now, but this time it sounded more pointed. "So that's, like, the fact that not everyone's tracking the same things, or presenting the data in the same way, stuff like that? Or is there more?"

"It's a little more complicated," Carter said. "So, Parks Canada hires ecologists to work in the national parks, and they're responsible for tracking populations and climate change and things like that. Ontario Parks has ecologists too, but there's no real oversight. Everyone's just out there doing their own thing, and none of the data is accessible to anyone. Of course scientists can apply for a research permit to come out and study what interests them on their own, but… the data is already there, so, I mean, it's kind of a waste of everyone's time and resources, and the reason it's a waste—"

"Is because scientists hate sharing data?" Jeff guessed.

Carter snorted. "So you've been paying attention to those rants."

"I'm a good listener." Jeff poked him. "Anyway, go on."

"Right. So I've been building a database of the research, trying to get in touch with someone at every park to contribute. Because climate and ecological science—the whole point is to conserve the natural world. The goal for most of these scientists is the same, and giving them the information will only benefit the parks system in the long run. But it's time-consuming."

"Hence the sleep you're still not getting?"

Carter groaned and hauled himself upright. "Speaking of the sleep I'm not getting." He glanced at his watch. "I'm supposed to coach T-ball in an hour."

Oh for fuck's sake. "You can barely keep your *dick* vertical," Jeff protested.

Carter raised an eyebrow. "You weren't complaining five minutes ago."

Fine. Jeff's remark was uncalled for, but—"Seriously. You look exhausted, babe. Not that you're not still ridiculously good-looking, but maybe this is one thing you can let go, you know?"

"I know," Carter admitted. Jeff almost had a heart attack from shock. "Except that means I have to find someone else to take over, and that's just one more thing to add to my to-do list."

Jeff huffed, thinking of his own to-do list and the ever-shrinking window he had to complete the items on it. "Tell me about it."

And then he had an idea.

Carter went off to shower and change, and Jeff pulled out his cell phone and sent a text message. *Hey so sorry if this comes across as stereotyping*, he said, *but you know how Carter coaches a T-ball team…?*

The reply came a few seconds later: *!!! No I did NOT know. Also, what stereotyping?* Following this, Kara sent a blurry picture of a dusty OV duffel bag with two metal bats looped through the handles.

Jeff smiled. *Do you and Jeri want to meet us at the diamonds in 25? Uh and also maybe I might invite Carter's queer niece?*

Please do!!!!

When they pulled up at the diamond, Carter frowned at the truck parked next to them. "Is that Kara's?"

Jeff cleared his throat. "Yeah. I invited her. Well. I might be attempting to recruit her."

Carter blinked at him, openmouthed, but before he could say anything, there was a spray of gravel as Charlie skidded into the parking lot on their other side.

"And also I did some networking on behalf of the baby queer? Come on, she'd be a cute bat girl, or whatever."

Finally Carter shook his head and unbuckled his seat belt. "Are you planning on swooping in like this to solve all my problems?" he asked, but he sounded reluctantly pleased and not at all resentful.

"Uh, yeah, whenever possible." Jeff nodded enthusiastically. He was getting a huge rush from being a good boyfriend, mostly because he was being a good boyfriend to Carter, who deserved it. "Until you, like, get tired of it or decide it's smothering or whatever."

But he just got a smile and Carter leaning over to kiss him. "Thank you. You might have to tone it down when the boot comes off, but right now I appreciate it. Although where did you get Charlie's number?"

"Your mom." Obviously. He reached for the door handle.

"You're not worried about a twelve-year-old fan having your phone number?"

Jeff paused for a moment and then lifted a shoulder. "I can get a new phone number. I'm more worried about a twelve-year-old fan having plenty of queer role models." It wasn't like he'd given her his email address. *That* would've been a pain. Besides, as Carter had already pointed out, she was used to living with fame. "Anyway, I owe her another guitar lesson. Gotta schedule it somehow."

Charlie greeted Jeff with attempted aloofness, which was pretty adorable. He introduced her to Kara and Jeri as he slung the equipment bag over his shoulder.

"Are we gonna get T-shirts?" Jeri asked, eyeing the way Carter filled out his. Jeff couldn't blame them.

Carter said, "Oh, I think we handed them all out—"

"We can get more printed," Jeff said, linking arms with Kara. "You should cut the sleeves off yours. It'll be hot."

"Read my mind. These kids absolutely need to see my cool tattoos."

Unsurprisingly, Kara and Jeri were a hit with the five-year-olds, and it didn't hurt that they creamed the red team.

"Isn't there supposed to be, like, a mercy rule?" Jeff muttered to Carter, *sotto voce*, as they sat on the bench at the bottom of the last inning.

Amanda ran home and high-fived Jeri on her way to the dugout. Kara offered a fist bump.

"We stop counting when we're up by more than ten," Carter said, shooting him a wry look. "But play continues until demoralization is complete."

Finally the red team managed a third out because the Rhodes's Garage runner tripped on his untied shoelace.

After the game, Jeff invited Kara and Jeri out for drinks down by the marina. It was a restaurant, not a bar, so they put Charlie's bike in the back of the truck and brought her along too. She seemed pretty happy to be sitting on the patio sipping a milkshake, asking Jeri about where they went to school and how long it took to become a vet.

Around nine thirty, Kara and Jeri said good night. "Some of us have to be in the office early for surgery," Jeri said. "Thanks for the drinks, Jeff."

He waved. "Thanks for your help with the team."

"Our pleasure." Kara nudged Jeri with her shoulder and shoved her hand in their back pocket as they turned to leave.

"They seem cool," Charlie offered when they'd left, and Jeff allowed himself a satisfied smile.

He dropped her off at her place—Dave and his wife had a five-bedroom, three-bath "cottage" on the lake, complete with a boathouse—and then Jeff drove them back to Carter's while Carter dozed in the passenger seat.

It felt strange to be crawling into bed before ten, but if Jeff didn't come to bed, Carter would find some reason to stay awake too, and he obviously needed rest, so Jeff brushed his teeth, washed his face, and crawled under the covers.

Carter huffed a little, obviously grumpy, and made discontented noises until Jeff curled his body into Carter's left side.

Jeff smiled into Carter's shoulder as Carter curled his arm around him. "You're such a baby."

"Because I like to cuddle?" Carter's sleep-heavy voice made it difficult to discern the words, but Jeff got it eventually.

"Because you throw a little tantrum when you don't get your way."

Carter snorted into Jeff's hair and kissed the top of his head. "Three more weeks."

Yes. Three weeks until Carter's cast came off and three weeks until, hopefully, Max was out of rehab. Jeff didn't love the overlap—he'd have loved a whole week to enjoy a healthy Carter first—but he looked forward to both. "Three more weeks," he agreed. "Good night."

Chapter Eighteen

NOW THAT he had a concrete deadline and something to work toward, Jeff didn't want to waste any more time. He insisted on driving Carter to work the next morning—if Jeff drove him, he could pretend Carter wouldn't take one of the park trucks out and drive it around—and then went to the cabin, where he spent two hours on the phone with Monique working out logistics.

Unfortunately, the cell phone signal really *was* weak—he could have a phone call just fine, if the day was clear, but loading anything more than text on his phone was a no-go. Which meant he needed to take a trip into town to meet with a real estate agent.

Corey Klein had gone to school with Carter's older brother, and she had time to meet with him that afternoon.

If she was surprised that he whipped out an NDA for her and her staff to sign right after they shook hands, she didn't let on. "I'll just get this to my receptionist," she said, smiling pleasantly. "One moment."

She was back five minutes later with copies, which she handed to Jeff in a neat folder as she resumed her seat at the desk. "Now, Mr. Pine. I admit you have my attention. What can I do for you?"

"I need to buy a house." No point wasting either of their time with a lengthy preamble. "A waterfront four-season would be preferable, but I'm in a time-crunch."

Corey flipped open a paper notepad. "How quickly are we talking?"

"Ideally, I'd want possession within three weeks. Faster if possible."

That *did* throw her; her eyes widened. He could practically see her calculating her percentage of what it would cost him to get what he wanted. He'd be excited about that too, if he were her. "I see. Have you been preapproved for a mortgage?"

Translation—How much are you willing to spend?

"I'll be paying cash." His selling estate agent told him the market was so bonkers at the moment he could get a near-immediate closing. That should cover a large portion of the cost. He had a few other options if it didn't. "I'd prefer not to spend more than three." He'd need to keep some funds in reserve for renovations. He couldn't just expect to find a place with the right acoustics for a recording studio.

He watched her process that yes, he meant three million dollars—not that that was an unusual price for a nice place on the water. "Okay. Let's talk about your must-haves."

They spent about twenty minutes discussing, and then Corey flipped the top of her notepad shut. "I think I have a good place to start. With your timeline, I'll be calling you later this afternoon to set up some appointments. What does your schedule look like?"

Jeff's only plans in the next three weeks included occasional T-ball games, naked time with Carter, and writing and polishing as many songs as he could squeeze out of his brain. He was just lucky that, with the prospect of leaving the label on the table, writing was coming a lot more naturally. "I'm pretty flexible." Except, shit, he wasn't supposed to tell Carter about the whole switching labels thing, and if Carter started asking questions, Jeff would fold like a wet paper bag. "Preferably regular business hours, but I can make evenings and weekends work."

"Business hours are great, actually, since most people are at work at those times, so the houses will be empty and you'll be one of the only ones looking."

"Great." He smiled and stood. "Then I look forward to hearing from you."

And spending a fuck ton of money. No big deal.

He picked up a few sandwiches and some veggies and hummus for a late lunch in the hopes that he'd find Carter in his office, doing whatever park naturalists did when they couldn't be in the field, but when he pulled into the parking lot, Carter was getting into a truck with Kara at the wheel.

Jeff hopped out, anxiety spiking. "Trouble?"

"Maybe not." Carter looked anxious to go, practically vibrating with nervous energy. "We got a report of a bear and cub, and the location doesn't match the trackers for the other mothers we know about. Kara's going to drive me out."

Grabbing the bag of food from the console, Jeff asked, "Can I come?"

Kara drove like she had to be reminded this was a conservation area, not a go-kart track. From the seat behind her, Jeff could see Carter's right leg twitching as if he wanted to hit a brake.

"I can't wait until that boot comes off," she griped. "Do you want to check this out before the bear disappears or not?"

"I'd like to get there in one piece."

Before Jeff could add his two cents—Carter did that to him all the time too—Kara wheeled around a curve and the seat belt tightened until he wheezed for breath. The bag of sandwiches fell to the floor.

Maybe Carter had a point.

They pulled to a stop just off the side of the road in an otherwise deserted area of the park. There was a walking trail on one side, and a bearproof garbage can stood where the trail intersected the road. Or perhaps *formerly bearproof*—it looked like someone had taken the curve too fast and hit the side of the can hard enough to dent it. It obviously didn't close properly anymore, and now garbage lay strewn across the road and down the path. *Something* had definitely been here.

"I don't suppose you'd be willing to stay in the car," Carter said, turning around.

Jeff gave him a flat look. "You literally have a broken foot, but *I* should stay in the car?"

"You both should stay in the car," said Kara, "but you're both stupid. Carter, get your air horn. Jeff, stay away from the bears. And cabin porches."

"Harsh."

They got out, leaving the doors open to avoid making any loud noises. Jeff worried about the damage running away from a bear would do to Carter's broken foot, but it turned out he didn't need to worry. As soon as they got out, Kara held a finger to her lips and pointed. She must have heard something.

Carter craned his neck over the bed of the truck but eventually shook his head. Then Kara climbed up on the back tire and pointed into the trees.

When Carter made to do the same on the opposite side of the truck, Jeff hissed, "*Absolutely not.*"

Rolling his eyes, Carter shuffled around the back of the truck, lowered the tailgate, and used the built-in step to gain a vantage point.

Fine. Not to be left out, Jeff climbed up after him. Carter's long legs made it look easy. For Jeff it was almost a jump instead of a step. He was afraid he made too much noise, but when he got his footing, Carter wrapped an arm around his waist, tugged him close, and turned his body so Jeff could follow the sight line from where he was pointing with his other arm. “There.” The smile came through in his voice, warm enough that Jeff felt it at the top of his head. “See them?”

Jeff looked.

It took a moment to discern the three dark shapes in the underbrush—Jeff really was going to have to get glasses, damn it—but when he did, he smiled. “Is that them?”

“No tracked bears in this area. And none of them have twins.”

Jeff leaned into Carter’s shoulder for a moment. “Well, what are you waiting for? Shoot her with a tranq gun or something and get another tracker on her! I can’t go through this again!”

“We didn’t really come prepared for that,” Carter said, amused. “We’re just here to check that she’s okay.”

“Ugh.” Jeff sat down heavily on the wheel well. “I could not do your job.”

They ended up eating lunch at one of the picnic areas, somewhat protected from the mosquitoes by the breeze off the water. Kara and Carter discussed the logistics of her T-ball takeover, which Jeff let pass easily over his head when he realized he actually had decent enough reception to load the pictures in the emails Corey had sent him.

He was thumbing through the options, debating whether he wanted to remodel a couple of bathrooms over the next few years if it meant he could have a gate, when Carter nudged him and he panicked and almost dropped his phone.

“Wow.” Carter’s eyebrows rose nearly to his hairline. “Are you looking at porn or something? I promise I won’t kink-shame.”

Jeff couldn’t decide whether to scramble for a lie or a snappy remark, so he felt relieved when Kara said, “Aww. The honeymoon’s over already.”

“If Carter’s asking about my kinks, I think we’re firmly in the prehoneymoon stage,” Jeff said wryly, grateful his phone screen had gone dark because he’d accidentally hit the button.

“Good point.” Kara crunched a carrot. “Don’t worry, Carter, I’m sure he’ll go slow with you at first.”

Between her words and Carter’s blindsided, half-offended expression, it was several minutes before Jeff could stop laughing.

AS WITH many other tasks, money made the process of buying a cottage infinitely less painful. It took Jeff a week to choose one, put in an offer, get an inspection, and close the sale. Thirty-six hours after that, Monique called to let him know his condo had sold and the deal was done.

Unfortunately, that left him with a number of other problems.

He still hadn't heard from Max. Everything else was just money; Jeff could always make more of it. He couldn't replace Max.

At least Trix seemed to have some contact with him, because she said, "He's going through some stuff. I promise he will talk to you eventually, but he has things he needs to apologize to you for, and he needs to work up to it."

Jeff just hoped he managed that before they had to play in Ottawa.

And then there was the cabin rental. Jeff wasn't exactly *broke*, but it didn't seem like a great idea to let the cabin just sit there once he owned property, especially considering his recent change in financial situation. *Especially* with the potential of Big Moose finding out what they were up to and blowing the whole thing out of the water.

After a week of agonizing, he amended his rental agreement the day the cottage closed. He'd have two days to get the rest of his things from the cabin and transfer them to his fancy new four-bedroom cottage on the lake (complete with boathouse). Most of his stuff was at Carter's by now anyway; he only used the cabin for songwriting.

The biggest problem *should* have been keeping his mouth shut about all of this to Carter, but Carter was still working like he could single-handedly save the planet. Eventually Jeff took to driving him to and from work every day just to curb Carter's habit of spending ten hours in the office.

Or so he thought, at least until, one evening in late June, he arrived at Carter's office at six thirty to find the building locked and the parking lot empty.

Typical.

At least Carter had the good sense to pick up on the second ring. "I'm late for dinner, huh?"

Jeff rolled his eyes. "You're late for a kick in the ass. Where are you?"

"Uh, Two Willows Point?"

God damn it. The road only went halfway out there. "Did you *walk*—"

"No, relax, we took a utility cart. We had a patron report a badger sighting. Had to check it out." He sounded so *cheerful*, like this was the best possible thing he could imagine. "Normally I'm pretty skeptical, but they were right. Which is a big deal, because there's fewer than two hundred badgers in Ontario, by the latest estimate."

It was difficult to maintain his grump in the face of Carter's enthusiasm. "Congratulations." The way Carter talked, he might as well have personally built the badger a guest house and rolled out the welcome mat. Which, considering that he was largely responsible for the stewardship of the park and creating, curating, and preserving its microhabitats, wasn't far off.

"Thanks," Carter said, as though Jeff had been completely sincere.

Jeff *had* been completely sincere. Damn it. "Want me to come meet you?"

So he drove off to pick up Carter from wherever his ranger of the day had carted him off to. For ten minutes Carter talked animatedly about the biodiversity returning to that area of the park, and then they hit the highway and he leaned his head against the window and fell asleep with the evening sun gilding his hair.

Jeff could hardly look at him, and yet he couldn't tear his eyes away. He was too beautiful and too good, and Jeff loved him to distraction. The next month was going to be terrible. If he could just get this last show under his belt, and if they could get their album written in time, and if the new label deemed it good enough, then he could have this life—this quieter, slower, warmer life—where he'd be gone for a few weeks a year instead of months on end; where he'd spend his life surrounded by people who knew him instead of people who simply adored his persona; where Carter would come home to him at the end of almost every day.

Even if he was late.

Late workday or not, Carter's car nap must have rejuvenated him, because when they got home, he shepherded Jeff into the bedroom and then rubbed his beard all over Jeff's thighs before taking him into his mouth. As soon as Jeff started to move his hips, Carter abandoned his dick, hard and leaking all over his stomach, in favor of fucking him open with two fingers.

Carter *really* didn't need any help finding Jeff's prostate now. He worked Jeff until Jeff was fucking back into every thrust, hands curled in the sheets, profanities falling from his lips. Jeff orgasmed on a half shout as Carter ran his teeth up the sensitive skin on his inner thigh that he'd just beard-burned, and didn't know how much later he tuned back in to reality to find Carter had three fingers in him now and was rutting unhurriedly against his thigh.

"Oh, did you want something?" Jeff asked, a little hoarsely.

"Hmm." And suddenly the fingers slid out and the head of Carter's cock nudged against his hole.

Jeff wasn't going to get a chance to finish that album because he was going to die of sex. He went hot all over as it popped in, only for Carter to withdraw and rub his dick in the slickness around Jeff's hole. Jeff groaned and hooked his ankle around Carter's waist, hoping to pull him closer. "You really love that, huh?" he asked, raising his eyes to Carter's face.

Carter tapped his cock against him obscenely. Jeff's stomach muscles clenched in anticipation. "*You* really love that," he corrected, his voice every bit as hot as his eyes, and he proceeded to fuck Jeff just like that until Jeff broke and wrapped a hand around his own erection and came everywhere.

So, yeah. Dead of sex. But what a way to go.

They spent the last rays of the afterglow on the back porch, polishing off the burgers and sweet potato fries Jeff had made for dinner. Jeff was halfway convinced that life would still be pretty great even if Carter continued being an irrepressible workaholic when his phone rang and dumped a bucket of cold water on all his warm fuzzies.

It was Dina.

Jeff cleared his throat before he answered, in the hopes that he would sound more normal. "Dina, what's up?"

"Have you heard from Max?" she said with no preamble. "I haven't been able to get ahold of him."

Fuck. Jeff was not telling her *anything* about that. "Did you leave a message? You know how he can get."

He meant *flighty artist*, but from Dina's response, she obviously thought he meant *high*. "I *do* know, that's what I'm worried about."

Well, she wasn't going to reach him at his rehab facility until his doctors cleared him to have his phone. Which would hopefully happen in the next two days, because that was how long they had before the next concert. "What do you need to talk to him for, anyway?"

Dina sighed. "I need to confirm travel arrangements and accommodations for Ottawa. He hasn't been answering my emails either."

Jeff had written her back to give the plans the thumbs-up a week ago. "I'm sure it's fine. Trix and I will make sure he shows up."

He crossed his fingers under the table, hoping she'd accept that and just move on, because Carter was already watching him with interest. Unfortunately, what she said was "Where is he?"

"I couldn't tell you," Jeff dissembled. "Sorry, Dina, but you're kind of interrupting dinner here. Do you need something from me?" He felt a little guilty about it; it wasn't her fault the label was full of fuckweasels.

She sighed heavily. "No, that's fine. Sorry for interrupting. Have a good night, Jeff."

Now he felt like an asshole. "Yeah," he said. "You too."

He hung up.

Carter regarded him curiously, head tilted to the side, one eyebrow raised. "Trouble?"

Jeff took a deep breath and slowly let it out. Max hadn't specifically asked him not to say anything, and it wasn't like Carter would rat him out to anyone. And he hated lying to Carter even by omission. He could at least offer a partial truth.

"Max is in rehab," he blurted. "He's been out of contact with everyone but Trix. Dina wanted to talk to him."

"Oh." Blinking, Carter furrowed his brow. "Dina doesn't know?"

He rolled his lips together and bit them. "Max didn't think it was any of her business. The rest of us agreed."

"No, I get it, I mean, you've had enough trouble with them. Why give them an inch?" But the frown hadn't gone anywhere. "Why didn't you tell me, though?"

It wasn't like Jeff could just say *Because if I told you that, I'd be that much closer to spilling the whole "getting out of our shitty contract" plan, and I signed an NDA*. If it was just him, he wouldn't worry about it. He trusted Carter implicitly. But it wasn't fair to ask Trix and Joe and Max to trust him implicitly too.

"I wanted to." He pushed his empty plate away from him, suddenly nauseous. "But it felt like it wasn't my story to tell."

"You've been a little off," Carter said gently. Of course he noticed. Of course he never said anything. Of course he waited for Jeff to bring it up. "Is this why?"

"It's part of it." Jeff didn't want to lie any more than he had to, but he didn't feel like he could admit there was more. All he needed was Carter mentioning something to his mother or someone offhand, and then townspeople asking about it. The cottage purchase would be public record; it wouldn't be difficult to find once someone was looking. And even if Jeff buying a cottage didn't raise any red flags for the label, him selling his condo in Toronto might. If they found out about the contractors he'd hired to soundproof a recording studio, that might.

If they found out Trix, Joe, and Max were coming to Willow Sound after the Ottawa show *with their instruments*, that *definitely* would raise eyebrows. Jeff needed to keep a lid on as many of the details as he could.

Carter's expression didn't clear. If anything, it grew more troubled. He pursed his lips, and his broad shoulders hunched in for a moment before he took a deep breath and straightened them. "Are you…?" He met Jeff's eyes. "Are we okay?"

What? Jeff's mouth dropped open. "Carter—yeah, of course we are. Why would you think…?" Had he somehow been ambiguous? He'd basically moved in. He didn't want to be anywhere else.

Then again, Carter didn't know Jeff had sold his condo or bought property locally.

Damn it. Jeff tried again as his stomach sank with the weight of his dread. "Are *you* unhappy?"

"No!" Carter said quickly, mouth opening in horror. "No, God, Jeff—I've never been this happy in my life and my foot's broken." He gave a breathy puff of laughter and shook his head. "Guess I should've been watching where I was going instead of flirting with you."

"Nah," Jeff squeezed out past the sudden tightness in his throat. "Who knows how long it would've taken me to get a clue if you hadn't?"

"I was thinking about engraving an invitation if the hike didn't work," Carter teased.

Jeff stuck his tongue out. "You could've said something, you know."

"Oh, like you did, you mean?"

Now that was just unfair. "How many thinly veiled Top 40 love songs do you need?" Jeff gently kicked his left ankle under the table. "I thought we weren't talking about them because you didn't feel the same and I made it awkward. I didn't know you were just being obtuse."

"Hey," Carter protested. "How was I supposed to know? And even if I thought maybe some of them were about me, was I supposed to assume you felt the same way more than ten years later? That you meant it the way I—I mean, lots of artists have muses—"

Jeff stared at him, openmouthed. "Oh my God."

Carter stopped, the apples of his cheeks burning red, and dropped his gaze to the tabletop.

"Oh my God," Jeff repeated. He'd been operating on the assumption that they were on the same page, but obviously Carter thought Jeff was still reading the introduction or something. *It's not like he doesn't know*, Jeff had written in that social media statement—but maybe, somehow, he didn't. "How do you not—Carter." Fuck this. He reached across the table and grabbed his hand, because by God he would have eye contact for this. "You are so lucky you have a big dick," Jeff said, "because if you haven't realized how stupidly in love with you I am, then you are *so dumb*—"

"Hey!" Carter said again, but he was laughing now, and the flush had calmed from embarrassed red to a pleased pink. "Don't ruin the moment."

"The moment was ruined when I had to do my love confession song live in front of five thousand other people," Jeff said dryly, "and apparently it didn't even *take* with the person I most wanted to hear it, so—"

Honestly, did Carter think Jeff made public statements about who he was dating for just anyone?

"All right." Carter tried to raise his hands in concession, but he was still holding one of Jeff's, so the gesture turned out kind of lopsided. "You made your point. I was dumb. I thought maybe you weren't ready."

"No shit."

Carter made a face. "In my defense, the first time I *wanted* to say it, you looked like you were going to have an attack of the vapors."

"Oh, I was," Jeff agreed easily. He knew exactly which moment Carter was referring to—that campfire-night comment and the way Carter had looked at him afterward, as though Jeff were the stupid one. "You wait fifteen years to hear that from someone, the idea that you might actually get what you want is kind of overwhelming."

Speaking of, Carter had not actually said the words yet. Jeff was trying to be patient, but like he said—fifteen years of waiting. Suddenly another fifteen seconds seemed like too long.

For a second, he wasn't sure if Carter was teasing him on purpose or just being dumb again, but then he caught the hint of a smirk in the corner of his mouth. "You're not gonna have one now, are you?"

Jeff sputtered. "Time will freaking *tell*—"

Carter kissed him, which was cheating and also probably the fastest way to get Jeff to shut up. The kiss was warm and sweet and full of promise, and at the end it got a little dirty, so that by the time Carter pulled away, Jeff was leaning in for more. Carter stopped him with a finger to his lips, and his blue eyes were soft and serious and so, so fond when he said, "I love you too."

So *that* was great.

Jeff got to bask in the glow of that for a whole twenty-four hours, and then he picked up the keys to his brand-new cottage, double-checked the cabin was empty, and went to sit on the dock of his brand-new multimillion-dollar gamble.

"No big deal," he told himself as he plucked out a few notes on the Seagull. "Just the possibility of getting everything you ever wanted." The Ottawa concert was the day after tomorrow. He didn't have time to panic.

The sound of tires on gravel pulled him out of his contemplation of the water. That would be the contractor. He went and let them in and gave them a quick refresher tour—they'd already had a basic one when he had the inspection done—and then his phone rang.

Ella Rhodes.

She must be returning his call from the other night. "Sorry, I have to take this."

"Sure," the foreman said. What was his name again? Gord? "I'll come find you if I have any questions, but I think we're all set here."

Jeff took the call in the office off the kitchen, sitting in a desk chair that was a little too worn to be comfortable and a size too big for him anyway. But he'd specifically asked for the house to come completely furnished because he didn't have time to buy everything by the time he needed it. He'd ordered new mattresses and linens and that was it.

"Hi, Ella."

"Hi, sweetheart. I got your message."

Yes, obviously. Only now Jeff had to talk to her about it. Ugh. "Thank you for calling," he said. "Um, I just… this is going to sound so bizarre."

"You and Carter didn't have a fight, did you?" She sounded concerned. "I know he can be stubborn. He's like his father that way."

That was the opening Jeff needed, but he hated himself for using it. "No, we're not fighting, but he…. Actually, that's…. I'm just wondering…." *Did your husband work himself into an early grave? And do you think he passed that on to your middle son?* Working yourself to death wasn't a real thing, was it?

"Honey, I've known you a long time, but you're going to have to give me a little more to go on."

Jeff groaned and resisted the urge to bury his face in his hands. For one thing, it'd make a really ridiculous noise on the phone. "Has Carter always been so… hardworking?"

Wow, did that make him sound like an asshole?

Ella hummed. "You mean has he always put in extralong days, taken on any extra responsibility he could find, and filled all his waking hours with activity?"

"*Yes.*" Jeff practically deflated in relief. "Why is he doing that?"

This time when she answered, her voice was as dry as the liquor store before a holiday weekend. "What am I, the oracle?" He could practically see her rolling her eyes. "I love my son, but I don't pretend to know all his secrets."

Shit. There went Jeff's hopes of getting an easy answer. He tried to explain. "I just wondered if he'd always been like this. The only time I managed to get him to relax at all was when he was with me in Toronto and Vancouver. I don't remember him being like this as a kid, but maybe my mind's just playing tricks?"

"No, you're right about that." She paused—a thoughtful silence. "I told you what he was like after his father died. He was trying to fill a hole that couldn't be filled."

Jeff resisted the urge to make a dirty joke. "Yeah, you said. But after that, I don't know… I thought…."

"Honestly, Jeff, those weeks he spent with you before the memorial were the most relaxed I'd seen him in months. Which is saying something, considering the park is mostly closed in the winter and he had very little to do."

Jeff had been afraid of that. "So this backsliding now…."

"You'd have to ask him about it," she said pointedly, which was fair. Jeff couldn't go running to Carter's mom every time they needed to have a difficult conversation. "But if I were you, I'd be asking myself what's changed."

Jeff was already writing an album; how much more self-reflection could one person do? "All right. Thanks," he said belatedly.

"You're welcome, sweetheart. You know you can ask me anything." Ella paused again, and this time when she resumed, amusement colored her voice. "Even if the answer is that you need to do the legwork yourself."

Jeff snorted in spite of himself. "I could use the frank talk," he admitted. He didn't exactly have much in the way of relationship role models, and Ella and Fred had been more in love in their forties than any other couple he'd ever met.

"Oh, I know it. And I know you make my boy very happy."

He could tell from the tone of her voice she was thinking about the time she'd walked in on them kissing, and he had to fight the urge to groan aloud again. "It's mutual."

Now she laughed. "Oh, Jeff. I never had any doubt about that."

He'd only just hung up when the foreman poked his head in. Jeff's heart sank. "Bad news?"

"Well, it's not great." He had a clipboard with him. "This is going to be a studio room, yeah? Lots of equipment for recording and… whatever?"

"Yeah, that's the plan." *Please tell me that can still be the plan.* "Is something wrong?"

"Ah, yes and no. Any idea how much power that equipment draws?"

Jeff didn't have a clue. "No… but I can call my setup guru? Or just give you her number. She can probably give you all the details more efficiently without me as the go-between."

"Right."

The guy looked like he had more to say. Jeff had never met a foreman who wouldn't speak their mind—they didn't get put in charge of crews by being afraid of telling people about problems—but maybe this was extra weird for him since Jeff was semi famous. "Look—Gord?"

"George," he corrected.

"Sorry. George." Jeff dropped his phone on the desk and sat forward with his hands between his knees. "Whatever's going on, it's not your fault and I'm not going to get mad at you or have, I don't know, some kind of rage fit like you see on MTV or whatever. So just spit it out. What's the problem?"

George practically sagged with the release of pressure. "The house is only wired for fifty-amp service." He showed Jeff the clipboard, which told him absolutely nothing, but he was a man, so he pretended it all made perfect sense. "You're going to need to put in a new breaker box."

Finally, a plan of action. "Okay," Jeff said. "Whatever it takes, just get it done."

George blinked. "That's it? You don't want a quote or whatever?"

There were two contractors in the area and the other was booked solid trying to get things done before high tourist season. "Are you going to stiff me, George?"

"No?"

"All right, then." Jeff handed him back the clipboard.

"Uh," George said.

Damn it, apparently he wasn't done.

"It'll take a few days to get an electrician out here."

Jeff didn't really have a few days, but whatever. "Can you continue what you're doing until then?"

George nodded. "Oh, yeah, sure, no problem."

That wasn't so bad, then. "All right."

"Um."

Jeff took a deep breath and counted to four, then let it out. "Something else?"

George held out the clipboard. "I need you to sign at the bottom?"

Son of a bitch.

LESSON SEVEN
A Relationship Is a Duet

SOMETIMES IT feels like it's you and your partner against the world, especially in a new relationship.

It's not.

I know, I know, I just finished telling you to make room for someone. And a relationship *is* a duet (or trio, or however many people are in your relationship), but while you're singing your guts out, who's playing the drums? Who's on guitar? Piano? Who's doing the lighting? Who's backstage stocking the snacks in the dressing room?

You decide together what song you're singing.

But you're not an island. When the shit hits the fan—and it will—don't forget about the other people in your corner.

For one thing, they'll make you feel really *stupid*.

Chapter Nineteen

SO JEFF was already stressed as he prepared to leave for Ottawa. He'd had almost complete radio silence from Max, broken only by updates via Trix, which came by text. Apparently he called her from the retreat's phone every few days to catch up. The contractors wouldn't be able to get an electrician in until after the holiday.

And Carter was being weird. He didn't linger over the good-morning kiss he gave Jeff when Dave picked him up for their workout, and he was unusually quiet during dinner too.

"Hey." Jeff put his hand over Carter's on the table.

Carter startled. "What?"

Jeff looked at him as though he'd grown another head. "I've been asking you the same question for three minutes and you haven't answered. Where are you?"

"Sorry." Carter looked down at his plate and shook himself. "Just… weird day."

"Yeah?" Was he going to talk about it or just sit there acting strange? "How so?"

He exhaled dramatically, puffing out his cheeks. "I just… do you ever get the feeling that someone's keeping something from you?"

Fuck. Alarm bells went off in Jeff's head, volume cranked to eleven. "I mean…. Max hid his drug addiction for the first couple years. We never really knew how bad it got until later." That totally wasn't what Carter meant, though. He meant Jeff. Unless…. "Did something happen at work?"

Did that come off as sounding hopeful?

Carter shot him a sideways look. "Kind of." Holy shit, really? Jeff couldn't believe he was getting off the hook. "See, this afternoon Kara's truck got a flat while she was out at the dog beach, so I had to go meet some people at the rental cabin."

Fuuuuck.

Jeff knew his panic was written all over his face. He could feel his blood draining into his toes. How could he have been so stupid as to forget that *Carter worked at the park he'd rented the cabin in*? How could he have thought he could keep it secret that he'd canceled that reservation?

He couldn't think of a single thing to say in his own defense.

"Because they rented it," Carter went on, pointedly.

Jeff closed his eyes. "I'm sorry I didn't tell you."

"I'm feeling kind of left out of the loop, here." Carter's even keel was one of the steadiest things about him; hearing the hurt and frustration in his voice made Jeff feel like crying. "What's going on? Are you… are you leaving?"

"No," Jeff answered sharply. "No, fuck. I mean, just to the concert in Ottawa."

"So you just moved in without telling me."

Shit. *Shit*, and he'd sold his condo in Toronto, and with the renovations going on at the cottage, he was kind of technically homeless. "I really want to tell you everything," Jeff forced himself to say. He looked at Carter when he said it, even though it hurt to see the betrayal and suspicion there. "And I will. As soon as I can."

As quickly as the storm had come, it blew past, and Carter turned his hand—still under Jeff's on the table—and squeezed their fingers together. "Just tell me it doesn't…. It's not about us? I mean—" He scratched at the corner of his jaw with his other hand. "—we did move kind of fast. Is it too much?"

"Carter, no." Were they going to have a talk like this over dinner every day? If so, Jeff was never signing another NDA without Carter being read in at the beginning. This was miserable. "I was serious about the matching slippers, okay?"

"That was my idea." But some of the worry smoothed from his brow. "Is everything else okay?"

No more lying. "It will be, I hope. I can't tell you all the details yet because they're not mine to tell. But I wasn't using the cabin anyway. It would be a waste for it to sit unoccupied when someone could be enjoying it."

"Mm," Carter agreed. He glanced down at their hands for a moment and then back up, and now his eyes held a bit of a smile. "Did you leave the blackout curtains?"

HE DIDN'T hear from Max until the morning he had to leave for Ottawa. Even then, it was just a text: *Let's do this!!!!* followed by a tower emoji and seven Canadian flags.

He figured that was as good as he was going to get until they saw each other in person, so he just texted back *Fucking right* and hoped Max understood that he meant *welcome back, I hope you're doing well.* For two people who communicated professionally, their language with each other could be kind of opaque.

He didn't have that much time to think about it because he was too busy double-checking he had everything packed into the truck and putting off saying his actual goodbyes to Carter.

Despite the resolution to their… whatever that was… things didn't quite go back to normal before Jeff left for Ottawa. Jeff couldn't blame Carter; obviously Jeff was only reaping what he'd sown. But it still sucked to be standing in Carter's driveway, getting ready to leave for a few days, and feel that things weren't right between them. He and the band could not finish this album soon enough.

"You're sure you don't want to come?" he asked for probably the third time. Carter was going to say no again, but Jeff had this dream that if he came along, they could go back in time a little, relive the Vancouver trip instead.

Carter shook his head. "I've had this cast on for six weeks and I'm not postponing my follow-up X-ray for anything short of Armageddon."

Well, when he put it like that. "*Fine.*" Jeff tried for levity. "You just don't want to sit in the car with me for five hours. I see how it is."

"It wouldn't be my first choice." Carter punctuated this statement with a kiss, though not as lingering as Jeff would've liked. "Drive safely and call me when you get there."

"I will." God damn it. It didn't feel right to leave like this, but he'd made his bed, and it was at a secret cottage. "I love you."

At that he got a real smile, if a small one. "I love you too." *And* another kiss—still not long enough but warmer and sweeter than the last. Their noses were still touching, Carter's clear blue eyes kind and warm and steady when he added, "Come home soon."

Jeff inhaled sharply. *Home.* Carter had used that word on purpose. How was Jeff supposed to leave now?

But he managed it somehow—he put Carter's house in his rearview and hit the road, furiously hoping this was not a preview of what might become a staple of their lives in the next two years.

One more month. He just had to hold out one more month, get the band to finish an album, record a demo, and he could relax. He could tell Carter everything. He'd be home free.

Sure, no pressure.

He met some traffic on the way to Ottawa, though there was a bit more of it leaving the city, heading out for the holiday weekend to camp or cottage. He stopped once for lunch and a bathroom break and made it to the hotel just before check-in—perfect timing.

He'd just dressed after a shower and was debating texting Trix and Joe to see about dinner when someone knocked on the door. Figuring it must be one of them, he answered, only to find Max standing there instead.

He looked… different. His cheeks were fuller, and the shadows under his eyes that Jeff had come to think of as a part of him had lightened.

He did look a little nervous, standing in the hallway and fidgeting with a paper envelope, avoiding Jeff's eyes.

"Hey, Max." Jeff tried not to let on that he was surprised to see him without Trix. "You want to come in?" He stepped aside.

Max's eyes flashed up to his, and he smiled a little. "Thanks."

Shit. Jeff hoped the concert wasn't going to be this awkward. He closed the door. "I was just about to text you guys and see if we had plans for dinner."

"Trix and Joe found some sushi place they're dying to try, I think." Max wiped one hand on his jeans. "So, uh." He blew out a breath and finally just handed Jeff the envelope. "Here. This is for you."

Bemused, Jeff took it. It was just a simple paper envelope, not particularly noteworthy… until he looked inside and—"Jesus." He almost dropped it. There had to be a thousand dollars—

Oh.

"I'm supposed to make amends," Max said. He rolled his eyes a little, but Jeff thought it was more at his own behavior than a commentary on the gesture. "I can't do much about all the times I got high and ended up in the paper or went to rehab and it didn't stick or was a dick to you. I can't give Carter back the pills I took. But I can pay you back the money I stole from you in February."

Jeff cleared his throat. "Thanks." He didn't exactly want to carry around a thousand bucks in cash when he wasn't planning to drop it on an old guitar, but never mind. He'd just pick up the tab for dinner. This was mostly a symbolic gesture anyway.

With a sound of frustration, Max flopped into the office chair. "Don't *thank* me. God. I'm here to apologize. It wasn't fair of me to do those things to you. I never should've made you feel like you had to cover for me. I shouldn't have stolen. I made you feel like you and Howl didn't matter. And I know you worried." He ran both hands back through his hair in agitation. "Never mind Trix, who blamed herself—" He let out a long, slow breath. "Anyway. I'm so sorry, Jeff. I hope I can earn your forgiveness."

"Earn?" Jeff couldn't help think about how much worse it could've been. No one had gotten hurt—not irreparably. The whole tour could've tanked, Max could've died, Trix would've been beside herself. They never would have recovered.

But Max made a small noise, looking like a kicked dog, and Jeff realized he'd misunderstood.

"Max, forget it. You don't have to earn my forgiveness, okay? All you had to do was want it." Oh God, Max was blinking too rapidly. Jeff took a few deep breaths of his own and scrambled for something to say to lighten the mood. "Rehab is pretty intense, eh?"

Max barked a quick, inappropriate laugh and ran a hand back through his hair, and suddenly he wasn't a jaded thirty-year-old rock star and recovering addict, he was the teenager Jeff had first met in detention, who'd offered Jeff one of the Twinkies in his pack in exchange for help with his English homework. "This one was totally different from the other times. Apparently the doctors think I'm bipolar? Which kind of explains…." He waved his hand as if to encompass the highs and lows of his erratic behavior over the past ten years. "Anyway. Apparently that lends itself to cocaine use. Surprise."

So lightening the mood had failed spectacularly. "Oh. Wow." Jeff forced himself to sit down on the end of the bed, because otherwise he'd pace. "So can they help?"

Max nodded. "Yeah, eventually. Turns out getting the right dosage of the right kind of brain meds is, like, 20 percent science, 80 percent dumb luck. I'm pretty fortunate it only took them two tries to find something that's working so far." He scratched at the back of his neck. "Not that I've been on them long enough to really test it."

"I'm glad it's working. Hopefully it, you know"—God, could he sound like more of an idiot?—"keeps working."

Meeting his gaze, Max intoned, "Wow, Jeff. Deep, man."

Oh thank God. Jeff laughed. Tension broken, finally. "Shut up. We good?"

"Yeah, we're good."

And they were.

Better than good was taking the stage in the middle of the afternoon on Parliament Hill the next day, to sweltering sunshine and more than ten thousand fans. Howl hadn't played a proper music festival in years, and Jeff had forgotten how much he liked it, even if the different audience demographic meant they had to change up their set list a little.

He was truly drowning in sweat this time, though. At least he'd opted for his Rhodes's Garage T-shirt instead of his usual black.

They capped off a performance of some of their tamer hits with a cover of the Hip's "Fireworks," and by the time they got offstage, Jeff could practically feel his nose freckling. He was definitely going to peel. Dina escorted them all back to the VIP tent, which was filled with a weird mix of musicians and political bigwigs, for water and snacks.

Trix poured an entire bottle of ice-cold water over her head and sank into the nearest chair. "Are we writing a song about global warming next?" she panted. As she slumped, the strap of her tank top shifted, revealing pasty white skin and highlighting the burn on her shoulders. The rear of the stage was covered—Jeff had only gotten burned because the angle of the sun lit the front of the stage—but evidently she'd spent enough time in the sun watching the other acts.

"Don't give him any more excuses to write love songs for Carter," Joe teased.

Jeff was too busy draining his second water bottle to defend himself, but Max passed each of them a clementine and said, "He doesn't need excuses. Great Bear Lake posted another video."

"Oh no," Jeff said out loud. He didn't think he could handle it. His face was already on fire from sunburn.

"Yes." Max cued it up and slid his phone to the middle of the table. He propped it up on its PopSocket.

The next musical act hadn't gone on yet, so they could all hear perfectly well as Carter went over some basic steps for celebrating Canada Day in an environmentally conscious manner.

"Fireworks can release toxic chemicals into the environment and can negatively impact local wildlife. Not to mention the noise can be stressful for pets and people with PTSD." On the tiny screen, Carter paused to pet a ginormous chocolate lab, who looked at him like he was made of bacon.

"Where'd he get a dog?" Trix asked.

"Are you kidding?" said Joe. "He probably just walked through the forest whistling a jaunty tune. I'm surprised he doesn't have a squirrel."

Jeff wasn't at all sure he wouldn't be coming home to a new roommate. He also wasn't sure he'd be able to voice a protest to it; Carter and the dog combined had too much puppy eye.

"If you do decide to set off fireworks, be sure to find an area where it's safe to do so, away from houses and only with appropriate supervision. Fireworks should never be set off in areas that are in drought. Look for these brands, which are rich in nitrogen and less toxic and smoky than other fireworks. And if you like sparklers, opt for bamboo over metal, since the chemicals in the metal ones mean they can't be recycled."

He took off his sunglasses and hung them on the front of his ranger uniform.

"Nooo," Jeff moaned quietly.

Max snickered.

The video switched to a scientific-looking area of the park buildings as Carter followed with his usual spiel about choosing products with eco-friendly, recyclable packaging. "And though most manufacturers these days have moved away from six-packs, remember if you do have any to cut apart the plastic rings before you throw them away, because they can be a danger to wildlife."

"Oh my God," said Trix. "He *does* have a squirrel!"

Jeff watched through his fingers—when had he put his hands over his face?—as Kara, her hands carefully gloved, brought out a frantic-looking squirrel. Carter used a pair of snub-nosed scissors to free it.

"Corporations, not individuals, are responsible for the vast majority of pollution and global warming. But that doesn't mean individuals can't make a difference. Happy Canada Day. Please celebrate responsibly."

"Your boyfriend is so cheesy." Max shook his head and popped a slice of clementine in his mouth.

"I know," Jeff half wailed. The thing is, he was so *sincere*. "I'm gonna marry him."

"You sound like you need a beer." Joe knocked on the table. "Uh, or are we not—?" He looked at Max.

Max waved him off. "None for me, but you go ahead."

"Make mine a radler, if they have it," Trix said.

"Two beers, one radler. Be right back."

He'd only been gone a few seconds when Jeff said, "Is it bad that I want to play the video again?"

"Oh, I love that guy," a voice said from behind him.

Jeff turned to see a woman he didn't recognize. From her summer-professional clothing, she was a politician, not a performer. "Yeah," he said dryly. "Me too."

"That's his boyfriend," Trix put in.

"Yeah, I know." The woman gestured to the empty chair next to where Joe had been sitting. "Do you mind?"

Somewhat bemused, Jeff said, "Go for it."

"Thanks." She sat and offered her hand. "Annemarie Jacoby."

The name rang a bell, but Jeff couldn't put his finger on where he'd heard it. In the news somewhere, doubtlessly. "Jeff. And this is Trix and Max." He sighed, possibly a little sunstroked, and gestured at the phone. "And I guess you know Carter."

"Canada's dreamiest park ranger."

Joe came back with their drinks and took the seat next to Annemarie. They introduced themselves, and then the conversation returned to Carter, as Jeff explained his actual job and how hard he worked and the whole debacle with the data sharing.

About five minutes in, Joe surreptitiously pulled Jeff's beer back and pushed another bottle of water toward him.

"Ugh, I'm rambling?" he guessed.

"Just a little." Joe grinned. "Have some more water. Maybe a Gatorade."

"Maybe a nap," Trix added.

"Maybe dinner," said Max. "Clementines or no, I'm starving. Anyone else?"

Joe's stomach growled as if on cue. "Okay, yes," he agreed. "Except I think Jeff needs to be inside in some air conditioning stat. Room service?"

They gathered up their things and said their goodbyes to Annemarie, but before they got far, Dina intercepted them. "Oh. Leaving already?"

Jeff wavered on his feet. He should've known they wouldn't get off scot-free. "Yeah."

Her mouth pinched. "I was hoping to talk to you about the album progress. I haven't been able to get hold of any of you for weeks—"

Maybe because we are not a goddamned juke box, Jeff thought.

"—I need an update, please."

"Don't worry," Trix assured her. "We're gonna get right on that as soon as we get back from this gig, all right? But Jeff's going to pass out if we don't feed him."

"That—" Jeff wanted to defend himself, but he wanted to avoid talking to Dina more. "—is probably true."

"We'll text you," Max said cheerfully. "Enjoy the rest of the concert."

THEY PACKED their stuff into Jeff's truck for the drive back to Willow Sound, and it felt like the early days of the band, driving to gigs in a beat-up van that broke down every other month. Except a lot more comfortable. The cooled seats were a particularly welcome improvement.

"So, tell me about this house," Joe said, leaning back in the front seat. "Like are we going to have to do an exorcism?"

"I don't think it's *that* old," Jeff said. Though probably if it only had fifty-amp service installed, it was pretty old.

Trix had her feet up on the console. "Do you have a hot tub?"

He rolled his eyes. "No. But there's a soaker tub in the master bathroom."

"Acceptable."

"Water access?" Max asked.

At that, Jeff smiled, because this was the best part. "Private lake." The only boat launch was on private property. Even if the general public figured out his address, they couldn't just get in a boat and swing by his dock to spy on him.

"Nice," Joe approved as they turned down the winding lane that would eventually lead to the cottage.

"Do you have a boat?"

"Maybe after the next tour," Jeff said dryly. Then he didn't say anything for a while; the road to the cottage was pretty twisty.

The construction crew was still at work when they arrived. Jeff introduced everyone and let Trix, Max, and Joe pick their rooms while he had a word with the foreman.

"Electrician's coming by in a half an hour or so," he said. "Should take an hour or two."

"Fantastic." In that case, Jeff had business to attend to. He left George in the soon-to-be studio room and went upstairs to poke his head in on Trix. "Hey. You good here?"

"I am never leaving," she said, lying flat on her back in the middle of the king-size bed. The balcony doors were wide open, letting in the breeze off the lake. "I live here now."

"You might change your mind when you find out how much rent is," Jeff said dryly. "I'm going to go say hi to Carter. His doctor's appointment was today."

"Say hi to his dick from me."

"Fuck off, I will." He rolled his eyes. "Fridge should be stocked. I had a service swing by. Call me if you need me." At some point in the next few days, he'd need to figure out how to either tell Carter his friends were in town and needed to borrow his truck or figure out where to rent them a car. In the meantime he had a boyfriend to make up with. Properly this time. "See you later."

"I doubt it," she shouted after him as he hightailed it down the steps.

He texted Carter before he got in the car, but the only reply he got was "thumbs-up emoji," read through the truck's Android Auto feature in its hilarious toneless inflection. Good enough for him. GPS said he'd be there in twenty minutes.

He made it in fifteen, feeling vaguely guilty for the excessive speed.

Then Carter came out of the house, no boot in sight, and Jeff somehow teleported from inside the truck into his arms.

"Hi," Carter said into the side of his neck when the kiss had tapered off into a tight hug. Jeff could feel his smile. "Someone's in a good mood."

"You got freed from the boot?" Jeff verified, pulling back a little.

"Doc says it healed beautifully." Carter made a face. "Although despite the exercise, it turns out returning to a regular stride takes practice."

Jeff watched him as they went into the house, and yeah, it was lopsided. "Did they send you for physio?"

"No." Carter shot him a dry look. "They told me to try not to favor it and just walk it off, basically. Except the ligaments don't want to bend enough for that. It doesn't feel natural. So I've been doing a one-man Ministry of Funny Walks since the thing came off at ten this morning, trying to get everything stretched back out."

"I want to see them all," Jeff proclaimed. "But, like, later." He sat on the couch and held out his hands to indicate Carter should sit with him. Carter did, more heavily than Jeff expected, and Jeff finally noted the bags under his eyes. "Long day?"

With a sigh, Carter turned his face against Jeff's shoulder. "I feel like a wuss, but apparently walking around with no cast on is exhausting now."

"Poor baby." Jeff maneuvered them until he was sitting in the corner, Carter lying with his head in his lap. A more carnal reunion could wait. "You want to have a nap?"

"I want to have *sex*," Carter grumbled against Jeff's stomach as Jeff carded fingers through his hair, "but I'm too tired."

Wonders never cease. "It's fine," Jeff said. "Being like this is nice too."

"Mm-hmm," Carter said. His eyes closed, then opened again, and he rolled onto his back so he could look into Jeff's eyes. "Sorry I let you leave when things were still awkward. I trust you to tell me whatever's going on on your own terms."

One day Jeff was going to be worthy of this man. Meanwhile— "Sorry I couldn't just tell you everything. Or stay and fix things. I—"

His phone rang.

Carter's lips twitched the way they always did when he was fighting a smile.

Jeff sighed. "I swear to God. We're not only going to be cockblocked by every human in your family, we're also going to be conversation-blocked by my damn cell phone. I really do have to take this, though." The display said it was the contractor.

He should probably get up. If he didn't, there was every chance Carter could overhear, and he'd have questions.

But Carter was comfortable, and Jeff didn't *want* to move. He'd just said he trusted Jeff.

Jeff answered. "Jeff Pine."

It was George. From the tone of his voice, Jeff knew it was bad. "Hey, Jeff. I've got the electrician on the line for you. Do you have a minute?"

"Yeah," he said, but it barely made a sound. He coughed and repeated, "Yeah, of course."

The electrician didn't beat around the bush, and he didn't leave room for interpretation. He barely left space for Jeff to get a word in edgewise, more than *yes*, *no*, and *as soon as possible*.

It wasn't until he hung up that he felt the bottom falling out of his stomach, the disappointment squeezing his chest. That was it. Their best chance at getting out from this label had just gone up in smoke.

At least the cottage itself hadn't burned down yet, which according to the electrician's assessment of the existent wiring was an ongoing possibility.

Jeff set the phone on the arm of the couch and rubbed his hands over his eyes, trying to tamp down on his rising panic. How was he going to tell the band? There was no way they'd be able to use the cottage for songwriting, not for at least three weeks. That left them very little time to get anything recorded, and that was assuming the wiring job went as scheduled.

Fuck. *Fuck.*

Carter sat up. "Jeff?"

Jeff made a sound of pure frustration. Fuck it. It didn't matter if Carter found out now. The whole thing was a crabfuck. "How much of that did you hear?"

A pause. After a second Carter said, "Pretty much all of it? You have your volume turned up pretty high."

Jeff probably needed to upgrade the hearing protection he used at concerts. "Fuck."

Carter cleared his throat, and Jeff finally peeled his hands away from his face. Carter looked pensive. "Uh, I guess… I was wondering…. Wouldn't your condo building handle something like this?"

Finally Jeff laughed. There wasn't anything else to do. "Yeah, they would if I still owned it."

Carter's mouth dropped open. "You sold your condo?" He had a lot of face, and ordinarily Jeff would've enjoyed watching confusion and realization wage a battle over the real estate. "So what wiring problem was he talking about?"

Fuck it. "It's probably easier if I just show you."

Chapter Twenty

"YOU BOUGHT a house," Carter said twenty minutes later as he stared out the front window of the truck. The contractors had left for the day; there wasn't anything more they could do until the electrical work was finished.

"I bought a house," Jeff confirmed. "I mean, technically I think it might be a cottage, but it's supposed to be livable year-round."

Carter was still staring at it. "That's… a lot of house."

"Four bedroom, three bath," Jeff confirmed. "And a dock. And a huge kitchen, and a great room. And a studio. Well. Supposedly."

"And a huge garage," Carter pointed out. He sounded shell-shocked.

Jeff nodded along. "You should see the boathouse."

Now Carter laughed and covered his face with one hand. "The boathouse," he said. "Of course. So, what's the deal with the wiring?"

An elated whooping scream filtered up through the truck's open windows. A tremendous splash followed. "Apparently the house has some kind of shoddy plastic-coated wiring that's liable to go up in flames at any moment. Which is a problem because we need to record an album in three weeks so Spin Cycle will buy out our contract, and we can't do it anywhere Big Moose will find out or be able to claim they invested in it."

For a moment Carter just silently opened and closed his mouth. Then he said, "You sold your apartment to buy a secret cottage to record an album in and it didn't already *have* a studio?"

"I sold my apartment and bought a cottage for *us*," Jeff said before his brain could tell his mouth that was a bad idea. "Um. I realize that under ideal circumstances that would be something we'd talked about and discussed what we wanted beforehand, and then we'd have gone looking together, but we all kind of signed an NDA, because if the label finds out we're trying to screw them over, the other label could get sued. Among other problems."

"Huh." He shook his head. "All right."

"All right," Jeff echoed. Wait, what? "*All right*?"

Honestly, one day Jeff would earn this kind of devotion and forgiveness. "All right," Carter repeated. "Come on. I want a tour. And then, when that's done, I think you and… I'm assuming that's Max and Joe and Trix down on the dock?"

"I dropped them off here before I came to see you."

"Right. So give me the tour, and then you and me and Max and Trix and Joe are going to sit down and figure out a plan B."

As if it were that simple. "Carter—"

"Tour," Carter said firmly. "Come on."

So they did. Jeff led him through the cottage, which featured a gray water reclamation system and repurposed wooden flooring along with its creature comforts—a natural gas range in the kitchen, the soaker tub, a shower big enough for two, with dual rain-shower heads. Balconies in two bedrooms. From the one in the master, he pointed down to the boathouse. Unlike the main cottage, its roof wasn't shaded, and the previous owners had installed solar panels.

"It's not enough to live off the grid or anything," he said, embarrassed that these were the things he'd hoped Carter would appreciate. "But—"

"Jeff." Jeff shut up and looked at Carter, who was smiling more with his eyes than his mouth. "I think I've finally realized grand gestures are your love language. You can stop downplaying them now."

Jeff had never successfully downplayed anything in his life, but he decided it was better to kiss Carter than argue about it.

Finally they walked hand in hand down to the dock, where Trix sat under a huge umbrella reading her latest cozy mystery series, a bag of snacks open on the table next to her. Joe and Max were sunning themselves on the raft; Jeff hoped Max had remembered sunscreen.

Trix pulled her sunglasses off and tilted her head to say hi. "Hey. I thought this whole operation was on the DL? Uh, no offense, Carter."

Carter shrugged. "None taken."

Jeff grabbed the deck chair next to hers. "It was, but that kinda got blown out of the water. Hey, Max, Joe, you want to bring it in for a minute?"

The four of them told Carter the original plan for recording the album. Then Jeff sucked it up and explained the problem with the house. "So it turns out they don't just need to put in another breaker panel to up the service to the recommended 200. They need to rewire the whole house."

"Shit. Any idea how long that'll take?"

"At least a week, probably two. And the power will be off for a lot of it, not to mention the noise and disruption." Translation—they weren't going to be able to finish writing an album here, never mind start recording anytime soon.

Max cracked open a bottle of water from the cooler under the table. "Okay. Easy problems first. We could just rent another cottage and stay there."

"In Willow Sound in peak tourist season?" Carter said wryly. "Good luck."

"A motel, then." He shrugged. "It doesn't have to be fancy."

"The boathouse has a bathroom and kitchenette on the upper level," Joe said. "We checked it out earlier 'cause Trix has to pee all the time and she didn't want to walk all the way back up to the house—"

Trix tossed a handful of Cheezies at him.

"Anyway. The point is, we could just move some mattresses in and slum it."

"Yeah," Max said dryly. "We're really going to be suffering."

"I *will* be suffering," Trix said, "because you both snore like chainsaws, but I'm willing to put up with it. Problem solved."

"We could write there too, probably," Joe said, thoughtful. "No recording, because the water would be too loud, but there's probably space."

"Only if you picked the mattresses up every morning," Jeff said, shaking his head.

"What about the garage?"

He grimaced. "Almost definitely not." That place was crawling with spiders. Jeff wasn't going in there until it'd been visited by the pest-control man. Which he'd have to keep secret from Carter. But in this case, what Carter didn't know wouldn't hurt him. "There's barely any lighting, and it's full of junk."

"Uh, guys? And Trix."

Trix looked at Jeff first. "I like him," she said. Then she turned to Carter and gestured expansively. "You may speak, polite one."

"Thanks. Um, what exactly is required for a home recording studio?"

Max flipped his bottle cap with his thumb, then caught it. "Good soundproofing, adequate electrical service."

"Room for three guitars and a drum kit," Joe added. "Plus the recording and mixing equipment."

"And located somewhere we won't raise any eyebrows," Trix finished. "Like a unicorn. That's why Jeff, you know…." She gestured at the cottage.

"Also because he's super in love with you and can't be apart from you for two days without moping." Max held up his hands when everyone turned to look at him. "What? I only speak the truth."

Jeff was sitting in the shade and couldn't even blame the sun for the blush spreading over his face. He rubbed his forehead. "*Anyway*—"

Fortunately Carter didn't encourage Max by engaging with his comment, but he did smile and nudge Jeff's foot with his own under the table. The sap. "Right," he said. "That's sort of what I thought." He looked at Jeff. "And I think—I mean, if you're okay with it, I think I know the perfect spot."

Struck speechless, Jeff stared at him for a moment. How could he just have a perfect spot in mind? What could he—

And then it hit him.

"Oh my God."

Carter's dad's den.

"It'll mean reading in my family," Carter said. "You'll probably have to sign autographs for my niece."

"She's cool," Jeff said. "So far she hasn't sold my phone number to the internet."

"She *is* a cockblock, though."

"Is he allowed to say the C-word?"

"Not in front of his mom," Jeff and Carter chorused. They grinned at each other when everyone else stared at them in horror.

Then Jeff rapped twice on the cast-iron tabletop. "All right. All in favor of reading in Carter's family so we can get this in the can, raise your hand."

The motion passed unanimously.

THERE WAS a lot to do.

The electrical work wouldn't start until tomorrow, so they decided to leave the mattresses where they were for the time being. In the meantime, Jeff and Carter needed to meet with Ella.

"I mean, she's going to say yes," Carter said.

Jeff adjusted his grip on the prettiest planter he'd been able to find at the garden center. "Let's hope."

Ella did say yes, of course. Also, she cried.

Jeff met Carter's eyes over the top of her head and tried to convey *help, how do I do mom emotions* as she clung to him tightly enough that he started to worry about his circulation. But after a moment she pulled back, beaming, and wiped away a tear. "Your father would be beside himself with joy."

She meant Fred, and she was talking to Jeff, and now *he* was going to cry. Fuck it. "Thanks, Mom."

Everything was very manly for a few moments until they composed themselves. Then Jeff said, "Okay, well, let's get to work."

Before they could set up the recording equipment, everything had to come out of the man cave—old furniture, Carter's dad's record player, the hi-fi, the shelves. Carter, Jeff, and Dave moved it out and set it up in the downstairs living area instead.

At home later that night, when they fell exhausted into bed, Carter curled his arm around Jeff's shoulders. "So you never mentioned what this all means. Why you're going to all this trouble. I mean… okay, your current label sucks, but this is a lot of stress to put yourself through."

"Yeah," Jeff said, snuggling in. He turned his head so he could look at Carter. "The thing is, our current arrangement is pretty predatory. We didn't have our own manager when we signed, so we got taken advantage of. Even when they offered us better terms when we re-signed five years ago… it wasn't what it should've been. And we never had an advocate, so we've been running ourselves ragged."

Carter brushed Jeff's hair back from his face. Soon he was going to need a haircut as well as glasses. "I'm sorry. I didn't realize."

Jeff gave a wry smile. "It's not like you can really go around complaining about it. You'll get a bad reputation, and honestly, 'poor little rich guy,' right?" He shrugged and caught Carter's hand. "Part of the reason I came back here was to get away from that toxic atmosphere. I was debating just paying the penalty and saying fuck it to the whole thing—the band, the label, everything. The tour schedule is grueling."

"I can imagine."

He spent a moment sinking into the warmth and comfort of the bed, basking in it, before he continued. "I didn't want to do that again.

I'm exhausted, Max can't handle it, Joe's going to be a father. I want to be able to call someplace home and feel like it's true."

Carter brought their hands to his mouth and pressed his lips to the back of Jeff's.

And now he had to go one step further and just… say it. "I want to be able to spend time with you."

Carter bit his lips and shook his head minutely. From his expression, he knew exactly what Jeff meant. "You want to know something funny?"

Somehow Jeff doubted he was going to laugh. "Tell me."

"When my dad died, I started doing too much so I didn't have to think about it." He rubbed his thumb over the back of Jeff's hand, a hypnotic tic. "I didn't realize how much I'd missed out on until you showed up, and suddenly I was rearranging my schedule to spend time with you."

So he *had* known he was doing it.

But then Carter went on, "Only once we started dating, I worried. I knew you'd have to go back on tour, that I'd have to get used to you being gone all the time."

Understanding dawned. Jeff almost groaned aloud. They were both so dumb. "So, what, you decided to get used to never seeing me by making yourself insanely busy?"

"It seemed like a good idea at the time."

This time Jeff did groan. He rolled over to muffle it in his pillow, and when he lifted his face again, he caught Carter's eyes. "We're going to do better than this," he said with all the conviction he could muster. "No more workaholics in this house."

Carter raised an eyebrow.

Jeff relented, "After this album is done."

Carter smiled. "Deal."

WHILE THEY were doing the final touches on the studio—cleaning, ensuring they had enough outlets, double-checking with the electrician that the man cave could handle the equipment without tripping the breaker—Joe flew back to Toronto to spend some time with Sarah. He returned two days later in his SUV, with Jeff's favorite sound-equipment guru in tow.

Jeff and Carter had just finished bringing the last box down to the basement when Joe pulled into the drive. When they went out to say hello, Jeff only just made it down the stairs before he was attack-hugged.

"Oof!" he said as Sibel hit him at Mach 3. "Was driving with Joe that bad?"

"We almost got killed by a moose." She pulled back, bubbling with energy. "By which I mean there was one standing by the side of the highway. It was huge. For a second I thought it was a kaiju."

He snorted. "One pilot in each antler?"

"It was a girl moose. *Speaking* of moose." Sibel turned to look behind him. "Who's your friend?"

Well, Carter *was* pretty tall. "Carter Rhodes, please meet Sibel Ergener, sound tech extraordinaire. Sibel, this is my moose, Carter."

Carter gave him a long-suffering look, but he smiled at Sibel. "Nice to meet you."

"Yeah, you too." She nudged Jeff with her elbow and lowered her voice—though not quite low enough. "We'll talk later."

Jeff should probably just accept that he was going to get shit about this for the rest of his life, honestly. He clapped his hands. "Okay! Who's ready to plug things in?"

It took the four of them an hour and a half, but by the end of it, they had everything set up and working to Sibel's satisfaction. Jeff went to pick up dinner—and Trix and Max—and returned to find the extended Rhodes clan had descended on the house as well, also with food, and that Brady and Dave were putting all the extra leaves in the table.

"We're probably going to have to expand onto the deck," Ella said, glancing outside at where Trix had blatantly stolen Jeff's student and was teaching Charlie drumming rhythms on the deck railing. "I hope that's okay."

Jeff sidled up behind her and wrapped his arms around her waist. "It's perfect." If a little overwhelming. Jeff had never had much family, and now the two found families he had were together in one place so his first one could help the second.

"Don't get all sentimental on me," Ella warned teasingly.

Jeff kissed her cheek. "I'll get the plates."

Dinner set the tone for the week—namely chaotic and joyful and loud. While Sibel relaxed at Jeff's, Howl camped out in Ella's basement, fine-tuning what turned out to be a mostly complete album. Jeff came home every night wired but exhausted, and Carter made it home before him all but one day.

On that day Jeff was in the kitchen, trying to decide if he had the energy to put together something that could charitably be called dinner or if he was going to have a nap and then order pizza, when the front door opened.

"Jeff?"

"Hmm?" If he stared into the fridge for long enough, attractive low-energy food options would assemble themselves, right? That was how it worked?

That was how it *should* work. If a fridge could order groceries, surely it could tell you what to have for dinner.

"Do you—" He cut himself off. "Am I interrupting something? Do you and the fridge need a minute?"

Right, he was wasting energy. Jeff closed the fridge. "Me and the fridge need, like, at least half an hour. You know what I'm like." But something about Carter's demeanor seemed off—excited, but restrained, tentative. "What's up?"

Carter furrowed his brow. "Do you know why I just got a call inviting me to apply for a job as a research liaison and coordinator with the Ministry of the Environment and Climate Change?"

Jeff blinked at him. "No…?" Why would he know that? Unless—"Uh, who *is* the Minister of the Environment?"

"Annemarie Jacoby."

Oh God. A strangled, hysterical laugh slipped out.

"Oh no," Carter said. "What did you do?"

"Nothing," Jeff protested through a wheeze, holding himself up against the fridge. "She was at the Canada Day concert. She likes your videos."

Carter's eyes widened. "Oh God."

"You had to know," Jeff said. "Those things are everywhere. Didn't *As It Happens* call you for an interview?"

"I was busy," he said.

"Whatever. Your videos are internet catnip, even though you use YouTube like an old man."

"I told you, TikTok's portrait format—"

Jeff wasn't going to have this argument again when he was dead on his feet—even if he *could* recite his part in his sleep. "I mentioned you were working like crazy trying to get all this data for a colleague of yours, because you knew it had to exist but wasn't being used for anything. I didn't know she was your boss or whatever."

"She's not. She wouldn't be—it's a union job. I still have to apply, I…." Carter sat at the kitchen table. After a moment's consideration, Jeff did too. His feet thanked him. Carter let out a long breath and finally looked up. "It's a good job. Important."

So apply, Jeff thought. He was already doing the damn job anyway. But it had to be Carter's choice. Jeff propped his chin on his hand. "What're you going to do?"

"Honestly?" He looked kind of wild about the eyes.

"Honestly." Hopefully not try to work yet another job. Jeff would have to put his foot down about that.

For a few seconds he simply drummed his fingers on the table. Then he stood up and pulled Jeff with him.

Jeff blinked. "What?"

"I'm going to take my boyfriend out to dinner," Carter said. "And then we're going to come home…."

Oh, Jeff liked this plan. "I'm listening," he said. "Go on."

Smiling, Carter reeled him in until his thumb was gently caressing the skin on the inside of Jeff's elbow. "And we're gonna have a *nap*," he crooned.

Jeff truthfully could not have said if he was elated or disappointed. A nap with Carter sounded amazing.

However, Carter wasn't done. He kept moving his thumb in gentle circles, and now he leaned down, so tall it felt like he could block out the whole world and so close Jeff could've counted his eyelashes. "And then I'm going to make you come so hard you forget the words to every song you've ever written and neither of us is going to *think* about work until tomorrow morning."

It was fortunate that Carter had such a good grip on him, or Jeff might've hurt himself in his swoon. "That is the nicest thing you've ever said to me."

Carter snorted and kissed his forehead. "I'll make it up to you with dirty talk later."

If Carter said *fuck* twice within twenty minutes, Jeff would die. "Let me just get my shoes."

WITH SIBEL to mind the mixing board, actually recording the demo turned out to be the second-easiest part of the whole endeavor.

"I was expecting more yelling and cursing," she admitted as she pulled off her headphones. "Where's the drama?"

The observation threw Jeff for a loop, because she was right. The last time they'd recorded an album had been stressful and fraught with petty arguments. He glanced at Trix.

"I think we left it at our old label."

"Holy shit," Jeff said, shaking his head. After months of stress, they'd finally done it.

"I'm going to sleep for a *week*," Max said, sprawled out on the floor on his back. "Tell your mother-in-law not to move me."

"No binge-sleeping until we have a new contract," Trix said firmly. "First we get this to Monique, then we sign with the new label, *then* we sleep."

Sibel tucked her feet under her on the chair. "I think there's one thing you're forgetting, though."

"Did you hear something?" Joe said. "Because I didn't hear anything."

"Nope," said Trix. "Total silence."

Sibel ignored this. "What're you going to call it?"

Oh.

Jeff hadn't thought about it.

Max waved his hand. "That's easy. The rest of us voted."

Trix poked him with a drumstick. "You want to make it unanimous?"

It turned out Jeff did, but now he had another problem. "Shit," he said, rubbing a finger underneath his right eye. "I think I have to write another song."

Chapter Twenty-One

TWO DAYS later, Monique met them at LaGuardia.

Jeff had always liked New York City. New Yorkers had rules—not hassling celebrities in their off hours was one of them, mostly. Not that they were taking any chances. All four of them wore their most inconspicuous street clothing and let Monique, in a gorgeous cream linen suit with a teal silk shell, command people's attention.

They wouldn't be in town for long anyway, Fate willing.

The car picked them up right outside the airport and they quickly got in. Jeff leaned his head on the window and looked up at the skyline—well, he couldn't see all the way to the sky, but he looked *up*… and smiled. "Remember the first time we played in New York City?"

"Barely," Max admitted with the ghost of a smile. "Didn't you throw up?"

"Twice." Jeff didn't get nerves much as a rule, but playing NYC the first time had him ready to spit butterflies for a week.

Across from him, Joe grinned. "It was a wild time for everyone, if I recall."

That had been in his pre-Sarah days. Jeff had the vague feeling Joe had gone home with a pair of twins, but he wasn't going to ask about it. Although—"What did *you* do?" he asked Trix.

She stretched her legs out—sandals discarded on the floor of the car—and propped them in Max's lap. The two of them had shared a room for their first several years as a touring band. "Honestly? I went back to the hotel and sobbed in the shower for ten minutes because I couldn't believe we'd done it, and then I went to bed and slept for eleven hours."

"I remember that," Max said. "I thought you must've had way too much to drink. I tripped over my own feet when I got in and you didn't even move."

"Emotional catharsis is better than any sleeping pill." Trix rubbed the back of her neck. "Finally getting to prove people were wrong—that you could be a rock band with a girl drummer and she didn't have to fuck any of the guys to earn her spot…." She lifted a shoulder. "Sweet, sweet vindication."

Jeff let himself sink into the rightness of it. With the sun streaming down on his face, he felt like he'd been personally blessed by his decision to stick around. They hadn't given up. And now they could reap the rewards of their labor.

Monique cleared her throat as they passed the next block. "All right. Let's go over our plan for the meeting one more time."

She walked them through it—reiterating to make sure she knew exactly what they were asking for, reminding them to defer to her and let her do the talking if things didn't seem to be swinging that way. They hadn't booked return tickets, just in case they needed to stick around New York to label shop, but Jeff didn't think they'd have to.

This was the best album they'd ever put together. It might be their *Rumours*… and everyone knew that was Fleetwood's best album.

If these executives knew what was good for them, they'd give Howl whatever they wanted and be grateful for the opportunity.

Fingers crossed.

The car pulled up to the office a few moments later, and Monique strode to the reception desk in her sky-high Manolo Blahniks. "Monique Huberdeau and Howl for Zephyr Kendrick."

The receptionist looked up through thick-framed plastic glasses, wide-eyed. He took them in and then pressed a button on his phone. The elevator doors opened behind him. "Go on up. She's expecting you."

Jeff furiously ignored the churning cement mixer in his stomach. Suddenly he missed the butterfly effect.

Half of him expected a typical conference-room setup, but instead they were shown into a casual office with comfortable lounge furniture and a sound system that would've had Sibel diving for the manuals to drool over the specs.

A woman and a man met them in the lounge.

"Monique," the woman said, coming forward for a handshake—except once they clasped hands, they leaned in for a kiss on each cheek. Apparently this wasn't their first meeting. "How long's it been?"

"Let's not count the years since twelfth grade." Monique stepped back with a smile and gestured the band forward. This was Jeff's cue. "Zephyr Kendrick, may I present Jeff Pine, Trix Neufeld, Max Langdon, and Joe Kinoshameg, better known as Howl."

They went around with handshakes—the man with her was the label's executive vice president of A&R, Amir Basri—and then Zephyr gestured them to the couches. "So. Monique tells me you're ready to make the leap from Big Moose." She waved her hand. "Once some administrative details are out of the way, of course."

Jeff glanced at Monique for permission. She nodded infinitesimally. "Very," he said.

Zephyr smiled. "Well, then."

Jeff knew Monique had transmitted the files digitally in some supersecure manner, but he didn't know if Zephyr and her team had listened to them. Surely to God they weren't going to have to listen to an hour plus of their own music while sitting with a room full of music executives? There weren't enough antacids in the city of New York.

But the smile only widened. "Welcome to Spin Cycle."

THE INK wasn't even dry on their check—metaphorical check—when they booked their last-minute tickets back to Toronto. Jeff felt like he spent the entire flight bouncing his knee. He didn't dare text Carter, didn't dare even check to see if their trip to NYC had made the internet. None of that could matter until the contract with Big Moose was officially terminated.

Monique's superlawyer status must give her some kind of clout, because they didn't have to wait for an appointment there either.

Still grimy from the dual flights, punch-drunk with apprehension and relief, they followed Monique into the executive boardroom at Big Moose.

Dina was there, as well as Tim, which Jeff would've been angry about except that he was really going to enjoy watching the man's face as his golden goose crapped all over him.

Tim didn't even let Monique get a word in edgewise when they entered the room. "Ah, Howl. I hope you're here to deliver your album?"

Monique smiled like a shark, but it was Max who stepped forward.

"We're here to deliver our letter of resignation." Ignoring Tim completely, he stepped up to company president John Cannon's desk. "We're breaking our contract."

He slid the check across the desk.

Tim spluttered. "You can't—"

"They can," Monique interrupted. "I triple-checked. The payment's all there. My clients are free to sign with whomever they choose." For legal reasons, the actual agreement wouldn't be signed until tomorrow.

Cannon looked thunderous. "In all my years in the industry—"

Oh, fuck him. "What?" Jeff said. "No one's ever stood up to your predatory business practices?" He paused. "First time for everything."

Trix spread her hands in innocence. "We've always been trendsetters."

They all looked at Joe. It was definitely his turn for a parting shot. "Fuck you guys," he said with an eloquent shrug. "Dina, call me if you need a reference letter."

For the first time, Jeff looked at her and noticed she was biting both lips, wide-eyed. "For the record," he said, "we probably wouldn't have quit if Dina had been in charge from the beginning." She would've been, like, twelve when they started, but whatever. He didn't want her to get fired.

"Actually," she said, "you know what? I quit too."

"Nice!" Trix high-fived her.

Monique tilted her head toward the door, and Jeff was happy enough to take his cue. "All right, nonlawyers to the back. Drinks on Joe?"

"It's Trix's turn to pick up the tab—"

"I'll buy," Max broke in, prompting cheers.

Ahead of them, Monique offered Dina her arm. "So listen," she said, "I'm new to the music management business. I don't suppose you signed a noncompete agreement…?"

From *Guitar Hero Magazine*
September issue
Howling at the Blue Moon

IT'S BEEN a whirlwind summer for multiple Grammy nominees Howl. Between public indecency charges, headlining a Canada Day celebration, wrapping a tour, and cutting ties with Big Moose, it's been an eventful few months, to say the least.

And that's not even mentioning frontman Jeff Pine's fairytale romance with best friend Carter Rhodes, recently of @smokeybearlake fame, or the happy news of Joe Kinoshameg's impending fatherhood (his partner, Sarah Monague, is expecting their first child in December).

Somehow, on top of all of this, rehab and treatment for Max Langdon, and a handful of real estate transactions, Howl found time to record a new album and sign a new record deal, this time with NYC's Spin Cycle.

You might think that writing an album in the middle of such a tumultuous summer would result in a slipshod, unfocused effort, patched together through necessity. But you'd be wrong about this. I sure was.

While it's obvious that each member of the band has gone through their own struggles in the past year—drummer Trix Neufeld recently went public as a survivor of childhood sexual assault—their voices work together beautifully on the album, tied together by a common thread: that feeling of hitting your thirties and wondering, *What next? I'm not where I should be. I've fallen behind.*

"Our tour schedule with Big Moose was a lot," Pine, now thirty-one, tells me in the back booth of a family-owned restaurant in his hometown of Willow Sound, Ontario, a few hours out of Toronto. Far from the gaunt, hunted-looking man who graced covers of magazines internationally earlier this year at the end of the band's February tour, this Pine is tanned, round-cheeked, and dimpled, completely at ease. As we chat, he sips on a milkshake; a song he wrote plays on the diner's tinny overhead speakers. "I was exhausted, Max was spiraling, Joe just found out he was going to be a dad, Trix was working through her own shit. But none of us were talking to each other about it. I came out here convinced I was going to find the guts to go back to Toronto and quit for good, pay my way out of our contract and then, I don't know, write songs in a cabin in the woods for the rest of my life." He laughs. "Except there's, like, way too many spiders in the woods. So that wasn't going to work out."

Instead he opted for a cottage on the lake with his high school best friend and now boyfriend Carter Rhodes, a man many now speculate was the inspiration for more than a handful of early Howl hits. And as for the decision to stay with Howl….

"When I first came out here," he says, "I wanted a break, but what I got was some clarity, some perspective. I realized that I'd gotten so burned out I couldn't see past my own problems and that the way we were going was unhealthy for other members of the group too. It took a little break for me to realize they weren't the right target of my frustration. Once I figured that out, my whole plan changed."

The plan, as I've come to understand it—neither Pine nor any other member of the band will confirm or deny—seems to have hinged on securing a different label before their next album, the final on their contract to Big Moose, was due.

"I'm not going to talk about that," Pine tells me. He takes a break to sip his milkshake. "You know how it is."

Whatever the motivation behind it, Howl's latest album is far more than a cry for freedom. It alternates between emotional connection and catchy bangers and will resonate with any audience who's wrestled with past demons, uncertainty, and the dreaded third-life crisis. In the two hours I was permitted to spend for a sneak preview at Pine's cottage, tucked into a recording studio apparently put together for the specific purpose of making this record, I struggled not to see myself in every song. This is a collection of tracks that meets you where you are and tells you it's okay not to have all the answers.

This is the album we've been waiting for—even if the tour dates are farther out and significantly more scattered than we've gotten used to over the past ten years.

Rhodes's Garage comes to digital and physical stores near you this November.

"THAT'S THE last of it." Carter set the box on the tailgate and gave it a push. It just fit between the lawn mower and the Rubbermaid bin full of kitchen detritus.

Jeff closed the tailgate and leaned against it. "We going to do a last walk-through?"

Carter held out his hand. "Kinda feel like we should. Come on."

Casting one last look at the SOLD sign at the end of the driveway, Jeff let Carter lead him into the house.

It didn't look anything like it had the first time he'd been there. Instead of stacks of boxes and clutter, the hallway held nothing but the occasional shoeprint. It had been a rainy week, and it didn't make sense to take their shoes off every time they collected another box to bring out to the truck. The kitchen cupboards hung open, the better to verify they'd been emptied. Even the shower curtain had been packed, though Jeff had no idea what Carter was going to do with it. They certainly didn't need it at the cottage.

Carter's home office was bare save for the curtains and the pull-up bar installed over the door.

They paused in the bedroom—empty but for the two of them. Carter wrapped his arms around Jeff's waist and snuggled up behind him. "A few good memories here," Jeff commented as he folded his arms over Carter's.

Carter bent his head and nuzzled Jeff's ear. "We could make one more."

Jeff should've seen this coming. He squirmed a little—the prickle of Carter's beard against his neck, contrasted with the soft heat of his mouth, always got him hot, but it also tickled—and protested, "There isn't any furniture."

"Hmm," Carter said thoughtfully and bit gently at the side of Jeff's neck.

Then he spun him around, hoisted Jeff by his thighs, and pressed his back to the wall.

"Oh my God," Jeff said weakly as Carter held him up one-handed to fish a bottle of lube out of his pocket. He hadn't even known his dick could still *get* hard that fast; it was like being a teenager. "Okay, yes, but put me down so I can take my pants off."

Carter kissed him first, fast and dirty, and then pulled back far enough for Jeff to get his feet on the ground.

"Really glad the new owners wanted to keep the curtains," Jeff said, stepping out of his boxers. "Slightly—" He yelped when Carter lifted him again before he expected it. "*Slightly* regretting we tossed out the condoms." The ride to the cottage would be squishy.

Carter did the one-handed lift again and handed Jeff the lube with the other. Jeff opened it and poured and didn't pretend to be surprised when Carter pushed two fingers into him at once to smear the slick inside him.

Then Carter was pushing in—no teasing this time, just a fast, shallow thrust that had Jeff struggling for breath. He managed to squirt some lube in his own hand and was just about to wrap it around himself when Carter decided the angle didn't suit them and stepped *backward*, taking more of Jeff's weight and angling Jeff's lower body so Carter could nail him just right.

"Oh fuck," Jeff said, wrapping one arm around Carter's stupidly large forearm. This was not going to take long.

Sex with Carter was normally mind-bendingly, stupidly hot—Jeff loved being manhandled, and Carter knew exactly what to say or do or how to touch Jeff to set him on fire with pleasure. But right now Carter was lost in his own pleasure, chasing what felt good to *him*, and that was hot in a whole new way. The slap of skin against skin filled the room, echoing loudly without any furnishings to soften the noise. Jeff wrapped his legs around Carter's waist and watched his eyes go dark, and then he was lost too, stroking his cock in fast, tight strokes, desperate for orgasm.

He was almost there when he heard the knock on the front door.

"Are you fucking *kidding me*," he hissed when Brady's voice called out, "Carter? You guys here?"

Carter must have been close too, because he gave a particularly brutal thrust—Jeff's mouth dropped open and a breathy cry fell out—and his cheeks were flushed and his eyes bright when he yelled, "Go away! We're fucking!"

Jeff was so startled by the cursing that he laughed out loud, which made Carter groan and fuck in harder.

He vaguely heard Brady's "Oh my God, *gross*" filter through the house, but he didn't care because Carter was coming, dick jerking inside of him. Jeff could feel it dripping out of him, feel the suddenly overslick way Carter moved in his ass, and that as much as anything pushed him over the edge.

He came back to himself with Carter leaning against him, closer now that he didn't have anything left to prove. "I'm gonna set you down now," he said. "Okay?"

"Hnng," Jeff agreed. His legs were a little stiff when he uncurled them from Carter's waist, and they definitely weren't happy about supporting his weight. He glanced down at himself and the mess they'd made of each other. "We did leave hand soap in the bathroom, right?"

"And paper towels," Carter confirmed.

"Good." Any moment now Jeff was going to trust himself to stand without leaning on the wall. "We need to wash your mouth out."

"Not the orifice I was going to suggest, but let's see you try it." He held out a hand for Jeff to steady himself on… and then they both looked at their hands and grimaced. It was a miracle Carter hadn't dropped Jeff on his ass after he came. Jeff couldn't imagine getting a grip on *anything* with that much lube and come on it.

"Bathroom?" he suggested after a moment.

"Agreed."

When they'd dressed and come outside, Brady was sitting in his car with the music cranked so loud his fillings were probably rattling right out of his teeth. Carter was blushing furiously, but Jeff refused to be embarrassed. Maybe this would finally teach Carter's family to *call first*. He waved cheerfully.

Brady turned off the truck and made a show of looking at his watch and smirking.

"Think very carefully about how Christmas is coming up before you say whatever it is you're thinking," Jeff said cheerfully. "I always keep my receipts."

Carter gave him a sideways look. "It's the end of September."

"Which means I have several long months in which not to shop for Christmas presents." Jeff returned his attention to Brady. "What have we learned?"

Brady raised his hands. "Next time I'll call first?"

Now Jeff grinned. They *could* learn. "Good. You're in charge of teaching Mom."

"What're you here for, anyway?" Carter asked when Brady blanched. "Since it was so important you couldn't *call first*."

"Honestly, I just saw the truck was here when I drove by and thought I'd see if you needed an extra set of hands." He flushed bright red when he said it and covered his face. "I mean, obviously not. But I know campfire night starts at seven, and possession of the house is tomorrow…."

Right—Jeff was still getting reaccustomed to the whole "having family members who actually wanted to help" thing. "We're all finished here. See you at the park?"

"We'll be there. For a bit, anyway, until the baby has to go to bed."

Speaking of, they'd better get a move on. It was almost five and… well, Jeff needed a shower. "Sounds good. Tell Katie I'll save her a beer."

They ended up making it to campfire night *almost* on time, but when they pulled up in the parking lot, Carter made no immediate move to get out. Instead he pensively drummed his fingers on the steering wheel.

"Hey." Jeff covered his hand, trying not to let on. Carter wasn't supposed to know anything was up yet. This was just another campfire night—his last as Great Bear Lake's naturalist, but just another campfire night. "Second thoughts about leaving?"

Carter shook his head. "No." He'd applied for and gotten the job with the Ministry of the Environment and Climate Change. But civil service jobs involved a lot of hurry-up-and-wait to start with, and he had things to wrap up at the park too. He didn't want to leave them without a naturalist in high tourist season.

Jeff would have bet his next royalty check he just didn't want to give up campfire nights. He was pretty sure they were going to end up attending those anyway.

"I'll miss it," he said now, "but… I'm not actually going anywhere. I'll still have data to track in the park." That had been one of the things he'd asked about before he accepted the offer. "I don't even have to move my office. I don't know how they pulled that off."

Jeff didn't pretend to understand the complexities of federal vs. provincial jurisdictions when it came to parks or politics. The very notion of attempting to understand it gave him a headache. But he felt certain Carter was discounting a very plausible scenario. "Maybe they just like you."

Laughing, Carter finally reached for the door. "Yeah, maybe. Come on. I guess we'd better go."

He even grabbed Jeff's guitar out of the back seat for him. He was a gentleman like that.

The campfire had already started by the time they reached the amphitheater. Kids and adults, friends and family and park guests, gathered on the benches, chatting among themselves. A banner that hung between two trees—doubtless made of recycled paper—read *Congratulations, Smokey*. Someone had taped on a picture of Carter in his park naturalist uniform, doubtless from one of his YouTube clips.

Jeff was kind of hoping they'd let him keep the uniform.

Kara spotted them first and shouted, "*There* they are! I knew they'd be late!"

Max turned around with an enormous camera—a hobby he'd taken up since his stint in rehab. "Smile, losers!"

With all the kids around, Jeff had to quell the impulse to flip him the bird. He stuck his tongue out instead.

Carter turned to Jeff, half smiling. "Your work, I presume."

Jeff grinned. "My idea. I delegated the actual work."

Trix brought them drinks and executed a silly curtsy as she passed them over. "I see the honeymoon period continues."

Jeff accepted the drink. "I can neither confirm nor deny." He looked around. "Did Joe and Sarah make it?"

"Yeah, but she had to pee again, and you know how Joe hovers. He's probably, like, holding her purse." She smiled. "Have you seen her lately? She looks like someone shoved a basketball up her shirt. It's adorable."

Not since they finished recording the final cut of the album the month before. Frankly Jeff was just glad she'd finally been able to keep some weight on. "It'll be good to catch up with them."

He'd just spotted them emerging from the restrooms when Kara turned on the mic. "If I can have everyone's attention," she said. A smattering of whistles answered. "Thank you. We're here tonight to say so long to one of the park's best. He's not going anywhere; we just like to have parties."

"Anyway," she went on—behind her, Joe kissed Sarah's cheek and Sarah went to sit in the first row of seating, where Carter's mom had reserved her a spot—"I don't know if you know this, but Carter's got this connection to a semi local band. I've personally never heard of them—"

"Boo," Trix said, but she, like Joe and Max, was maneuvering to the side of the amphitheater.

That was Jeff's cue. He turned to Carter and held out his hands for the guitar case.

"You just can't resist a captive audience."

Jeff couldn't pass up a chance to play for him. "You know me." He leaned in for a quick kiss. "Go take a seat. Maybe see if Jeri has the s'mores up yet."

Carter rolled his eyes. "Yes, dear."

A man Jeff assumed to be one of the park guests must have overheard, because he badly disguised a laugh as a cough.

Half a minute later, Jeff had the Seagull slung over his shoulder, tuned and ready to go.

"Hi, everybody," Max said. "Thank you all for coming."

Jeff took a deep breath; it smelled like pine. If he concentrated, he could just hear the crashing waves of the Sound.

Joe took over. "We're not going to introduce ourselves because tonight isn't about us."

"It's about this guy Jeff knew in high school. He saved our band the same way he's trying to save the environment." Trix tapped out a quick rat-tat-tat. "He won't even pollute the air with swear words."

"That's not true!" Brady shouted from somewhere near the back.

Jeff grinned and winked at Ella, who had pulled Carter to sit down on her other side. "Carter loves campfire night," he said. Carter's pink cheeks told him he understood the subtext. "So I thought we'd have his favorite band play his favorite song."

But when he locked eyes with Max and played the iconic opening riff of "The Difference," Carter stopped him. "Jeff," he complained. "Come on."

God, Carter was such a sap. But, fine. It was his party. Jeff muted the strings and glanced at Max, then Joe. "Have it your way," he said, ignoring the heat in his own cheeks. The second Carter had heard that song, he'd claimed it as his new favorite.

It wasn't that Jeff didn't know that. It was just that most of the world hadn't heard it yet.

Well, never mind. The single would release tomorrow anyway. Jeff leaned into the mic and shook his head at Carter, but he wasn't upset.

Carter loved *this* song because it was the first one Jeff had written about himself. "This song is called 'Little Fish.'"

WILLOW SOUND GAZETTE
Local Artist Sweeps Grammy Awards
By Avery Cho

LAST NIGHT was an exciting night for fans of Canadian music. At the Grammy Awards in Los Angeles, pop-rock phenomenon Howl took home the first Grammy Award of their career.

And their second.

And their third.

Frontman Jeff Pine, thirty-one, accepted the first award for Best Rock Album. "We truly could not have done this without the support from our families and our fans," he said. "This is for you."

Last autumn, a local landmark, Rhodes's Garage, was used as a filming location for one of the album's music videos.

Pine and his partner, Carter Rhodes, live in Willow Sound.

ASHLYN KANE likes to think she can do it all, but her follow-through often proves her undoing. Her house is as full of half-finished projects as her writing folder. With the help of her ADHD meds, she gets by.

An early reader and talker, Ashlyn has always had a flare for language and storytelling. As an eight-year-old, she attended her first writers' workshop. As a teenager, she won an amateur poetry competition. As an adult, she received a starred review in *Publishers Weekly* for her novel *Fake Dating the Prince*. There were quite a few years in the middle there, but who's counting?

Her hobbies include DIY home decor, container gardening (no pulling weeds), music, and spending time with her enormous chocolate lap dog. She is the fortunate wife of a wonderful man, the daughter of two sets of great parents, and the proud older sister/sister-in-law of the world's biggest nerds.

Sign up for her newsletter at www.ashlynkane.ca/newsletter/
Website: www.ashlynkane.ca

String Theory
Ashlyn Kane & Morgan James

For Jax Hall, all-but-dissertation in mathematics, slinging drinks and serenading patrons at a piano bar is the perfect remedy for months of pandemic anxiety. He doesn't expect to end up improvising on stage with pop violinist Aria Darvish, but the attraction that sparks between them? That's a mathematical certainty. If he can get Ari to act on it, even better.

Ari hasn't written a note, and his album deadline is looming. Then he meets Jax, and suddenly he can't stop the music. But Ari doesn't know how to interpret Jax's flirting—is making him a drink called Sex with the Bartender a serious overture?

Jax jumps in with both feet, the only way he knows how. Ari is wonderful, and Jax loves having a partner who's on the same page. But Ari's struggles with his parents' expectations, and Jax's with the wounds of his past, threaten to unbalance an otherwise perfect equation. Can they prove their double act has merit, or does it only work in theory?

"Kane writes with a huge helping of heat and heart.... This is a treat."
—*Publisher's Weekly*

THE INSIDE EDGE

ASHLYN KANE

What does a work-life balance look like to recently retired professional athletes?

Ex-hockey player Nate Overton is trying to find out, but dipping his toes in the gay dating scene post-divorce is a daunting prospect even without the news that his show is on thin ice. Before he can tackle either issue, he skates headfirst into another problem—his new cohost. Former figure skater Aubrey Chase is the embodiment of a spoiled rich playboy. He's also flamboyant, sharp, and hot as sin.

Aubrey knows how important it is to get off on the right foot. He's just not very good at it outside the rink. Having spent his life desperate for attention, he'll do anything to get it—even the wrong kind.

For Nate and Aubrey, opposites don't so much attract as collide at center ice. But while Nate's everything Aubrey has scrupulously avoided—until now—Aubrey falls suddenly head over heels, and Nate's only looking for a rebound fling. Can Aubrey convince Nate to risk his heart again, or will their unexpected connection be checked at the first sign of trouble?

CPSIA information can be obtained
at www.ICGtesting.com
Printed in the USA
LVHW051604051021
699598LV00009B/523